America's greatest weapon

could be its worst enemy...

continued . . .

THE CARDINAL OF THE KREMLIN
*The superpowers race for the ultimate Star Wars
missile defense system . . .*

"*CARDINAL* EXCITES, ILLUMINATES . . . A REAL
PAGE-TURNER."   —*Los Angeles Daily News*

CLEAR AND PRESENT DANGER
*The killing of three U.S. officials in Colombia ignites the
American government's explosive, and top secret, response . . .*

"A CRACKLING GOOD YARN."   —*The Washington Post*

THE SUM OF ALL FEARS
*The disappearance of an Israeli nuclear weapon threatens the
balance of power in the Middle East—and around the world . . .*

"CLANCY AT HIS BEST . . . NOT TO BE MISSED."
                    —*The Dallas Morning News*

WITHOUT REMORSE
*His code name is Mr. Clark. And his work for the CIA
is brilliant, cold-blooded, and efficient . . . but who is he really?*

"HIGHLY ENTERTAINING."   —*The Wall Street Journal*

Novels by Tom Clancy

THE HUNT FOR RED OCTOBER

RED STORM RISING

PATRIOT GAMES

THE CARDINAL OF THE KREMLIN

CLEAR AND PRESENT DANGER

THE SUM OF ALL FEARS

WITHOUT REMORSE

DEBT OF HONOR

EXECUTIVE ORDERS

RAINBOW SIX

THE BEAR AND THE DRAGON

RED RABBIT

THE TEETH OF THE TIGER

SSN: STRATEGIES OF SUBMARINE WARFARE

Nonfiction

SUBMARINE: A GUIDED TOUR INSIDE A NUCLEAR WARSHIP

ARMORED CAV: A GUIDED TOUR OF AN ARMORED CAVALRY REGIMENT

FIGHTER WING: A GUIDED TOUR OF AN AIR FORCE COMBAT WING

MARINE: A GUIDED TOUR OF A MARINE EXPEDITIONARY UNIT

AIRBORNE: A GUIDED TOUR OF AN AIRBORNE TASK FORCE

CARRIER: A GUIDED TOUR OF AN AIRCRAFT CARRIER

SPECIAL FORCES: A GUIDED TOUR OF U.S. ARMY SPECIAL FORCES

INTO THE STORM: A STUDY IN COMMAND
(written with General Fred Franks, Jr., Ret., and Tony Koltz)

EVERY MAN A TIGER
(written with General Charles Horner, Ret., and Tony Koltz)

SHADOW WARRIORS: INSIDE THE SPECIAL FORCES
(written with General Carl Stiner, Ret., and Tony Koltz)

BATTLE READY
(written with General Tony Zinni, Ret., and Tony Koltz)

TOM CLANCY'S GHOST RECON

TOM CLANCY'S ENDWAR

TOM CLANCY'S SPLINTER CELL
SPLINTER CELL
OPERATION BARRACUDA
CHECKMATE
FALLOUT
CONVICTION

Created by Tom Clancy and Steve Pieczenik

TOM CLANCY'S OP-CENTER	TOM CLANCY'S NET FORCE
OP-CENTER	NET FORCE
MIRROR IMAGE	HIDDEN AGENDAS
GAMES OF STATE	NIGHT MOVES
ACTS OF WAR	BREAKING POINT
BALANCE OF POWER	POINT OF IMPACT
STATE OF SIEGE	CYBERNATION
DIVIDE AND CONQUER	STATE OF WAR
LINE OF CONTROL	CHANGING OF THE GUARD
MISSION OF HONOR	SPRINGBOARD
SEA OF FIRE	THE ARCHIMEDES EFFECT
CALL TO TREASON	
WAR OF EAGLES	

Created by Tom Clancy and Martin Greenberg

TOM CLANCY'S POWER PLAYS
POLITIKA
RUTHLESS.COM
SHADOW WATCH
BIO-STRIKE
COLD WAR
CUTTING EDGE
ZERO HOUR
WILD CARD

Tom Clancy's
SPLINTER CELL®

CONVICTION

WRITTEN BY
DAVID MICHAELS

BERKLEY BOOKS, NEW YORK

THE BERKLEY PUBLISHING GROUP
Published by the Penguin Group
Penguin Group (USA) Inc.
375 Hudson Street, New York, New York 10014, USA
Penguin Group (Canada), 90 Eglinton Avenue East, Suite 700, Toronto, Ontario M4P 2Y3, Canada
(a division of Pearson Penguin Canada Inc.)
Penguin Books Ltd., 80 Strand, London WC2R 0RL, England
Penguin Group Ireland, 25 St. Stephen's Green, Dublin 2, Ireland (a division of Penguin Books Ltd.)
Penguin Group (Australia), 250 Camberwell Road, Camberwell, Victoria 3124, Australia
(a division of Pearson Australia Group Pty. Ltd.)
Penguin Books India Pvt. Ltd., 11 Community Centre, Panchsheel Park, New Delhi—110 017, India
Penguin Group (NZ), 67 Apollo Drive, Rosedale, North Shore 0632, New Zealand
(a division of Pearson New Zealand Ltd.)
Penguin Books (South Africa) (Pty.) Ltd., 24 Sturdee Avenue, Rosebank, Johannesburg 2196,
South Africa

Penguin Books Ltd., Registered Offices: 80 Strand, London WC2R 0RL, England

This is a work of fiction. Names, characters, places, and incidents either are the product of the author's imagination or are used fictitiously, and any resemblance to actual persons, living or dead, business establishments, events, or locales is entirely coincidental. The publisher does not have any control over and does not assume any responsibility for author or third-party websites or their content.

TOM CLANCY'S SPLINTER CELL®: CONVICTION

A Berkley Book / published by arrangement with Ubisoft, Ltd.

PRINTING HISTORY
Berkley premium edition / November 2009

Copyright © 2009 by Ubisoft, Ltd.
Excerpt from *Tom Clancy's Splinter Cell: Endgame* written by David Michaels copyright © by Ubisoft, Ltd.
Tom Clancy's Splinter Cell: Conviction copyright © 2009 by Ubisoft Entertainment. All rights reserved.
Splinter Cell, Ubisoft, and the Ubisoft logo are trademarks of Ubisoft in the U.S. and other countries.
Cover illustration provided by Ubisoft, Ltd. Stepback digital composite by Diana Klosky. Cover design
by Rita Frangie.
Interior text design by Kristin del Rosario.

ISBN: 978-0-425-23104-3

BERKLEY®
Berkley Books are published by The Berkley Publishing Group,
a division of Penguin Group (USA) Inc.,
375 Hudson Street, New York, New York 10014.
BERKLEY® is a registered trademark of Penguin Group (USA) Inc.
The "B" design is a trademark of Penguin Group (USA) Inc.

PRINTED IN THE UNITED STATES OF AMERICA

10 9 8 7 6 5 4 3 2 1

1

SO confident was the target in his invincibility that Sam Fisher had little trouble finding him, and even less in determining how to best take him down. Then again, as jobs went, Romain Doucet wasn't the toughest nut Fisher had ever cracked. Not even close, in fact. He did, however, rank high on Fisher's "Waste of Humanity" list.

As he had been for the last hour, Doucet was holding court, as it were, on the bleachers beside a basketball court off rue Voltaire, under the shadow of the Cathedral of Notre-Dame. Physically, the Frenchman was impressive: almost six and a half feet tall, 270 pounds, with a weight lifter's body. On the other hand, his powder blue gangsta-style tracksuit and gold chains were something less than magisterial.

Fisher, sipping coffee and reading his copy of *L'hebdo du Vendredi*, watched, trying to guess what topics someone like Doucet might be covering. Judging by the guffaws and gaping of his five compatriots, the man's proclamations involved whatever women happened to stroll by on the sidewalk. Fisher caught only a few snippets of conversation, but most of Doucet's comments seemed to be anatomical in nature. This was no surprise. In fact, it was Doucet's lack of impulse control that had brought him into Fisher's sights.

Romain Doucet fancied himself an up-and-coming Mafioso of sorts, though most of his crimes involved strong-arm robbery and burglary. But his crew was loyal and the residents of his neighborhood frightened, so Doucet never wanted for an alibi, and this, sadly, was the case in the recent rape of a local man's fifteen-year-old daughter. The police had investigated, of course, but with no forensic evidence, and eyewitnesses placing Doucet elsewhere at the time of the crime, the city prosecutor had been forced to drop the case. The girl's father refused to accept this, and word quickly spread that the father would be willing to pay for retribution. Reims was a relatively crime-free city, however; what few solicitors the father received had clearly been unequal to the task. For his part, Fisher had, over the last year, realized the mercenary business was one of feast or famine (too often the latter), so he had taken the job. Any other time and he would happily have done the job for free, simply because Doucet deserved it, but men of Fisher's ostensible vocation weren't known for their sentimentality, and he dared not show any now. Plus, the five thousand euros—almost seven thousand U.S. dollars—would cover his expenses for the next week or so, until he received his next payment from his German friend. What interested Fisher most, however, was one of Doucet's side businesses: identity theft. If one knew where to look, money was fairly easy to come by, but not so with passable identity documents. For what he had to accomplish over the next month, he'd need plenty of those.

RODOLPHE Vernier spent thirty-two years making his fortune from a chain of high-end brasseries in Paris and Marseille before retiring in 1999 and turning the business over to his sons. A widower, he retired to Reims, where he met his current wife. Shortly after they married, Vernier adopted the woman's daughter, Marie. He loved the girl as his own, he'd told Fisher during their first meeting, and if not for his advanced age and prominence would have happily handled Romain Doucet himself. From any other man it might have come off as a boast, but the hard sadness in Vernier's eyes told Fisher the man was telling the truth.

"You found him?" Vernier now asked Fisher. They were sitting on Vernier's cobblestoned garden patio, beside a trickling fountain—a puffy-faced marble cherub spitting water in a high arc. "He was where I said he would be?"

"I found him," Fisher replied in French. He wore a disguise, not a good one, but enough that Vernier would have trouble giving an accurate description: a ball cap that hid Fisher's shaggy hair, dark glasses, and five days' worth of stubble.

"You can do it?" Vernier asked.

"Yes. I won't kill him, though."

"No? Why not? If it is money—"

"It's not money. Neither of us needs the trouble. If you hurt a deserving man, the police will smile in private; if you *kill* a man—even if he's deserving of it—the prosecutors will force them to do their job. Trust me: When I'm done, Doucet won't ever be the same."

Vernier considered this, then nodded. "Do you want part of the money now?"

"No." Again Fisher felt a pang of guilt: If not necessary to his larger mission, he would tell Vernier to keep the money. Handling Doucet was a necessary public service. Even so, Fisher now gave Vernier instructions on where and when to leave the cash. "Once I've done the job, I'll pick it up. How is your daughter getting along?"

Vernier shrugged. "A bit better, we think. She is seeing a therapist. She has started talking to us, taking an interest in things. I want to thank you for—"

"Thank me by forgetting me. Forget me. Forget you hired me to do this. Don't talk about it to anyone. No bragging. For the next twenty-four hours, go out with your family and be seen. Do you understand?"

"An alibi."

"Yes."

Vernier studied Fisher for a few seconds. "Aren't you going to threaten me—tell me not to talk to the police?"

Fisher gave him a hard smile. "You won't tell the police."

"No, I suppose not." Fisher held his gaze until he said it again: "I won't."

"They will come see you, ask you questions. Don't be too quick with your alibi. Let them do the legwork. Tell them you're not sorry about what happened to Doucet, but you and your wife and daughter are just trying to move on with your lives. For a while everyone will assume you're responsible. Stick to your story and it will pass. Understood?"

"I understand."

"Keep your eye on the news Sunday. Leave the key for me later tonight. I'll collect." On Fisher's instructions, Vernier had left a manila envelope containing the money in a locker he'd rented at a local hostel. Once certain Fisher had in fact done the job, Vernier would leave the key under a bird feeder in the backyard.

Fisher stood up and extended his hand to the Frenchman. "Good luck to you."

"And you."

DOUCET and his gang of five had watched too many episodes of *The Sopranos*, and perhaps the *Godfather* trilogy a dozen too many times, going so far as to have their own social club/communal apartment: a 2,500-square-foot Quonset-style warehouse in a largely abandoned industrial park on Reims's western outskirts. Every weekend night, after trolling the city's bars, they returned to the warehouse—sometimes with women they'd picked up but more often alone—where they drank and watched bad kung fu movies until dawn.

FISHER tailed them on foot for an hour, just long enough to be sure they were sticking to their Saturday-night routine of barhopping, then walked back to his car and drove to the industrial park. He found a spot a half mile from the warehouse, then walked the remaining distance, making a complete circuit of the side streets before spiraling inward to the bolt-hole he'd scouted earlier. It was nearly eleven, so the area was dark and quiet. He found the thicket of trees that bordered the warehouse's loading ramp and settled down to wait. He had time to think.

In the space of a year his life had taken a dramatic turn. Not that he hadn't expected it, but the adjustment had been tougher than he'd anticipated. *Before . . . now,* he thought. Before: a covert soldier, a Splinter Cell for Third Echelon, the NSA's top secret operations branch. Now: a countryless mercenary. A murderer. No, it was worse than that, wasn't it? He was a man who had betrayed and murdered one of his oldest and finest friends: Lambert. None of it seemed real, as though the whole thing were a fuzzily remembered movie he'd seen long ago.

Someday, perhaps, the truth would come out and the situation would be judged differently, but today wasn't that day, and there was no guarantee that day would come at all. For now he would deal with what was in front of him and keep looking for the light at the end of the tunnel.

At this thought, Fisher smiled. *What was that old saying? "Be careful the light at the end of the tunnel isn't an oncoming train."*

Overhead spread a rumble of thunder, followed moments later by a flash of lightning to the south. A soft rain began to fall, pattering on the leaves around him. He pulled up his hood and kept watching.

SHORTLY before 1:00 A.M., Doucet's rust-on-white, hubcapless Citroën Relay van pulled into the driveway alongside the warehouse and followed it to the circular turnaround behind the loading dock. With a soft squealing of brakes, the Relay pulled to a stop twenty feet from where Fisher crouched. From inside, there came laughter and shouting. No female voices, as far as Fisher could tell. The Relay's side door slid open, and the Doucet gang came tumbling out, each of them barely negotiating the step down to the tarmac. This, Fisher thought, was going to be disappointingly easy. In his weeklong surveillance of the gang, he'd seen no guns but plenty of knives and truncheons. The two acts of violence he'd witnessed—group beatings administered to passersby for some slight, real or imagined—had confirmed what Fisher had already guessed: Doucet and his gang were bullies, but they were also good street fighters. No matter. Tonight good wasn't going to be good enough, and he had no intention of letting it descend into a fight—at least not a fair one. No such thing in this business.

Doucet emerged from the van. Despite the chilling

rain, he wore red nylon Nike track pants and a tight white T-shirt that accentuated his muscles.

"Hey, André, get the damned door open, huh!" he yelled.

André hurried up the loading-dock steps to the door. He looked up, noted the dimmed light fixture Fisher had disabled earlier, and gave it a tap with his finger. The light stayed dark. Another tap. Still dark.

"André!" Doucet drunkenly stumbled toward the steps. "Forget that!"

André got the door opened, and Doucet stepped through, followed by the rest.

FISHER gave them ten minutes to settle in, grab a fresh round of beers, and start whatever kung fu movie was on the night's playbill; then he shed his rucksack and retrieved the pair of two-by-fours he'd stashed under a pile of leaves earlier that day. He walked down the driveway to the front of the building and braced the first two-by-four under the front door's knob, then returned to the rear and did the same to the loading-dock door. He returned to the trees and retrieved his rucksack.

At the top of the loading ramp, he boosted himself onto the railing, then, with one hand braced on the wall, leaned forward until he could reach the defunct, car-sized air-conditioning unit affixed to the warehouse's back wall. Once he had a good grip on the unit, he stepped off the rail with his left foot and placed it on a flange jutting from the AC unit. He followed with his other hand and foot, then boosted himself atop the unit. From there it was a short climb up the utility ladder to the roof. Walking catfooted, he crossed the corrugated sheet metal until he reached the skylight; this, too, he'd already surveyed. He'd found it unlocked, but the hinges were squeaky, so he'd fixed them with a few squirts of silicone grease from a flip-top travel bottle. He lowered himself flat, pressed his ear to the sheet metal, and listened: laughter and, in the background, melodramatic martial-arts shouting and tinny movie music. Fisher lifted the skylight hatch until it rested against the roof, then slipped his legs through, feeling around until his right foot found a ladder rung. He climbed down a few feet, reached up, and closed the skylight, then climbed down to the floor. He was in a closet adjoining the bathroom. The previous owner had turned the warehouse's raised office area, which occupied the rear third of the space, into an open apartment that now overlooked the Doucet gang's social club—a collection of tattered recliners and couches clustered around a fifty-inch LCD TV.

Fisher pressed his ear to the door. He heard no one in the bathroom. He opened the door, took a moment to grease the hinges, then stepped past the toilet and sink on the right and eased open the exterior door; this one made no noise.

Directly ahead of him, spanning the width of the loft apartment and ending at a set of steps along the opposite wall, was a waist-high steel railing. To his right were a small kitchen, a breakfast nook, and a laundry area, each separated by a hanging mustard yellow bedsheet. The loft's width was divided every ten feet by load-bearing stanchions.

Clink. A dish. Fisher froze.

As he watched, one of Doucet's men—Pierre, it looked like—appeared, moving from right to left. He trotted down the stairs and out of sight. Fisher eased forward along the short wall until he could see over the railing. The gang was all there, still drunk and clearly entranced by the movie, occasionally shouting curses at characters and standing up to mimic a particularly pleasing kick or punch.

Fisher returned to the closet, retrieved what he needed from his rucksack, then shut the door, leaving it cracked open. Now he would let nature do its work.

THE wait was short. Ten minutes later he heard the clunk of feet coming up the steps. Ten seconds later the bathroom door swung open. Through the gap between the closet door and the jamb, Fisher saw the one known as Louis walk in. Fisher let the man position himself before the toilet, then swung open the door, stepped out, and tapped him hard behind the ear with a lead-and-leather sap. Louis dropped straight down. Fisher caught him by the collar and lowered him noiselessly to the floor. He quickly secured Louis's feet and hands with plastic flex-cuffs, then flushed the toilet, ran the faucet for a few seconds, and moved into the kitchen.

He opened the door under the sink, knelt down, stuck his head in the cabinet, and then called in guttural French, "Hey, Pierre!"

No response.

"Hey, Pierre!"

"What?"

"Gimme a hand here. Something's wrong with the sink!"

Footsteps thumped up the stairs, then across the floor into the kitchen. Head still inside the cabinet, Fisher stuck his hand out and waved Pierre forward. He knelt down to join him, and as his head slid inside, Fisher brought his seven-inch Gerber Guardian dagger up and laid the edge under Pierre's jawline.

"Not a word," Fisher whispered, "or I'll open your throat for you. Nod if you understand."

Pierre nodded.

"No matter what happens, your friends won't be quick enough to save you. Understand?"

Another nod.

"We're going to stand up and move to the bathroom. Nice and quiet now . . ."

Fisher got Pierre on his feet and herded him into the bathroom. When Pierre saw Louis's prostate form, he stiffened and started to turn around, but Fisher was ready with his sap. With a groan, Pierre dropped in a heap atop his friend. He bound them together, flex-cuffed hands and ankles interlocked.

Two down. Three to go.

Had this been a Third Echelon–sanctioned mission, his standard operating procedure would have been ano- nymity above all: no muss, no fuss, no footprints. In this case, however, disruption was everything. Romain

Doucet was about to experience, in a dramatic way, the law of cause and effect.

FISHER made no attempt to hide himself coming down the stairs. Even so, he'd nearly reached the bottom before Doucet noticed him. "Who the hell are you?"

"Meter reader."

"What?"

"Census taker."

Now Doucet and the other three—Georges, Avent, and André—were on their feet.

"How did you get in here?" This from Avent. The top of his right ear was missing; the crescent shape suggested he'd been Mike Tysoned.

Fisher circled the group, keeping them on his right with a couch between them. He kept his eyes fixed on Doucet. No one would move without a sign from him.

"I said, how did you get in here?"

"Pierre and Louis let me in," Fisher said. "You can ask them yourselves when they wake up."

Four pairs of eyes darted up to the loft, then back at Fisher. The fact that Doucet was still talking rather than attacking told Fisher the Frenchman dealt poorly with uncertainty. This brazen stranger in his house had upset the order of things. Had interrupted his Saturday night.

"This is a mistake, asshole," Doucet growled. "Do you know who I am?"

"You mean aside from a general dirtbag? No, I can't think of a thing."

"You're dead, mister! Georges, call the others and get them over here. We're going to need help burying this guy."

Georges pulled the cell phone from his pocket and dialed. He stared at the screen, then frowned. "No signal."

Fisher pulled a cigarette-pack-sized black box from his jacket pocket and held it up for them to see. "GSM signal jammer. Range is about thirty feet. You might have better luck outside."

At Doucet's nod, Georges headed for the door. It didn't budge.

"Almost forgot," Fisher said. "I locked us in."

"Locked us in?" Doucet repeated with a smirk. "Why the hell would you want to do that?"

"I don't want any interruptions."

Georges had returned to Doucet's side. The four of them glared at Fisher. Doucet said, "You've got five seconds to get out of here alive."

Fisher let the half smile he'd been wearing fall from his face. "Stop running your mouth, Lurch, and let's get to it."

Fisher barely got the words out before Doucet stepped forward, grabbed the arm of the couch, and tossed it aside as though it were a plastic chaise lounge. Fisher heard the distinctive *snick* of a switchblade opening a split second before Avent charged. The man was fast, but predictable, telegraphing his moves with his shoulders. He slashed wide at Fisher, who stepped back far enough to feel the blade's passage under his chin but close enough that a quick step forward brought him inside Avent's circle. He grabbed the knife arm at the wrist and the elbow, then dropped his own hips and twisted, putting all his weight into the torque. Avent's arm shattered at the elbow. From the corner of his eye, Fisher saw movement—two smaller figures, Georges and André—so he spun again, levering the screaming Avent's arm until he came around into their path. Fisher kicked Avent in the back of the knee, dropping him, then shoved him into Georges's legs. Georges stumbled forward. Fisher met him, sidestepping left to keep Georges between himself and Doucet. As he drew even with Georges's head, Fisher lashed out with a side fist that landed on the point of his jawbone, just below the ear. There was a muffled crack as the bone shattered. Georges gasped and went down, writhing. Seeing his two comrades down, André hesitated, but only for a moment before he, too, charged in, arms flailing in windmill punches. Fisher took a step back, waited until André's weight was on his lead foot, then toe-kicked him in the kneecap, shattering it. As he pitched forward, Fisher rammed his knee forward, catching him on the point of the chin. His head snapped back and he slumped backward, unconscious.

For a long ten seconds Doucet stared at Fisher, his chest heaving, the veins in his beefy neck pulsing. He glanced around, gave Fisher a sneering grin, and then walked over to one of the recliners. Beside it lay a cricket bat. Doucet hefted the thirty-eight-inch, three-pound length of white willow and squared off with Fisher again.

"Want to run now, asshole?" Doucet asked.

"No, thanks. In fact, that bat will suit my needs perfectly. I'm going to take it away and use it on you."

"How do you figure?"

Fisher let the smile drop from his face. "You're still running your mouth."

Doucet charged. He hadn't taken two steps before Fisher's Gerber was out of its sheath. Doucet's left leg was just coming forward when the dagger slammed, hilt deep, into his thigh. The left foot came down and immediately slipped from under the Frenchman as though he'd stepped onto an ice rink. He went down, knife hilt first, into the concrete. Then came the screaming.

IT took ten minutes to get Pierre, Louis, Georges, André, and Avent cuffed and arranged on the couch. Doucet, who'd received a sedating tap from Fisher's sap, was barely conscious, moaning gibberish as Fisher secured him to the sturdy oak coffee table, wrists and ankles cuffed to the legs.

Fisher made himself a cup of tea, sat down in one of the recliners, and waited until the others regained consciousness. Doucet was the last to come around. Fisher had bound the thigh wound using a sweatshirt he'd found stuffed between the couch cushions. Fisher's aim had been true: The Gerber had struck no arteries, just muscle.

Pierre was the first to speak. "What the—"

"We're done with questions, gentlemen. Now's the

time for answers. You run a thriving identity-theft business. I want to know where you keep your stock."

Louis said, "We don't have—"

Fisher silenced him with a raised hand. He picked up the cricket bat from beside his chair, then stood up and walked over to Doucet, who gaped at him. "I'm going to start hurting your boss," Fisher said. "How badly is up to you. The quicker you give me what I want, the less pissed off he's going to be at you." Fisher brought the cricket bat level with his waist, extended his arm, let the bat hover over Doucet's kneecap for a moment, then let it drop.

Crack!

Doucet screamed. Fisher let him get it out of his system, then said, "That's not even broken, guys. Next time I'm going to put a little heart into it."

"Tell him," Doucet said.

No one spoke. They looked everywhere but at their boss.

"Tell him, or God help me!"

Louis said, "Behind the dryer. There's a satchel."

"Don't go anywhere," Fisher said, then went upstairs, retrieved the valise, and came back down. "One more piece of business. Romain, you've been misbehaving—"

"I didn't—"

"Shut up. You've been misbehaving and now it's time to atone. I'm going to do some things to you, and it's going to involve a lot of pain, but you'll survive. While you're recuperating, I want you to remember this night. If you so much as litter or steal a magazine or curse at an old woman, I'll come back here and kill you." Fisher looked at the others, staring at each face in turn. "All of you. And I'll take my time doing it, too. Understood?" Six heads nodded.

Doucet said, "Hey, hey, you don't have to do this. I can give you—"

"There's nothing you can give me, and there's nothing you can say. You're a bully. Bullies' brains are wired differently. To truly get it, you need an unforgettable lesson."

"Please, don't—"

"Too late for that," Fisher said. He hefted the cricket bat, tested its weight, then walked closer to Doucet, who was openly sobbing now. "Don't worry," Fisher said. "You'll pass out quickly."

2

AT eleven the next morning, Fisher's taxi pulled onto rue de Vesles. Fisher let it go another hundred yards before asking the driver to stop. He paid the fare and climbed out. The block was lined with boutique clothing and shoe shops. Fisher crossed the street and walked another hundred yards, past the intersection of rue Marx Dormoy, then back across again. No sign of watchers. Once on the opposite sidewalk he reversed course again, past Marx Dormoy, and then into a tunneled alley called passage Saint-Jacques. Once through the alley he found himself in a warren of tree-lined courtyards and tall wrought-iron fences.

He found the right house number and pressed the buzzer. A moment later a wheezy voice replied, "Yes?"

"It's François Dayreis."

The door buzzed and Fisher pushed into the alcove, then down a short hall to a stairwell. He took it down one flight to the basement apartment and knocked. Fisher heard the shuffling of feet on carpet. Down the hall a ceiling fixture flickered, went dark, then flickered back to life. Abelard Boutin opened the door and gestured for him to enter. Boutin was as close to a human gnome as Fisher had ever met. In his late fifties, he was five feet, four inches tall and stoop shouldered, with only a few wisps of greasy gray hair to cover a skull so dented it reminded Fisher of a golf ball. Boutin's black-rimmed Coke-bottle glasses completed the look. Boutin cared little for appearances, Fisher had learned, at least those in the "realm of the animated," as Boutin called it. The Frenchman had only one interest: forgery. Like a mathematical savant who lived his life immersed in numbers, Abelard Boutin lived his life for the perfection of falsification. There were plenty of forgers in France but only a handful of Boutin's caliber.

It was that and one other trait of Boutin's that had brought Fisher here. Boutin could be trusted to do whatever it took to keep his beloved world intact. Clients who threatened that integrity were culled from the herd.

"How can I help you today?" Boutin asked wheezily. Clearly he was a fan of Gitanes: His apartment stunk of them. He shuffled Fisher into the apartment's sitting/ TV/work room. The center of the space was dominated by a ten-by-five-foot maple workbench equipped with all the tools of Boutin's trade. A perpetually burning electric brazier at each end of the workbench ensured that unexpected police guests would find no documents, only the tools of an avid fly-fishing-lure maker: swing-arm halogen magnifier lamps; miniature, multiarmed clamp vices; delicate pens and paintbrushes; a high-end copier-printer; and a laminating machine—for making weather-resistant shipping labels, Boutin had explained to Fisher on their first meeting. The forgery-specific tools and supplies Boutin likely kept in a well-concealed safe.

"I need these altered," Fisher replied, dropping the driver's licenses for the Doucet gang down on the table.

Boutin waddled over, snatched up the licenses, studied each in turn, then shrugged. "Easy enough. You have pictures?"

Fisher handed him the strip he'd taken in a do-it-yourself photo booth.

"The usual names?" Boutin asked.

"No, these." Fisher handed him a typewritten list.

"How soon?"

"How much?"

"Depends on how soon."

"Later this afternoon."

"Sixteen hundred for all."

"Eight hundred."

"Out of the question. Fourteen."

"One thousand, and let's be done with it. I'm sure you don't want me here any longer than is absolutely necessary."

This did the trick. Boutin waggled his head from side to side, thinking, then nodded. "Come back at five."

Fisher walked the half mile toward the city center, to a Sixt rental car agency on Aristide Briand, rented a white Ford Fiesta, then drove north out of the city on the D931. He reached Verdun just after noon. One of the handful of forgers on par with Boutin lived in an apartment near the quai de Londres on the Meuse River.

During World War II, Verdun and Reims were informal sister cities, together having been fortified into a loosely connected defensive line. Verdun's other claim to fame, one which was not found in many guidebooks, was that Adolf Hitler had served briefly in Verdun during World War I.

Fisher found Emmanuel Chenevier in a postage-stamp courtyard off his ground-floor apartment, apparently asleep in a redwood lounger, a copy of *The Count of Monte Cristo* lying open on his chest. As Fisher approached, Chenevier turned his head, shaded his eyes with one hand, and smiled.

"Afternoon, Sam."

"Emmanuel."

Chenevier was not only the one man in France who knew his true identity, but also one of the only "off the books" friends he had here. An old Cold War veteran, Chenevier had spent thirty years in the DGSE, the Direction générale de la sécurite extérieure (General directorate for external security). They'd become friends in the early nineties and had stayed in touch. Chenevier was a loyal Frenchman down to his bones, and while he knew Fisher had been disavowed, they'd struck a bargain: Fisher wouldn't harm Chenevier's beloved "Hexagone," and Chenevier would keep his secret.

"Please sit down, Sam." Fisher took the other lounger. "You cut your hair," Chenevier said. "And your beard . . . I can't recall the last time I've seen your face. You're moving on?"

"Soon."

"You need documents?"

"Alteration."

"Our bargain still stands, yes?"

"Of course. Had a situation in Reims yesterday, but nothing you wouldn't have done."

Chenevier pursed his lips. "I saw something on the news this morning. Some injured men in a warehouse?"

Fisher nodded.

"They deserved it?"

"They deserved worse."

"I have trouble imagining such a thing, Sam. As I recall, one of them had his arms and legs broken: tibia and femur in both legs, radius and ulna in both arms. They found him strapped to a table."

"I thought there were three bones in the arm: radius, ulna, and humerus."

"So there are. Sam, you frighten me sometimes."

Fisher didn't reply. Chenevier let it go. "Let's go inside. I'll make us some lunch."

AFTERWARD, Chenevier looked through Fisher's take from Doucet's warehouse, separating the items into piles: credit cards, driver's licenses, passports, and, as Fisher had already discovered, a surprise: thirty or so cell phone SIM (subscriber identity module) cards.

"These could be handy," Chenevier said with a low whistle. "I'll have to check them, of course, but if even a few are usable, you'll be like a ghost. As for the credit cards—"

"Just need them for reservations. Hotels and cars."

"I can do that. A few of the driver's licenses might be of use—"

"Forget those. I've already been to see Boutin."

Chenevier frowned. "He's untrustworthy, Sam. And when he sees the news about that warehouse business . . ."

"I know. He won't make the call until I'm gone, though."

Chenevier smiled. "You're right, of course. Monsieur Boutin has a finely honed sense of self-preservation, doesn't he? Why go to him at all?"

"I need to shake the tree. See what falls out."

"Ah, I understand. The passports are your safest course."

"Agreed."

"I can get six to eight out of this bunch. When do you need them?"

"Day after tomorrow."

"*D'accord*."

"I can give you—"

"You can give me nothing, Sam."

"*Merci*, Emmanuel."

"You look tired. Tell me: Will you ever be able to go home again?"

Fisher considered this. "I don't know."

FROM Verdun, he drove north and west, meandering his way through the villages of Forges-sur-Meuse, Gercourt-et-Drillancourt, and Montfaucon-d'Argonne before turning back toward Reims. While he doubted he would be using an alternate route to the border, the more familiar he was with the countryside, the better. Chances were, his dash from Reims would take him straight to Villerupt and Russange, but he was also aware of the old adage "No battle plan survives contact with the enemy," and unless he was wrong about Boutin, the enemy would soon be here.

Only two questions remained: How good would they be? And what would be their orders?

HE was back at Boutin's apartment shortly after five. The forger had the altered licenses ready. Fisher checked them, then handed over the money. "Nice work."

"I am aware. So, where will you go from here?"

"Who said I'm going anywhere?"

"I just assumed. . . ." Boutin gestured to the forged licenses.

Fisher shrugged. "Switzerland . . . Italy. I've got a friend who has a villa in Tuscany."

"A lovely place, Tuscany. When will you be leaving?"

"Tomorrow or the day after."

"Well, safe travels."

FISHER left Boutin's apartment and walked down the block to Jules, a clothing store on the corner of de Vesles and Marx Dormoy, and spent fifteen minutes perusing the racks by the window overlooking both entrances to passage Saint-Jacques until Boutin emerged from the courtyard. Being the devout indoorsman he was, the forger took the shortest route to the nearest *cabine*, or telephone booth, where he spent thirty seconds before retracing his route to his apartment.

Good boy, Abelard.

LIKE Emmanuel Chenevier, Boutin the Gnome would have little trouble with arithmetic. The man he knows as François Dayreis arrives at his apartment with five driver's licenses, and within hours those same names appear in the news: a brutal assault on the outskirts of Reims. A lone perpetrator. François Dayreis was more trouble than he was worth—a customer whose continuing business was more a liability than an asset to Boutin. By the time he'd placed his anonymous call to the authorities, Boutin had probably suspended his business and secreted his tools and materials. If Dayreis was captured and tried to implicate him, all the police would find was an old man running a fly-tying business in his basement apartment. As is the nature of their trade, forgers know how to hide things.

Now came the waiting. Boutin would be visited; of that Fisher was certain. His cutout had been clear about that much. The timelines and scope of the response would be telling. Who? How many? And, most important, what were their rules of engagement?

Fisher checked his watch: almost 7:00 P.M. Boutin was savvy; he wouldn't have said anything to the authorities about forged documents, but rather that he knew of the man described on the news. François Dayreis was his name. The report would go to the local police, the Police municipale, who would pass on the tip to the Police nationale. As Doucet and his cohorts would have reported the theft of their driver's licenses (but not the loss of their satchel full of stolen IDs, passports, and SIM cards), the Police nationale would assume the attacker planned to use the stolen licenses, which would necessitate the involvement of Interpol and the Direction centrale du renseignement intérieur (Central directorate of interior intelligence), or DCRI, France's version of the FBI. From there, electronic ears would take note of the name François Dayreis and alarms would be raised. In all, Fisher estimated he had six hours before someone in the United States pushed the panic button.

3

FISHER was awoken by the cricket chirp of his iPhone. Having set the ringtone to match only one incoming number, he knew the alert meant visitors had arrived. He checked the time: 11:15 P.M. He sat up in bed and looked around, momentarily confused by his surroundings—the by-product of moving around so much. The decor and layout of chain hotel rooms tended to blur together.

The good news was that the visitors weren't his but rather Boutin's. The night before, Fisher had planted a homemade motion detector around Boutin's apartment door: the tremble sensor from a vehicle's antitheft GPS tracker wired to a prepaid cell phone. The tremble sensor was buried beneath Boutin's doormat, and the cell phone buried against the wall a few feet away, its antenna jutting up among some weeds. Lacking the technological edge that working for 3E had provided, Fisher had, during the last year, become a fair inventor.

Having adopted the habit of sleeping in his clothes, he had only to grab his rucksack and head for the door.

HIS hotel, the Monopole, was a couple hundred yards north of Boutin's apartment, on place Drouet d'Erlon. The proximity was a risk, he knew, but having disposed of the François Dayreis alias and checked into the Monopole with one of Emmanuel's superbly altered passports, he felt relatively secure.

Outside, the streets were deserted and dark, save the yellow glow of the streetlamps reflecting on the damp cobblestones. He walked north, turned right onto rue de l'Etape, then immediately left into passage Subé, which took him south along an alley lined with boutiques and side entrances to restaurants until he was within sight of rue Condorcet. He stopped a hundred feet short and found a darkened doorway. Across the street lay a kebab restaurant, and to the left of it the tree-lined northern entrance to the courtyard outside Boutin's apartment.

From his rucksack he withdrew his EOS 1D Mark III. He affixed the AstroScope Night Vision, powered up the Canon, and brought the viewfinder up to his eye. In the greenish glow of the NV, he scanned the courtyard. Standing so still was the figure that he passed it twice before he realized what he was seeing. Japanese, medium build, shaved head—in his mid-twenties, too young to

be bald. An aesthetic choice. Fisher zoomed in, switched
the selector to burst mode, and pressed the shutter button. He stayed focused on the man, waiting to see if he
was smoking or waiting for someone, but for a full two
minutes the man stayed stock-still. *Disciplined.* The man
had "operator" written all over him.

Fisher moved on, scanning deeper into the courtyard.
There were too many trees. If he was right about the
Japanese guy, there would be others. This one was covering the northern entrance to the courtyard. . . . Would
he have partners at the west and south entrances? *Time
to move.*

Moving with exaggerated slowness, Fisher backed out
of his doorway and retraced his steps until he reached
the intersection of passage Subé and passage Talleyrand,
where he turned west. He emerged back on Drouet
d'Erlon, just south of his hotel, turned left through the
square, around the fountain at its center, then onto Marx
Dormoy. Ten feet from the west entrance to the courtyard, Fisher stopped short. He scanned his flanks with
the Canon, then moved up and peeked with the Astro-
Scope around the corner.

Like the Japanese man, this one was hidden in the
trees directly across from Boutin's apartment door. She,
too, was as still as a statue, save her eyes, which kept up
a constant scan. Fisher shot a burst of her, then zoomed
in and panned left. He stopped, panned back. In the NV,
there was no way to be sure of the hair color, but the
face looked familiar. . . . He zoomed in again. Kimberly
Gillespie. Fisher lowered the camera from his face, took

a deep breath, and squeezed his eyes shut. His situation had just gotten exponentially more complicated. *Damn*.

Fisher retraced his steps again: north to the square, then left and left again down rue Théodore Dubois to where it intersected rue de Vesles, then east for a hundred yards to the ATM just outside the courtyard's southern entrance.

He ducked down, crab-walked up the alley gate, and peeked around the corner and into the alley.

He froze.

The third watcher was standing thirty feet away, just inside the archway. Fisher kept still, barely breathing, until his eyes readjusted to the darkness and he could see a silhouette of the figure's face: thin and wiry with a hawk nose. Another familiar face? Fisher waited until the face rotated left, toward the interior of the courtyard; then he raised the AstroScope and zoomed in. The face turned again, back toward Fisher and into three-quarter profile. Fisher took a quick burst, then lowered the camera and froze. The man's eyes seemed to fix on Fisher's position. Five seconds passed. Ten. Thirty seconds. The face rotated again. Fisher ducked back and let out his breath.

He brought the Canon up to his face and switched on the LCD screen. He clicked through the last series of pictures. No mistake. He knew this one, too: Allen Ames. As it invariably did, the name caused Fisher's subconscious to start whispering. Something about Ames didn't sit right.

Fisher brought his mind back on track. So, three on overwatch, which meant at least one person inside talking to Boutin—no, there'd be two inside with Boutin, so five in all. One team leader and two pairs. A standard field team. There was no doubt about the opposition now.

Next: *transportation*. They wouldn't rely on taxis or mass transit, which meant rental cars, at least two of them. Using the AstroScope, Fisher scanned up and down rue de Vesles; the street was under partial construction with temporary NO PARKING signs every thirty feet. The cars would be close, but not too close. A quarter mile or less.

Fisher started walking.

It took fifteen minutes. On rue de Thillois, a few hundred yards southeast of Boutin's apartment, he found a blue Opel and a green Renault parked nose to tail. Both bore Europcar CDG stickers—Paris's Charles de Gaulle airport. This told him something. Someone had been lazy with tradecraft.

Fisher walked to the park across and down the street and found his spot: a bench sheltered by the low-hanging boughs of a tree with a clear sight line to the cars. He did a quick circuit of the park, checking approaches, exits, and angles; then he returned to the bench, pulled a rolled-up newspaper from his pocket, lay down, and covered himself with a hobo blanket. He completed the disguise with a half-consumed bottle of wine, which he placed on the ground beside the bench's leg.

Twenty minutes later the Japanese man and Kimberly appeared to the east on rue de Thillois. They were a quarter mile away and heading toward the cars. Fisher looked around. *Where are you? . . . There.* Fifty yards to the west, at the corner of rue des Poissonniers, stood a wiry figure. Ames. *Good tradecraft.* Kimberly and her partner—Fisher had started thinking of him as a Japanese Vin Diesel—would do a walk-by of the cars, looking for signs of tampering or surveillance while Ames did the same from his static position.

At the next intersection, Kimberly and Vin split up: Kimberly going straight ahead, Vin crossing over. As she passed the Opel and the Renault, she reached up with her left hand and adjusted her beret: an "all okay" signal to Vin, who replied by taking his right hand out of his pocket. Vin reached Ames's corner and turned left. Kimberly kept walking, crossed the intersection, then took up position in a sunken doorway before a pharmacy. She muttered something—into her SVT (subvocal transceiver), he assumed—then went still, watching. This, Fisher knew, would be the final check-in with Vin and Ames before everyone rallied back at the cars. A nice bit of discipline. It was all too easy to dismiss such precautions as excessive—which they often are—but overcautiousness was an operator's best friend, one of those habits that would, if you stayed in the business long enough, save your life one day. Fisher had seen the lack of it kill plenty of otherwise good spooks.

Who would it be? Fisher wondered. So far he recognized two of the three opposing players. Would he recognize the other two? He'd know soon enough. He tried to look ahead, tried to visualize the surrounding streets as a chessboard, placing Kimberly and Ames on their respective squares. Vin was still moving, probably circling the block; they'd want to triangulate on the cars' position. . . . *There.* Vin appeared at the intersection to the west and stopped, taking up a static overwatch post. That meant the team leader and the remaining team member would be coming from the north, probably down rue Jeanne d'Arc.

As if on cue, two figures turned the corner opposite Vin and started toward the cars. Fisher remained perfectly still. The team would be at its most alert now, as it reunited. *Eggs in a basket.*

When the new pair was fifty feet from the cars, Vin, Ames, and Kimberly left their posts, collapsing toward the cars. The newest pair, a man and woman Fisher could now see, reached the Opel. The woman, a blonde, peeled off and walked around to the driver's side. Vin was right behind her, getting into the rear as the woman unlocked the doors. The man walked around the front of the Renault to the driver's door. Kimberly walked past Fisher's position, got in the front passenger seat as Ames got in the rear. Fisher lifted the AstroScope, focused on the Renault's driver, shot a burst, then lowered the camera.

Within seconds, the cars pulled out and drove down the block. At the intersection the Renault headed north, the Opel south. Once the engines faded, Fisher called up the last batch of shots on the Canon's LCD. In all but two of the pictures the driver's face was partially obscured by a patch of reflection on the Renault's windshield. The last two were enough. Fisher smiled. *Ben Hansen.* A decent choice for team leader. *Nice to see you alive, Ben.* Fisher hoped he didn't regret playing a part in this.

HANSEN would want to talk to the still-recuperating Doucet and company, but it was after midnight, well past visiting hours at the Centre Hospitalier Universitaire, so the visit would have to wait until morning—assuming they'd gotten into Reims late. If so, that left Hansen two options: settle in for the night or visit Doucet's warehouse and see what they could see. Fisher guessed the latter; Ben Hansen was proactive, to put it mildly. A "bulldog" was perhaps a better term. Though the police wouldn't have found anything of use at the warehouse, Team Hansen would be looking for altogether different evidence.

Fisher let five minutes pass, then walked back to Boutin's block. It was time for another field exam. From the trees beside the kebab restaurant, he watched Boutin's courtyard for fifteen minutes. Nothing moved. He moved in.

In the glow of his red-hooded penlight, he lifted the doormat. The tremble sensor had been moved, ever so slightly. Fisher checked the cell phone. It, too, showed signs of having been touched. *Fail*, he thought. Someone—probably Hansen—had either spotted or looked for the sensor. Having found it, he and his team should have doubled back and set up on Boutin's courtyard to see if anyone came to collect the device. So far, it was a mixed report card: some good tradecraft but some dumb mistakes and a missed golden opportunity.

FISHER drove to Doucet's warehouse and drove around the industrial park until he spotted the team's cars; this time they'd parked a quarter mile apart. Hansen was learning.

He found a scrap yard, parked beside the hurricane fence enclosing the lot, then shook the fence a few times until certain no guard dogs were present. He then climbed atop the car, scaled the fence, and dropped down to the other side. On the west side of the dirt lot was a car compactor, next to it a crane with a glassed-in control booth. He climbed the ladder and slipped inside. A quarter mile to the north, over the tops of the stacked cars, he could see Doucet's warehouse. He lifted the Canon to his eye and zoomed in. For five minutes nothing moved, and then, from the skylight hatch on the roof, a darkened figure appeared. Then a second. They padded across the roof and down the same air-conditioning unit he'd used to gain entry two nights earlier.

In the corner of the AstroScope he saw a glimmer of light. He panned that way but saw nothing, so he returned his focus to the warehouse. Another glimmer. He snapped around in time to catch it.

In a parking lot across the street from Doucet's warehouse, a lone black Range Rover sat under a tree. Fisher zoomed in and adjusted the NV contrast until two man-shaped silhouettes came into view. He couldn't make out faces, but there was no mistaking the object the passenger was holding: a spotting scope. Aimed at Doucet's warehouse.

4

FOLLOWING the extended arm of the lot attendant, Fisher pulled his rental car into the parking space and got out. He handed the rental agreement to the attendant, waited while she checked the car's mileage and condition, then took the receipt, grabbed his blue duffel bag, and started walking. The bus station was two blocks away; twenty minutes later he was heading west toward Villerupt.

He was exhausted. It was, in fact, hell getting old, Fisher decided. True enough, he was in far better shape than 90 percent of the people half his age, but the little aches and pains that at one time went unnoticed were harder to ignore now. The same went for sleep deprivation, but that wasn't anything that couldn't be cured by a tall cup of dark roast. And so far the aches were no match for a couple of tabs of ibuprofen. He checked his watch. Not quite eleven. Once he reached his destination he'd catch a couple of hours' sleep, then prep for the border crossing.

The night before, in Reims, he'd sat in the crane's control booth and watched until the rest of Hansen's team emerged from Doucet's warehouse and rallied back at their cars, with the mysterious Range Rover following, headlights off, at a discreet distance. The watchers themselves were being watched. But by whom? It was a question that would have to remain unanswered for the time being. Fisher watched from his perch until one of the team's cars and the Range Rover disappeared east down the D980, then headed back toward Reims, returned to his hotel, slept for four hours, and got up and headed north.

He pulled into the Villerupt terminal just before noon and checked into a hostel using one of Emmanuel's clean passports. No credit card was required. He paid cash for three days. Unless something went wrong, he would be staying only the afternoon.

AT three o' clock Fisher left the hostel and walked a half mile west to the Sixt office on place Jeanne d'Arc and rented a sun yellow Chevrolet Aveo using Louis Royer's driver's license and one of Emmanuel's sanitized Master-Cards, then drove to a Lacoste outlet store and paid cash for three outfits: a red polo shirt over green trousers, a yellow polo over sky blue trousers, and khaki trousers with a long-sleeved navy blue button-down shirt. He completed the ensembles with a similarly mixed-and-matched trio of designer baseball caps and sunglasses. He used the changing room to don the red and green outfit, then stuffed the rest of the clothes in his rucksack and left.

Finally, he took the D16A northeast two miles to Russange, which straddled the border along with the Luxembourgian village of Esch-sur-Alzette, just two miles north up the D16/18. He found a local bike-rental shop, made the necessary arrangements, and then, following his guidebook, he found the Café Entrepôt on rue Napoléon 1er and parked. Out his passenger window, a quarter mile to the northeast, he could see the France–Luxembourg border crossing.

He checked his watch. An hour had elapsed since he'd rented the Aveo, forty minutes since he'd made his purchases at the Lacoste store. If Hansen and his team were in close contact with home—which Fisher knew they would be—news of his purchases may have already reached them. Given his sudden appearance in Villerupt, not a stone's throw from the Luxembourg border, they would have to assume he was running. Fisher doubted Hansen would want to waste the two-plus hours it would take to cover the 140 miles to Villerupt. And, with no TGV routes available, that left one option: charter plane. As the crow flies, it was an eighty-five-mile trip.

Fisher started his mental clock. Ninety minutes. No more.

ON an impulse that he would soon wish he'd ignored, Fisher drove to the nearest airport, which in this case was an airstrip four miles southwest of Villerupt and just out-side the village of Errouville. The runway was little more than a dirt tract hemmed in by farmers' green fields.

Fisher parked beside one of the three outbuildings that seemed to serve as the strip's terminal, hangar, and office. Four parking spaces down were a pair of SUVs, both Renault Koleoses: one in black, the other silver. He pushed through the door marked BUREAU. Sitting behind the counter was a paunchy woman with bright red hair.

"Vous désirez?" she asked.

In French, Fisher explained that he was expecting some friends later that afternoon, but he wasn't sure what flight they were on. "Five of them," he finished.

The woman checked her log, frowning and clicking her tongue as her finger traced the columns. "Nothing later this afternoon. We do have five coming in . . ." She trailed off, walked over to the radio set on a nearby desk, and had a rapid-fire exchange over the hand mic. She came back. "Three minutes. A charter from Verdun."

Fisher's heart lurched. *Stupid, Sam.* Of course Han-sen would have gone to see Emmanuel. His old friend wouldn't have given them anything, but when word of his car rental reached Hansen, he and his team were virtually halfway to Villerupt. By car it would've been a seventy-five-minute trip, by charter twenty minutes. That told him something: His pursuers were, in fact, keen to intercept him before he crossed the border.

Fisher thanked the woman and walked out to his car. To the south he could hear the drone of an airplane engine. He turned and scanned the skies. Seconds later he could see it, a white sliver dropping altitude on its way into the airstrip. On a hunch, Fisher walked down to the parked Renault SUVs. In the back window of each was the familiar orange and silver Sixt logo.

He got into the Aveo, started the engine, and sped off.

HE was back at the Café Entrepôt in Russange thirty minutes later. Another check of the watch: twenty minutes to go. The sun was already arcing toward the western horizon.

He needed to keep Hansen and his team close, but not so close that they could impede his progress or, worse still, capture him—a task hard enough in its own right and made harder still by the nature of his pursuers: trained but largely untested. They were likely to make a lot of mistakes on which he could capitalize, but they were just as prone to mercuriality. An operator of his own caliber would react to situations, not predictably, but coolly, logically. Equanimity under fire was usually found only in seasoned operators. He would have to pay close attention to his own assumptions. Hansen and his team might zig when they should have zagged.

Fisher had chosen this section of the border because it was straddled by sister cities—Russange in France and Esch-sur-Alzette in Luxembourg. Except for lightly patrolled wilderness areas, urban confluences like this were usually the easiest to cross. Employees lived on one side, worked on the other; friends lived virtually within shouting distance, but were separated by a border; restaurants and taxi services shared customers; French doctors would refer patients to Luxembourgian dentists. Fluidity and proximity demanded indulgent border standards.

As luck had it, the weekend's unique festivities would further help Fisher's plan. The old Audun-le-Tiche station and rail line that once connected Russange and its environs to Esch-sur-Alzette had, despite the protests of nostalgic French and Luxembourg citizens alike, been slated for decommissioning. Carnivals at stations on both sides of the border were to begin at sunset with the departure of a nineteenth-century locomotive and three carriage cars from Audun-le-Tiche. The one-mile journey would take ten minutes; revelers of both nationalities could travel back and forth to the celebrations free of charge throughout the weekend, once an hour, on the hour. Those who chose to forgo the train could walk, drive, or bicycle. Of the forty thousand or so residents in the area, some five thousand were expected to attend the celebrations.

TEN minutes later, on schedule, the bike shop owner's ten-year-old son pulled into the Café Entrepôt's parking lot and braked to a stop beside Fisher's open window. Fisher gave him a five-euro tip and told him where to leave the bike.

"Merci," the boy called and pedaled off. The sun was setting now, casting the village in shades of gold and red.

The timing was mostly guesswork, more an art than a science: From touchdown at the Errouville airstrip to the Sixt office would be forty minutes. Hansen would immediately contact 3E with the make and model of Fisher's rental, and the NSA's potent electronic ears would begin scanning radio traffic for any mention of such a vehicle in the area. While hoping for a break, the team would begin scouring the area for the car, probably splitting up to first check Villerupt, and then Russange.

Fisher let five minutes pass, then drove a few blocks south to the McDonald's on rue du Luxembourg. He made one circuit of the parking lot, during which he found a man sitting alone in his car, eating a Big Mac. His expression, Fisher felt, was sufficiently dour to suit his purposes. Time to make sure Hansen and his team were moving in the right direction. He pulled to a stop ten diagonal feet from the man's rear bumper, then stepped on the accelerator. The crunch of bumpers echoed through the parking lot. Fisher grabbed his duffel bag and got out. The other man did the same and immediately began screaming in French, gesticulating wildly at his car. Fisher shouted back, waved the duffel bag menacingly, then suggested the man frequently enjoyed carnal knowledge of his own mother. The man's face turned red. He charged Fisher. Fisher turned and ran into the McDonald's, shoving people out of the way and shouting and generally wreaking havoc before darting out the side exit. Behind him the man began yelling, "Police! Police!"

Half stumbling, half sprinting, and casting dramatic looks over his shoulder, Fisher headed north toward the Audun-le-Tiche station. Farther up the tracks he could see rhythmic plumes of smoke over the treetops as the train returned from its run to Esch-sur-Alzette.

Behind him came the distant warble of police sirens. He reached the station, pushed his way through the crowds at the west entrance, and out onto the platform. *"Excusez-moi . . . pardonnez-moi. . . ."* Followed by the words "mother," "sick," and "hurry." The platform was festooned with balloons and colored flags. Portable stalls shaded by awnings of red, blue, and white stripes—the flag colors of both Luxembourg and France—sat along the perimeter of the station, selling souvenirs, drinks, and snacks. Yellow candle lanterns swayed from wires suspended between the streetlamps and the station's eaves. Giggling children darted about with fizzling sparklers. Somewhere nearby a band played French folk music.

With a chugging sigh of steam, the train stopped at the platform. The incoming passengers were disembarked by black-capped, bow-tied conductors, who then unclipped the velvet ropes and began ushering the departing passengers aboard. Once aboard, Fisher turned right, found an aisle seat in the last carriage before the caboose, and sat down. He unzipped his duffel, pulled out his rucksack, and shoved the bag under the seat.

The seconds turned into minutes as stragglers came aboard and found seats. With a cry of "All aboard!" in French, the locomotive whistled and the car lurched forward. In the corner of his eye Fisher saw sudden movement on the platform and turned in time to see Vin and the blond woman appear in the station doorway, their heads swiveling. Fisher leaned back in his seat, and the platform slid from view.

He checked his watch. Damn, they were quick.

5

LIKE the Audun-le-Tiche station, the rail line was deco-
rated: Old-fashioned replica conductor's lanterns, blin-
kered in blue and red, were mounted on posts every
hundred yards or so. Moving at a mere eight miles per
hour, the train covered one post every thirty seconds,
so Fisher had no trouble keeping track of his position.
At the twelfth post, just over the Luxembourg border,
the train approached a curve. Fisher stood up, walked
to the back of the car, and without looking back, opened
the vestibule door and stepped out onto the coupling
platform. It was fully dark now. Beneath his feet the
levers and wheels rattled. To his right, on the other
side of the embankment, lay a line of trees; to his left,
across a ditch, the two-lane road linking Russange and

Esch-sur-Alzette. Cars tooled along in both directions, honking and waving at fellow revelers.

He waited until the train was halfway between two lighted posts, then tossed his rucksack and jumped after it. Just before hitting the ground, he dropped his shoulder, rolled into the impact, and let himself go flat. He watched the train disappear around the bend, then groped around, found his rucksack, and crawled up the embankment and into the trees. He stopped to get his bearings.

These machinations—the fracas in the McDonald's parking lot, his theatrical dash to the train station, the bicycle he paid to have deposited along the D16/18, the change of clothes—were admittedly overengineered, but his trail into Luxembourg needed to be not only cold, but convoluted. The more he could split the team, both physically and mentally, the better. Not only would it keep them at bay, but it would, hopefully, reveal weaknesses he might use later.

He used the stone obelisk across the road and the lantern posts to fix his position. Unless the boy hadn't followed through, the bike would be lying in the tall grass of the embankment, fifty yards up the road. Fisher stood up and began picking his way through the trees. Across from him, the cars continued in steady north and south streams. Horns honked. Laughter and friendly shouting echoed in the darkness. Out of the corner of his eye, he caught a flash of chrome in the moonlight: the bike. He stopped, crouched down. He looked up and down the road. All was clear. Hunched over, he ran down the slope and up the other side. He was ten feet from the bike when, fifty feet to the left, he noticed a pair of SUVs—one silver, one black. He dropped flat. Ten seconds passed. Nothing happened. He began wriggling backward down the slope.

The black SUV's rear driver's-side door opened, and out stepped Kimberly. A moment later Ames and Blondie came around from the other side. Each wore a long trench coat. Together they began walking toward the bike. Fisher kept going, reverse crawling to the bottom of the ditch, where he crabbed around and started up the opposite slope toward the trees.

The trio started running. Fisher did the same. Within seconds he was in the trees and heading east. He recalled his mental map: a hundred feet to the reservoir, two hundred feet to the opposite shore, then a dirt road bordered by forest.

Using what little light filtered through the canopy above, he ducked beneath branches and dodged trunks until he broke into the clear and found himself skidding down another embankment. He dropped into a baseball slide and dug his heels into the moist earth, coming to a halt with his legs dangling in space. Ten feet below was the surface of the reservoir. *Damn.* Here was a reminder: The map is not the territory. Having not anticipated needing to run this way, he'd relied solely on Google Earth, which, of course, didn't show this miniature cliff along the shoreline.

From the trees behind him came the crunch of footfalls.

He spun himself on his butt, pushed off, and dove into the water. Instantly he felt a wave of relief, an old habit from his SEAL days: Water was cover, escape, safety. He scissored hard for thirty feet, broke the surface for a lung-ful of air, then dove again, this time kicking straight for the bottom, eight feet below. When his outstretched hand touched mud, he began kicking. After thirty seconds his lungs began to burn; he heard the pounding of blood in his head. He kicked off the bottom and broke into the air.

He heard a muffled *pop*. He knew the sound all too well. Even as the voice in his head said, *Cottonball*, he felt the projectile strike the back of his head. The tang of the aerosol tranquilizer filled his nostrils. He snorted and ducked under again, shaking his head to get the aerosol out of his hair. He was only marginally successful. Within seconds his field of vision began to sparkle; he felt slightly drunk. Clearly, Third Echelon's weapons geeks had improved the LTL (less-than-lethal) projectile. This Cot-tonball's tranquilizer was much stronger and much faster acting. He'd gotten only a quarter dose, he estimated. If he'd been hit on land, he'd be asleep right now.

Focus, Sam, focus. . . . Keep going. Distance was survival.

He rolled onto his back and porpoised upward so only his mouth broke the surface. He sucked in a breath. Another muffled *pop*, this one sharper, but also familiar: a 5.56mm bullpup round from a SC-20K rifle. The round slapped the water two feet from his head. *A mistake or—*

Pop!

The second round zipped past his ear. *No mistake.*

He dove again, rolled over, scissored hard for the bottom. He covered ten feet . . . twenty . . . thirty. . . . He stretched out his right hand. *Come on, come on!* His fingers touched something vertical—mud, weeds. He grabbed a handful of roots and pulled himself forward until he was pressed against the mud. He surfaced amid the weeds drooping over the embankment. He caught his breath. He now knew something else about his pursuers: They either didn't have goggles or were choosing to not use them lest they stand out. Third Echelon standard-issue NV headsets gave Splinter Cells not just night-vision capabilities but also EM (electromagnetic) and IR (infrared, or thermal). Using the latter, they would have seen him here—a man-shaped blob in various temperature-shades of blue, yellow, and red.

Fisher parted the weeds and peered across the reservoir. Kimberly and Ames were nowhere to be seen. He kept scanning, checking the length of the embankment before moving up to the trees. *There*. Three figures lying prone, barely visible in the underbrush of the tree line. Their scopes would be panning his side of the reservoir, looking for movement, ready to zoom in. . . . The question was: What were their fire selectors set to? And exactly what were the rules of engagement they had been given? If it had been Kimberly shooting at him, then, clearly, in her eyes their previous friendship had lost its charm. If it was Ames . . . well, no surprise there. As for Blondie, she was, at this point, a question mark.

There was no way he would make it up the ten-foot embankment. The climb was doable, but the movement of the weeds would give him away. He looked left. A hundred feet away the reservoir's north end was bordered by an abandoned municipal swimming pool surrounded by a cracked, weed-covered cement deck whose outer wall plunged vertically into the reservoir. Fisher couldn't see them in the dark, but Google Earth had clearly shown two squared-off alcoves where steel-rung ladders were cut into the wall. The alcoves were three feet deep—enough, he judged, to impede Kimberly's and Ames's lines of fire.

He sucked in a lungful of air, dropped beneath the surface, and began using the roots to pull himself along the embankment. At the halfway mark he again pulled himself against the mud wall and carefully surfaced in the weeds. He caught his breath, ducked under again, and thirty seconds later his outstretched hand touched concrete. He turned right, dragging his fingertips over the rough surface until he felt the wall turn inward. Two kicks brought him to the ladder. He pressed his head into the corner and surfaced. No shots came. He rotated his head and peeked around the corner.

With the increased distance, it was impossible to tell if Kimberly and Ames were still in position. He waited. Two minutes . . . five. He climbed the ladder, rolled onto the concrete deck, pressed himself flat, then began snaking his way through the weeds until the concrete gave way to open ground. He was three hundred yards from the opposite shore—a tough shot but not impossible. Still, he needed to be seen.

He took a deep breath, curled his legs beneath him like a sprinter, then took off, heading for the road fifty yards away. He'd covered half the distance when he heard the *smack-thump* of a bullet striking the earth to his right. He resisted the impulse to dodge in the opposite direction, instead turning into it, zigzagging until he reached a slight depression before the road, where he dropped flat again. He checked his watch. It would take them sixty or seventy seconds to move from their shooting position to the pool, then another sixty seconds to clear the deck and the surrounding undergrowth before pushing toward this road. Right now they'd be on their SVTs, radioing the other SUV: *Circle north and west to the dirt road, and we'll drive him from the west.* A smart plan, Fisher admitted. Keep up the pressure; don't let the quarry rest. Unfortunately for them, he wasn't about to let himself slip into the quarry mind-set.

He shed his clothes, trading the red on green outfit for a dark blue sweatshirt and a pair of old French army fatigue pants he had picked up at a surplus store. The Aloksak bag had kept them perfectly dry. He stuffed the discarded outfit under a bush, careful to leave a bit of red showing.

He let a minute pass, then got up and ran, hunched over, north along the depression to where it intersected with a stand of pine trees. He paused to pull out his red-hooded penlight, then kept moving until he estimated he had enough cover. He stopped and ducked behind a fallen trunk.

A branch snapped. *South.*

Partially obscured by the trees, a lone figure crossed the open ground, heading west. The build told Fisher it was a woman. *Kimberly.* She stopped. Her head swiveled, scanning the pine trees. *Good girl.* She'd neither heard nor seen anything, of that he was certain, but she was thinking: *If Fisher had cut to the north instead of crossing the road, he'd be in there. . . .* What to do? Abandon the pincer plan, leave her partner alone and search the trees, or—

She kept moving.

It was the smart move. She was going to kick herself later, but clearly she'd been paying attention during Small-Unit Tactics.

He waited until she'd moved out of view, then continued east, slowly at first and then more quickly as he gained some distance, until he could see car headlights on the D16/18. When the trees thinned enough that he could see the cars themselves, he stopped. He opened his rucksack and found the two Aloksak bags he needed. He traded his fatigues and sweatshirt for the yellow Lacoste polo over sky blue outfit, then got out his binoculars—a pair of night-vision Night Owl Explorers. Not the same caliber as Third Echelon's DARPA-produced headsets, but as he was something of a beggar these days, he'd renounced choosiness.

He powered up the Night Owls, crawled to the lip of the embankment, and panned the highway. There were four SUVs in view, but none of them Renaults. A half mile to the northeast, across the highway, he could see the lights of Esch-sur-Alzette's CFL (Chemins de fer Luxembourgeois) train station. Almost there. Fifteen minutes and he'd be gone. He'd have some breathing room. At least for a while.

He put away the Night Owls, waited for a lull in traffic, then stood up and walked down into the ditch and back up the other side. He was stepping onto the dirt shoulder on the far side of the road when, to the right, he heard the roar of an engine. Out of the corner of his eye he saw a single headlight bearing down on him.

6

THE instinctive part of Fisher's brain reacted instantly, registering the motorcycle a quarter second before sending the "jump" impulse to his legs. The nearest oncoming car, moving at a leisurely fifteen miles an hour, was twenty feet away. To avoid Fisher, the motorcyclist could either go right, into the ditch, or left, into traffic. Fisher gambled and went in the latter direction, spinning on his heel back into the path of the oncoming car, landing in a half crouch, with his legs spread, ready to dive away if the car didn't slow. To his left, the motorcycle's brakes locked up. The headlight shuttered with the sudden deceleration, then veered right and down into the ditch. There came the sound of wrenching fiberglass. The car bearing down on Fisher slammed on its brakes. Horns began blaring. Car doors opened and witnesses began jogging toward the scene.

Blend, Fisher commanded himself. "Help me—he's down here!" Fisher called in French, then trotted down into the ditch. The rider lay in the tall grass on the other side of the embankment; ten feet away his motorcycle was a tangled heap. Fisher and four others reached the rider at the same time. He was barely conscious. "Stabilize his head," Fisher commanded, then lifted the visor on the man's helmet. The face didn't look familiar. Just bad timing, he decided.

Voices began babbling: "Idiot tried to pass . . ." "Did you see him? . . . almost hit . . ."

Fisher said, "He's in shock. I'll find a blanket. Stay with him. . . ."

"Oui, oui . . ."

Fisher trotted north, up the road. He glanced over his shoulder. A dozen or more people were now at the bottom of the ditch, tending to the motorcyclist. From the border came the whine of sirens and flashing blue lights. He put another fifty yards between himself and the commotion, then walked back into the ditch, up the other side, and into the trees beyond. He paused to get his bearings, using the highway to his left and the soccer stadium lights to his right as navigation points. *The CFL station would be . . . that way.* Another two minutes of walking brought him to a weed-covered gravel lot surrounded by a dilapidated hurricane fence, half of which jutted from the ground at wild angles, while the other had collapsed altogether. In the center of the lot was what had looked like, on Google Earth, an abandoned prison, with high brick and corrugated-steel walls topped by conical watchtowers and arched mullioned windows. It was, in fact, a deserted steel foundry. Early twentieth century, Fisher judged. A hundred years ago European industrialists often chose the ornate over the pragmatic, assuming a happy worker was a productive worker.

It was as good a place as any for another clothing change, he decided. His second clothing change had been for his pursuers' benefit; having likely found the first outfit east of the swimming pool, they would have assumed he'd adopted night-friendlier clothes. If spotted now, he'd be another local in colorful springtime garb.

He spotted a vertical slit in the foundry's sheet-metal wall and headed for it. A quarter mile to his left, back on the highway, he saw a pair of headlights do a quick U-turn, then a second pair. At this distance he couldn't make out the makes and models, but the shapes suggested SUVs. They began heading south, in his direction.

What the hell?

Fisher sprinted for the wall, pried back the sheet metal, and stepped through the slit. He glanced back. The SUVs had drawn even with the foundry driveway and stopped, turn signals blinking, as they waited for a gap in traffic. Fisher wriggled through the opening, then did his best to wrench the metal closed behind him.

He pulled out his penlight and looked around. In the darkness, the scene was jumbled: vaulted concrete ceilings dotted with broken skylights through which moonlight streamed, crumbling plaster-covered brick walls, ladders and catwalks and spiral staircases, a labyrinth of overhead iron girders and concrete lintels. The floor was ankle deep in ash, dust, and accumulated silt. Weeds and spindly trees sprung from the loam. Somewhere overhead he heard the leathery flapping of wings. The echo told him the space was cavernous.

He took a step. His foot plunged through the soil and into empty space. He shined his light down. The floor was made of heavy four-by-four wooden beams. Through the hole in which his foot had slipped, he could see crisscrossing pipes and, beyond that, the glint of water. *Man-made canals,* he thought. Older foundries relied on them to cool equipment.

From the lot came the skidding of tires on gravel. Car doors opened, slammed shut.

Don't think, run!

He pushed up, levered himself onto his belly, then jerked his leg free; he flexed it. Nothing broken. He got up and ran, steering for the nearest wall, hoping and assuming the beams would be stronger nearer the joists. The dancing beam of his penlight picked out a staircase rising against the wall. He sprinted for it, leapt onto the third step, then stopped. He looked back; his footsteps were as clear as if he'd left them in snow. To his right a series of forearm-sized pipes stretched beneath a concrete lintel. Fisher mounted the handrail for a better look. *Maybe. It would be tight, but—*

Voices shouted outside. The sheet metal at the entrance rattled.

Fisher grabbed the nearest pipe, pushed off the railing, then swung, hand over hand, until he reached an intersection of beams. He flipped his left leg up, hooked his ankle on the pipe, shimmied another three feet, then chinned himself level with the pipe, reached over with his left hand, found purchase, and levered himself atop the pipe run. He straightened his legs and tucked his arms flat against his thighs. It was a tight fit. He went still and took three calming breaths to slow his heart rate. He craned his neck to check his surroundings.

Five feet above him was another concrete lintel, this one running perpendicular to the pipes on which he lay; there would be a matching shelf along the opposite wall, he assumed. Four feet above this lintel, through a tracery of pipes, he could see the underside of the second floor.

From below came the violent wrenching of sheet metal, then silence.

Whispered voices.

Come on in, Fisher thought. *But watch your—*

As if on cue, he heard the splintering of wood, followed by a curse in Japanese. The accent was American, though, which told Fisher a bit more about the man.

Step.

"Help me, goddamn it!" a voice rasped.

"Hold on, hold on . . ." This was a woman's voice. Not Kimberly, he didn't think. Blondie, then. Hansen, the team leader, would be working solo while the other four were paired up. Blondie and Vin were here; Kimberly and Ames would probably be on the east side, looking for an entrance. As for Hansen—

More cracking of wood, another curse. This one from Blondie.

There were thirty seconds of grunting and whispers as the two extracted their legs and feet from the floor traps, followed by muffled feet padding through the loam and moving toward the stairs. A foot clanged on the metal steps, then stopped.

"What?" whispered Blondie. Clearly these young Splinter Cells had a few things to learn about CommSec—communication security. SVTs did, in fact, take some getting used to—as well as a bit of ventriloquial talent—but this was Stealth 101.

Silence now.

Fisher leaned his head to the side, just enough for one eye to clear the pipe run. Directly below him was a clean-shaven head. Vin. Fisher eased his head back. A flashlight clicked on and panned left to right, pausing on piles of debris and shadowed corners until the beam had made a 360-degree circuit. The flashlight went dark.

Then came on again. The light angled upward, tracking slowly over the pipes and beams. After a long thirty seconds, the beam went out.

Above, Fisher heard a crack, not of wood, but of rock on concrete, followed by a series of metallic clangs. Something hard thumped into his thigh, then rolled off and hit the ground with a powdery *fwump*. They were trying to flush him out. Another rock smacked into the lintel over his head. It ricocheted upward, hung there for a moment, then came back down, *ting*ing loudly in the darkness before zipping past Fisher's face.

"Nothing there," Blondie whispered. "Come on."

"Yeah, okay."

Footsteps clanked up the steps, then faded.

Fisher let out a breath. He drew his legs forward, under his chest, then stood up. Arms extended above his head, he grabbed the edge of the lintel, chinned himself up, then rolled onto the shelf. He was twenty feet above the floor; unless one of them found the perfect viewing angle through the pipes below, he was effectively invisible.

Next step, he thought. He had three options: hunker down and wait until they moved on, wait for a chance and slip away, or create his own chance and slip away. The first option was the worst of the three. With five people and at least a nominal equipment loadout, they could exfiltrate the foundry and stake it out electronically. He needed to be gone before the plan occurred to them. That left the third option: create some chaos and use the confusion to break out. How, though?

The answer presented itself with the sound of splintering wood above his head. The floor planks split. Ash and dirt funneled through the opening. The dust cleared to reveal a leg jutting through the hole, wriggling like a worm on a fishing line. To his or her credit, the person above made no sound, not even a gasp of surprise.

Fisher dug into one of his rucksack's side pockets and came up with ten-foot coil of Type III 550 paracord. This was one of Fisher's many "desert island staples," along with duct tape, Swedish FireSteel, and superglue for on-the-fly wound repair. He tied a quick running bowline in one end of the cord, then lassoed the dangling foot, looped the free end twice over a pipe, and finished with a cinch knot.

The leg jerked once, then again.

"Shit," a voice rasped from above. Sounded like Hansen.

Gonna need help, Ben.

Fisher didn't wait for it to come but rather dropped back down to the pipe run and followed it across the space, ducking under beams and around pipes, until he reached the opposite lintel, where he chinned himself up. Through the floor he heard the rapid padding of footsteps. Two people, it sounded like. Hansen had called for help.

Fisher followed the shelf south, past Hansen's position, until he reached the far brick wall. Below him and to the right he could see a steel ladder affixed to the wall. Arms outstretched like a trapeze artist, Fisher leaned out from the lintel, let himself fall forward, and then, at the last second, pushed off, snagging a pipe with both hands. He let himself swing twice, then hooked a lower pipe with his heels, reached forward, and grabbed the next pipe over. He wriggled his trunk forward until the pipe under his heels rode up under his butt, and then sat down. Next he rolled over so the pipe was pressed into his quadriceps and let himself slide off until his hands caught the pipe. Two hand-over-hand swings brought him to the ladder.

He stopped, listened.

From the floor above, he could hear shuffling and whispered voices: "Snagged . . . Go down there . . ."

Fisher climbed the ladder to the open floor hatch and peeked up. Thirty feet away he could see Hansen's

hunched form. Standing behind him were two figures—
Kimberly and Ames, judging from their outlines.

"Go down there. . . ."

Kimberly trotted off toward the stairs. Ames stayed
behind.

Fisher climbed the last few feet and crab-walked away
from the hatch, then stopped behind a stack of bricks. An
impulse popped into his head; he debated it briefly, then
flipped a mental coin. *More chaos it is, then.*

The ankle-deep loam on the floor made the crossing
almost too easy. Twenty seconds after leaving his hiding
place, he was standing behind the pair. Hansen, stuck up
to his crotch in the floor trap, couldn't turn around; Ames
could do nothing but stand watch over his team leader.

Fisher waited until Hansen said via SVT, "What? What
kind of cord?" then reached forward, circled his right arm
around Ames's throat, and clamped down with Ames's
larynx in the crook of his elbow, his left fist pressed against
Ames's carotid artery. He leaned back, lifting Ames free
of the floor. Fisher began reverse walking, taking wide,
balanced strides on flat feet to compensate for the extra
weight. The levered grip on Ames's throat took immediate effect, shutting off the oxygen spigot to his brain and
rendering him limp within four seconds.

Occasionally glancing over his shoulder, Fisher
retreated to the hatch, where he stopped and stepped
sideways behind the brick pile. He laid Ames flat, stripped
the OPSAT (operational satellite uplink) off his wrist,
then unhooked his SC-20 from its shoulder sling. He
smelled the barrel; it had been fired recently. He ejected

the magazine and found only two rounds missing. He hadn't been the only one shooting at the reservoir.

Fisher laid the SC-20 aside and took Ames's SC pistol from the holster and stuffed it into his waistband. He turned his attention to the OPSAT, tapping buttons and scrolling through menus until he found the first screen he wanted. In sequence, he tapped the buttons marked POSITIONING > ONBOARD GPS > OFF, then scrolled back to the diagnostics screen and tapped SELF-REPORT > SVT > MALFUNCTION > TRANSMIT INOPERABLE, then hit SEND. Next he switched screens to TACTICAL COMMS > INTRAUNIT, then called up the on-screen keyboard and typed, MOVEMENT ON LOWER FLOORS, NORTH SIDE; INVESTIGATING, then hit SEND again.

Across the floor Hansen was moving, rolling to the left and withdrawing his leg from the hole. Kimberly had freed him. Fisher strapped the OPSAT to his wrist, returned to the hatch, and started downward. Footsteps clanged up the ladder across the room and, as his head dropped below floor level, he saw Kimberly's figure sprinting across to Hansen, who was climbing back to his feet. Hansen's taut posture told Fisher the team leader had failed to see the humor in his paracord trick.

Fisher repeated his trapeze act until he was back on the lintel shelf. Crouched over and taking careful, quiet steps, he headed south, stopping every ten feet to listen. Whether his ruse was working, he couldn't tell. As he drew even with the hole in which he'd entered the foundry, a pair of figures—Vin and Blondie—appeared on the floor below, silently sprinting north, trailing a cloud of dust. Fisher stopped, crouched down, and checked the

OPSAT. It appeared Hansen had bought, at least for the time being, Ames's malfunction message, having used his command function to switch the team's comms from VOICE to VOICE + TEXT TRANSCRIPTION. As the transcription was coded by OPSAT number rather than name, Fisher couldn't tell who was who, but with Ames having gone solo, Hansen would have teamed up with Kimberly. In near-real time, Fisher watched the dialogue pop on the screen:

In subbasement, north side . . . nothing yet . . .
Third-floor north clear, heading south . . .
Ames, report. Say position. Ames, respond . . .

Starting to get worried now, Fisher thought. He stood up and continued on.

Hansen was sharp; at most, he'd give Ames another minute to respond and then order a regroup. If he and Kimberly had, in fact, seen the footprints heading toward the ladder hatch, Hansen would realize his mistake, his assumption. By then it wouldn't matter. With the now-four-person team converging on the second-floor north wall, he would be moving south, toward—

Even before Fisher shifted his weight to his forward foot, he knew something was wrong, could feel the sole of his boot sliding sideways on the spot of grease or rainwater or whatever it was on the concrete. Before he could react, he was falling through space. The floor loomed before him. At the last moment he reached out and smacked his palm against a section of pipe. He twisted sideways, slowed ever so slightly; then his body was horizontal and falling again. He curled himself in a ball, arms wrapped around his head, legs tucked to his chest.

The loam softened the impact, but he still felt as if he'd taken a body blow from a heavyweight boxer. Swirling sparks burst behind his eyes.

He heard a *crack*, then a *pop*, then silence.

The floor splintered beneath him; then he was falling again.

— 7 —

HAVING punched a ragged, man-sized hole through the floor, Fisher found himself falling amid a cloud of dust and ash that obscured his vision save for a few jumbled glimpses of concrete, steel pipes, and moonlight glinting off water. *Water. The canal.* With no way of knowing how deep it was, he scrambled to right himself, twisting his torso and flailing his arms until his internal gyroscope told him he was right side up. He spread his limbs like a parachutist, sucked in a breath, and set his jaw.

The impact felt like someone had slapped him in the sternum with a twelve-inch plank. His world went dark and quiet. Despite being shielded from the sun, the water was surprisingly warm. His head broke the surface. He checked his waistband: The SC pistol was still there. He checked his wrist: The OPSAT was gone.

The stench of algae, mold, and animal decomposition filled his nostrils. The surface was covered in patches of greenish gray slime. Here and there he saw clumps of what looked like fur and feathers. This answered one of his earlier questions: This canal, wherever it began and ended, saw little freshwater circulation. Flanked on both sides by narrow concrete walkways and high walls interspersed with arched doorways, the canal was about thirty feet wide; whether it extended the length of the foundry proper, he couldn't tell.

Through the hole in the floor/ceiling he saw the glimmer of approaching flashlights accompanied by the muffled plodding of multiple sets of feet. Fisher looked around. The canal walls were smooth, vertical concrete rising at least four feet off the water's surface. Thirty yards away, on the right side of the canal, he could make out a set of steps rising from the water and, opposite them, an archway through which pale moonlight streamed. He'd never reach the steps in time, and with the team's adrenaline and anger levels spiked, he had to assume at least one of the gun barrels about to be jammed through the ceiling hole would be spitting bullets. Above, powdery loam gushed through the hole as feet skidded to a stop at its edge.

Fisher blew out all the air in his lungs, refilled them, and ducked beneath the slime. Immediately, he realized his belly-flop entry had been the right move: The canal's muddy bottom was only four feet down. His submersion had improved his situation only slightly. They would see the ripples he'd left behind. He was just rolling over, sweeping his arms and legs into a powerful, scissoring sidestroke, when he heard the first *pfft* strike the water behind him. Whether it was a bullet or an LTL projectile, he didn't know, but the first shot was immediately followed by several more, then a dozen in rapid succession, punching into the water to his right, to the rear, and in front as the shooters tried to bracket him.

He arched his back into a left-hand turn, heading for the canal wall, hoping the combination of the acute angle and the hole's jagged shape would make aiming more difficult. It did. The gunfire tapered off, then died away. Fisher kept stroking, gaining distance until he judged he was opposite the steps. Using his palms against the wall to control his ascent, he stopped a couple of inches below the surface. The murk made it impossible to see either the hole in the ceiling or any signs of light. He shifted his head a bit so he was centered under a plate-sized patch of slime, then let his eyes break the surface. He blinked rapidly to clear his vision. Now he could see the hole. Nothing moved. No light visible. Someone was there, if only to serve as overwatch as the rest of the team tried to find a way down to the basement. He couldn't wait any longer.

Keeping his head still, he reached behind his back, drew the SC out of his waistband, brought it around, and shut off the LAM, or laser aiming module, with his thumb. No use advertising his intentions. He let the pistol slowly rise to the surface until just the barrel was exposed. The angle was difficult and he was shooting from the hip, and he was trying to miss—a contradiction at which the tactical part of his brain balked.

He fired. The bullet punched into the closer edge of the hole. Another equipment improvement: The SC's noise suppressor was quieter still; the shot was no louder than a gloved hand clap. Fisher snapped off three more shots, then dove under, pushed sideways off the wall, and kicked to the steps. Five seconds later he was out of the water, through the arch, and crouched against the brick wall.

He was in a courtyard, roughly a hundred feet square, bordered on the left and right by window-lined wings of the main building; opposite him, a twelve-foot-high hedgerow leading . . . where? In the distance he heard the faint roar of a crowd and a tinny voice speaking through a loudspeaker. *The soccer stadium.* Fisher thought it over: It might work. First, he'd have to get there in one piece.

He heard the screeching of rusted steel. He looked up. On the wing's fire escape, a door was being shoved open. A body appeared in the gap, trying to push its way out. Fisher glanced across at the hedgerow, then back at the emerging figure.

A voice shouted, "In the arch! Three o'clock low!"

That settled it. Fisher dashed back through the arch, turned right, and sprinted down the walkway. The basement was cavernous, at least the length of a football field. He reached the far wall, turned left onto a catwalk suspended over the canal, then left again onto the walkway, then a quick right into the next arch. He stopped, listened. In the courtyard the door gave one final shriek, then slammed open. Boots pounded the fire-escape stairs. He closed his eyes, trying to gauge how many sets of feet; it was impossible to tell.

Fisher clicked on his penlight. He was in a maintenance tunnel. Just a few inches wider than his shoulders and lined with yet more conduits, pipes, and wall-mounted ladders, it ran from south to north. He tried to place himself on the mental map he'd been keeping. He was somewhere beneath where he'd first entered the building. He turned off his penlight.

The pounding of boots stopped, and in his mind's eye he could see figures racing across the courtyard.

Give them something to think about. Slow them down.

He ducked around the corner, took aim on the center of the canal, and fired three shots. All three rounds impacted within a half inch of one another. A second later a pair of figures—one on either side of the courtyard arch—peeked around the corner.

Fisher took off, sprinting on flat feet until he reached the first ladder. He started upward. After ten feet he found himself enclosed in a shaft; another twenty feet brought him to what, in the dim light, looked like a door. He clicked on his penlight, saw a rusted doorknob, clicked it off again. First floor, he assumed. He kept climbing, passing the second and third floors. The ladder came to an abrupt end. He groped above his head and traced out a square of sheet metal. A hatch. He found the handle and gave it a test push, expecting to feel resistance and hear the grating of steel on steel. Instead, the hatch opened smoothly, noiselessly. He froze. Someone had been here recently.

Probing with his index finger, he found one of the hinges; it was coated in oil. He brought his finger to his nose and sniffed. Then smiled. Bacon grease. This ruled out Hansen and company and ruled in urban explorers or, more likely, poor teenagers looking for a nocturnal adventure in their small Luxembourgian town.

Down the shaft he heard the scuff of a boot, followed by a pebble skittering across concrete. He eased the hatch shut and turned himself on the ladder so he was pressed against the wall. A flashlight beam appeared in the maintenance tunnel, widening and growing brighter as its owner approached. The flashlight went dark.

Then on again—this time pointing directly up the shaft. Half expecting this, Fisher had shielded his eyes with his palm. Still, he felt a deer-in-the-headlights moment of panic. He quashed the sensation. He was sixty feet off the ground. The flashlight beam was strong, but not strong enough to reach him. If, however, the person at the end of the beam decided to fire an exploratory shot . . . The cliché "fish in a barrel" came to mind.

The flashlight blinked off. Fisher took his hand away in time to see a figure move past the shaft opening and out of sight. *Where's your partner? Come on . . .*

A second flashlight popped on, probed the shaft, then went out again.

Fisher waited a full minute, then eased open the hatch, lifted the prop-arm into place, then climbed out and shut the hatch behind him. The E-shaped flat roof was an expanse of patchy gravel, peeling tar paper, and exposed ceiling planks interspersed with skylights and squat brick chimneys. On the western side he could see the roofs of three of the complex's watchtowers, for lack of a better term. He assumed they'd served as control booths from which foremen oversaw the foundry floor. To his east were upper (north) and lower (south) arms of the E—the two wings enclosing the courtyard. Overhanging the north wing's roof, and silhouetted against the night sky like a massive ball of cotton, were the boughs of an oak tree.

Not the most noble of exits, Fisher thought, scrambling down a tree like a kid, *but it would work all the same.*

Taking careful steps and sticking to exposed wood, he picked his way across the roof to the north wing. Closer up, the oak was even more massive than he'd imagined, reaching nearly 120 feet into the sky. The smallest limb overhanging the roof was the size of his waist. He'd taken his first step onto the branch when he heard a female voice behind him say, "Don't move a muscle."

Fisher neither turned nor hesitated. He jumped.

8

FISHER bolted awake to screaming and the pounding of feet, but his mind immediately clicked over, translating the sounds from potential threat to reality: children giggling as they ran down the hall outside his room. *Youth hostel . . . Luxembourg city.* He checked his watch. He'd been asleep for four hours. It took a few more moments to piece together the events of the night before.

Knowing the oak was sturdy enough to take his weight, he had been less worried about plunging to the ground after leaping off the foundry's roof than he was about catching a bullet in the back. Whether the shooter, whoever she was, had been too startled to fire or had simply decided her chances of a hit were nil, Fisher didn't know, but his descent through the boughs had prevented any further attempts. So far Blondie and Kimberly had exercised good fire discipline; it seemed unlikely they'd hose down the oak.

Mostly bouncing from limb to limb but occasionally managing to swing himself closer to the trunk, Fisher crashed through the tree, picking up plenty of bruises and scratches but no serious injuries. He managed to arrest his fall ten feet from the ground. Hanging from the lowermost limb, he waited for his body to stop swinging, then dropped the remaining distance.

He raced across the side street behind the foundry, rue Barbourg, then zigzagged his way through alleys while keeping the lights of the soccer stadium in view. Three minutes after dropping from the tree, he was standing at a ticket booth outside the main entrance, and a minute after that he was in the stadium itself, along with five thousand cheering fans who'd come to see the match starring the home team, the Jeunesse Esch. He took a few moments to consult a Plexiglas board showing the stadium's layout, then found a bathroom and ducked into a stall, where he changed clothes. A quick stop at a souvenir shop and he had a Windbreaker and baseball cap bearing the team's distinctive black and yellow logo. Finally, he made his way around the field to the east-side exit, then across the frontage road and down another embankment into some trees.

The CFL train station was now out of the question; upon realizing they'd lost him at the foundry, it would be the first place they'd stake out. The same with

Esch-sur-Alzette. They would assume he'd look for the next easiest mode of escape, namely a bus or rental car; with the town's population less than twenty-seven thousand, Hansen and his team would have little trouble scouring stations and agencies. Fisher needed distance, as much and as quickly as he could manage.

Fisher got out his iPhone and called up Google Earth. To the east were three towns within three miles: Rumelange, Kayl, and Tétange. Fisher chose the latter. It had a train station and the intervening terrain was mostly farm fields and forest. After downing an energy bar with a few gulps of water, he started running.

IT took him forty minutes to reach Tétange's western outskirts. From there it was a quarter mile stroll to the station. His luck was holding. He bought a ticket on the night's last train heading north and, after a brief stop in Bettembourg, he was on his way toward the city of Luxembourg—and a youth hostel full of, predictably, young tourists and their even younger children. On the plus side, Luxembourgian hostels were rarely fully occupied, so he had a communal room to himself and, most important, no credit card was required.

He made his bed, then opened his rucksack and removed its contents and went about checking supplies. The SC he'd taken off Ames was gone, disassembled and tossed into a river during his jog to Tétange the night before. The rest of his delicate gear seemed undamaged, tucked safely away in Aloksaks. He would need to restock his staples, but a few quick stops to military surplus, hardware, and hobby shops would do the trick. Of course, with any luck by dawn tomorrow he'd have all the gear he needed for the foreseeable future.

He repacked everything but his clothes and stuffed all of those into a garbage bag, except for a pair of dark khaki trousers, a long-sleeved navy rugby shirt, and a pair of brown loafers. Finally, he shaved, showered, re-dressed, and left, tossing the garbage bag into the Dumpster behind the hostel. It was almost nine, so he had an hour to kill.

In contrast to most of the rest of the city, the hostel itself was contemporary in design, with a stark white-stucco and glass facade; it lay situated between the Pfaffenthal Viaduct, an elevated, arched train overpass, and a park of labyrinthine and concentric hedgerows.

The city of Luxembourg started in the fourth century as nothing more than a Roman watchtower at the intersection of two roads and remained that way for another six hundred years before the construction of the Lucilinburhuc, or Little Fortress. Over the next three centuries Lucilinburhuc morphed into Luxembourg. For Fisher, who had spent a good portion of the last eighteen months traveling Europe, Luxembourg epitomized Old World charm, with rolling cobblestone streets, some barely wide enough to accommodate two cars; winding rivers and moats; and steeply sloped and spired rooflines.

Fisher got to the meeting place, a shop-lined alleyway on rue de l'Eau, a few blocks from the Grand Ducal

Palace, an hour early, then found a small restaurant with a terrace overlooking a park and ordered breakfast. He hadn't eaten a real meal in two days, so he asked for *uitsmijter*—bread, Gouda cheese, Ardennes ham, and fried eggs—along with *quetsche tort*, all followed up by two cups of Ethiopian Yirgacheffe coffee.

He felt better, both physically and mentally. He had some breathing room, some time to think and plan before Hansen and his team would reappear. Whether they would be able to track him here on their own, he didn't know, but he was doubtful: He'd paid for his CFL ticket using cash and an Emmanuel credit card; he'd changed out of his black and yellow Jeunesse Esch–fan outfit before reaching Bettembourg, and both the train and the station at Luxembourg had been all but deserted.

Fisher sipped at his third cup of Yirgacheffe, then checked his watch.

Almost time.

TEN minutes later a slight man with blond hair and wire-rimmed glasses came beetling through the park toward the restaurant. Of course, "beetling" wasn't exactly right, was it? Fisher thought. Vesa Hytönen's movements were more birdlike. Somehow Hytönen managed to exude both furtiveness and inconspicuousness at the same time. To passersby he was, Fisher suspected, just another funny little man—a cloistered scientist or a persnickety librarian, someone you found momentarily interesting but almost immediately forgot.

If Vesa ever decided to graduate from information cutout to full-fledged agent or intelligence operative, the espionage world might never be the same.

Of Finnish and Belgian descent, Vesa was, in fact, a scientist—a biochemist—but he also held postdoctorate degrees in European literature and African history and had begun tinkering in the field of robotics and artificial intelligence, both of which were, according to Vesa, merely hobbies to help pass the time.

When he reached the edge of the park, Vesa gave no sign that he'd seen Fisher but rather turned left down the block, bird-walked his way around a couple of pedestrians, then into a bookshop. He emerged carrying a newspaper in his right hand and headed down the block away from Fisher. Vesa dropped the newspaper. When he retrieved it, he folded it lengthwise and stuffed it into his outside jacket pocket with the top headline showing. Fisher got up and followed. After twenty minutes of dry-cleaning, Fisher decided neither of them was being watched. He gave Vesa the all-clear signal—a simple scratch of the ear while they waited, with some other pedestrians, at a crosswalk—then broke off. They met back at the City Central Park and sat down on a bench near a fountain.

"Good to see you again, Vesa," Fisher said.

Hytönen darted his eyes to meet Fisher's for a moment, then bobbed his head. "And you, and you."

"What do you have for me?"

"I've been told that the man you're interested in will in fact be at his Vianden home for the next three days."

The man in question was a man named Yannick Ernsdorff. An Austrian in his mid-fifties, Ernsdorff had until ten years earlier worked as a legitimate, if ruthless, investment banker in Vienna. Why and exactly how Ernsdorff had chosen the profession that had occupied him in recent years was anyone's guess, but he had become the go-to financial manager to the underworld's überwealthy. What Einstein and Planck were to physics, Ernsdorff was to the sheltering and laundering of money. To even get the Austrian on the phone, prospective clients had to have a minimum net worth of one hundred million dollars.

As of late, however, Yannick Ernsdorff had expanded his menu of services to include the role of banker for a very special auction, the details of which were what Fisher required before he could make his next move. With luck, Ernsdorff's secrets would be the shove Fisher needed to set the dominoes falling.

"Security contingent?" he now asked Hytönen.

"I should have satellite imagery by this afternoon."

"Blueprints?"

"The same. I did, however, come across an item in the news that I thought would interest you." Hytönen handed Fisher a newspaper clipping.

Fisher scanned it. Yannick Ernsdorff, it seemed, was either a philanthropist or he'd decided the appearance of philanthropy was a deductible business expense: The previous year he'd spent three million dollars building an Outward Bound–style children's challenge course on the grounds of his five-hundred-acre waterfront estate outside Vianden. Starting that summer, underprivileged children from across Europe could come to enjoy rock-climbing walls, zip lines, rope bridges, obstacle courses, spelunking treasure hunts, and hide-and-seek among dozens of multilevel tree-house complexes.

"Almost makes me wish I were a kid again," Fisher replied dryly. "Please tell me this place isn't named Yannickland."

"Challenge Discovery Park," replied Hytönen. "There's a website. Many pictures and maps."

How nice of Yannick, Fisher thought. "I need you to pass along a few questions."

"Go ahead."

"One, ask about ROE," Fisher said, referring to the rules of engagement. "Not mine. She'll know what it means."

"Very well."

"Two, our Japanese friend seems to have attracted some attention. I need to know everything she knows. And three, I'll need all their operational frequencies, both data and voice, and the makes and models of any cell phones they're carrying."

Hytönen nodded. He'd written nothing down, having filed the information away in his mental vault. Fisher had seen a number of keystone spook traits in Vesa, but near the top of the list was his astounding memory. Fisher had no doubt that if asked, Vesa could draw an exact map of Ernsdorff's property from his brief visit to the Challenge Discovery Park website. Likewise, the queries he'd just recited would be passed along, verbatim.

"I will strive to have answers by this afternoon."

"Thanks. What about the caches?"

"There are three of them within the borders of Luxembourg, and another four in northern France, eastern Belgium, and western Germany—"

"No more borders for a while." More often than not, border crossings went smoothly, but they were in Fisher's mind a lot like air travel: Most aircraft accidents happen during takeoffs and landings, and the odds of an incident occurring increased with repetition.

"Of course. The key codes are unchanged, and the equipment is of the penultimate generation."

"'Penultimate?'"

"It means—"

"I know what it means. Second to latest. I've just never heard anyone actually use the word in a sentence."

"Thank you. Standard antitampering measures are in place, so if you—"

"Everything goes boom."

"Well, yes, I suppose so," Hytönen said with another birdlike head bob. "You'll want to exercise caution."

Fisher smiled ruefully. "Story of my life, Vesa."

THEY made plans to meet again later that afternoon; then Fisher walked a few blocks to a mom-and-pop car agency and rented a dark green 2001 Range Rover. He used a pair of Emmanuel's sanitized passports and credit cards; he still had the Doucet batch but would not use any of those unless absolutely necessary. He'd ridden that particular trick pony hard during his Esch-sur-Alzette border crossing, and while Hansen and his team would have no choice but to investigate should he use the IDs or cards again, Fisher doubted they would fall for such a ruse so completely again.

Before leaving the parking lot he got his iPhone, called up the maps application, and punched in an address in Bavigne, a quaint village of 125 souls, sitting along a channel of the Sauer River about sixty kilometers northwest of the city of Luxembourg. He took his time with the drive, exploring and enjoying the Luxembourgian countryside before finally pulling into Bavigne shortly before one. He found a restaurant, the Auberge, and ordered what turned out to be one of the best meals of his life: lobster soup with langoustine tails, Ardennes salad, game terrine on a bed of salad, confit of red plums, and a lemon *tartelette* for dessert.

One for the list, Fisher decided. As of late he'd started a mental list of potential retirement spots. Bavigne had just jumped into his top ten. Quiet, secluded, and bucolic.

He lingered over coffee for another hour, then paid the bill and drove out of town, following the iPhone's on-screen directions: first heading northeast, then south again along the Sauer, between farmers' fields and the tree-lined banks of the river, until he crossed over a covered wooden bridge and found himself in a clearing dominated by a log cabin. He got out, mounted the porch, and knocked on the door. There was no answer. He knocked a second time and waited a full minute before circling the cabin and checking windows and satisfying himself that no one was home.

He walked back to the rear and down six steps to a wooden root cellar door. The padlock hanging from the hasp was relatively new, an all-weather Viro marine model; at the turn of Fisher's key it snapped open smoothly.

The root cellar was dark and cool, the temperature hovering in the mid-sixties. Fisher clicked on his flashlight and entered. Momentarily caught in his beam, a rat skittered across the dirt floor and disappeared. Fisher stopped in the center of the cellar, took a moment to orient himself, then walked to the southeast corner, shoved some empty fruit crates out of the way, and set his flashlight on one of them. He knelt down and began brushing at the dirt with both hands until a four-by-three-foot rectangular outline appeared. He felt along the edges until he found a thumb hole and lifted the hatch, revealing a shallow dugout. At its center sat a black plastic case the size of a large suitcase. It was in fact a DARPA-modified model 1650 Pelican case complete with an encrypted-keypad lock and an antitampering system that consisted of a C-4-shaped charge designed to destroy the case's contents.

Fisher lifted the case out of its hole and laid it flat on the ground with the keypad facing him. He pulled out his iPhone, called up the calculator application, then punched in the cabin's latitude coordinates, subtracted the longitude, and divided the resulting number by the current algorithm, a random four-digit number spit out by the mainframes at Fort Meade every month. Fisher took a deep breath, tapped the code into the keypad, and pressed ENTER. A series of six red lights across the front of the pad began flashing, and then slowly, one by one, began turning green. There was a soft beep followed by a triple mechanical *snick*.

Fisher flipped open the latches along the perimeter of the Pelican's lid, then lifted it. He smiled. "Hello, old friends."

FISHER was back in Luxembourg by five. He and Hytönen met at yet another park, this one was across town. As he sat down, Vesa dropped a tiny object to the ground between them; Fisher glanced at it. A key. He covered it with his foot.

"A storage locker at Findel airport," Hytönen said. "All the information you requested."

"Thanks."

"I have a special message from our mutual friend. She says there's a mole."

"Say that again."

"There's a mole. Someone inside the group following you."

"She's sure?"

"Reasonably so, I expect, or she wouldn't have mentioned it."

"Good point."

"How or to whom the information is going, she doesn't know."

"But it involves me," Fisher said.

"Yes. She is working on the problem, but she suggests, and these are her words, 'Don't hold your breath.'"

Fisher smiled. "That sounds like her."

"Will you be needing me again?"

"Probably. I'll keep you posted via the Lycos account. Check the drafts folder every morning. If it's more urgent, I'll leave a message for Heinrich."

"I will. Good luck to you."

And then Hytönen was gone, walking down the path with his birdlike steps.

9

THE next morning Fisher pulled to a stop in a parking lot overlooking the Our River and shut off the Range Rover's engine. Vianden had just jumped onto Fisher's retirement list above even Bavigne. Situated in a shallow valley along the Our River, Vianden and its fifteen hundred residents lived in what looked to Fisher like a Grimms' fairy tale come to life, with gingerbread-style homes in muted pastel shades, cobbled river walkways, and arched stone bridges. He could see castles rising from the mist atop several nearby hills, their lower reaches shrouded in trees. Fisher shook himself from his reverie and got out.

The night before, after picking up the cache outside Bavigne and meeting with Hytönen, Fisher had first stopped at the airport to retrieve the USB flash drive Vesa had left for him, then checked into the Hilton Luxembourg on rue Jean Engling. He spent an hour going over Vesa's information. Everything he requested was there: the encrypted frequencies for the Hansen team's OPSATs; the makes and models of their cell phones; and the team's rules of engagement—*apprehend, maximum priority; lethal force authorized as a last resort.* Either Ames had a low threshold for "last resort," or his live fire at the Esch-sur-Alzette reservoir had been a mistake.

Next Fisher had turned his attention to the cache and found no surprises. A standard equipment loadout: subvocal transceiver; OPSAT; Trident goggles equipped with night-vision, infrared, and electromagnetic settings; SC pistol; SC-20K AR MAWS (Modular Assault Weapon System) with all the goodies, including ring airfoil grenades, Sticky Shockers and Cameras, and gas grenades; Mark V Tactical Operations RhinoPlate suit; and six grenades (three XM84 flashbang, two M67 fragmentation, and one AN-M8 HC White Smoke). He checked each piece for damage; field stripped, cleaned, and reassembled the weapons; then ran internal diagnostics on the OPSAT and Tridents. Everything was operational; everything felt familiar. It felt good to be back in the saddle, as it were.

THE scooter shop was two blocks away, beside a restaurant whose patio jutted over the river's slowly churning waters. Having called ahead, Fisher found the proprietress, a matronly gray-haired woman named Vima, ready for him. She spoke Luxembourgish and a little stilted German, so their conversation was limited, but she beamed and nodded as Fisher inspected the sky blue Vespa scooter, then paid cash for a day's rental. Within minutes he was puttering down Vianden's main street, which took him northwest out of town along a series of switchback roads. Twenty minutes later he was descending again, the trees alongside the road giving way to farmers' fields; the dirt was coal black.

Ernsdorff's estate sat on the western side of a kidney-bean-shaped lake a few miles out of town along with four other mansions, each one occupying a section of the southwest and southeast shorelines. Fisher tooled around the lake's perimeter, occasionally stopping to take pictures, taking care to get plenty of shots of Ernsdorff's acreage. Even from the opposite shore, almost two miles away, Fisher could see glimpses of the Challenge Discovery Park: labyrinthine rope courses, wooden bridges, vertical climbing walls, and, jutting from the treetops like multicolored circus tents, rainbow-striped tree-house roofs.

Fisher spent two hours exploring the lake, using his watch's timer function, his camera, and the Vespa's odometer to stake out angles and distances he would use that night. Aside from a chest-high, rough-hewn brick wall running along the perimeter of the grounds and a wrought-iron driveway gate set on motorized rollers, he saw no physical security measures. The trees were thick enough, however, that his Canon's zoom lens could penetrate only a few hundred yards into the grounds; if there were guards, dogs, or more fencing, they were closer to the house itself. These were bridges he would cross when or if they arose.

Shortly before 11:00 A.M. Fisher saw a white panel van come down the driveway through the trees and stop at the gate, which rolled back to let the van pass. As it turned south, heading back toward Vianden, Fisher zoomed in and snapped a dozen pictures. He called them up on the LCD screen.

On the van's side in red letters were the words DATA GUARDIANS INC.

HE returned to town and, after having lunch at the restaurant next door to the scooter shop, Fisher followed Vima's directions to Scheuerof, a neighboring village a mile to the north, where he found a family-owned KOA-style campground. It was empty save for a mid-twenties blond couple in red, green, and yellow Rastafarian knit caps, swinging from a pair of canvas chairs suspended from a tree beside their tent. They gave him a wave; he waved back, the brim of his baseball cap pulled low over his eyes. He found a suitable site at the campground's northernmost boundary. Hemmed in on all sides by thick trees, and accessible by only two footpaths, it lay within a half mile of the bridge Fisher had spotted earlier on Google Earth.

He set up camp—a tent, lawn chair, cooler, and a clothesline from which he hung a few items of clothing—then called Vesa Hytönen's apartment, got the machine, demanded that "Heinrich" pick up immediately, then cursed, and hung up. Next he used his iPhone to log into the Lycos e-mail account, typed up his query, and saved it as a draft.

While waiting for a response, he went for a hike, using his handheld Garmin 60Cx GPS unit to time himself and mark waypoints. From his campsite to the lake it was 1.32 miles—forty minutes at a leisurely pace. He added 30 percent to that figure to account for darkness and another 30 percent to account for potential pursuers. So, roughly two hours and fifteen minutes round trip. He saw only three other hikers, none of them equipped with anything more robust than a lumbar pack. Day travelers. In all likelihood he'd have no company on the trail later.

He checked his watch. Eight hours until nightfall.

HE spent the remainder of the afternoon at his campsite, sitting by the fire, eating hot dogs, drinking beer (non-alcoholic to keep a clear head), whittling, and generally behaving like a normal camper until six o' clock, when he climbed into his tent and closed his eyes. He was awoken ten minutes later by his iPhone's incoming e-mail chime. It was Vesa:

> Data Guardians Inc. (DGI) a privately owned Luxembourg company. Specializes in home networking, information security, and storage. Our mutual friend investigated. According to internal company records, DGI installed IBM

System x3350 server two months ago; routinely
scheduled maintenance call logged this date.
Service-fee schedule suggests special-needs
installation. Details, countermeasures, penetration software available no later than 2100 local
time via uplink. Remote penetration problematic; physical link required.

Fisher mentally translated Vesa's message: DGI
designed and installed a beefed-up file-storage server for
Yannick Ernsdorff. Fisher's OPSAT would be updated
with everything he needed to do the hack, but he had to
be plugged into Ernsdorff's server first.

HE slept for five hours, waking shortly after eleven. He
strolled to the bathroom/shower shelter at the center of
the grounds, then walked back. No one else had checked
in during the day. His neighbors, the blond couple, had
retired to their tent for the night, and he could see their
silhouettes in the yellow glow of a lantern.

Back at the Range Rover, he carried the Pelican case
into the tent. He powered up the OPSAT, waited for
it to run through its self-diagnostics, then called up the
COMMS screen and initiated the uplink. As promised, the
update was waiting. He watched the progress bar crawl
across the screen until it reached 100 percent, then
waited as the OPSAT recycled. He took a moment to
review the package, which included a spec sheet and
schematic of the IBM System x3350, then read through

the hack instructions. Next he called up the map of the area and punched in the latitudes and longitudes he'd recorded throughout the day; they appeared on the OPSAT's screen as pulsing red pushpins. He tapped the one representing his campsite and the screen zoomed and recentered: WAYPOINT 1 RECORDED. He set the OPSAT to STANDBY. He donned his tac-suit and gear, then returned the case to the Range Rover and locked up. Finally, he scanned the campgrounds with NV and IR and found it still empty, save for his Rastafarian friends, who appeared to be asleep, their prostrate forms coming through in infrared shades of blue, yellow, and red.

Fisher ducked onto the trail and headed out.

10

HAD he been operating on a strict schedule, it would have been derailed in the first ten minutes. A hundred yards over the bridge he heard faint voices down the trail. He slipped into the undergrowth and scanned ahead. The NV showed little, so dense were the trees; the IR wasn't much better, but patience paid off, after thirty seconds of watching, as he caught glimpses of four ghostly rainbow shapes moving through the trees. They were approaching. Fisher switched the IR to standby and huddled down to wait. As the group approached he smelled cigarette smoke and heard giggling. *Teenagers*, he thought. Two boys and two girls. As the group drew even with his hiding place, it turned onto a smaller trail and stopped at a picnic site. A small fire crackled to life.

Fisher could see the four of them sitting on fallen logs around the flickering light. Clearly they wouldn't be moving on anytime soon.

Moving on flat feet, Fisher backed away from the trail. When he'd put enough distance between himself and the teenagers, he turned back to the east and began picking his way through the trees until he'd looped back to the main trail. Forty minutes later he heard a double beep in his subdermal, indicating he'd reached his final waypoint. He was now within a couple of hundred yards of the western edge of Ernsdorff's estate. He stopped and did an IR/NV scan and was about to move on when something caught his eye to the right: a too-straight vertical line among the trees. His first thought was a sensor or camera. Keeping his eye on the object, Fisher picked his way closer until he could identify what he was seeing: a diamond-shaped sign atop a fence post. In what he assumed was red lettering on a white background, it stated in Luxembourgish, German, and English: PRIVATE PROPERTY—KEEP OUT.

Either Ernsdorff had claimed a bit more land than he owned or the survey maps and records were mistaken; from what few glimpses Fisher got from Google Earth, the brick wall surrounding the grounds lay three hundred yards ahead. Either way, the sign told him something he'd already suspected: Ernsdorff and/or his security consultants had decided he wasn't a high-value target, at least for murder or kidnapping. People who are truly concerned about their personal safety don't try to warn off attackers, but rather they let their security measures handle intruders. Fisher would, of course, be thorough, but it was unlikely Ernsdorff had guards roving the property. If there was security here, it would likely be found inside and in close proximity to the house itself.

Fisher spent the next twenty minutes mapping sign placements, adding digital pushpins to his OPSAT, until he had the western edge identified. Near each sign he had stopped to scan the ground ahead with night vision, infrared, and electromagnetic, and each time he saw nothing bothersome. He continued forward, taking his time, sidestepping twigs and fallen branches, occasionally cycling through the Tridents' settings until at last the outer wall came into view. Unlike the wall he'd photographed on the lakeside of the property, this one was higher, perhaps six feet, and topped with shards of jagged ceramic embedded in mortar. This was of little concern to Fisher; the shards would barely scratch his RhinoPlate. What concerned him was what he saw when he studied the wall with the Tridents' EM mode: Every third brick in the row just below the shards was pulsing with energy. The Tridents' EM wasn't sophisticated enough to tell him the precise nature of the energy, but experience told him *radio waves.* Fisher zoomed in and switched to night vision, then infrared. The former showed no signs of cameras or directional microphones; they were perfect replicas of weatherworn bricks. Infrared, however, showed that each third brick was warmer than its neighbors, which suggested it was being fed electricity. So: not visual, not auditory. *Pressure or tremble,* Fisher thought. If something of roughly human weight climbed the wall, the faux bricks would send a signal—probably to a monitoring center in the house.

He had two options. He could make his way to the front of the property, to the chest-high wall, but that would do him little good if it were similarly monitored. He'd clear the wall more quickly, but an intrusion-detection signal would nevertheless be sent. He would make his penetration here, he decided. If nothing else, it would establish the quality of guards with which he was dealing.

Fisher backtracked, found a jumble of fallen logs about fifty feet from the wall, and crouched down. Ernsdorff's security experts had done something else right: They'd trimmed the nearby oak trees so no branch thicker than a thumb extended over the wall. There'd be no Tarzan-style penetration this time—unless he wanted to climb a hundred feet, tightrope walk thirty or more feet, then rappel back down. That, he decided, would be plan B.

At least the weather was cooperating. Shortly after he'd left his campsite the wind had begun to pick up, and now it was gusting to thirty miles per hour and driving a light rain before it. Heavy wind blew down branches, and rain made otherwise diligent guards lackadaisical.

Fisher curled himself into a kneeling firing position, braced the SC-20 on a log, laid his cheek against the stock, and zoomed in on the swaying canopy far above. He picked and rejected a number of candidate branches before finding the one he wanted. He fired. A miss. He took aim, trying to compensate for the branch's movement, looking for a pattern. . . . *Pop*. As he'd intended, his second shot struck the branch just off center, so it didn't part cleanly but tore free, leaving behind streamers of bark. The branch plummeted, crashing wetly through the canopy before slamming into the top of the brick wall. Fisher started the timer on his watch. Now he moved the SC-20's selector to STICKY CAM and swung the barrel around, zooming in on a bridge connecting a pair of tree houses on the other side of the wall. With a muffled *thwump*, the camera sailed over the wall and affixed itself to the bridge. Using the OPSAT, Fisher tested the cam, panning and zooming until satisfied it was operational. He aimed it in the direction of the main house and set it to SLOW AUTOPAN.

Eighty-seven seconds after the branch stuck the wall, the guards appeared: two Cushman electric carts, each carrying two guards, speeding down the gravel trail. When they reached the wall, the carts split off, each one slowing to a walk as the occupants shined flashlights along the wall and surrounding underbrush. Fisher took control of the Sticky Cam and followed the cart that had gone left. It stopped beside the fallen branch, which lay perched atop the wall like a seesaw. The driver got out, jerked the branch free of the shards, then examined the severed end. Apparently satisfied that the break was an act of nature, he tossed it aside. A radio came up to his mouth. What the guards did next told Fisher they weren't your run-of-the-mill rent-a-cops, as each pair spent another five minutes patrolling the area, playing flashlights over the wall, the foliage, and up among the tree houses, dangling ropes, and zip lines.

Nicely done, gentlemen, Fisher thought. *Now let's see how you deal with frustration.*

* * *

THRICE more over the next forty minutes Fisher repeated the process, taking care to choose branches at random locations but within range of the Sticky Cam. The first two times, the guards appeared in less than ninety seconds and performed with the same diligence: check the branch, check the surrounding area, then depart. But the third time, it took nearly two minutes and twenty seconds, the guard who removed the offending branch simply tossed it away, and their inspection of the area was perfunctory before returning to the house.

Fisher shot one more branch, this one directly above his head, then collected it and crawled out from his hiding place. After a final check of the wall through the NV, IR, and EM, he sprinted to it, tossed the branch over, then backed up ten feet and charged the wall again, this time vaulting at the last minute and snagging the top with both hands. He was on the other side four seconds later; ten seconds after that he was scaling the nearest tree-house ladder; a minute after the intrusion alarm would have gone off in the monitoring center, he was lying flat atop the tree-house roof.

It took the guards nearly three minutes to arrive. Fisher didn't bother following their movements on the Sticky Cam. He didn't need to. He could hear their curse-laden exchanges over their portable radios as they moved below him on foot and in their Cushmans. He saw flashlight beams flitting in the trees around him, but they came nowhere near him and ended quickly. A short while later he heard the whirring of the Cushmans departing. Fisher checked his watch. For the sake of continuity he would have to down one or two more branches before he left for the night.

He climbed back down to the ground, called up the Sticky Cam on the OPSAT, tapped DISENGAGE, then collected the camera where it had fallen a few feet away. One of the improvements Third Echelon had made was reusable adhesive pads for the Sticky Cams and Sticky Shockers, a feature that cut down not only on pack weight but also on after-the-fact detection. Sometimes having an enemy know that someone *had* been there was as bad as having them know someone *was* there.

He moved out, leapfrogging from cover to cover, using the walls and pits of the obstacle course and the thick oak trunks to close in on the house, until finally he saw the exterior lights filtering through the trees. He was a hundred yards away, and the oak trees were giving way to pine and poplar. He stopped and spread himself flat beside a curved concrete sewer pipe turned pirate cave.

The lights he was seeing were decorative—low-voltage path lights and mission-style sconces along the exterior walls, but Fisher had no doubt there would be spotlights somewhere, either set to automatic to detect motion or controlled by the monitoring center. Ernsdorff's home was a three-story affair done in French-country style, with white stucco walls, heavy shutters, and dark wooden beams buttressing the rooflines and eaves. Conversely, the backyard was all Zen garden: winding paths of pristine white gravel, rock gardens with combed sand, short-span bridges over trickling streams, and stands of Japanese maple.

As was his habit, he scanned the ground ahead through his Tridents. Night vision showed nothing unusual, same for infrared. But, as it had at the wall, the electromagnetic scan revealed something unexpected: a laser intrusion-detection system unlike anything he'd seen before. Unlike most LIDSs, this one was neither steady nor arranged with horizontal or diagonal beams. It was, rather, made up of vertical, pulsating bars. Running from the north wall to the south, the "laser cage" was twenty yards deep and seemed comprised of an evenly spaced emitter grid, perhaps one emitter every six inches. Like some wild rock concert show, the emitters shot random beams of light into the trees, as though coupled to the beat of a noiseless song. Of course, it was run by computer, most likely a software algorithm designed to generate an ever-changing, patternless grid.

Fisher was impressed, and that small part of his brain that loathed the idea of turning down a challenge was whispering to him, but he shut it out and brought himself back on point: the mission. He looked around, scanning his surroundings, until the kernel of an idea formed. Fisher smiled at the thought. If Ernsdorff wanted to go high tech, that was fine. Fisher would find an old-school solution.

He backtracked to the nearest ladder and climbed the trunk to the tree house above. Hunched below the foreshortened ceilings, he made his way through the tree house's connecting rooms until he found a bridge connecting to the neighboring house. Once there, he stepped out onto a six-by-six-foot wooden platform enclosed by rope rails. At the edge of the platform, tied off to one of the rails, was a zip-line chair. The corresponding platform was fifty feet away, standing at the edge of the laser cage.

Fisher got into the chair, grabbed the overhead rope with his left hand, and flipped the release with his right hand. The angle at which the zip line was built was slight, a few degrees at most, lest the kids get more of a ride than they bargained for, but Fisher's adult weight made the chair lurch forward, and he had to clamp down on the rope with both hands to keep from racing toward the opposite platform.

Hand over hand he eased himself across the gap until he was almost two-thirds across. He stopped and took stock, eyeballing distances and making his best guess about momentum and swing. If not for the pine and poplar trees interspersed within the laser grid, and the gusty wind, what he was planning would not work. Satisfied he'd made the best guesstimate possible, Fisher reached behind his head, drew his legs up to his chest, and shimmied backward until he was dangling behind the chair. Now he raised his legs and gave the chair a shove. With a rasping sound, the chair glided toward the far platform, and with a soft metallic *snick*, it locked into place. His anchor, he hoped.

He was committed. Hanging by his right hand, he drew his knife with his left hand and used the serrated edge to begin fraying the rope. Here, again, he had to put himself in the mind of whoever would find the parted rope; he needed to create the appearance of natural failure rather than malice.

It took three minutes of patient scraping, but finally the rope was down to one pinkie-finger-sized strand. Fisher sheathed his knife, hooked his left hand next to his right, and bounced once, twice, then a third time, and the rope parted.

The platform post rushed toward him. He twisted his torso right, swung his legs, and swept past the post with inches to spare. Then he was into the trees, branches slapping at his face and, unseen below him, laser beams parting in the boughs' wake in what he hoped looked to the monitoring center like a particularly strong gust of wind. His swing reached its zenith, paused, then started back in the other direction. Fisher let go and curled himself into a paratrooper ball, taking the impact and rolling with it.

He got up, took ten seconds to smooth out the pine needles where he'd landed, then sprinted to the left, back into the trees, skirting the edge of the laser cage until he reached what he could only assume was an Old West town, complete with main street, livery, saloon, jail, and hotel. Everything, of course, was done in half scale, so he had to drop into a crouch to slip into the livery. Behind him, through the trees, he saw spotlights pop on.

This close to the house, the intrusion-detection system drew a quick and robust response. Through the slats in the livery's plank wall, Fisher watched three Cushmans and six guards arrive. After an initial inspection of the area, which included a flashlight sweep through the Old West town, the trio of Cushmans converged on the laser cage. After a minute of searching, one of the guards' flashlight beams picked out the rope dangling in the branches. He raised his radio to his mouth to turn off the laser cage, Fisher assumed. The six guards moved into the trees, scanning the ground and branches above them until they reached the zip-line clearing. Fisher would know momentarily whether his ploy had worked.

After much discussion and even an inspection of the parted rope by one of the guards standing on the shoulders of another, the group seemed satisfied that nothing was amiss. They retraced their steps back to the Cushmans, and a quick radio call from the leader brought the laser grid back online. The guards mounted up and drove away, the soft hum of the Cushmans' engines fading into the darkness. Fisher let himself take a deep breath and let it out.

TEN minutes passed before the spotlights went dark and the decorative lighting returned. All was again well at Schloss Ernsdorff. The guards probably didn't feel that way, of course, having been dispatched on five wind-related goose chases, but unless one of them gave Fisher no other choice, at least they would live through the night.

Fisher picked his way northwest, out of the Old West town, through the pirate cove/Barbary Coast shantytown, and around the far end of the obstacle course, until he was within sight of the wall bordering the front of the property. Here the landscaping was more natural, the shrubs and undergrowth having been left unattended on purpose, Fisher suspected, to create the wall of vegetation he'd photographed during his lakefront surveillance. At last he reached the gravel driveway. Across this and through another three hundred yards of trees, he'd inscribed a wide arc around the home's front door, a U-shaped portico turnaround flanked by river-rock columns.

Forty minutes after leaving the Old West town, Fisher crept up to the northern wall and followed it alongside the house, paralleling a lighted walkway to the servants' quarters. Fisher was playing a hunch. As his visit here was so brief, it seemed unlikely Ernsdorff would bring along a contingent of servants. Ahead, at the end of the path, he could see the quarters, a cluster of three whitewashed Caribbean-style bungalows enclosed by a six-foot cedar stockade fence.

Fisher crept up to the fence and knelt down. He withdrew the flexicam and wriggled it between the fence's slats. On the OPSAT screen, the flexicam's fish-eye lens showed the outer wall of the nearest bungalow. He panned up, left, and right, looking for lights or movement in the windows, but saw nothing. He withdrew the flexicam and tucked it away. After a quick NV/IR/EM scan, he was over the fence and on the other side.

He made a quick circuit of all three bungalows to confirm that they were unoccupied, then returned to where he started. He checked the side door for alarms and found none, so he picked the lock and slipped inside. Off the kitchen he found what he'd come for: a sliding-glass door leading to an arched, glassed-in breezeway. The terra-cotta tiles, rattan furniture, and potted palms told Fisher this was Ernsdorff's version of a solarium. Keeping to the shadows, and careful to avoid patches of moonlight slicing through the glass ceiling, Fisher crossed the breezeway to the opposite door, this one made of thick oak and equipped with an industrial-grade Medeco dead bolt but no alarm sensors. It took him two minutes' work to open the Medeco. When the lock snapped open, he put away his tools, drew his SC pistol, crab-walked backward, and crouched beside a potted palm. He waited. If he was wrong about the sensors, or someone had heard the click of the lock, he'd know shortly.

He gave it five minutes. Nothing moved.

He holstered the SC and returned to the door. The gap beneath it was an eighth of an inch—too narrow for the flexicam—so he gently turned the knob, paused for thirty seconds, then eased the door open a half inch, and slipped the flexicam through the gap. The fish-eye lens revealed a short hallway bordered on both sides by pantries and a kitchen done entirely in stainless steel and black granite. It suited what Fisher imagined was Yannick Ernsdorff's Teutonic personality: cold and utilitarian.

Fisher eased open the door, stepped through, and eased the door shut. Somewhere in the kitchen he heard the click of footsteps on tile. He ducked into the pantry. He drew his sap and went still. The light in the kitchen came on, casting stripes down the short hall before him. A drawer opened; silverware rattled; the refrigerator door opened and shut. The soft pop of a Tupperware lid being removed. The lights went out. Fisher peeked around the corner, then padded through the kitchen, around the center island, and up to the still-swinging door through which the snacker had entered. Fisher caught the door with his fingertips and pushed it open until he could see a figure in a black Windbreaker retreating down the wide, dimly lit hallway. Fisher recognized the Windbreaker: one of the guards. Like the kitchen, the hallway's decor matched Ernsdorff: blond hardwood floors covered in a carpet runner with a jagged red, white, and black pattern. The guard turned left at the end of the hallway and disappeared.

Fisher retreated to the pantry, took the OPSAT off standby, and scrolled through until he found the blueprints of Ernsdorff's home. The main floor was devoted to living spaces—kitchen, living room, dining room, family room, and three bathrooms—while the second floor was all bedrooms and guest rooms. The third floor was divided into office space, storage, a library, study, and exercise room. Though it wasn't listed on the plans, based on where the guard seemed to be heading, the monitoring center was in the basement. He needed to make sure of that before going any farther.

The carpet runner was thick and absorbed the sound of his feet easily. He reached the end of the hall and stopped short, sliding along the wall to the head of the stairs. One set went upward, another down. From below he heard muffled voices, a few chuckles. Fisher descended, pausing every few steps to listen. The stairs turned right at the landing, doubled back on themselves, and ended at a six-by-six-foot foyer. The light from the hallway above had all but faded, casting the foyer in deep shadow. To the left was an archway. Fisher drew his pistol and stepped up to the threshold. To his left a narrow hallway disappeared into darkness; near its end, on the right, he saw a sliver of horizontal light near the floor. A door. He flipped his Tridents into place and selected NV to confirm. There were three other rooms in the hall, one at the far end and two on the right. The lighted room was equipped with a biometric keypad lock; the others, standard knobs.

The door to the monitoring center opened, casting a rectangle of white light on the opposite wall. Fisher's heart lurched, but he controlled it and drew back smoothly, stepping through the arch and turning left into the corner, where he dropped the SC to his side and stood erect. A figure appeared through the arch and started up the stairs. Fisher lifted the barrel of the SC at his waist and tracked the man up the stairs and around the landing until he disappeared from view. Fisher followed, taking the stairs two at a time on flat feet, pausing only briefly at the top to check the corner. One of the doors in the hallway was closed; having checked it already, Fisher knew it was a bathroom. The toilet flushed. Fisher crossed the hall and stepped into the linen closet. The bathroom door opened. Footsteps padded away. Fisher waited until he heard the soft buzz and click from the biometric pad outside the monitoring center, then stepped out of the closet, walked back across the hall, and started up the stairs.

He paused at the second floor only to count open and closed doors and to confirm that the layout matched his blueprint, then continued to the third floor. A few steps from the top, he froze. He crouched down. Directly across from him lay the library. The double mahogany doors were opened. Inside, silhouetted against the mullioned windows on the far side of the room, was a figure. Fisher smelled cigar smoke, and as if on cue, a dime-sized cherry glowed to life in the dark. Whoever it was in there, he was facing Fisher. *Ernsdorff himself*, Fisher thought. According to his intel, Ernsdorff was traveling alone, having left his wife and two young daughters behind in Vienna.

The cherry came to life again, this time moving, turning back toward the windows. Fisher switched the Tridents first to infrared, then to EM, and saw nothing unusual, so he stood up and walked across the carpeted hall to a seating alcove beside the library doors. He crouched against the wall nearest the doors, then withdrew the flexicam, let it peek around the corner, and waited.

Ernsdorff was in no hurry. Fisher could hear him pacing in the library, not with the insistent stride of a worried man, but more contemplative, as though he hadn't a concern in the world. And he didn't—at least not from Fisher, at least not on this night. Of all the players he would likely visit before this job was over, Ernsdorff was the one whose disappearance or death would cause the most harm. If Ernsdorff went down, the others would go to ground. Then again, Fisher thought, if Ernsdorff was intent on spending the rest of the night smoking and pacing in the library, he might have to force the matter.

It didn't come to that. Ten minutes later Ernsdorff emerged from the library. He was wearing a red silk robe and black silk pajama bottoms. Without a backward glance, he trotted down the stairs to the second floor. Fisher put away the flexicam and ducked into the library.

He switched to night vision. The space was enormous, with a domed ceiling and built-in shelves so tall they warranted a rolling ladder. There must have been thirty thousand books, Fisher estimated. The carpet was dark, perhaps olive, and the desk and side chairs were heavy teak. Fisher switched to EM and turned in a slow circle. Aside from the pulses and swirls of hidden electrical cables, television cables, and phone lines, the room was electromagnetically quiet. If Ernsdorff's server was here, it was well shielded. Once certain he hadn't missed any nooks or crannies or hidden alcoves, Fisher switched back to night vision and headed for the door.

He stopped.

A flashlight beam was coming up the stairs.

Fisher retreated. He trotted across the carpet to the desk and crouched down. The flashlight beam grew wider, cutting a pie slice into the library. The guard stepped up to the threshold and panned the light around for ten seconds, then moved on. Routine patrol. Fisher checked his watch: 1:00 A.M. on the dot. Hourly patrols, starting on the top floor and moving downward. Standard stuff. The rest of the guard's circuit took a mere five minutes; the second floor, which was all bedrooms, would take even less. The man would be back with his buddies in the monitoring center in twenty minutes.

Fisher waited until the man was headed back down the stairs, then stepped out, moved to the railing, and peeked over. *Interesting*. The guard had bypassed the bedroom floor altogether.

Fisher moved on to the next room—a study furnished almost identically to the library save for the domed ceiling and bookshelves. A quick scan with the EM showed nothing of interest.

Next room. Ernsdorff's office. Unlike the previous two,

the office decor was contemporary: quasi-industrial-style shelving and furniture, an all-glass crescent-shaped desk, and area rugs in red and black. Fisher did his EM sweep. *Strike three*. What had he missed? Given the size of the house, and without knowing the exact location of the server, Fisher had been forced to make an assumption, namely that since the server was business related it would be stored in a business-related area. Now Fisher rethought this. Ernsdorff kept his servants' quarters separate from the main house; he kept his security personnel in the basement; he probably forbade the guards to patrol the bedroom floor. Would he treat the computer nerd of Data Guardians any differently? Fisher doubted it. The next likely location for the server seemed to be the basement, near the monitoring center. He should have scanned the hallway for EM signals. Live and learn.

Fisher returned to the head of the stairs and waited at the railing—crouched down with the flexicam curled over the edge and doing the watching for him—until the roving guard reappeared in the first-floor hallway and headed back down to the basement. Fisher followed, moving quickly, more confident in the layout and the guards' movements. He stepped through the arch outside the monitoring center and switched the Tridents to EM.

Fisher smiled. *There you are.*

The door at the end of the hall swirled with various shades of blue electromagnetic waves. Fisher checked his watch: thirty-five minutes before the next roving patrol. Stepping carefully now, he moved past the monitoring center and knelt down before the server room. He tried the knob; unsurprisingly, it was locked. Yet another Medeco industrial-grade dead bolt—one for which only Ernsdorff had the key, Fisher suspected. This lock took four minutes; while no more complex than the one he'd encountered in the breezeway, this one happened to be within a few feet of a room full of security guards. Here silence, not speed, was his primary concern.

The lock snicked open. Fisher switched to night vision, gently swung the door inward, then crab-walked as he closed the door behind him. The home's utility room was the size of a small bedroom and divided by a half wall, one portion devoted to the water heater, furnace, and air-conditioning unit, the other portion to telephone lines, coaxial and Ethernet cables, modems, and routers—and sitting alone on a shelf on the wall like a pizza box: Ernsdorff's IBM System x3350 server.

Now came the easy part. Having been preloaded with the requisite software, the OPSAT simply needed a digital handshake with the server. To accomplish this, Fisher fitted the OPSAT with its Ethernet adaptor, then plugged the cable into the server's empty dual gigabit port. The OPSAT went to work, its screen flowing with the numbers and characters that were the language of digital computing. Little of it was recognizable to Fisher, but the script was quick enough. Two minutes after he initiated the handshake, the OPSAT's screen announced:

process complete . . . establishing up-link . . . uplink established . . . uploading . . . upload complete.

Fisher unplugged the cable.

HE retraced his steps—back down the main hall, through the kitchen and the breezeway to the servants' quarters, then back over the fence and along the wall to the property's western edge—the lakefront side. Here he repeated his windblown branch routine, vaulting the wall and leaving the branch teetering in place before sprinting down the drainage ditch running along the wall. By the time the Cushmans arrived, he would be a quarter mile away. Ahead lay an intersection: One road curved northwest along the shore, a second headed roughly west in the direction of the bridge near Fisher's campsite, and a third swung south and east, meandering its way back toward Vianden. The wind was still gusting, whipping branches and causing the canopies to sway against the night sky, but the rain had slackened to a drizzle.

As he approached the bend, a pair of headlights appeared over the grassy berm. The car was moving so fast Fisher barely had time to dive headfirst into the weeds at the bottom of the ditch. Then the car was gone, its engine fading.

Tires screeched. He heard the clunk of a transmission being shifted, then the unmistakable whir of an engine in reverse. Fisher didn't bother looking, he simply got up and ran.

— 11 —

HE didn't have time to think, to entertain the only question that popped into his head: *How did they find me?* He only had time to react. His mind switched over to evasion-and-escape mode.

He sprinted down the ditch, around the bend, then up the slope, across the road into the opposite ditch, and then through a hedgerow bordering a farmer's field. Now on even ground—the field had not yet been tilled—he picked up speed, running southeast in the general direction of Vianden; the road back to town was to his right, a hundred yards away.

He covered the quarter-mile field in just over a minute. He was almost to the far tree line. *Come on, come on . . .* If it was Hansen and his team, they would be in two cars. *Do your job.* . . . He glanced over his shoulder and saw a dark sedan turning onto the Vianden road. A figure was leaning out the driver's-side rear window, panning a handheld spotlight over the ditch and the field beyond. Fisher slowed his pace ever so slightly, and as he closed to within twenty feet of the tree line, the spotlight pinned him. A moment later he was in the trees. He ran for another twenty feet and stopped to catch his breath. He checked the OPSAT, pulled up the area map. This stand of trees was merely a border between two fields. If the sedan kept going, after another five hundred feet the road would curve again, coming within twenty feet of the next field over. If the team was going to try to flush him, that was where they would start. He had a hunch about the other car, but only time would tell if he was correct.

He took off running again, heading due east. The trees gave way to a strip of open ground, then another hedgerow; Fisher pushed through this and into the next field and kept running. To his left, across two more fields, Fisher could see a pair of headlights heading east down the bridge road. Though he couldn't make out the model, it was similar to the first car. Hansen was learning. Rather than going "all in" and sending all his troops on a foot chase, he'd split his forces and hedged his bets in case Fisher decided to double back—which was exactly what he'd done. With team members probably in the trees behind him and the second sedan on the bridge road to act as a blocking force, they had him in a nicely designed pincer movement. Unfortunately, nicely designed wasn't going to be good enough. He hoped.

He kept running due east. The car on the bridge road had spotted him but hadn't stopped, acting instead as forward observer for the flushing team. The next hedgerow came into view. The field beyond was rectangular and separated from the road by a narrow wedge of trees. When Fisher was fifty feet from the hedgerow, the sedan disappeared behind the trees. He veered left and put everything he had into a full sprint, covering the distance to the road in thirty seconds. He slid headfirst into the ditch, crawled up the other side, and stopped a few feet short of the shoulder. The sedan was still moving east, negotiating a slight incline. As its taillights disappeared over the top, Fisher stood up, ran across the road and into the trees beyond. Another short sprint brought him within sight of the southern wall of Ernsdorff's property. He turned right—east—and kept going until the trees to his right thinned out slightly. He stopped and dropped flat. A few moments later the sedan came speeding back west. Having reached the eastern edge of the wedge and realized Fisher had not kept to his course; they'd doubled back. They would search the wedge of trees first, then the ditches, and only then would they realize he'd taken to the larger forest—thousands of acres' worth.

Fisher got up and kept running.

HE put another half mile between himself, Ernsdorff's estate, and Hansen's team, then stopped. He needed to process what had just happened. Unless he'd made a huge mistake at some point in the last two days, Hansen and company shouldn't have been able to track him here. Fisher mentally retraced his steps, starting with his boarding of the train in Tétange and ending with his arrival at the campsite outside Scheurerof. His credit cards and passports were sanitized; he'd given no one specifics of his plans; his comm protocols were streamlined and compartmentalized. . . . So how had they known to come here? Only one answer popped into his head, and the thought of it made his stomach churn. It didn't seem possible; at the very least she wouldn't have been that sloppy. If he were wrong, however, he'd just uploaded the contents of Ernsdorff's server to the one person who shouldn't have it.

HE crossed the bridge adjoining the camping grounds thirty minutes later, found the trail, and made his way back to his site. Through the trees he saw a glimmer of light and realized it was a car's dome light. Fisher crouched down and got his bearings. He was in the right place. He got up and crept closer. When he was within twenty feet of his Range Rover, he knew there was no mistake: The tailgate was open. Fisher drew his pistol. Silhouetted by the dome light, a figure was leaning into the Range Rover, rummaging through Fisher's belongings. The figure turned his head, and in the dim light Fisher saw a red, green, and yellow knit cap on the person's head. One of his campsite neighbors. The idiot was pillaging his vehicle. Fisher couldn't help but smile. If this didn't take the prize, he didn't know what would. He barely survives a hairy exfiltration only to find himself being burglarized by a Luxembourgian hippie, probably so high he was simply looking for Twinkies. So surreal was the situation that it took Sam a couple of moments to wrap his mind around it.

He pulled the Nomex balaclava down over his face, tucked the SC next to his leg, and stepped from the bushes. "Stop right there," he said in rough but passable Luxembourgish. "Police."

The hippie froze.

"Hands up. Turn around."

The hippie complied, and Fisher saw what looked like a bayonet in his right hand, but in the next instant realized it was a lock shim. The hippie had some skills; opening automatic locks with a shim took a fine touch.

Suddenly, to Fisher's right came a woman's scream. He flicked his eyes that way—saw another flash of red, green, and yellow—and thought, *Hippie girlfriend*.

The woman ran screaming in the direction of the main road.

For a split second Fisher's instincts took control, and he brought the SC up and around, drawing a bead on her back. He caught himself and turned back to the hippie boyfriend, who hadn't moved a muscle.

"Leave," Fisher said.

The hippie hesitated.

"Go!" Fisher barked.

The hippie took off, sprinting after his girlfriend.

Damn it.

* * *

FISHER checked the Pelican case; thankfully, it was unmolested. In addition to miscellaneous bits of gear, the case contained all his credit cards and passports. He had little to worry about, actually. As with everything it modified, DARPA had engineered the case not only to be tamperproof but also to withstand a remarkable amount of abuse.

He slammed the tailgate shut, got into the Range Rover, and started the engine. He reached the site's main entrance a few seconds after the hippie couple and caught a glimpse of them pounding on the door of the caretaker's cabin as he swept past them and turned onto the dirt tract. Thirty seconds later he reached a blacktop road, rue de Sanatorium, turned east toward Scheuerof, drove fast for a quarter mile, then slowed down to the speed limit. He wasn't happy about heading into town, as the Scheuerof police department would be the first to get the call from the distressed hippies, but his only other choice was to backtrack through Vianden, an even larger population center. The sooner he could get through Scheuerof and onto the rural roads that ran along the German border, the safer he would be.

As he passed through the center of town, he saw the flashing lights of a police car heading in the opposite direction down a parallel street. A couple of minutes later, as Fisher reached the northern outskirts, he saw a second police car, which he hoped made up the entire complement of Scheuerof cops.

He approached a slope and a gentle turn to the east, and soon the road was hemmed in by thick stands of fir trees. The lights of Scheuerof faded behind him, and he took a deep breath and let it out.

A pair of headlights appeared on the road behind him, almost a mile back but gaining ground quickly. He saw no flashing lights. An unmarked police car, perhaps? He doubted it, not in such a small town. So, either a local in a hurry or . . . Fisher felt his belly turn over. He had to assume the worst. He jammed the gas pedal to the floor and the Rover's engine revved. The speedometer swept past 115 kph and kept climbing. With one hand and one eye on the road, Fisher took the OPSAT off standby, called up the map screen, and touched the keys: RECENTER, ZOOM 4×, and TRACK. He needed something and he wasn't sure what. But if, in fact, it was Hansen and his team on his tail, he needed to end the chase sooner rather than later. As the speedometer climbed past 130 kph, Fisher watched the OPSAT screen reorient itself, auto-scrolling with the movement of the Range Rover. The German border was a mile to his left, and given the rolling hills and thick vegetation he doubted there would be fencing. The nearest border checkpoint would be where? . . . Probably Bettel, about six miles ahead. He had to make his move before then.

The headlights reappeared over a crest behind him, a half mile back. Fisher looked again: two sets of headlights. They'd cut his lead by a half mile in four minutes, so whatever they were driving had some horsepower. Some model of Audi, Fisher suspected. He glanced at the

OPSAT. On the screen, a thread of a road appeared two miles ahead and off to his left. He zoomed in on it and traced its zigzagging course deeper into the forest, along the German border, and then across. It was unnamed. A fire road or construction site? It didn't matter. He would take it. The Range Rover's higher clearance and four-wheel drive would hopefully negate his pursuers' advantage in speed. The problem was, they would catch up to him before he reached the turnoff.

Fisher switched the OPSAT map to topographical view. The two-lane road had turned into a series of humps and dips a few hundred yards apart. Each time he topped a crest, he saw that his pursuers had shaved a little more off his lead, until a mile from the side road they were only a crest behind. The slope before the side road was steeper, at least thirty degrees, which meant the downward slope would be just as dramatic.

Time to throw a wrench into the works.

Fisher reached the trough and started up the incline. When the Range Rover's engine began to protest and he began bleeding speed, he downshifted hard and stomped on the accelerator. The Rover lurched ahead, topped the crest, and started down the backside. Fisher let himself get a third of the way to the bottom, then slammed on the brakes. The steering wheel shuddered in his hands and the Range Rover yawed, first left, then right, before straightening out. He came to a stop. The side road was a hundred yards ahead, marked merely by a gap between the trees. He turned off the headlights and waited.

Fifteen seconds. No more. He started counting.

At twelve seconds, the first set of headlights popped over the crest. As soon as the headlights angled downward again, Fisher flipped on his headlights, tapped the brake lights twice, then shifted into reverse and jammed the gas pedal to the floor.

The tires let out a squelch, and then the Range Rover began accelerating toward the oncoming headlights.

_12_

FISHER'S gambit was a double-edged sword. If his pursuers were not quick enough to react, they would rear-end him, and if they reacted quickly but poorly, they might lose control and crash into the trees bordering the road. He wanted them off his trail, not dead.

He'd closed to within fifty feet of the car before its driver reacted, sending the car into a skid, turning it broadside as it slewed past the Range Rover and onto the right shoulder. Fisher could now see that the car was, in fact, an Audi, a black A8 twelve-cylinder model, which explained how it had gained so much ground so quickly. Just as the Audi slipped off the dirt shoulder and down into the ditch, the driver corrected, got the nose pointed back toward the road, and accelerated back onto the blacktop and screeched to a stop. Fisher slammed on his brakes, shifted into drive. Behind him, a second Audi crested the hill. This driver reacted just as quickly as the first, braking hard but then overcompensating, sending the car into a flat spin that took the Audi down into the left-hand ditch. As its taillights disappeared over the berm, Fisher punched the accelerator and aimed the hood of the Range Rover at the first Audi, which sat at a forty-five-degree angle, front tires on the blacktop, back tires on the shoulder.

A split second before he slammed into the Audi's front door, Fisher gave the steering wheel a jerk to the left. His headlights filled the side window, and he caught a glimpse of Ben Hansen's face squinting at the oncoming lights. The Range Rover hit the Audi broadside, side panel to side panel, shoving it sideways over the shoulder and down into the ditch. The Range Rover glanced off the Audi like a billiard ball as Fisher gave the steering wheel one more jerk; then he was accelerating again, straightening out and heading for the side road. As he drew even with it, he tapped the brakes twice, turned the wheel again, and shot into the gap between the trees. Within seconds the headlights of the Audis faded behind him.

NONE of the occupants was injured, Fisher guessed. Shaken up, yes, but uninjured. Having not seen how it came to a stop, he didn't know if the second Audi was drivable, but the first one certainly was, and with any luck, they would spend some time trying to get the second car back onto the road rather than piling into the first and giving chase.

The road ahead was narrower than it had looked on the OPSAT screen—barely fifteen feet wide and slightly overgrown by tree limbs that slapped at the Range Rover's hood and side panels. Fisher had the vague sensation of moving through a car wash. The rain had started falling again, light but steady. Ahead, his headlights illuminated a tree directly in front of him, and he spun the wheel, taking the left-hand turn too fast. The Range Rover's wheels stuttered, then found purchase again, sending up a rooster tail of dirt and gravel. Over the next hundred yards the road zigged four more times, each turn at a right angle to its predecessor. Fisher glanced out the side window, and in the amber glow of the Range Rover's side lights he saw a wall of dirt and foliage appear as he moved into a ravine. The branches that had been clawing at the windshield rose up and began scraping at the roof.

He caught a glimmer of light in the rearview mirror; then it was gone. He craned his neck around to look out the rear window. Nothing. Five seconds later the glimmer was back. Fisher turned again and saw headlights slicing through the trees; the lights blinked on, off, as the Audi negotiated the hairpin turns.

"Damn it!"

They'd recovered more quickly than he'd anticipated.

He depressed the gas pedal another inch, pushing the Range Rover harder. His headlights picked out a basketball-sized rock in the middle of the road. He swerved right. The Range Rover's front right quarter panel plowed into the berm, coughing out a horizontal rut; mud and gravel and vegetation pressed up against the side window. His front tire bumped against the rock and he corrected, bringing the Range Rover back onto the center of the road. He glanced at the rearview mirror, saw headlights—two sets of them now—then returned his attention to the road.

Rock! This one was bigger, roughly the size of a lawn chair.

This time there was no time to swerve. Fisher slammed on the brakes. The Range Rover bucked. A cloud of dirt enveloped him, obscuring the road, then cleared in time for him to see the rock looming before the hood. With a crunch of fiberglass, the bumper hit the rock. Though Fisher was half expecting it, the *pop-hiss* of the air bag expanding caused his heart to lurch. He was pressed back against the seat. A plume of talcum powder effluent filled the car.

Knife . . . knife . . .

He groped with his right hand, down his leg to his calf, felt the sheath, then drew the knife and began hacking at the air bag, holding his breath and squinting against the powder. The air bag collapsed like a sun-warmed, partially deflated balloon, and Fisher kept slicing until it came free of the steering wheel. He tossed it aside and glanced at the rearview mirror. The Audis were coming on fast, only two hairpins behind.

Fisher shifted the Range Rover into reverse, stomped on the gas, then the brake, and then shifted into drive and accelerated around the boulder. *Give them something else to think about.* He slammed on the brakes, rolled down his window. He plucked the M67 fragmentation grenade off his harness and pulled the pin. He checked the rearview mirror. The lead Audi had cleared the second closest turn and was accelerating. *This would be a lot easier with real bad guys,* Fisher thought. He counted three more seconds, then let the M67's spoon fly, let the grenade cook for one second, then hurled it into the dirt berm. He hit the accelerator and lurched forward. As he skidded into the next turn, the grenade exploded. Fisher heard the skidding of tires on dirt, then the familiar crunch of fiberglass.

Another deposit lost, Fisher thought with a grim smile.

HE pushed the Range Rover as hard as he dared on the dirt road, which was growing muddier with each passing moment. The four-wheel drive helped, but with the road so narrow, Fisher found himself glancing and bumping off the dirt walls, leaving sod and branches and shredded foliage in his wake.

Suddenly the road widened into an oblong clearing covered in mulch and chopped tree branches. *A loggers' dumping ground,* Fisher thought. Ahead, the road split— the center branch continuing straight, west, the other two heading to the north and the south. Though he'd seen no signs, he assumed he'd crossed the German border. The sooner he could find a major highway, the sooner he could widen the gap between himself and Hansen's team.

He slowed, letting the Range Rover coast, and checked the OPSAT map. The L1 highway, which ran north to Neuscheuerof and beyond and south to Obersgegen and Körperich, lay two miles down the center road. He needed a highway, and they probably knew he needed a highway. *Take the road less expected,* Fisher's instincts told him.

He spun the wheel to the left and accelerated out of the clearing and onto the north road. Again he found himself immediately bracketed by trees. This road was narrower than the previous one by at least two feet but so far appeared less winding. He accelerated to 80 kph, just over fifty miles an hour, and didn't slow for a quarter mile until the road veered right. He eased into the turn, then followed the road back to the right and onto another straightaway. Ahead, the road started up an incline. When the Range Rover was twenty feet from the crest, he took his foot off the gas pedal, bleeding speed; then the car was up and over and back on level ground. A wooden bridge loomed through the windshield. Even as his brain analyzed the structure and warned, *Too old, too rickety,* the Range Rover's front tires were thudding over the uneven planks. He heard a soft crunch, like a hiker's foot plunging through the crust of a rotted fallen log, and then the Range Rover was tipping forward and plunging into darkness.

FISHER felt the car go vertical and had a momentary wave of vertigo. The Range Rover stopped, tailgate jutting skyward through the bridge's deck. Fisher had a split second to refocus, and then the car was moving again, plunging straight down. He felt his belly fill his throat. The headlights illuminated only blackness, but then Fisher saw a shimmer of water, wet stones, steep-sided rock walls. The hood crashed into the ground. Fisher was thrown forward against his seat belt. His chest slammed into the steering wheel. The horn began blaring. *Shit!* . . . He pushed himself off the steering wheel and pressed his back into the seat. The horn kept blaring. He switched off the ignition. The horn went silent. He switched off the headlights. Through the windshield he could see water rising over the hood. He turned around, looked out the tailgate window. The red taillights were glowing eerily against the underside of the bridge.

Moving slowly, carefully, with the sound of gravel grating on steel, the vehicle was moving again, tail end tipping forward. With a surprisingly gentle crash, the Range Rover landed on its roof, rocking gently a few times before coming to a stop. Upside down, Fisher looked over his shoulder and saw the creek water begin rising against the tailgate window and trickling through the weather seals. He took stock of the Rover; the steel cage had done its job. Aside from a slight dent in the sheet-metal roof, the cabin seemed undamaged. Nor was the rising water a worry. The creek was shallow, a foot or two at most. His driver's window was still open, and through it water had begun to trickle. It was surprisingly cold, almost instantly numbing the skin of his hand.

His big problem was the horn. As he had, upon reaching the clearing Hansen and the others would have probably stopped. Faced with no tire treads to follow in the mulch, they would have had to explore each road, if only for a few dozen feet to determine if the Range Rover had passed that way. The blaring horn had just negated that delay.

Right palm braced against the roof, Fisher unbuckled his seat belt with his left and eased himself down, then turned onto his belly and crawled into the backseat. Working from feel alone, he found the handle to the Pelican case and dragged it forward onto the passenger seat. He spun himself around again, stuck his legs out the open window, and began crawling backward, dragging the case out with him. Once clear of the car, he got up, stepped out of the water onto the bank, and found a clump of bushes where he crouched down.

He took stock of his surroundings. The ravine was no more than twenty feet deep, but the walls were nearly vertical, with only the sparest of weeds and plants growing from the dirt. It was climbable, Fisher decided, but he doubted he had the time. To his left, past the bridge, the ravine disappeared into the darkness. To his right, a hundred feet away, was something interesting: a clearly man-made concrete wall sitting at a forty-five-degree angle to the streambed. After a few more moments, his eyes adjusted and he could make out a darker rectangle set into the facade. *A mine?* he wondered.

From the road above came the revving of an engine. Headlights swept over the bridge's uprights.

Time's up.

Fisher got up, hefted the Pelican case over his shoulder, and sprinted for the concrete facade. He was there ten seconds later and immediately realized it wasn't a mine. The rectangle he'd seen was actually a rusted steel door flanked by angled facades. On the door a square white sign with red letters told Fisher where he was: VERBOTEN. SIEGFRIEDSTELLUNG WESTWALL.

This was no mine entrance, but rather part of the Siegfried Line, a span of defensive forts and bunkers built by Germany during WWI and again in the 1930s in answer to France's Maginot Line. The Siegfried stretched almost four hundred miles from Kleve, on the border with the Netherlands, to Weil am Rhein, to the north on the border with Switzerland, and was made up of almost twenty thousand bunkers, tunnels, ramparts, dragon's teeth tank traps, and termite-mound machine-gun emplacements.

Aside from selected locations along the line that had been rendered safe and turned into tourist attractions or museums, the Siegfried Line was closed to the public. It was, however, one of the biggest draws in Europe for urban spelunkers, which probably explained the rusted padlock and snipped chain lying at the foot of the door Fisher now faced. Several of the hinges had been pried free as well, and the door hung askew. Water poured through the gap, trickled down the jumble of smooth stones Fisher had traversed to get here, and then down into the ravine.

He looked over his shoulder in time to see one of the Audis pull up to the bridge. Fisher set the Pelican case down, grabbed the edge of the door with both hands, and heaved. With a squeal, the door opened a few more inches. He heaved again and gained another three inches, then once more and the door shuddered open enough for him to squeeze his hips through. He reached back and pulled the Pelican in behind him just as a flashlight skimmed over the concrete facade.

Whether he'd been spotted, he didn't know. It didn't really matter. They knew he wouldn't have had time to climb out of the ravine. The bunker was his only chance.

13

FISHER stood in the dark for a few moments, catching his breath and thinking. The fight-or-flight response in his brain was advocating the latter, but he quashed the impulse. There was a damned good reason the German government had closed the Siegfried to the public. After almost eight decades of, first, bombardment, and then neglect and exposure to the forces of Mother Nature, these bunkers were death traps. Dozens of careless explorers had died or disappeared in these catacombs over the last ten years, most of them having stumbled off blind drops or through crumbling concrete floors. Fisher checked the OPSAT, hoping against hope he might find some semblance of a map of the bunkers, but there was nothing.

Decide, Sam. Act.

Hansen was sharp and learning quickly; how the team had reacted upon spotting him outside Ernsdorff's estate had proven that. Similarly, here Hansen would not put all his eggs in one basket but would probably split his team. Two would come straight after him, and two would circle around and look for another entrance. And one would stay behind at the cars, standing guard over the entrance should Fisher reemerge.

Fisher opened the Pelican case, stuffed the remaining contents, including his credit cards and passports, into his formfitting Gore-Tex camelback rucksack, then shoved the case aside. He found another short coil of paracord in his sack's side pocket and knelt before the door. He flipped the Tridents down and switched to night vision. In washed-out green and gray, the rusted door filled his vision. Above the latch was a U-shaped handle. Fisher gave it a tug and found it surprisingly solid. He rolled onto his butt, pressed the soles of his feet against the door, and shoved once, then again, and the door groaned shut.

He looped one end of the paracord through the handle and secured it with a taut-line hitch, then threaded the other end through a rusted eye bolt in the jamb. He repeated the process, knotting and looping until he was out of line. He cinched the paracord with a bowline and stepped back to examine his handiwork. It wasn't perfect, he decided, but it would slow them down. The door hadn't sealed completely, but the gap was narrow enough that it would take some steady pressure on the door and persistent knife work to saw through the paracord.

He took a moment to get his bearings. The origin of the "creek" was a jagged, ten-foot-long crack in the ceiling through which a thin sheet of rainwater was pouring. In the night vision he could see this wasn't an unusual feature of the bunker: Water sluiced down the walls, gushed from holes in the ceiling, and ran in rivulets across the concrete floor, in some places pooling in corners and depressions, in others finding yet more cracks in the floor. From somewhere below, Fisher could hear the splattering of water.

The bunker was laid out along a center alley roughly thirty feet wide and who knew how long. Branching off from both sides of the alley were concrete stairwells, one leading up to pillboxes and machine-gun emplacements, the other leading downward into what Fisher assumed had once served as living quarters and storage areas. Fisher walked to the nearest stairwell and peered down. There was nothing. The concrete had long ago collapsed, filling the shaft halfway to the top. He mounted the steps leading up to a pillbox and, careful to stay below the horizontal firing slit, climbed up. He crawled to the wall and peeked up. Beyond the slit lay a field of high grass. To the right and below his perch he saw movement. He adjusted position until he could see down. Twelve feet below, a pair of figures in tac-suits was creeping along the bunker's exterior wall. As if on cue, he heard a meaty *thud* on the entrance door as though a shoulder had given it a test shove. A vertical line of light appeared at the doorjamb. Fisher descended back to the alley.

Once again he was dealing with expectations. What

did Hansen and company expect him to do? Most often, doing the unexpected was the best course, but in this case that meant going deeper into the bunker complex and using the labyrinth to lose his pursuers. However, his discovery of the collapsed stairwell had changed his mind. Even if he managed to reach the lower levels without injury, there was no guarantee of finding a safe exit. He could, by being too clever for his own good, find himself trapped. So, he would go up. Somewhere there had to be escape ladders. Ceiling hatches.

Behind him the door groaned again, steel scraping on concrete. Walking on flat feet, Fisher crept up to the door just in time to see a double-edge knife slip between the gap. Like a probing finger, the knife touched the paracord, retreated, then reappeared again. The blade began sawing.

Time to go.

Fisher turned and started down the alley and had taken a dozen steps when he felt the floor shift beneath his feet. He backpedaled. As he did, a crack in the concrete spread, following him like a snake. He sidestepped toward a stanchion and watched as the crack slowed, then stopped.

An idea popped into his head. He switched the Tridents from night vision to infrared. Down the alley as far as he could see were pulsating columns of blue and green. The image that flashed in Fisher's mind was that of a field of psychedelic mushrooms like something from a bad 1960s movie.

The plumes were in fact air from the cooler lower

levels rising through gaps and weak spots in the floor.
The deeper the blue of the plume, the cooler the air and
the more easily it was passing through the floor. These
would be holes and wider cracks; the greenish blue
plumes indicated slightly warmer air that had been stalled
below the floor before seeping up through weak spots.
The air nearer the ceiling, having been warmed by sunlight conducted through the concrete, was a yellowish
orange.

He heard a soft *twang* and turned around. He switched
back to night vision. Two loops of paracord dangled from
the door handle. They were making fast progress.

He switched back to infrared and headed out, moving quickly but carefully between the plumes and sticking to the darker patches of what he hoped was in fact
solid concrete. If his reading of the IR scan was mistaken,
he might have only a split second to react before plunging through a hole. Two minutes passed. He'd covered
a hundred yards. He stopped, unslung the SC-20, and
aimed it at the far door, zooming until the door handle
filled his vision. The knife was still sawing, having parted
all but one loop of paracord. Fisher crouched down,
curled his finger on the trigger, then took a breath and
let it out. He fired. The 5.56mm round thudded into the
concrete beside the doorjamb. The knife jerked back. He
waited for five beats, then fired a second round in the
same spot. He slung the rifle back over his shoulder and
kept going.

After another hundred yards he reached an intersection. The alleyway continued straight and branched to

the left and right; each of these branches ended at a large garage-style steel door set into an outward sloping wall, and beside each large door was a pedestrian entrance like the one through which he'd entered. Fisher unslung the SC-20 and checked each door. The one down the left-hand alley looked closed; the one to the right was open a few inches.

Fisher switched his Tridents back to infrared and started jogging, following a serpentine pattern between the colored plumes. Ahead a dark rectangular shape appeared in the center of the alley, rising toward the ceiling. As Fisher drew nearer he switched to night vision and could see it was a stanchion, but wider, measuring nearly three feet across. Fisher stopped beside it, circled it. In one of the sides was a waist-high opening. Fisher stooped down and peered inside. A ladder.

Where there was a ladder, there had to be an exit.

From down the alley came an all-too-familiar sound— the grating of a steel door being forced open.

He crab-walked into the shaft, grabbed a rung, and gave the ladder a few tugs. The lag bolts affixing the ladder to the concrete were loose in their sockets but appeared solid enough for his purposes. He craned his neck upward and saw nothing but blackness. The night vision illuminated only a few rungs.

Distantly there came the echo of footsteps—soft but moving quickly.

Fisher peeked out and around the corner of the stanchion. He switched the Tridents to infrared. Down the alley, in the middle of the intersection, was a pair of figures in red, blue, green, and yellow. In unison, the figures crouched down. Hands went up to unseen Trident goggles, flipping through NV, IR, and EM as heads swiveled this way and that.

So close, Fisher thought, *but not close enough.*

He ducked back into the shaft, turned around, and started climbing.

PASSING the tenth rung, Fisher estimated he was twelve feet off the ground—the approximate height of the ceiling. He was now "outside" the bunker itself and moving into an exterior battlement or bulwark he hadn't been able to see from the ravine entrance.

The ladder shifted. Fisher froze. Then, accompanied by what sounded like a brick being scraped over a layer of sand, the lag bolt before his eyes wriggled free of the concrete. Another one, somewhere below his feet, let go with a *pop* and dropped down the shaft, pinging off rungs until it clattered to the floor below.

Fisher turned himself sideways and, without unslinging the SC-20, flipped the selector to STICKY CAM, glanced into the scope, then fired. He took the OPSAT off standby and panned the Sticky Cam so it was aimed through the opening at the bottom of the shaft. He closed his eyes and listened, and after a few seconds heard the scuff of footsteps; they'd heard the falling bolt and were looking for the source.

He kept climbing. He ignored the grating of the lag bolts as one after another began to tear free of the concrete. His right hand, reaching for the next rung, slammed into something solid. Fisher stopped, looked up, saw a circular hatch equipped with a dogging wheel. Knees jammed against the ladder uprights for support, he reached and gave the wheel a test turn. It didn't budge. He set his teeth, took a breath, tried again. The wheel moved an inch, then two, then let loose and spun freely. He pushed open the hatch.

He checked the OPSAT screen. In the greenish white of the Sticky Cam's fish-eye lens he saw a pair of booted feet standing a few feet outside the opening. He pulled an XM84 flashbang grenade from his harness, armed it, and dropped it down the shaft. His aim was true. In the NV he watched the flashbang bounce once, strike the upper edge of the opening, then roll out.

It detonated, instantaneously releasing 170 decibels of noise and eight million candela of stark white light. Having been exposed to flashbangs both in training and on missions, Fisher was all too familiar with the effects: It was like getting simultaneously blasted by a 747 jet engine and a marine-grade halogen spotlight. Regardless of the target's preparedness and physical condition, a close hit by a flashbang was a mind- and body-jarring experience.

It would be at least ten seconds before those below could orient themselves and take action, and Fisher took advantage of that, climbing up through the hatch and shutting it behind him. Another length of paracord looped around the dogging wheel and tied off to a nearby floor cleat locked the hatch behind him.

He looked around. He was in an artillery emplacement

measuring roughly twenty feet by twenty feet and ten feet tall. The gun had long ago been removed, of course, leaving behind only the mounting structure in the floor. About six feet up each of the four walls was a horizontal firing slit wide enough to accommodate the barrel of a cannon. Fisher took a moment to get his bearings. He was a half mile or so north of where he'd entered the bunker. Hansen and his three assistants—or four, if they'd decided against leaving an overwatch at the bunker entrance—were somewhere below him. Was he assuming too much? Even without his paracord lock on the hatch, Hansen was too smart to try to breach it. Fish in a barrel. So, had he retreated, returned outside, and set up on the bunker, waiting for Fisher to reappear? Still, his options were limited: He needed a vehicle, which meant he had to get out and double back. *Divert and run*, Fisher thought.

He moved to the east wall, fished a chem light from his rucksack, crushed it, then reached up and tossed it through the slit. He would have two or three seconds before the chem light glowed to life. He hurried to the opposite wall, stopping a few feet back.

Three one thousand . . . four one thousand . . .

He charged the wall, leapt up, grabbed the edge of the firing slit, then boosted himself up and rolled through the opening, reversing his hands so he was dangling down the exterior wall. He'd heard no gunshots, but as they were armed with SC-20s he couldn't be sure. He looked down. Eight feet below, a concrete lip jutted from the wall; below that, a wall sloped to the ground.

Fisher took a breath, released his hands, and pushed off with his toes. The concrete lip flashed before his vision. He felt his palms slap against it. He curled his fingers. He jerked to a stop, paused a moment, then let go again, twisting as he fell. He hit the sloped wall on his butt and felt the shock travel up his spine. Then he was on the ground and rolling. He went with it, pushing off with the balls of his feet until he'd reached the tall grass he'd glimpsed on his slide down the wall. He spread himself flat and went still. Nothing. If Hansen had posted overwatch snipers on this side of the complex, they would have zeroed in on him by now. He waited another thirty seconds, then began back-crawling through the grass until he reached a slight depression, where he turned himself around and kept going, following the bunker's sloping wall south, back toward the ravine. The grass turned into undergrowth, and that turned into a patch of trees. Fisher got up, kept moving. He made quicker progress than he had inside the bunker, and within five minutes, he was crouched behind a fallen log overlooking the lip of the ravine.

A hundred feet to the south he could see the bridge; the team's two Audis sat at its head. His own vehicle, the belly-up Range Rover, lay in the creek where he'd abandoned it. *What do we have here?* Three figures stood on the shoulder of the road before the bridge. He unslung the SC-20, laid the forestock on the log, and zoomed in on the trio. He was surprised to see only one familiar face: the Japanese Vin Diesel, whose narrowed eyes and furrowed brow told Fisher that the other two men, who stood side by side across from him, were not friends.

The first man was fortyish, bald, with a wrestler's build; the second was gaunt and pasty with dark black hair. They were standing in profile to Fisher, the stout one closest to him, the taller one closer to the road and standing a couple of feet back from his partner. As had Vin's eyes, their postures told Fisher this was a bad situation about to get worse.

The stout man shifted his feet, turning slightly, and now Fisher could see the squarish outline of a semiautomatic pistol dangling from his left hand. Fisher panned slightly to the right and scanned the gaunt man: He, too, was armed.

Could these two men be the tail he'd spotted at Doucet's warehouse outside Reims? Who were they, and was their interest in Vin alone or Hansen's team or Fisher himself? None of that mattered right now, of course. As he watched, the stout man raised his semiauto to his waist and leveled it with Vin's belly. Fisher couldn't hear the man's words, but Vin's reaction told the story: He clasped his hands behind his back and knelt down in the dirt. *Execution.*

Fisher zoomed out slightly, adjusted his aim. As the stout man raised his weapon, extending it toward Vin's forehead, Fisher laid the SC-20's reticle over the upper rim of the man's ear and pulled the trigger. Even as he was dropping like a puppet whose strings had been cut, Fisher was adjusting his aim. His second shot came less than a second after the first, the 5.56mm bullet drilling into the tall man's head two inches behind his temple.

Fisher zoomed out and refocused on Vin. He was still

kneeling, gaping at the two crumpled forms before him. He rotated his head right, looking for the source of the shot, then rose from his knees into a crouch and began sidling right, reaching for something—his own gun he'd been forced to toss away, Fisher assumed. He adjusted aim again and fired a round into the dirt six inches from Vin's groping hand. Vin froze, raised his hands above his head, and gave an "okay, okay" shrug.

Eyes fixed on Vin, Fisher got up and picked his way through the trees along the edge of the ravine until he was within twenty feet of the bridge. When he stepped from the trees and crouched down, Vin saw the movement and began to turn his head.

"No," Fisher ordered. "Face the cars."

Vin complied. "Was that you?"

"Was that me, what?"

Vin jerked his head toward the two dead men. "Them."

"I needed their car. Something told me they weren't the cooperative type."

"Well, thanks."

"Don't mention it."

Fisher flipped the selector to COTTONBALL and fired one into the point of Vin's right shoulder. Vin gave out a slight gasp, then toppled over sideways, unconscious before he hit the ground. Fisher got up and walked over. He frisked Vin's would-be executioners and found a few hundred euros, a set of car keys, two passports, and a half dozen credit cards between them. The money was real enough, but not so the passports and cards, he suspected.

He took everything. Next he checked Vin's pulse; it was steady.

Time for an eye in the sky. Fisher thumbed the selector on the SC-20 again and pointed the barrel into the sky at a seventy-degree angle over the bunker. He pulled the trigger. The projectile was of course saddled with an alphanumeric DARPA-inspired name, but Fisher had long ago dubbed it the ASE, or All-Seeing Eye—essentially a miniaturized version of a Sticky Cam embedded in an aerogel parachute.

Consisting of 90 percent air, aerogel could hold four thousand times its own weight and has a surface area that boggled the mind: Spread flat, each cubic inch of the stuff—roughly the size of four nickels stacked atop one another—could cover a football field from end zone to end zone. In the case of the ASE, its palm-sized, self-deploying aerogel chute could keep the camera aloft for as long as ninety seconds, giving Fisher a high-resolution bird's-eye view of nearly a square mile.

He lifted the OPSAT up, tapped a few buttons, and the ASE's bird's-eye view appeared on the screen. He switched modes from night vision to infrared; doing this drew enormous power from the ASE's internal battery, cutting its life nearly in half, but the view was rewarding. From five hundred feet above the ground, Fisher had a view of the bunker and the field to the east. In familiar rainbow hues he could pick out two figures lying prone in the field, their SC-20s aimed at the bunker. A third figure was walking across the bunker's roof near the emplacement where he had exited. The fourth figure was nowhere to be seen. Probably still inside, Fisher assumed. He tapped a few more keys on the OPSAT's screen, sending a self-destruct command to the ASE, which triggered an overload in the battery, frying the camera's internal circuitry.

One last task.

He got out his Gerber Guardian and went to work.

14

FISHER sat before the computer screen, sipping a double shot of espresso and occasionally clicking on the browser's REFRESH button. The Internet café was busy, filled with late-morning commuters stopping by for a caffeine fix before work and the early-lunch crowd looking for a boost to get them through the afternoon. The babble was all in German, and Fisher used his waiting time trying to catch snippets of conversation; his German was good, but it could always be better.

He hit REFRESH once more and was rewarded with a newly saved message in his drafts folder. He clicked on it, scanned the contents, and nodded. Finally, the answer he wanted. His request for a meeting—if only a voice-to-voice one—had been met with resistance. Until now.

The night before, after punching holes in the rear tires of both Audis, Fisher had taken the dead men's car, a Volvo, and driven to the L1. He headed south to Obersgegen, and then northeast for twenty miles to Bitburg, a city of thirteen thousand. It was nearly dawn when he pulled into the city limits. He drove through downtown, the eastern edge of town, following signs for an overnight rest stop where he pulled in, changed out of his tac-suit, and caught four hours of sleep in the Volvo's backseat.

Now, shortly after eleven, rested and alert after three double espressos, he reread Vesa's message one last time, committed the details to memory.

Meeting approved. Proceed immediately to Aachen.

There was a street address, but it was unfamiliar to Fisher. He deleted the message, signed off the computer, got a coffee to go, and left.

He arrived in Aachen ninety minutes later and, after consulting his iPhone's map, found a crowded shopping area, where he abandoned the Volvo, then caught a taxi and rode aimlessly for thirty minutes before telling the driver to stop. He spent another hour walking, checking for signs of surveillance, before stepping into an Enterprise office and renting a BMW 7 Series. Twenty minutes later he pulled to a stop before a brownstone apartment on Kockerellstrasse. He got out, trotted up the steps, and punched the correct code into the keypad lock; as with the Pelican case, the code consisted of the brownstone's latitude and longitude coordinates combined with some division and subtraction.

He heard a soft buzz, then a click, and the latch opened under his hand. There was no one home, of that he was certain—or mostly certain. He wouldn't have been sent here if the safe house were occupied. Even so, with his SC pistol at his side he searched the apartment's two floors. The decor and furnishings had been chosen straight from a hotel supply catalogue: comfortable but without personality. On the second floor he found a similarly furnished office. One wall was dominated by a fifty-inch LCD television monitor. Sitting on the dark cherry desk, on a leather blotter, was what looked like a standard telephone. He punched SPEAKERPHONE, waited for the dial tone, then hit the pound button three times and the asterisk button twice. The speaker emitted thirty seconds' worth of squelches and clicks as the encryption buffers engaged; then a computerized, Stephen Hawkingesque voice came on the line. "Please hold . . . transferring . . ."

Then a female voice: "Sam, are you there?"

"I'm here, Grim."

IT had been eight months since he'd heard Anna Grimsdóttir's voice, and a lot longer than that since they'd stood in the same room together. The LCD monitor glowed to life, and on the upper edge of the TV's case a tiny green light blinked on, indicating the built-in webcam was on.

Grimsdóttir's face and shoulders resolved. Fisher didn't recognize the background, but it clearly wasn't anywhere at Fort Meade. He guessed that she, too, was using a Third Echelon safe house.

She looked the same as she had the last time they'd seen each other. Despite his misgivings about his old friend's loyalty, it was good to see her. He missed his old life.

"You look tired, Sam," Grim now said.

"I am tired. When was the last time you heard from Hansen?"

"Couple of days. I'm afraid we might have a mutiny on our hands."

"How so?"

"The team knows we're holding back on them. Moreau's got his hands full."

"He's in the field?" Louis "Marty" Moreau was one of Third Echelon's best technical operations managers—in other words, a Splinter Cell "handler."

Grim nodded. "Coordinating. And getting shot at."

Fisher smiled. "But surviving, right?"

"Right. Anyway, Hansen's trying to keep the team on track, but I can hear it in his voice: He knows something isn't kosher. There's more than a little frustration there, too."

"Don't blame them. Well, for what it's worth, they haven't been making it easy on me. Almost had me a few times."

"Uh-huh," Grimsdóttir replied skeptically. "You've given them some breaks."

"Some. Have to make sure the show's convincing enough to sell Kovac," Fisher replied, referring to the National Security Agency's deputy director, Nicholas Andrew Kovac. Grimsdóttir's boss. In addition to being an all-around idiot and dyed-in-the-wool bureaucrat, Kovac was also on their too-long list of high-ranking NSA Brahmins who may have sold out the United States. Until Fisher and Grimsdóttir finished this mission, she would have to placate Kovac. Unfortunately, that meant fielding a team to hunt down Fisher.

"So far, so good," Grimsdóttir said.

"Grim, we've got a problem. They were in Vianden— Hansen and the others. They almost caught me in Ernsdorff's backyard."

"What?"

Fisher brought her up to speed, starting with his arrival in Vianden and ending with his escape from the Siegfried-Line bunker. He left out any mention of Vin's close call at the bridge.

"They shouldn't have been there," Fisher explained. "I left them no trail to follow."

"You're sure?" When Fisher didn't reply, Grim said, "Of course you didn't."

"There are only a couple of ways they could've gotten there."

"Me and an outside information conduit."

Fisher nodded.

"It wasn't me, Sam."

Fisher almost said, *Convince me*. It wasn't necessary.

He'd known Anna Grimsdóttir too long, and the expression on her face told Fisher she was telling the truth.

"So that leaves a conduit. Moreau?"

"No chance."

"The mole, then," Fisher replied.

"Has to be."

"And you're sure about that part?"

Grim nodded. "There's a cutout. Code name is Stingray. He or she was in the Russange-Villerupt area the same time you were. Someone on the team is getting fed. We just don't know who or why."

"I'd like to think we could rule out Hansen."

"Me, too. But we can't. Not yet."

"Ames."

Grimsdóttir sighed. "He's a weasel, but beyond that there's nothing that points to him."

"He took a couple of shots at me—at the Esch-sur-Alzette reservoir."

"He reported it to Hansen. Fell on his sword. Said he got a little jumpy and fired warning shots."

Fisher considered this and shrugged. "It happens." Fisher changed topics: "Put their feet to the fire," Fisher said. "Right now, they're pissed off and frustrated. Threaten to pull them out of the field if they don't tell you how they got to Vianden. Hell, threaten to investigate them, kick them out of the program, take away Christmas. They're good, all of them, but they're green. Use it."

Grim nodded. "I'll do it."

"By the way, who are the other two? The blonde and the Japanese Vin Diesel."

At this Grimsdóttir laughed. "Maya Valentina and Nathan Noboru. I'll download their bios to your OPSAT."

"You may have a problem with Noboru. When I came out of the bunker, he was seconds away from getting a bullet in the head. Two men—one short and stocky, the other tall, anemic looking."

"Those would be misters Gothwhiler and Horatio. Mercenaries. Noboru did a job for a group called Gothos a few years back, but there was a woman and child involved, so he aborted mid mission. Gothos stiffed him, so Noboru hacked into its account and liberated his fee—he only took half, though, since he didn't do the woman and child."

"Interesting. I think I like him."

"You said, 'seconds away,'" Grimsdóttir prompted. "I assume that means you—"

"I did. Seemed like the right thing to do. Where are you with the data from Ernsdorff's server?"

"Still working on it. Heavily encrypted stuff, but there's gigabytes' worth, so at least we know we're digging in the right place. Hopefully, I'll have something in a few hours—at least a direction I can point you."

"I'll need something to satisfy Hans."

"You'll have it. How soon?"

"I meet him in Hammerstein tomorrow."

For the sake of appearances, when Yannick Ernsdorff had come to Third Echelon's attention Grimsdóttir and Fisher—who was already on the run and well established in the mercenary community—had looked for other agencies with an interest in Ernsdorff's activities. They found their stalking horse in Germany's BND, the Bundesnachrichtendienst, or Federal Intelligence Service. Fisher's BND contact, Hans Hoffman, hadn't specified what kind of information they were seeking, instead giving Fisher plenty of latitude. "Whatever you can find, *ja?*" had been Hoffman's vague instructions, which told Fisher that the Germans were in just the initial stages of mounting an operation against Ernsdorff or against someone Ernsdorff serviced. Either way, during the months running up to Fisher's penetration of Ernsdorff's estate the BND had supplied him with dribs and drabs of peripheral intelligence, which he had dutifully funneled back to Grimsdóttir at Fort Meade. None of the information had been, in and of itself, earth shattering, but it had given them a few insights into the man. Now Fisher had to report back to his customer and turn over the information he'd gathered—at least such information as Grimsdóttir deemed juicy enough to satisfy them but benign enough to keep the BND behind Third Echelon's own investigation. Until they were done with Yannick Ernsdorff, he needed to remain untouchable.

"When are you going to have your come-to-Jesus meeting with the team?" Fisher asked.

"Hansen's set to call in within the hour."

"Keep me posted."

"As soon as I have something, I'll call. The safe house is solid. You won't get any unexpected company. Stay there, get some rest."

"Twist my arm."

"Hang in there, Sam. I think we're in the last innings."

Fisher nodded and smiled wearily. "Unfortunately, that's usually when the rain starts falling."

IGNORING the instincts that had for the past year kept him constantly moving from city to city and country to country, Fisher took Grimsdóttir's advice. He had a long, hot shower, washed his clothes, then laid out all his gear, inspecting and cleaning each piece until satisfied everything was working as designed. At three o'clock he walked down the block to a sporting goods store and bought a Deuter Quantum 55+10 backpack, large enough to accommodate all his gear, and an assortment of kayaker's dry bags, then found a grocery store and bought some fruit, cheese, sourdough bread, sliced turkey and roast beef, and a six-pack of Berliner Kindl Weisse, then returned to the brownstone and ate at the dining room table.

At five he heard a soft double *bing* from upstairs. He walked into the office and touched the phone's SPEAKER button. Grimsdóttir's face appeared on the LCD. "You look a little better," she said.

"I feel a little better. Might be the two Berliner Kindl Weisses, though."

"What?"

"German beer."

Grimsdóttir screwed up her face. "Too stout for me."

Fisher shrugged. "What do you know?"

"I talked to Hansen and his team. I think I talked them down. Rattled their cages a little bit. It won't last forever, though—especially with him. He knows something's off about their mission, but at least for the near future he's willing to take some things on faith."

"Good. And Vianden?"

"They took some initiative and played a hunch. They still buy that you're freelance, and they assumed Luxembourg had something to do with a job. Noboru still has contacts in that world, so he came up with a few names of players that are still in the know. Ames made a few calls and got a hit."

"Explain."

"It's a small world you're in, Sam, and somebody of your caliber stands out. According to Ames, it was just a matter of asking about jobs in Luxembourg and U.S. government covert operatives gone bad, so to speak. Nobody had your name, but somebody had Ernsdorff's. They drove up from Luxembourg city, started scouting the area, and the rest is bad luck."

"How did they catch up to me after I lost them the first time?"

"Police scanner. Something about a man with a gun in a campsite."

"Hippies were robbing my Range Rover."

"Pardon me?"

"Forget it. So, you buy it—Ames's story?"

"It's plausible."

"Do we know who Ames got the tip from?"

"Somebody named Karlheinz van der Putten."

Fisher smiled. "I know the name. Half-German, half-Dutch guy. Used to be Fernspäher—special-forces reconnaissance unit. He's got to be in his sixties by now. His nickname was Spock."

"Why, does he have some kind of ear fetish? Something sexual?"

"Not so much sexual as surgical. He used to take ears as trophies."

"Very nice," Grim muttered. "Well, his trophy days are over, evidently. According to Noboru, van der Putten went into the information business."

"How much did Ames say he paid him?"

"Fifty thousand."

"Where's he living now?"

Grimsdóttir paused a moment and looked down at her PDA. "Spain. A village called Chinchón southeast of Madrid. Why?"

Fisher didn't answer. "Where did you leave it with Hansen?"

"They're back in Luxembourg, regrouping. Kovac's breathing down my neck, so I'll have to put them on the road again soon. Check your Lycos account tomorrow after Hammerstein."

"And Ernsdorff's server?"

"I've downloaded the package for Hoffman to your OPSAT. Should be plenty there to make the BND happy and keep them busy for a while."

15

IT was a leisurely two-hour drive from Aachen to Hammerstein, and the road meandered east before turning south through Cologne, then to Bonn, where Highway 42 took him along the east bank of the Rhine down to Hammerstein. Fisher met Hans Hoffman at a small, locally owned winery called J. P. Zwick Weinstube Weingut. The day was bright and sunny, the surface of the Rhine ruffled by a slight breeze. Fisher could see barges and pleasure boats in the main channel. Horns and whistles echoed across the water.

He found Hans Hoffman seated at a table in a rear courtyard surrounded by hedges. Sitting on the kelly green tablecloth were four empty wineglasses. He was sipping his fifth.

"How long have you been here, Hans?" Fisher asked as he sat down. There were only five other people in the courtyard: two couples sitting several tables away, and a thick-necked, broad-shouldered man in a black suit standing near the courtyard's rear wooden gate. *Bodyguard*, Fisher thought. This told him something he'd suspected about Hoffman: The man was fairly high in the Bundesnachrichtendienst. This was the first time, however, that Hoffman had brought along protection.

Hoffman smiled, shrugged. "Long enough to sample four . . . no, five wines," the BND man replied in lightly accented English. "They don't give you much to try, you know. Would you like—"

"No, thanks." Fisher shifted in his chair ever so slightly so he could see both the bodyguard and the courtyard's main entrance. "Who's your friend?"

"Dietrich."

"He needs to smile more."

Hoffman chuckled. "He is very stern, isn't he?"

Fisher said nothing but held Hoffman's gaze. Finally the BND man waved his hand dismissively. "Nothing to worry about, Sam. Another matter altogether. Apparently not everyone I deal with likes me as much as you do."

It was a lie. A well-told lie but a lie nevertheless. Fisher offered Hoffman a hard smile. "Who said I like you?"

Another laugh. Hoffman was the quintessential jovial German. Dietrich, on the other hand, was the quintessential stone-faced Teutonic knuckle dragger. His suit was also poorly fitted. Fisher could see the outline of a semiautomatic in a paddle holster at his waist.

"We're good friends, Sam."

"I'll take your word for it. His coat shouldn't be buttoned, you know."

"Pardon me?"

"Dietrich. His coat. It'll cost him a second or more when he goes for his weapon."

Hoffman glanced at his bodyguard and frowned slightly. "I'll see to it. Tell me how you fared in Luxembourg."

In answer, Fisher placed a 4 GB USB flash drive on the table and slid it across. "A lot of information. Whether it's what you're after is for you to judge."

Hoffman touched the flash drive with his index finger and slid it to the edge of the table, behind his collection of wineglasses. "I'll arrange for your fee to be transmitted when we're done here."

Fisher nodded. "Hans, just so we're clear: If you've set me up, I'll put two bullets in your heart before Dietrich can even reach his buttons."

Hoffman's face went slack. He cleared his throat. He shifted in his seat. "I don't know that I would it call it a 'setup.'"

"What would you call it?"

"An order from on high. I got a call from Pullach," Hoffman said, referring to the BND's headquarters in Pullach.

"From whom, exactly?"

"Does it matter? Someone called him, and someone had called the person before him. They wanted to know if I was working with you. What could I say?"

Nothing, Fisher thought. Unless Hoffman was lying

and the request had come from outside the government—
and his motivation was personal gain—he was taking the
only option open to him. Besides, Fisher had just given
Hoffman a flash drive full of useless information, so they
were even.

"Who's coming for me?" Fisher asked. "Some of
yours?"

"No, but I do not know who."

"Do they know what I'm driving?"

"If they do, it's not from us."

"How soon?"

Now Hoffman smiled. "Why, when we meet, of
course. At two o'clock."

Fisher checked his watch. It was one fifteen. "Thanks,
Hans."

"For what? I showed up early to enjoy the wine, and
here you were."

"Anything else you can tell me?"

"No, I'm sorry. If I had to guess, however, I would
say they are flying in."

"Which means Cologne Bonn Airport."

"Yes."

From the airport to Hammerstein it was an hour's
drive south on Highway 42. At least he would know
from where the threat was coming—unless they were
already here, that was.

"Frankfurt is only ninety minutes to the south. Big
city. Plenty of places to lose yourself."

Fisher stood up and extended his hand. "Do me one
more favor."

"Certainly."

"In five minutes call the local police. Tell them a madman in a BMW is smashing into cars in the marina parking lot south of the winery. Tell them he headed south down 42."

Hoffman pursed his lips in confusion but nodded. "Five minutes."

"Thanks." Fisher turned to go.

Hoffman said, "Just tell me one thing: If you hadn't liked the answer I gave you, would you have shot me?"

"Yes. But I wouldn't have enjoyed it."

He turned and headed for the rear gate, leaving Hoffman chuckling at the table.

FISHER went around the winery and came through the trees in the side yard. He stopped beside the bushes and looked around. Across the highway a couple dozen cars were parked in the boat-launch lot. It was busy for a weekday, with cars and boat trailers jockeying around one another, waiting for a chance to launch or leave.

Fisher watched, looking for anomalies. It didn't take long. Two men and two women dressed like locals, but not quite like locals, were moving through the lot, pausing at cars, peering in windows, and keeping one another in sight. Ames, Valentina, Noboru, and Kimberly Gillespie. He should have known that forty-five minutes was enough of a head start. Like any good operative Hansen had moved his team into position well before his quarry was set to arrive.

Speaking of Hansen . . . Fisher watched him emerge

from between a pair of cars in the lot and step over the guardrail and onto the shoulder of the road. He waited for a break in traffic, then started across toward the refinery.

Fisher didn't hesitate but stepped out from between the bushes and started toward his BMW. Hansen spotted him immediately and picked up his pace. *Not quick enough,* Fisher thought, and kept walking. When he was ten feet from the BMW, Hansen called, "Don't, Sam, we've got you."

Fisher didn't reply, didn't look up.

Hansen hesitated; his pace faltered. "Fisher!" It was almost a shout.

Fisher was five feet away. He pointed the key fob at the BMW and unlocked the door. In the corner of his eye he saw Hansen's right hand reach into the folds of his black leather jacket. Fisher reached for the door handle, lifted it, and opened the door, only then looking up at Hansen, who'd just reached the edge of the winery parking lot. Fisher gave him a curt nod and got into the car. As the door shut Hansen muttered, "Damn!" then turned and sprinted back across the highway. Fisher started the engine, did a Y-turn in the lot, and pulled onto the highway, heading south.

Indecision and youth, he thought grimly.

WHETHER born of his own suspicions about their mission, Fisher's saving of Noboru at the Siegfried Line, or something else altogether, Fisher didn't know, but clearly Hansen hadn't yet crossed the threshold.

As advertised, Fisher sped to the marina a quarter mile south of the winery, pulled into the parking lot, and side-swiped a dozen unoccupied cars before pulling back onto the highway and continuing south. He glanced in his rearview mirror. Several cars sat at the exit to the boat-launch lot, but none had emerged since he'd left the winery.

He made no attempt to blend in with traffic, and made no turns, but headed straight south, pushing the BMW as fast as he dared, weaving around slower cars until four minutes later he saw the sign for Neuwied. He glanced in the rearview mirror. Two miles back a pair of sedans was swerving over the center line, leapfrogging around slower cars; far behind them Fisher could see flashing blue lights.

He had no intention of letting this turn into a pro-tracted chase. Hollywood portrayals notwithstanding, urban high-speed chases *always* attracted the police, and the police usually won in the end. Plus, in the back of Fisher's mind he knew he'd been lucky too many times over the last few days. In broad daylight, with two cars to Fisher's one, Hansen would get the upper hand sooner rather than later. What he needed was to end the chase quickly and dramatically—and in a way that would not only allow his escape but also complicate Hansen's situation.

Sitting at the table with Hoffman, Fisher had reviewed his mental map of the area and picked his spot.

AS he sped past the Neuwied city limits sign the traf-fic thickened, and he slowed to 60 kph. Highway 42 swung west, looping around the city, and changed into the L258. Another half mile brought him to a cloverleaf. He followed the Highway 256 exit, which swung south and east, back into Neuwied proper. As the waters of the Rhine came back into view, he looked in his rearview mirror but saw nothing. But they were there, matching his speed, flowing with the traffic, trying not to attract attention. The police from Hammerstein were also nowhere to be seen, but witnesses from the marina would have been certain of the BMW's direction. By now, the Neuwied police were on alert.

Fisher passed a sign that read RAIFFEISENBRÜCKE 3 KM. He punched the gas pedal and the BMW's powerful engine responded instantly. As the speedometer swept past 100 kph, then 120, he swerved around cars ahead of him, honking and flashing his lights and gesturing wildly. A half mile back a pair of Mercedes did the same, moving into the passing lane and accelerating.

There you are. . . . RAIFFEISENBRÜCKE 2 KM.

Now he could see it, the two-lane Raiffeisen Bridge rising from the river, its central A-shaped pylon jutting 150 feet into the sky, angled support cables stretching out like threads from a spider's web. In the passenger side mirror he saw flashing blue lights. He glanced over his shoulder. A pair of police cars raced up the Sandkauler on-ramp and fell in behind Hansen's Mercedes.

Two more curves and another kilometer brought Fisher to the bridge. He tapped the brakes, jerked the BMW left, around a slow-moving lorry, and then he was on the span and over the water. To his left, over the railing, he could see the curved dagger shape of Herbstliche Insel—Autumn Island—in the middle of the channel.

Fisher felt his pulse quicken. What he was about to do would either kill him or allow him to slip away and leave no trail whatsoever.

He waited until he saw Hansen's Mercedes appear on the bridge a few hundred yards behind him, then pushed the accelerator to the floor, putting some distance between himself and the closest following cars. He then slammed on the brakes and skidded to a stop, with the BMW's tires straddling the center line. Tires screeched. Horns began honking. Across the center guardrail, traffic in the eastbound lanes was slowing to a crawl.

Fisher closed his eyes for a moment, took a breath, tried to block out the blaring car horns, the warbling of the approaching police sirens, the shouting. . . . He looked in his rearview mirror. People were now getting out of their cars, peering at the lone BMW sitting still in the middle of the span. Fisher leaned over, pulled his backpack off the passenger floor, tossed it into the backseat, then closed each of the dashboard vents in turn.

Not going to get any easier, Sam, he told himself.

He shifted the BMW into reverse, spun the wheel, and backed up until his rear bumper thudded into the center guardrail and his hood was pointed at the opposite guardrail. He unbuckled his seat belt.

He shifted into drive, took a final calming breath, then jammed the accelerator to the floor.

_16_

IF not for the BMW's six-liter, 537-horsepower engine, Fisher's escape attempt would have ended before it started, when the car's front bumper hit the guardrail. But the engine, combined with fine German crafts-manship, was no match for the waist-high rail and the abutting suicide-prevention hurricane fencing—a bit of irony that didn't escape Fisher's attention as the BMW tore through the fence and plunged toward the river below. The drop was fifty feet, but trapped inside the car, listening to the banshee wail of the engine and watching horizon and sky and water turn to a smudge before his eyes, it might as well have been a thousand feet.

As it had hundreds of times before, Fisher's training took over when every muscle of his body wanted to freeze up. He rolled over and threw himself over the seats and onto the floor in the back, atop his backpack. Most victims of bridge collapses die in the front seat, arms braced against the steering wheel or dashboard, every muscle in their body tensed as they stare, transfixed, at the water's surface rushing up to meet them. Whether being in the backseat would provide any great protection, he was about to find out. He took a deep breath, let it out, and commanded his body to relax.

The BMW stopped dead, as though it had hit a brick wall, which, in terms of physics, was more true than not. From fifty feet up, the car had gained enough momentum that the water's relative solidity was equal to that of concrete. Fisher was thrown against the seats, and the seats tore free of their floor mounts and slammed into the dashboard and windshield. He felt the BMW porpoise— the hood plunging beneath the surface, then breaching again as the rear of the car slammed down. With a prolonged sputter the engine died.

Fisher groaned, tried to push himself off the seat backs. White-hot pain arced through his chest and he gasped. Having experienced the sensation before, he knew he'd bruised a rib, perhaps more. He craned his neck and peered between the seats. The windshield was intact. He could feel the car settling lower, could see the water boiling up over the windshield and side windows. He heard the gurgle of it pouring through the nooks and crannies in the engine compartment. Water began gushing through the vents. Fisher felt a flash of panic. Words and half-formed images flashed through his mind:

trapped, drowning, tomb, slow death . . . He pushed the panic back and focused. He *was* sinking, but he wasn't trapped, not yet at least, and he'd be damned if he was going die trapped in a BMW 7 Series at the bottom of the Rhine River.

People who survive bridge collapses only to drown in their cars invariably make one fatal mistake: They try to keep the water out, realizing only too late that it is the water pressure that's keeping them from opening the doors or rolling down windows. Panic sets in, the mind freezes up, and they drown.

Most modern cars are equipped with thick and precision-fitted weather seals, and Fisher's BMW was no exception. While water was gushing from the vent slats, the door seals were holding, save dozens of rivulets streaming down the glass. These would get worse as the water pressure increased, but he still had time. Teeth set against the pain in his chest, he rolled over and looked out the back window. Light from the surface was fading rapidly; he estimated the car was dropping past twelve feet. The current, which ran at an average of four miles per hour—a walking pace—had taken hold. It would be ten minutes or more before rescue craft arrived on the scene. By then, provided the Rhine was as deep here as he'd guessed, he and the BMW would be a half mile downstream.

NINETY seconds later he was passing thirty feet, and the BMW slipped into complete darkness. Fisher dug an

LED headlamp from his jacket pocket, donned it, turned it on. The backseat was bathed in cold, blue-white light. The water pouring from the vents had reached the mangled steering wheel. All around him the car popped and squelched as the exterior pressure increased. Occasionally pockets of air in the engine compartment would find their way out, then bubble past the windows and disappear into the gloom.

Almost time, Fisher told himself. *Gear check.*

Working under the headlamp's beam, Fisher unzipped the backpack and pulled out a black aluminum cylinder the size of a Pringles potato chip canister. Modeled on the commercial version known as Spare Air, this DARPA-modified miniature scuba tank had been named OmegaO by some long-forgotten techno-geek with a dark sense of humor. Omega for "last," and *O,* the symbol for oxygen—*the last breath you're likely to take.* Despite its diminutive size, the OmegaO was something of a marvel, able to hold 2.5 cubic feet, or 70 liters, of air, which translated into roughly forty-five to fifty lungfuls. For an experienced diver this could mean as much as five or six minutes underwater, enough for a strong swimmer to cover a quarter mile or more. Fisher was a strong swimmer.

FED by spring snowmelt, the water was shockingly cold but not so much so that hypothermia was a worry. Not yet at least—not as long as he got out of the water within the next half hour. Fisher wondered how Hansen and his team had reacted. Whether they believed he was dead was a toss-up, but he wasn't counting on that but rather on the mess with which he'd left them: a high-speed chase ending in a car plummeting off the bridge into the Rhine. If nothing else, his pursuers would be occupied for the next hour or more.

The water was roiling now, being forced into the car under ever-increasing pressure. The level reached his chest. One final time, he checked the OmegaO hanging from the strap around his neck.

With a grating jolt, the BMW hit the riverbed; the car continued to slide for another ten feet until the tires sunk into the mud, bringing it to a halt. He could feel the current buffeting the sides. Water bubbled up to his chin. He got to his knees and, head pressed into the ceiling, donned his backpack. He put on the regulator and punched the button to test the airflow and was rewarded with a short hiss. He took a breath; the air was cool and metallic tasting. He closed his eyes and the water enveloped him.

Silence.

He sat still for a moment and listened to the ticks and pings of debris washing over the BMW, then opened his eyes. His headlamp beam was a cone of white before him. He checked the windows but saw only darkness and occasional bits of swirling sediment and plant matter. In which direction had the car settled? He pressed his hand first against the passenger-side window, then the driver's side; here he felt more pressure against the glass. He scooted back to the other side, lifted the handle, and put his shoulder to the door. It burst open. Fisher tumbled out and landed on his side, buried up to his collarbone in mud. Loosened by the impact, his headlamp slipped off his head and slipped away. He snagged it, settled the straps back on his head, and cinched them down.

He started swimming.

THE current, combined with his paddling, doubled his submerged speed. With his vision narrowed to what the cone of light from his headlamp illuminated, he had the sensation one got on an airport's moving walkway. With no fixed references to latch on to, his brain was telling him he was swimming at a normal pace, but his body knew otherwise. Counting seconds in his head, Fisher swam hard for a minute, then turned left on the diagonal, aiming for the Rhine's western shore. After another two minutes he felt the current suddenly slacken, and he knew he was clear of the main channel. He felt something soft slide over his chest and belly, and it took him a moment to realize it was mud. The bottom was rising. Twenty feet, he estimated. He was perhaps thirty feet from the bank. He had no fixed plan, but knew he needed to surface close to land, close to cover, lest he be spotted by rescue boats or an onlooker.

The current changed again and he felt his body spiraling left into some kind of vortex. His kicking feet touched mud, and then the water was calm again. He angled upward. The light increased. The surface came into view. Using his hands like flippers, he backpedaled in the water, slowing down until he was hovering a few feet below the surface. Directly ahead he could see trees: fuzzy broccoli shapes silhouetted against the sky. There was a gap between them. An inlet. He turned over, dove to the bottom, and swam on, using only his feet, arms spread wide, until he felt his fingers trailing over soil walls. The inlet continued to narrow and bottom out until his chest was scraping the bottom. He rolled onto his back and used his heels to wriggle forward until his head broke the surface. He blinked his eyes clear and found himself staring at tree branches, so close he could have reached out and touched them. He was right: an inlet. Shaped like an elongated V, it was at least two hundred feet deep. At its midpoint was a wooden footbridge. Someone was standing on it. No, two people. A man and a woman with their backs to him—watching the show in the main channel, he assumed. Moving with exaggerated slowness, Fisher reached up and removed the OmegaO's mask.

It was ten long minutes before the couple moved on, crossing to the southern bank of the inlet and disappearing from view. Fisher rolled back onto his belly and began crawling.

At what he assumed was the end of the inlet, he instead found a choke point of dead branches and fallen logs draped by low-hanging boughs. On the other side of the natural dam he found a knee-deep creek enclosed in a tunnel of yet more undergrowth and trees. He followed the creek for a half mile, pushing deeper inland, occasionally glimpsing houses and cul-de-sacs through the trees until finally, after forty minutes of plodding through the water, he saw a raised concrete bridge ahead. He heard the rush of traffic, heavy enough that he realized he was near a major road.

He moved to the bank and found a comfortable place to sit down. He shrugged off his backpack, rummaged around until he found the Aloksak containing his iPhone; he pulled it out and powered it up. After tapping into a nearby wireless network, he called up the map feature and pinpointed his location. He was on the northern outskirts of Weißenthurm, the town across the Raiffeisen Bridge from Neuwied. The bridge ahead of him was part of the L121—Koblenzer Strasse. As the crow flies, he was less than a mile from where he'd gone off the Raiffeisen but almost twice that in the water and on foot.

He checked his watch. It was almost four o'clock. Three hours until nightfall.

17

HAVING been out of contact longer than he'd anticipated, Fisher, upon landing at the Madrid Barajas International Airport, took a taxi downtown to the first
touristy landmark that came to mind, the Monasterio
de las Descalzas Reales on Plaza de las Descalzas. The
forty-minute drive gave him time to do some passive
dry-cleaning. The driver, whom Fisher felt certain had
been rejected by a Spanish demolition-derby show, made
countersurveillance an easy task as he weaved in and out
of traffic, ignored the speed limits, and showed a love
for impromptu turns and narrow, one-way streets. By
the time they reached Plaza de las Descalzas, Fisher was
beyond certain he'd picked up no tails.

The previous night, after sitting on the bank of the inlet

for five hours, he had waded out beneath the Koblenzer Strasse bridge, then walked north through farmers' fields and down riverside hiking trails to Andernach, two miles north of Weißenthurm. By the time he found an appropriately anonymous hotel, the Martinsberg, his clothes were dry and he was presentable enough to arouse no suspicions from the night clerk. Once in the room, he first called the Frankfurt Airport's Iberia desk and booked a late-morning flight to Madrid; his second call was to a local limousine company to arrange for a pickup. Both of these reservations he made using yet another pair of Emmanuel's clean passports and credit cards. Unless he was recognized between Andernach and the airport, he would be leaving behind an ice-cold trail.

After a hot shower and a late room-service supper, Fisher spent ten minutes probing his rib cage until satisfied nothing was broken, then took four 200 mg tablets of ibuprofen and went to sleep. He awoke the next morning at eight, found a local address for a DHL office, and took a taxi there, returning thirty minutes later with a box and packing materials. He packed up his non-airport-friendly gear and weapons, sealed the box, and addressed it to the DHL office in Madrid and left it at the hotel's front desk for pickup.

Now, just before noon Madrid time, he found himself standing before the Monasterio de las Descalzas Reales. He paid the driver, waited for the car to squeal around the corner and out of sight, then walked four blocks southeast to an Internet café on Calle de la Montera.

Fisher got signed in, left his passport at the counter as

requested, then found an open computer cubicle and sat down. There was a draft message in his Lycos mailbox. It read simply:

21 Calle de la Concepción Jerónima
Apartment 3B
Key, baseboard

This would be another safe house. Fisher memorized the address, deleted the message, and was out the door and in a taxi two minutes later. It wasn't until the car pulled onto the narrow street that Fisher realized the apartment faced the building housing Spain's Ministry of Foreign Affairs and Cooperation. *Nice touch*, he thought as he got out.

As advertised, beside the door to apartment 3B Fisher found a loose baseboard, and behind it a key that opened the apartment door. Inside there was nothing. Where the German safe house had all the charm of a hotel chain, this studio apartment was completely empty, save for a familiar-looking keypad lock on the bedroom door. He punched in the correct code and pushed through. Inside was, of all things, a red beanbag chair sitting before an LCD television. On the floor next to the chair was a speakerphone. Fisher typed in his pound/asterisk code, and sixty seconds later Grimsdóttir appeared on the monitor.

"You're alive," she said simply.

"So it appears. They were tipped off, Grim."

"What?"

"You heard me. If Hans Hoffman hadn't grown a

conscience, they would've been on me when I walked out of the winery."

"Explain." Fisher did so, and Grim said, "So Hoffman gets a thirdhand call that trickled down from the top, which means the original call had to come from someone with horsepower."

"I got the impression it came from outside the BND. One of those 'step aside and let nature take its course' orders."

"Kovac?"

"That was my first thought. What better way to undermine you than to arrange my capture? He makes some calls to ally agencies, cashes in a few favors, gets lucky. . . ."

"No proof, though," Grim replied. "No one in the Bundesnachrichtendienst or the German government would cross Kovac."

"Agreed." Fisher moved on. "What do Hansen and his team think?"

"About your stunt? They're skeptical, but the rescue workers haven't even found the car yet, let alone a body. Truth is, I think they're all in shock. They all think you did it on purpose; most of them think you thought you'd survive and were wrong."

Fisher nodded. This was one of the outcomes for which he'd hoped. The other involved the Neuwied police. He asked Grim about it.

"The second Mercedes—with Valentina, Ames, and Noboru—managed to take off before the cops arrived on the bridge. Hansen and Gillespie talked their way out of it. They told the police they saw a dangerous driver and were trying to keep it in sight until the police arrived. Apparently, aside from your BMW, the Hammerstein cops couldn't identify any of the cars involved in the chase." Grim asked, "How'd you do it?"

Fisher recounted the incident, from his car's impact with the water to his arrival in Madrid.

"Why the limousine?"

"The opposite of anonymity is—"

"Ostentatiousness," Grim finished. "Hiding in plain sight."

"Something like that. Were they even covering the airports?"

"No, they drove straight back to Cologne Bonn Airport. I pulled them back to Luxembourg and put them in a holding pattern. I assume you're in Madrid to visit the local ear collector?"

"You assume correctly," Fisher replied.

Karlheinz van der Putten, a.k.a. Spock, lived in Chinchón, twenty-five miles to the south. Ostensibly, Ames, using Noboru's contacts in the mercenary world, had produced the lead that had led the team to Vianden. Fisher wanted to know if, in fact, van der Putten was the source of the information. As Grim had said during their previous teleconference, the scenario was plausible, but something about it wasn't sitting right in Fisher's belly. What he couldn't quite figure out was whether the suspicion was born of instinct or of his dislike for Ames.

"How long is van der Putten going to take?" Grim asked.

"If he's home, I'll have my answer before morning."

"Good, because your next stop is right next door—Portugal."

Third Echelon's mainframe was still chewing on the bulk of the data Fisher stole from Ernsdorff's server, but, Grimsdóttir told him, an interesting lead had bubbled to the surface: the name Charles Zahm—a person also known as Chucky Zee. Fisher had plodded through one of Zahm's novels, *Myanmar Nightmare*—250 pages of an *In Like Flint*–style secret agent karate-chopping his way through hordes of turtleneck-wearing villains and sleeping his way through gaggles of impossibly buxom women in beehive hairdos. At last count, Zahm's series had grown to thirteen books and publishing contracts worth millions, all predicated upon the fact that Charles Zahm had, until seven years earlier, been a member of the Special Air Service, or SAS, Britain's elite counterterror-ism force.

According to Ernsdorff's private investigating team—most of the members of which were culled from Brit-ain's Security Service, also known as MI5—Zahm hadn't restricted his postretirement exploits to paper but had also gone into crime. Along with five of his former SAS mates, Zahm was the leader of what London's tabloids had dubbed the Little Red Robbers, based on the Mao Tse-tung masks they'd worn during their robberies of two armored cars, four jewelry stores, and four banks. Whether Zahm had ever read or even heard of Chairman Mao's famous Communist treatise, known in the West as *The Little Red Book*, was a hotly debated topic in the country's gossip rags. What wasn't in doubt, however, was the Little Red Robbers' willingness to use violence. In all, six innocent bystanders had been beaten nearly to death during the robberies as preemptive warnings to would-be heroes, the police suspected. One woman lost her unborn child in the process.

"I don't buy it," Grimsdóttir told Fisher.

"I disagree," Fisher replied. "The SAS doesn't induct idiots. Maybe Zahm *is* just that smart. Write a bunch of critically panned novels that make millions and hide in plain sight as a dim-witted former soldier."

"While pulling off some of the biggest heists in Britain's history," Grim finished.

"He's got the training. With his money and contacts, it wouldn't have taken much to learn the ropes. There are plenty of retired thieves who'd gladly pass on their knowledge for a price. How solid does Ernsdorff's info look?"

"Very. Names, dates, accounts, sexual predilections . . . In fact, it looks like a blackmail file. But for what purpose?"

"Can't be money," Fisher replied. "Ernsdorff has more money than he could spend in ten lifetimes. My guess: He's leveraging Zahm—using his Little Red Robbers for a job or jobs."

"That seems out of character given what we know about Ernsdorff. He's been exclusively a background player"

"We know he plays middleman for bad guys and their money. And we know he's playing bank for this auction. From that, it's not that big a leap to other kinds of services."

18

ONE of the benefits of hunting people who live on the fringes of society is that they also tend to gravitate toward the fringes of communities. When you kill and steal and blackmail for a living, and have even a modicum of karmic awareness, you tend to worry about your deeds someday coming back to haunt you. Aside from the very rich, who could afford to live apart from the world and surrounded by security, or the very careful, who left no footprints that would lead enemies to their door, the bad guys who survive the longest are the ones who ignore that reclusive impulse and choose, instead, to dwell in plain sight, disguised as average citizens.

Luckily for Fisher, Karlheinz van der Putten, a.k.a. Spock, was neither wealthy nor karmically self-aware.

Upon retiring from active mercenary life and setting himself up as an information clearinghouse, van der Putten moved to Chinchón, a town of five thousand whose two claims to fame were its central square, which served as a temporary bullring, and the church of Nuestra Señora de la Ascunción, where Francisco Goya's *Assumption of the Virgin* was housed.

After signing off with Grimsdóttir and picking up a rental car, Fisher made two stops: one to replenish his basic traveling supplies, including an economy-sized bottle of ibuprofen for his bruised ribs, and the second to pick up the DHL box containing his weapons and gear. He was heading south out of the city by three and arrived in Chinchón an hour later, in the middle of siesta, the traditional Spanish period of late-afternoon rest and rejuvenation. He wore Bermuda shorts, sandals, and an "I ♥ Madrid" T-shirt.

Chinchón was perched on the eastern slopes of Spain's Sistema Ibérico mountain range, so the narrow cobble and brick streets rose and fell and branched at unexpected angles. The architecture was what one would expect from a village born during the Middle Ages: buildings of heavy, dark chiseled beams stacked closely together, faded stucco walls of yellow ocher and pale mocha, half-hidden courtyards, balconies fronted by ornate black iron railings, and a sea of undulating roofs covered in U-shaped terra-cotta tiles.

Fisher found a parking spot behind a tavern a few blocks from the Plaza Mayor and got out to stretch his legs. The streets were eerily quiet and deserted, save for the handful of people Fisher could see sitting on front porches and swinging in hammocks. A lone dog—a mix between a beagle and a husky, Fisher guessed—padded across the street and into a shaded alley. He stopped to give Fisher a glance over his shoulder, then trotted off into the shadows.

Fisher wandered for a few minutes, enjoying the quiet, then made his way toward what he hoped was the Plaza Mayor. It wasn't hard; all the roads and alleys and paths seemed to converge on the town's center. The bullring was up, Fisher saw: a six-foot-tall bloodred-and-yellow-striped fence enclosing a dirt clearing about 120 feet across. Surrounding the ring, like bleachers, were three-story galleried houses fronted by dark green railings. The sun reflected off the taupe-colored dirt, causing Fisher to squint. He caught a whiff of manure on the breeze.

A hand-painted sign on a nearby fence post announced that the bullfight would take place the next morning. With luck, he'd be gone by then. Not only did he have no love for the sport, but he needed to get on with the business of paying Charles "Chucky Zee" Zahm a visit and finding out precisely what he and his Little Red Robbers had been doing for Yannick Ernsdorff.

FISHER returned to his car and meandered through town to the southwestern outskirts and followed the signs for Castillo de Chinchón until he pulled onto the tree-lined dirt road that led him to a small gravel parking lot. As castles went, Chinchón's was probably underwhelming for the unseasoned traveler; Fisher had seen enough of these to know that was more the rule than the exception. Built on a square and anchored on each corner by a turret barely taller than the crumbling stone walls, the *castillo* was not quite two hundred square feet; it was, however, built on a slope overlooking the entire town, which, during its prime, likely compensated for its size.

There were only two cars in the lot and both looked local.

FISHER parked, got out, and walked across the bridge through the portcullis, pausing to grab a brochure from the wall-mounted box. Once inside he walked across the courtyard to the northern wall and followed the steps up the battlement. He was alone; if the two cars in the lot belonged to attendants, they were probably on siesta somewhere.

He pulled his binoculars from his rucksack and panned down the green fields between the castle and the town, picking out landmarks until he found what he was looking for. Karlheinz van der Putten's home, a two-story red-roofed villa surrounded by a low outer wall built under the shadows of mature olive trees, sat by itself on a dead-end road. Judging by the built-in swimming pool, lined with blue and white arabesque tiles, and the travertine flagstone deck, van der Putten had done well since going into business for himself. A balcony fronted by hand-chiseled cedar rails overlooked the pool deck; spanning the balcony's width were sliding-glass doors through which Fisher could see a master suite. A matching set of sliding doors on the ground floor led to what looked like a living room, a breakfast nook, and a kitchen.

Fisher scanned the patio until he saw a lone man sprawled on a chaise lounge beneath a potted lemon tree. The angle made positive identification difficult, but the face seemed to match that of van der Putten. Fisher smiled. It seemed the man had spent a good portion of his profits on groceries. Van der Putten was pushing the scales at nearly three hundred pounds. His height, five feet six, combined with his choice of swimwear, a pair of red Speedo trunks, did nothing for him. The image of a sausage ringed by a too-tight rubber band came to mind. Still, Fisher could tell there was a layer of muscle beneath the layer of fat. He'd take care not to underestimate the portly mercenary's experience and familiarity with violence—in fact, the story behind his nickname, Spock, told Fisher that van der Putten was not only familiar with violence but that he enjoyed it.

A woman appeared on the patio, carrying a pair of margarita glasses. She gave one to van der Putten, then lay down on the neighboring lounge. She had long brown hair, was supermodel thin, and was taller than van der Putten by a good four inches. She wore owl sunglasses that dominated her gaunt face, giving her a distinctly alien appearance. Only extraterrestrial origins or an abiding attraction to money could explain her choice of companion, Fisher decided. *To each her own.*

Fisher kept scanning, studying the other homes on van der Putten's road, looking for likely infiltration and exfiltration routes, and good cover, until finally lowering his binoculars. As he did so he caught a flash of reflected sunlight to his left. Instinctively he knew it hadn't come from a windshield or window or mirror but rather a lens of some kind—spotting scope, binoculars, or camera. Fisher leaned forward, pulled the brim of his cap lower over his eyes, and rested his arms on the stone, casually looking around as tourists tend to do. He stopped the rotation of his head just short of the flash's origin and used his peripheral vision to watch for it. A few moments later it came again. Fisher raised his binoculars and pointed them skyward, ostensibly watching the hawk riding the thermals above the castle but flicking his eyes left. A few hundred yards to the north and west, a cluster of villas sat atop a lesser hill. Parked at the head of an east-facing empty cul-de-sac was a gray compact car. Two men stood outside it. Both were armed with either cameras or binoculars. Above Fisher, the hawk cooperated and banked west. He followed it, one eye fixed on the two men until they came into complete focus. Neither looked familiar; both were well tanned, with black hair. Locals, he guessed. One of them was pointing a camera at van der Putten's home; the other, a pair of binoculars at Fisher himself.

Competition, Fisher thought. Of what type, it was too soon to tell.

Fisher took his binoculars off the hawk and lowered them, resuming his touristlike scan of the lush fields beneath the *castillo*. After a few more minutes, the two men got back in their car, backed down the cul-de-sac, and disappeared from view, only to reemerge on Cuesta de los Yeseros, the east–west road a quarter mile below. He watched the car meander east, then disappear again, then reappear on Calle del Alamillo Bajo, the road he'd followed twenty minutes earlier to reach the castle.

This could not be a coincidence.

He briefly considered bluffing it out as a tourist, but if they were curious enough to drive up here, they would also be thorough enough to memorize his face and record the make and model of his car. He didn't have time to get away, not in the car, at least.

He waited until the gray compact disappeared behind a line of scrub pines, then pulled out his Canon, zoomed in on van der Putten's, and took five sets of bursts, then put the camera and binoculars away and returned to the courtyard. He followed the brochure's map to the eastern wall, then down a set of steps the led beneath the wall, into a short tunnel, then outside through an arch built into the sloped foundation. He turned left, jogged to the base of the southwest turret, and peeked around the corner. He saw no one. He pulled back and waited.

A few minutes later he heard the crunch of tires on gravel, then the soft squeal of brakes. Two car doors opened, then shut, and then he heard feet scuffing over dirt. In his mind's eye he imagined the two men walking to his rental car and taking down the particulars before heading for the portcullis bridge. The footsteps went quiet as they crossed onto stone. Fisher peeked around

the corner and saw the tops of two heads moving toward
the portcullis. He heard the soft bang of the brochure
box's lid falling shut, then counted to ten, stepped out,
and walked quickly but quietly west along the wall. He
was under the bridge and at the southeast turret seventy
seconds later. He didn't pause, didn't look back, but kept
going until he reached the copse of cypress bordering the
entrance road. Once in the deep shade, he laid himself
flat, scooped the loam into a berm before him, and went
still.

His visitors took their time, spending almost thirty
minutes in the castle before emerging from the portcullis and crossing back over to the parking lot. A minute
passed without the sound of car doors. Two minutes.
A door opened and closed, followed by a second. An
engine revved up, and moments later the car was moving down the entrance road above Fisher's hiding spot.
He gave them five minutes, then retraced his steps to the
castle, back through the courtyard, and across the bridge
to the lot.

His car looked undisturbed, but he knew better than to
take that on faith. He found the GPS transmitter—a DIY
affair consisting of a prepaid cell phone, a plastic project
box, and glued-on neodymium magnets—attached to a
bracket on the engine's firewall. *Interesting*. They were
observant and thorough but were using a homemade
tracker. Fisher had seen their type: mercenaries or contract security consultants who were good but underfi-
nanced. Entrepreneurs trying to break into the business.
Fisher reassembled the tracker and put it back.

He lay in the cool shade beneath the car for a few minutes, thinking. He'd found himself in a wheels-within-wheels situation. Were these men watching him or van der Putten? If the former, were they watching him *because* he was watching van der Putten, or because he was potential competition or a threat? If their primary interest was van der Putten, they could be anyone: enemies, personal or professional; potential employers doing homework; law enforcement; intelligence operatives. . . . Fisher realized these mental aerobics were largely unnecessary. Bottom line: He needed to talk to van der Putten, and he needed to do it before these new players did whatever they'd come to do.

FISHER'S solution to the GPS tracker was to play his tourist role to the hilt. He left the castle and drove through Chinchón until he reached the M-316, which he took northeast toward the town of Valdelaguna three miles away. Soon after leaving Chinchón's outskirts, the gray compact appeared in his rearview mirror and followed him into Valdelaguna. Fisher spent an hour ignoring his pursuers, who seemed to worry less about being seen as time went by and Fisher went about his photography tour, snapping dozens of shots of architecture and scenery before finally heading back to Chinchón.

By the time he got back, siesta was over and the townsfolk were moving about. Fisher found a hotel, Casa de la Marquesa, within view of the bullring, and checked in, making sure to ask the desk clerk in halting Spanish about the bullfight the next day and nearby photography hot spots, in case his watchers should decide to ask the clerk about his gringo guest.

Once in his room, a quick peek through the curtains revealed his watchers had taken up station on the patio of a cantina down the block. After a half hour, they left. Fisher checked his watch: six thirty.

19

HE waited until dusk, when the town's lights began to flicker to life. He wandered down to the bullring and found it had been converted into an outdoor dance hall complete with pole-mounted torches and loudspeakers through which strains of *jota* music drifted. Fisher wore brown trousers, hiking sandals, and a dark blue polo shirt over a white T-shirt, both untucked to cover the butt of the SC pistol and the folded Nomex balaclava in his waistband. He'd debated bringing more equipment, at least the Tridents or the Night Owls, but given Chinchón's close-set houses, narrow streets, and the celebratory mood of the town, his chances of encountering a civilian were too great.

Though night had not yet fully fallen, half the town

seemed to have already converged on the ring; it was standing room only. Fisher spent twenty minutes picking his way through the throng, smiling and greeting revelers and enjoying the spectacle, all the while keeping his eyes open for his watchers. They were nowhere to be seen, and this told Fisher something else about them: They probably had no backup, and they relied too heavily on the GPS tracker, a dangerous approach, especially in a town where a person could walk from edge to edge in ten minutes. Then again, he'd given them little reason to further pursue their curiosity about him. Clearly, he was a shutterbug tourist who happened to be in the same area as their target.

Sticking to side streets, Fisher proceeded south, using the decorative lights of the castle on the hill as his guide until he reached Cuesta de los Yeseros, where he stopped beneath the sidewalk trees and watched and listened. He then walked across the road, scaled the shrub-covered embankment into the field beyond, and turned west. Another hundred yards brought him opposite van der Putten's rear patio, fifty feet across the road and situated atop a berm of scrub grass. Tiny halogen theater lights set into the patio wall cast soft white cones on the flagstone, and submerged lights glowed amber beneath the pool's surface. Van der Putten's master suite was dark save for a half dozen glowing candles. As Fisher watched, a door opened and in the rectangle of yellow light stood the silhouetted form of van der Putten's companion. She stood still for a moment, one leg before the other, arms lightly braced on the jamb, clearly showing off for van der Putten, whom Fisher could now see was lying on the bed. He was still wearing his red Speedo trunks. The woman flipped off the light and the room went dim again.

Through the ground floor's sliding-glass doors Fisher saw a circle of red appear, pan quickly across the kitchen, then go dark again. Only someone interested in preserving their night vision would use a red flashlight. His friends in the gray compact were making their move.

Fisher drew the SC, pushed his way through the undergrowth, zigzagged down the embankment, then sprinted across the road and up the berm to van der Putten's patio wall. Through the ground-floor glass he could see two shadowed figures moving through the living room toward the front of the house—toward stairs, Fisher assumed. He rolled over the wall and ran, hunched over, around the pool until he reached the sliding-glass doors, where he crouched down. He tried the door. Locked. He drew the Gerber Guardian from its calf sheath. He laid the SC down, then used his right hand to pull the door to the right, while wedging the tip of the Guardian into the latch mechanism. With a click, the lock popped open. He sheathed the Guardian, picked up the SC, crab-walked inside, and paused to slip on his balaclava.

From upstairs came a woman's scream, then a *thump*, like a body hitting the floor.

SC extended before him, Fisher moved through the kitchen, checked the foyer, then peeked around the corner up the stairs. Somewhere upstairs a light was on. Another scream. Fisher mounted the stairs, stepping carefully and steadily until the second floor came into view. At the end of a ten-foot hall, the door to the master suite was partially open. He could see a nightstand and a lamp, which was the source of light.

He heard a soft *thwump*, like a gloved hand striking a heavy dictionary.

Noise-suppressed weapon, a detached part of Fisher's brain told him. Either van der Putten or his girlfriend had taken a bullet, and the woman's scream that came a second later gave Fisher his answer. It wasn't a scream of pain but of resignation, of anguish. They'd killed van der Putten. Fisher quashed the urge to charge the door. The woman was still alive. The intruders had other business, or else she'd have already gotten her bullet.

Fisher took two more steps down the hall and stopped at an open door on his right. A bathroom. He stepped in, carefully groped with his hand until he found a heavy, glass soap dish. He switched the SC to his left hand, picked up the dish with his right, then stepped back into the hall.

"Hurry up, Rodrigo!" said a male voice in Spanish.

"This ain't as easy as it looks, damn it!" came the reply.

Fisher took a step forward, pressed himself against the left-hand wall. Now he could see around the lamp. On the bed were two pair of calves—one set on the bottom, unclothed and toes pointed up; the second wearing pants, toes pointing down. Their owner was kneeling on the bed over van der Putten. The bed was rocking from side to side.

Fisher cocked his right arm, took aim, and hurled the

soap dish into the master suite. The dish flew true, striking the sliding-glass doors dead center. Even as the glass
shattered, Fisher was moving through the door.

At the threshold he looked right and saw one man
standing over van der Putten's naked girlfriend. He had a
booted foot pressed into her neck and a noise-suppressed
9mm pointed at her skull. Predictably, he was gaping at
the shattered doors. Fisher spun, shot the man in the
head, and he stumbled sideways and slid down the wall.
Fisher turned again and took aim at the man kneeling
over van der Putten.

"Don't move," Fisher ordered in Spanish.

The man had been in middle of turning his head. He
stopped, his face in profile. His hands were out of sight,
held in front of him.

"Let me see your hands," Fisher ordered.

The man didn't move.

Fisher repeated his order.

The man raised his left hand above his head; it was
bloody up to the wrist.

"The other hand."

Fisher knew what was coming. He could see it in the
man's posture, in the flick of his eyes.

The man turned his head back toward the sliding-glass
doors, and said, "Okay, okay . . ."

Fisher took a wide step to his left, and a half second later the man made his move. Left hand still raised
above his head, the man spun his torso counterclockwise,
revealing his right hand and the 9mm it held. The muzzle
flashed orange. The bullet thunked into the wall where

Fisher had been standing a moment earlier. Fisher fired twice, both bullets entering within an inch of each other directly beneath the man's armpit. Both bullets shredded his heart. Already dead, he pitched forward over the edge of the bed, his legs jutting skyward for a few moments before he crumpled into a ball on the carpet.

Behind him the woman whimpered.

"Don't move. Don't look up," Fisher told her. "You're going to be okay."

She didn't answer.

"Say yes if you understand me."

He got a feeble *sí* in response.

Fisher walked to the doors and pulled the curtains shut, then checked van der Putten. The former mercenary lay facedown on the bed, a Rorschach of blood staining the white sheets beneath him. He'd been shot once behind the right ear—or what little remained of the right ear. It had been sawed off, along with the left, by the bloody tanto knife that lay beside the body. The ears lay side by side on a nearby pillow. They looked like miniature, dehydrated pork chops.

Karma, Fisher thought.

HE quickly searched both men, taking everything he found, then grabbed a spare blanket in the linen closet and covered up the woman. After some coaxing, she got to her feet, and Fisher led her out of the bedroom and downstairs to the living room couch.

"What happened?" she murmured, barely coherent.

She was in shock. "Who were those men? Why did they kill Heinzie? Who are you? Why did they . . . ?"

Fisher let her ramble as he went into the kitchen and found a plastic grocery bag, into which he dumped the men's wallets, pocket litter, and a set of car keys. He then went back upstairs and rummaged in van der Putten's medicine cabinet, where he found a bottle of Ambien. He gave the woman a tablet and a shot of Scotch, both of which she accepted without protest. He knelt before her.

"What's your name?" he asked.

"Isobella."

"Isobella, does Heinzie have a safe? Someplace he keeps important information? Maybe a hiding place?"

"What?" Fisher repeated the question, and Isobella shook her head. "He just has a watch and some rings. No jewelry—"

"I'm talking about documents. Important papers."

"Why do you need that?" For the first time since sitting down, Isobella lifted her head and seemed to truly focus on Fisher. Seeing his balaclava-covered face, she withdrew and her eyes went wide.

"I'm a friend," Fisher said. "I'm sorry I didn't get here in time to save Heinzie. Those men were after information." This was likely untrue, but the woman wasn't coherent enough to dissect the argument. "If I don't find it and get it out of here, more men will come. Do you understand?"

"More? More men?"

"That's right. Where did Heinz keep his important documents?"

"There's a safe. Upstairs. Under the sink . . ."

"Do you know the combination?"

"My birthday."

Fisher felt a fleeting pang of sadness. Clearly, Isobella had meant more to van der Putten than Fisher had guessed. "What's your birthday?"

Isobella blinked a few times and her head lolled. The Ambien/Scotch cocktail was taking hold. "What?"

"What's your birthday?"

"June 9, 1961."

Fisher laid her down on the couch, then went back upstairs. As advertised, he found a safe built into the floor of the bathroom vanity. He pushed aside the rolls of toilet paper and bottles of cleaning solution and spun the dial to 6-9-61. Nothing. He tried different combinations and sequences until 61-19-6-9 produced a click. Inside the shoebox-sized safe Fisher found nothing except a 2 GB SD memory card. He pocked it and went downstairs.

"I'll call the police," Fisher told Isobella. "You rest."

She nodded wearily, then rolled over on the couch.

Fisher left.

They'd parked their gray compact two blocks away. He searched it, taking every pertinent scrap of paper he could find and dumping it into the grocery sack before locking the doors and tossing the keys down a nearby sewer drain.

_20_

"**IT'S** possible," Fisher told Grim, "but I've never been a big believer in coincidences."

"Me neither," she replied from the LCD screen. "With luck, I'll have something for you in a few hours."

The night before, after dumping the keys to the gray compact in the sewer, Fisher had walked back toward the center of town, stopping briefly to buy a newspaper, in which he wrapped his blood-speckled polo shirt. When he reached the bullring, the community party was in full swing and a huge bonfire was burning. He tossed the newspaper and shirt into the blaze, then spent fifteen minutes dancing and drinking and generally making a spectacle of himself before walking to another convenience store, this one close to his hotel. He used the pay phone to dial 112—Spain's version of 911—and told the dispatcher in hurried Spanish that he'd heard gunfire near the intersection of Cuesta de los Yeseros and Calle del Alamillo Bajo. He'd then hung up and returned to his hotel.

The choice to call the police and remain in town rather than simply driving away was a tactical gamble, Fisher knew, but given Chinchón's size a foreigner leaving town in the dead of the night following a brutal triple murder wouldn't go unnoticed.

Fisher completed the ruse by waking up before dawn the next day, dropping his packed duffel bag off the balcony, and stopping in the lobby to ask the clerk when the bullfight was to begin and how to reach Guadalupe and whether the monastery there was open to the public. Once out the door he picked up his duffel, walked to his car, and drove away, taking the M-404 west out of town before turning north at Ciempozuelos and heading for Madrid and the Third Echelon safe house, where he packaged up his take from van der Putten's killers and sent it via International Next Flight Out. Grim had the package sixteen hours later.

"One thing I can tell you is that the SD card you got from van der Putten's safe looks like bank account info," Grim now said. "As you'd expect, he had several—two of them hidden behind front companies. I'm working on it. If Ames paid him in anything other than cash, it should be there."

"Good."

"Back to our noncoincidental coincidence: It could

mean either Noboru or Ames was lying about van der Putten."

"It's worse than that," Fisher replied. "It means one of them is the mole."

THERE were a few seconds of silence as Grimsdóttir absorbed this. On the screen, her brows furrowed and she let out a sigh. "It could be worse than that. If van der Putten wasn't the source of the lead that pointed Hansen and his team to Vianden, that leaves only three people who could've tipped off Ames: me, Moreau, and Kovac."

"You know who gets my vote," Fisher replied. "The question is, did he do it to make you look bad, or is it something else?"

"Such as?"

"Ernsdorff. When did you tell Kovac I was moving toward Vianden?"

"About four hours before Ames got his tip."

"As soon as he realized I was moving toward Vianden and Ernsdorff, he got nervous and ordered Ames to cut me off. Problem was, I'd already penetrated Ernsdorff's estate."

"If all that's true, why didn't Kovac simply call Ernsdorff and warn him?"

"Hard to say. Insulation, maybe. Maybe Kovac and Ernsdorff are separated by layers—if so, that means there're bigger fish out there."

"Big enough to pull the strings of a deputy director

of the NSA and Europe's premier black-market banker. Scary thought."

THEY talked for a few more minutes; then Fisher disconnected and made two more calls: one to Iberia to book an evening flight to Lisbon, and a second to DHL to arrange shipment of his gear. He then went out for a bite to eat, caught four hours of sleep, and then took a taxi to the airport. His flight departed at eight thirty. Owing to the time difference and distance, the seventy-minute flight put him in Lisbon ten "clock" minutes after he departed. By nine he was on the road, and an hour later he pulled into Setúbal and checked into the Hotel Aranguês.

Located on the Tróia Peninsula and the Sado River estuary, Setúbal was a town of 120,000 built around the sardine-fishing industry, which had been a booming business since the early 1900s. According to the plethora of well-crafted if melodramatic minibiographies and magazine profiles Fisher had found of Charles "Chucky Zee" Zahm, the former SAS commando turned novelist/master thief was himself a fan of fishing. Game fish, however— not sardines—were why he'd moved to Setúbal. Accompanying many of the stories were in-action photos of Zahm straining at a fishing rod on the afterdeck of his hundred-foot Azimut Leonardo 98 yacht, standing at the wheel of his hundred-foot Azimut Leonardo 98 yacht, sitting in scuba gear on the gunwale of his hundred-foot Azimut Leonardo 98 yacht. . . . It took little imagination to guess Zahm's favorite pastime, nor his most prized possession. This was understandable, of course. The Azimut Leonardo 98 sold for 4.9 million euros, or roughly 6.8 million U.S. dollars. The pictures of Zahm's ocean-view villa, down the coast from Setúbal in Portinho da Arrábida, further confirmed the man's love of the nautical life.

Fisher gave this some thought and decided the temptation was too great to resist. It was time to find out exactly how far Zahm's love of the ocean went.

FISHER was up and out the door shortly after dawn the next day, and by the time the sun's upper rim rose over the ocean's surface he was out of the city and winding his way south along the coast road. He stopped at a small restaurant called the Bar Mar, on Figueirinha beach, then continued on, arriving in Portinho da Arrábida ten minutes later. Of the short list of possible retirement spots he'd accumulated, the village immediately jumped to the top.

Nestled at the foot of the Serra de Arrábida—*serra* translates as "saw," an apt term for the mountain range that rose behind the village—Portinho da Arrábida was a ready-made postcard, with red-roofed bungalow houses perched atop lush slopes, white-sand beaches, and crystalline blue-green waters enclosed by a crescent of rocky shoreline.

Following a series of screen captures he'd sent to his iPhone from Google Earth, he drove through the village, then followed a switchback road into the mountains until he found a scenic overlook that offered him the vantage point he needed. He got out and walked to the wooden railing, where a bank of pole-mounted binoculars had been installed. He dropped a fifty-cent euro piece into the slot and pressed his face to the viewer.

His first view of Zahm's home told Fisher two things: One, the term "villa" was a gross trivialization; and two, the pictures hadn't done the place justice.

At three-thousand-plus feet, the ranch-style structure clad in floor-to-ceiling windows sat atop a hillside in a saddle between the Serra de Arrábida escarpment and a cliff overlooking the ocean. A ten-foot-wide moat-like swimming pool encircled the rear two-thirds of the house, while in the front a set of stone steps spiraled down to terraces set into the cliff, one containing a negative-edge pool that seemed to hang in midair above the water a hundred feet below. The second deck was covered in lounges, chairs, and blue-and-white-striped umbrellas, plus a freestanding cedar shack Fisher guessed served as a changing room/bathroom. At the bottom of the steps a two-hundred-foot stone jetty led to a trio of skiffs equipped with outboard motors, but there was no sign of Zahm's yacht.

Fisher scanned farther out, checking the ocean's surface from horizon to horizon until he spotted her anchored off an island five miles down the coast. He could see six men on deck, all shirtless and bronze in the morning sun. A fit group, he decided. Though from this distance they were mere specks, he saw a familiar economy and confidence in the way they moved. It was the kind of bearing gained from spending years in an elite military outfit, in this case the Special Air Service. The man at the center of the group—Zahm, Fisher assumed—sat in a fighting chair on the afterdeck, heaving and leaning on a ten-foot fishing pole. Fifty yards off the stern a marlin broke the surface and arced into the sky, trying to shake the hook, its black back glistening in the sun before it plunged beneath the surface again. A silent cheer went up on the yacht's afterdeck.

Fisher pulled his face away from the viewer.

"Going to be tricky," he muttered.

Handling one SAS soldier was nothing to take lightly. Handling six SAS soldiers was a do-or-die proposition. Do it right, without mistakes, or you won't survive the encounter. The fact that the group had been retired for quite some time improved Fisher's odds, but not by a comfortable margin. A lot would depend how much of their old ways they'd retained.

AFTER another hour the yacht hauled anchor and got under way. It took less than a minute for the twin 2,216-horsepower engines to bring her up to a cruising speed of thirty knots—almost thirty-five miles per hour—which meant they would be back in ten minutes or so. Fisher spent the time taking eighty-five pictures of Zahm's über-villa, focusing on sight lines, angles, entrances, points of cover, and possible infiltration and exfiltration routes. The house's floor plan was open, with most rooms carpeted and separated by hanging walls or fabric panels, which made surveillance easy but movement inside problematic: Thick carpet was a double-edged sword.

Eleven minutes after it left the island, the yacht was pulling up to the jetty. The man himself was at the wheel atop the flying bridge. He deftly spun the hundred-foot craft in a sliding Y-turn before reversing the engines and easing her alongside the jetty's bumpers. Fisher could now see the yacht's name etched on the stern—*Dare*—a play on the SAS motto, *Who dares wins,* Fisher guessed.

Zahm's buddies were moving before the *Dare*'s engines were shut off, jumping to the dock and securing lines while Zahm barked orders and gesticulated. Seemingly satisfied all was in order, he climbed down from the bridge, leapt onto the jetty, and the group proceeded toward the steps.

What they did next told Fisher much. A few minutes after they settled onto the second terrace deck, a trio of white-smocked servants emerged from the house carrying trays of tall glasses and pitchers filled with something other than lemonade. Zahm was a gin-and-tonic man, and it stood to reason that his entourage followed suit. Another thirty minutes of watching proved Fisher's theory as the group grew steadily more boisterous. Twice more the servants returned with refills and took away the empties. It was not yet nine in the morning.

The world at their fingertips, and Zahm and his Little Red Robbers pass most of their time drunk, Fisher thought. While pathetic of them, this was good news for him.

* * *

HE spent the remainder of the morning touring the mountains above Zahm's villa, stopping whenever he came across a valuable vantage point. By the time the sun reached its zenith, he'd taken nearly two hundred photographs of the villa and surrounding terrain. Many of the shots would probably turn out to be duplicates or near duplicates, but that was the beauty of digital cameras, Fisher had learned: massive storage capacity and the DELETE button. Also, even seemingly identical pictures often revealed useful details when viewed at full screen, zoomed in, and through image filters.

He spent another hour doing reconnaissance on Portinho da Arrábida's beaches, below Zahm's villa, then drove back to his hotel in Setúbal. The DHL box containing his gear was waiting for him. Once in his room, he dug out the OPSAT, powered it up, and established an encrypted link with Grimsdóttir. A message was waiting:

Spock financial accounts cracked.
No evidence of deposits within last two weeks.

Ames had lied. He hadn't gotten the Vianden tip from van der Putten.

21

GIVEN the party habits of Zahm and his friends, Fisher saw no benefit in postponing his infiltration much beyond nightfall. For all he knew, the band slept in the afternoon and stayed up all night, and Fisher didn't have the time to conduct protracted surveillance. At 9:00 P.M. he left Setúbal and arrived in Portinho da Arrábida thirty minutes later and retraced his route into the mountains. His Garmin 60Cx led him back to the hiking-trail parking lot he'd spotted earlier. There were no other cars in the lot. He got out, opened the trunk, and changed from civilian clothes to his tactical gear, then set out.

The hiking trail to the escarpment above Zahm's villa was less than a half mile long, but it crossed two ridge lines and covered a thousand feet of descent, so it was just after ten when Fisher saw the lights of the house appear through the trees. He dropped to his belly and crawled to the edge of the escarpment.

He had an ideal view of the villa, encompassing the entire west side and the deck and pool terraces; the party was in full swing on the latter, and Fisher could see that Zahm had guests—all of them female, all wearing bikinis. Fisher could hear strains of salsa music emanating from hidden speakers, and the area was lit by kerosene torches along the railing. Including Zahm and his men, Fisher counted twelve bodies—a couples get-together—but none of them appeared to be servants, which meant he could explore the villa without much worry of being interrupted. That was the only good news. With so many partygoers, separating Zahm from the pack would be dicey. Save for the glow cast from several recessed pot lights, the interior of the villa was dark.

Fisher stayed still, watching until he was certain he hadn't missed anyone in the house, then took a final night-vision/infrared/electromagnetic scan. Then he crawled backward into the trees, stood up, and followed a zigzagging trail down the face of the escarpment, using boulders and undergrowth to shield himself until the terraces disappeared from view below the top of the cliff. By the time he reached the saddle in which the villa sat, he was fifty feet west of the euonymus hedges bordering the property. After a quick night-vision/infrared check through the Tridents, he got up and ran, hunched over, to the hedges. On the other side of these he could hear the gurgle of the moat pool's filtering system. The offshore wind had picked up, carrying with it sounds of laughter and splashing intermixed with salsa music.

Fisher eased forward, following the hedges until they ended at the stone patio, where he peeked around the corner, then kept going. A short sprint over a decorative, wooden bridge took him over the moat to the villa's rear French doors. The right-hand door swung open under his hand. He slipped inside and shut it behind him. Despite the wind outside, the air conditioner was on and the temperature hovered in the mid-sixties. Fisher picked his way through the house, pausing at the entrance to every hallway and door to check for signs of alarms or sensors, but found nothing until he reached what he assumed was Zahm's master suite, near the front of the house and overlooking the ocean and Portinho da Arrábida. The terra-cotta-tiled floor was bare save for a tatami runner around its perimeter; through the EM, Fisher saw a lone rectangle of swirling blue waves emanating from beneath the runner. Directly above this spot was a framed painting. Fisher couldn't help but smile: Master thief Charles Zahm had gone with, of all things, a wall safe hidden behind a bad Monet reproduction. Fisher crossed the room to the painting and, careful to stay off the runner, examined the frame and the wall behind it for more sensors. There were none. He found the hidden latch on the frame's left side and swung it open, revealing a two-by-two-foot recessed wall safe. While Zahm had chosen the obvious route for the safe's location, he'd spared no expense on the safe itself. Bypassing the electronic lock would take time Fisher didn't have, and blasting the door open would also demolish much of the master suite. He needed Zahm's cooperation.

He was considering his options when he heard the opening of a sliding-glass door. Fisher stepped to the bedroom door and peeked around the corner, down the carpeted hall, in time to see a man and woman stepping into one of the guest bedrooms. The door clicked shut, and moments later came a woman's giggle.

Fisher stepped out, crept down the hall to the door, pressed his ear to the wood, and heard the creak of bedsprings as the man and woman lay down. Fisher drew the SC pistol and with his thumb flipped the selector to DART, then reached down with his left hand and gave the knob a test turn. Unlocked. He turned the knob an inch, paused, then another inch, then another until the knob reached its stop. He swung open the door and stepped through to the left. From his reconnaissance he knew the layout of the room, and now he turned right, bringing the SC up. Neither the man nor the woman had heard him enter. Fisher fired a dart into the man's shoulder blades, then sidestepped right and fired again. The second dart struck the woman in the side of the neck. They both went limp, unconscious. *Two down.* Fisher pulled the bedspread over the bodies, then left, shutting the door behind him.

Another giggle. The slap of flesh on flesh. A squeal. The noises were coming from outside.

Fisher pressed himself against the wall, eased up to the corner, and poked his head around it. Another couple appeared at the top of the terrace steps and crossed the patio to the sliding doors. Fisher stepped backward down the hall until he was deeper in the shadows, then crouched down and raised the SC.

Ten seconds passed.

From another part of the villa a door slammed, followed by the distinctive hum of an automatic garage door opening. An engine revved to life. A few moments later the garage door closed. Four down, Fisher thought. He couldn't afford to assume anything about this latest couple's departure, however. They could be gone five minutes or the rest of the night. He would assume the latter.

It was time to gamble. Fisher went back into the guest bedroom and found the unconscious man's Hawaiian shirt lying beside the bed. He slipped it on over his tac-suit, then went out the front sliding doors, paused to put aside his rifle, pistol, and Tridents, then took a deep breath and walked to the terrace steps, careful to allow only his head and shoulders to appear over the cliff's edge.

"Hey, Chucky, phone!" he called through cupped hands in his best British accent.

In unison, the group around the pool stopped and looked up at him.

Fisher felt his heart lurch. After five long seconds of silence, Zahm yelled back, "Don't call me that, damn it! I told you!"

Oops. Fisher gave a mea culpa shrug of his shoulders, then shouted, "Phone for you!"

Zahm handed his drink to one of the girls and headed

for the stairs. Fisher sprinted back to the villa, scooped up his gear, and then returned to the hallway where he shed the Hawaiian shirt. He brought up the SC pistol, took a step forward. The sliding door whooshed open, then banged shut. When Zahm appeared in the living room and started toward the kitchen, where the phone was located, Fisher tracked him for two seconds, then fired. The dart hit Zahm beneath the right earlobe. He gasped, stumbled; then his knees went out from under him and he collapsed. Fisher crossed to him and snagged him by the collar and dragged him down the hall into the master bedroom, where he flex-cuffed his hands and feet. *Five down or out of the picture.*

He gave Zahm a quick pat down and found a Colt .25 semiautomatic pistol in his waistband. This complicated things. If the boss was armed, the underlings would be armed. Probably. Another assumption Fisher had to make. He considered trying a Cottonball shot, but the distance and the wind made accurate hits difficult. He would need to get close and dart them. And that was iffy. Even in their drunken state, the remaining three men were ex-SAS. They'd lived and breathed firearms for many years; even if they were drunk, Fisher didn't put his odds above 50 percent.

Alternatives, he thought.

The kernel of an idea formed in his head.

He found the servants' changing room, a small closet off the laundry room, by the garage door, and found a white smock and a pair of khaki pants and sandals that fit reasonably well, then went to the kitchen.

* * *

SITTING on the counter were a dozen liquor bottles, but the emptiest ones seemed to be those needed for mojitos. Perhaps it was time for a special Sam Fisher concoction. He found a glass pitcher in one of the cabinets, mixed up a batch of mojitos, then set it aside and turned to his SC-20. *How many?* he wondered. *Three men, four women, all already drunk* . . . He ejected five Cottonballs from the rifle's modular magazine, dropped them in the pitcher, and then, using a long grilling fork, probed the liquid until he'd perforated all the Cottonballs. He waited three minutes to let the tranquilizer diffuse, then gave the pitcher a good stir, added ice, found a silver tray and six highball mugs, and poured. Finally, he shoved the SC pistol into his waistband and headed for the door. He paused before the foyer mirror to check himself, then stepped out.

He was halfway down the terrace steps before he was noticed. Welcoming shouts and cheers rose from the group around the pool, and by the time Fisher reached the deck they were walking toward him. Fisher's Portuguese was rudimentary, but his French was better, so he switched mental gears and said in French-accented, halting Portuguese, "Mojitos. Senhor Zahm's compliments."

The sweating glasses disappeared from the tray. Fisher turned to leave but was stopped short by a shout from one of Zahm's men: "Hey, I thought Charles gave you guys the night off."

Fisher turned. "No, sir. I am here."

"You're not Alberto." The man pointed a wobbly finger at the embroidered name on Fisher's smock.

"No, senhor. Pierre." Fisher gave the man a subservient smile.

"Huh. Pierre."

"Yes, senhor."

"Okay, then. Keep 'em coming, Pierre."

"Yes, senhor."

Fisher walked back to the steps and started upward. When the curve of the stairs blocked the pool area from view, he stopped, crouched down, and set aside the tray. He crab-walked back down until he could again see the pool. He was under no illusion about his Cottonball ruse: The tranquilizer would probably not be enough to render everyone unconscious. What it would do—what he was now seeing—was effectively double the group's inebriation level and give him the advantage he needed. One of the women, the skinniest of the group, was the first to react, stumbling toward a chaise lounge, where she collapsed, giggling and holding her mojito glass aloft in a babbled toast.

Fisher gave it another ninety seconds, then retrieved his tray and trotted back down the steps. As he walked onto the deck, he held the tray up to shoulder height with his left hand as though announcing the arrival of another round, while reaching behind him and gripping the butt of the SC with his right hand. He walked directly to the densest cluster of people—two of the men and two of the women—and closed the distance to ten feet before he was noticed.

"Hey, there!" one of the men called. "More—"

Fisher let the tip of his foot catch a seam in the deck and

stumbled forward, dropping the tray as he did so. As it sailed toward the group's feet, he drew the SC, brought it up, and fired three times in rapid succession, taking down both men and one of the women. The fourth one reacted surprisingly fast for a drunk, spinning on her heel and running toward the couple who stood twenty feet away. She got halfway there before Fisher's dart in the nape of her neck took her down. Even before she sprawled to the deck, Fisher shifted aim and fired again, taking out the woman on the chaise lounge. He turned, focused on the couple. From eight feet he fired twice, but a gust of wind took both darts wide, giving the man a chance to reach toward the gun in his waistband. Fisher fired again and this time the dart struck home, hitting him in the hollow of the throat. Beside him, the woman stood still, her arms raised and her mouth agape.

"Please, don't—"

Fisher darted her in the thigh. She went down.

He spun, SC extended, looking for more targets. There were none.

FISHER immediately realized he'd made a mistake, but given the plethora of fatal errors that accompanied all missions, it was an oversight he could manage: He'd brought flex-cuffs enough for only Zahm's men, so after dragging the bodies closer together he secured the three men and four women in a convoluted daisy chain, wrists and ankles crisscrossing one another until the group resembled a Twister game that had gone awry. Even sober, the best the group could manage would be a disjointed scuttle across the deck; the stairs would be impossible.

Fisher trotted back up to the villa, trussed together the couple in the guest room, then returned to where he'd left Zahm. He was still unconscious. Fisher pulled his balaclava down, then checked his watch. He waited another ten minutes, then went into the kitchen, filled up a pitcher of ice water, and dumped it over Zahm's upturned face. The improvised waterboarding had the desired effect. Zahm convulsed and sputtered and rolled onto his side, where he vomited. Fisher let him catch his breath, then knelt down beside him and stuck the barrel of the SC into his eye socket. Hard.

"Hey! Who—"

"Shut up."

Retired or not, drunk or not, Zahm's soldier instincts kicked in at once. He snapped his mouth shut in midsentence and studied Fisher with a special operator's gaze.

"I want the combination to your safe," Fisher said.

Zahm didn't answer.

"You can talk."

"Go to hell, mate."

"Is that your final answer?"

"And if it isn't, what? You're going to shoot me?"

Fisher shook his head. "Yes or no?"

"No."

"I thought as much. On your feet."

22

FISHER cut Zahm's feet free, then stood back as the man got up. Normally, Fisher would've felt confident keeping a couple of arms' lengths from an adversary. Zahm rated three.

"What now?" Zahm asked.

"That depends. The safe?"

"Can't help you, mate."

"It looks like we're going fishing."

"Huh?"

Fisher jerked his head toward the door, then followed Zahm down the hall and out the sliding doors toward the terrace steps. Zahm started down. Fisher kept his eyes alternately fixed on the small of Zahm's back and his shoulders; if the former SAS man tried to make a move, one or both of those spots would telegraph his intentions, giving Fisher the extra split second he needed.

The lack of any computers in Zahm's home suggested that the man was technologically unsavvy, but Fisher didn't believe this. Zahm led one of the most successful gangs of thieves in British history and hadn't even come close to being caught. So the question was, why no computers? Fisher suspected Zahm simply didn't trust digital storage. While he wasn't certain he'd find what he was looking for in the safe—or that it even existed—it seemed the logical place to start.

His choice regarding Zahm's interrogation, however, was based solely on instinct: The former SAS man wasn't likely to crack under normal methods. What Fisher had planned was abnormal in the extreme.

When Zahm reached the pool deck, he stopped and stared at Fisher's handiwork. "They dead?" he asked.

"No."

"What did you do to them?"

"Stop talking. Keep walking."

When they reached the beach, Fisher ordered Zahm to the jetty.

"Stop here," Fisher ordered as Zahm drew even with a skiff. "Get in."

Zahm turned and gave Fisher a smarmy smile. "Sure you don't want to take the *Dare*? Great boat."

"This'll do. Get in." Gun trained on Zahm, Fisher knelt down and steadied the boat's gunwale as Zahm stepped aboard. "Sit in the bow, facing forward."

Zahm complied. Fisher cast off the painter, then

stepped down and took his seat at the motor. It was a low-powered trolling model with electronic ignition. At the touch of the button the motor gurgled to life and then settled into a soft idle. Fisher cast off the stern line, then twisted the throttle and pulled out, aiming the bow for open ocean.

WHEN he was a mile offshore, he throttled down and let the boat coast to a stop. Almost immediately the boat began rocking in the wind. Water lapped at its sides. He shut off the engine.

"So, what now?" Zahm asked again. "We reenacting the Fredo scene from *The Godfather*? 'Cuz I—"

Fisher nudged the SC's selector to DART and shot Zahm in the right bicep. It was a grazing shot so the drug took longer to do its job, but after ten seconds Zahm slumped forward. His head hit the gunwale with a dull *thump*.

Fisher holstered the SC, drew his knife, and went to work.

WHEN Zahm awoke twenty minutes later he found himself hanging over the side of the rowboat, his flex-cuffed wrists secured to the cleat. "What the hell is this!"

"You're in the water."

"I can see that. . . ." Zahm struggled, trying to chin himself up, but gave up after ten seconds. "What the . . . What's around my legs?"

"The anchor."

Now Fisher saw the first signs of fear in Zahm. The man's eyes flashed white in the darkness as he turned his head this way and that. "What the hell is this?" he shouted again.

"Psychologists call it a stress trigger," Fisher replied. "I've got a theory about you, Zahm: First you volunteered for one of the toughest units in the British military. Probably saw your fair share of action, I'm assuming?"

"Yeah, so?"

"Then you leave the SAS and dive headfirst into writing novels; then you buy a seven-million-dollar yacht and spend most of your time at sea."

"What's your point?"

"My theory is this: When something scares you, you attack it. The more it scares you, the more of it you do."

"Go to hell."

"You're afraid of the water, Chucky."

"No chance, mate."

"Drowning, sharks . . . Whatever it is, you hate the ocean."

Zahm shook his head a little too quickly.

"Let's put it to the test," Fisher said, then scooted forward, drew his knife, and flicked the tip over Zahm's forearm, opening a one-inch cut. Blood trickled down his skin and began plopping into the water.

Now Zahm's eyes bulged. He thrashed in the water.

"Wouldn't do that," Fisher said. "Sharks love that. What kind do you have in these waters? Tiger? Bull? Great white?"

"Come on, mate. Get me out of here."

"As soon as you tell me what I want to know."

Zahm didn't reply immediately. He craned his neck around, checking the water around him. "What . . . what did you say?"

"As soon as you tell me what I want to know I'll bring you back aboard.

"Talk! Come on!

"You and your Little Red Robbers—

"Hey, that's . . ."

Fisher stopped talking. He simply stared at Zahm until the man barked, "Okay, okay . . ."

Fisher continued. "You and your Little Red Robbers did some work for a man named Yannick Ernsdorff." This was half a hunch, but with men like Zahm, bravado was currency. "I want you to tell me what you did for him. The what, the when, the where—everything."

"And if I do?"

"Are you bargaining with me, Zahm?"

Zahm jerked around in the water. "Something bumped me! Something bumped my feet!"

"Didn't take long, did it?" Fisher observed. "That bump is a test. It's trying to figure out if you're a threat. Next it'll give you a test bite."

"Oh, God . . ."

"You done bargaining?" Fisher asked.

"Yeah, sorry, sorry . . ."

"Here's the upside for you: One, you stop being live bait. Two, we part company and never see each other again. And three, I'll keep your sideline job a secret—

providing you and your boys retire permanently. I assume you can afford to do that."

"Yeah, we're set."

"Do we have a deal?"

Zahm nodded. "Now, for the love of bloody Christ, get me out of here!"

Fisher hauled him over the gunwale, leaving his feet jutting over the side and the anchor line trailing in the water. Fisher rolled Zahm onto his back and waited until he'd caught his breath. "Yannick Ernsdorff," Fisher prompted.

"Yeah, he hired us about eight months ago. One job, six million dollars, U.S. Don't know how he found us, but he had proof—enough to put us away for good. Knew every job we'd done. He never said the words, but I got the message: Do the job, take the money, and stay out of jail."

"Where was the job?"

"China. Someplace in China, near the Russian border. I've got documents in my safe."

Fisher smiled. "I thought you might. Insurance?"

"With a guy like Ernsdorff? Hell, yes, I got insurance."

"You deal with anyone other than Ernsdorff?"

"Nobody by name."

"Descriptions?"

"A Chinese bloke . . . lean, hair graying at the temples; a Russian . . . hoop earring and ponytail; an American . . . gray hair, crew cut."

"Okay, go on."

"So we spend three months prepping for the job.

Turns out the place is a government-run research laboratory in the middle of nowhere. Disguised as a chicken farm. Good internal security but almost no external stuff. Tough nut, that place."

"But you did the job?"

"Yeah, yeah. Ernsdorff didn't tell us what we were after. Just told us where to go and what to look for. Just shipping crates—high-end Lexan stuff—with serial numbers on it. He told us not to look inside."

"But you looked inside," Fisher said. "You took pictures."

"Damn straight we did. One of my guys is good with seals. We broke open the cases, took inventory, then sealed them up again, pretty as you like."

"And? What was inside?"

"Weapons," Zahm said.

"I assume we're not talking about AK-47s."

Zahm shook his head. "No, mate, we're talking about World War III stuff."

23

HAPPILY, Fisher found he was wrong about Zahm's technological foibles. The man had no issues with modern conveniences. He simply enjoyed life too much to partake in them. In that alone, Fisher admired him.

What he'd found upon opening Zahm's safe was not only a cardboard accordion folder filled with document scans and four-by-six photos in both color and black and white but also a Sony 4 GB Memory Stick Pro Duo.

After making sure Zahm's guests were still bound and unconscious, Fisher made sure the former SAS man understood both the benefits of forgetting what had occurred over the past two hours and the consequences of pursuing the matter after Fisher's departure.

* * *

IT was almost 3:00 A.M. before Fisher returned to his Setúbal home. Just before 8:00 in Washington. He inserted
the Memory Stick into the OPSAT's multiport, uploaded
the data, then waited for a response from Grim. It didn't
take long:

> Data received.
> Proceed ASAP to Madrid safe house.
> Lisbon Portela Airport. Flight 0835. Ticket at
> Iberia desk.
> Contact upon arrival.

Short and sweet, Fisher thought. He'd worked with
Grimsdóttir long enough to know what that meant:
She'd found something of value.

HE caught three hours of sleep, then got up, packed, and
drove his rental car to Cabo Espichel, a promontory overlooking the ocean. There he set the OPSAT for timed
self-destruction and dropped it, along with the rest of
his gear, in the backpack, into the ocean. However slight
the chance of its being noticed, he was wary of repeating
his DHL gear-shipment procedure one too many times.
Patterns attract attention. And, though Fisher was not a
superstitious man, he half believed in not pushing one's
luck too far.

He arrived at the Lisbon airport an hour before his

flight, had a bite of breakfast in one of the concourse food courts, then boarded his flight, arriving in Madrid an hour later, two hours on the clock. He was at the safe house by eleven thirty, and talking to Grim on the LCD a few minutes after that.

"We got a break," she announced. "Multiple breaks, in fact."

"You have my attention."

"First, this is mostly hunch work, but the three men other than Ernsdorff that Zahm claims to have dealt with . . . I think I know who they are: Yuan Zhao, Chinese intelligence; Mikhail Bratus, GRU, Russian military intelligence; and Michael Murdoch, an American. Does import and export, runs a handful of companies, most of them tech related. He's also elbow deep in defense contract work.

"Second, we extracted another name from Ernsdorff's server data: Aariz Qaderi, a Chechen from Grozny."

Fisher knew the name. Two years earlier, after assassinating his predecessor, Qaderi had taken control of the Chechen Martyrs Regiment, or CMR. It was well financed, tightly organized and disciplined, and made no bones about its mission: the subjugation or eradication of all nonbelievers.

"What kind of data?" Fisher asked.

"Just his name, an account number, and a pending payment of ten million U.S. dollars."

"Big money. Pending to whom?"

"Ernsdorff. Or whomever he's fronting for. Here's part two of the story: One of the serial numbers from Zahm's China job—"

"He didn't remember where exactly. . . ."

"The Jilin-Heilongjiang region, near the border with Russia, about a hundred miles northwest of Vladivostok. Anyway, one of the serial numbers from Zahm's job turned up during a raid of a CMR weapons cache outside Grozny. It was a land mine."

"Hardly worth ten million dollars," Fisher observed.

"No. I'm thinking the ten million is buy-in. The land mine was a teaser—a freebie to get Aariz Qaderi interested.

"That's the bad news. I've waded through Zahm's 'insurance' records from the theft. What Ernsdorff had him hit was a doppelgänger factory."

Fisher paused, sighed. "Oh, hell."

For decades China's foreign intelligence agency, Ministry of State Security—the MSS or Guoanbu—had been focused on industrial espionage. Through its Tenth Bureau, Scientific and Technological Information, the Guoanbu had been successfully targeting private military contracts in the West. The existence of doppelgänger factories— laboratories applying the raw intelligence data gathered by the Guoanbu—had been suggested by the CIA in the late nineties, but solid evidence had never been found.

Doppelgänger factories were dedicated to one purpose: creating perfect knockoffs of the West's latest and greatest weapons, often systems that weren't yet even in use by Western militaries.

"The official name was Laboratory 738," Grimsdóttir said. "But based on Zahm's data, there's no doubt what it was."

"You said 'was.'"

"I went back and checked the satellite imagery. About a month after Zahm's job, all activity at that chicken farm stopped. In the space of forty-eight hours it became a ghost town."

"Can't say I blame them," Fisher replied. "What else are they going to do? Admit to the rest of the world they stole the biggest and baddest secrets, then used those secrets to create an überarsenal that they then lost? What are we talking about, Grim? What kind of weaponry?"

"I'll download the encrypted list to your new OPSAT when you're ready, but suffice it to say that Zahm wasn't exaggerating: If this arsenal falls into the wrong hands, they'll become a first-world power overnight."

HERE was one of the reasons—the other had been settled months earlier—Fisher had been on the run for the past year and a half. Long before Lambert died he'd become one of the few U.S. intelligence officials convinced that doppelgänger factories were, in fact, real. Worse still, Lambert had come to believe the Guoanbu had been getting help from within the Pentagon, the private defense industry, and the U.S. intelligence community, including high-level NSA officials—all of whom were, in essence, sowing the seeds of America's destruction. Armed with the most sophisticated—and often improved-upon—weapons and systems, China, its nuclear weapons, and its billion-strong People's Liberation Army would become invincible.

While it hadn't taken much time for Lambert to convince Fisher and Grim that his theory was sound, it had taken much more to convince them that his plan was their only viable course. In killing his boss, Fisher had not only laid the groundwork for his entry into the mercenary underworld, but he'd also removed the specter of Lambert uncovering the corruption and treason that had infected virtually every aspect of the U.S. military-industrial complex. With Lambert dead and Fisher on the run and hunted, those involved would breathe a sigh of relief, go about their business, and hopefully make a mistake on which Fisher and Grimsdóttir could seize.

"So let's put the pieces together," Fisher said. "Ernsdorff is playing money man to whomever hired him to hire Zahm."

"Mister X," Grimsdóttir suggested.

"Okay. Mister X takes delivery of the 738 Arsenal. . . . Did Zahm indicate where this happened?"

"Korfovka, Russian Federation, about sixty miles from Laboratory 738 and five miles over the border. I'll send you the particulars later."

"Mister X takes delivery of the 738 Arsenal, then uses Ernsdorff to put the word out to the world's major terrorist groups about the auction. They invited anyone with the resources to provide the ten-million-dollar ante. To sweeten the deal, he sends out party favors—like the land mine they found at the CMR cache."

"I can buy that."

"What was it, by the way? The mine, I mean."

"Antitank. Essentially a miniature MIRV," Grim replied, referring to a multiple independently targetable reentry vehicle. "It uses range and bearing tremble sensors to target multiple tanks. When they're in range, the mine pops up and launches up to six kinetic-energy armor-piercing penetrators—tungsten carbide combined with depleted uranium—moving at about eight thousand feet per second."

"About five thousand miles an hour," Fisher added. "Even with a thirty percent miss rate, one of those things could take out a tank platoon."

"In the space of about ten seconds," Grim added.

"**OKAY,** it's a safe bet Aariz Qaderi and the CMR are invited to the auction. Do we know where Qaderi is now?"

"As of two days ago, still in Grozny. I'm retasking a satellite right now for a pass over his house. We'll know something in about four hours. In the meantime, we've got a problem we have to solve first."

"Which is?"

"Our tracking method just got flushed down the toilet—or at least partially."

Four months earlier, having decided the arsenal auction was genuine, Fisher and Grimsdóttir began searching for a method, not only to tag and track the weapons once they left the auction site, but to find the auction site itself. Standard GPS-oriented tracking methods were a nonstarter. With hundreds of millions of dollars at stake, Ernsdorff and his employer would make sure the attendees and the weapons were clean when they arrived at the auction site. No matter how small and how well disguised, GPS trackers emit electromagnetic waves. It was the unavoidable nature of the beast. If Fisher was going to have any chance of making sure the weapons didn't disappear into the black hole of the terrorist underworld, he needed an unorthodox tracking method.

As it turned out, such technology existed, but it did not belong to the United States or any of her allies but was instead the brainchild of private Italian researcher named Dr. Terzo Lucchesi, one of perhaps six scientists who had pushed the field of nanotechnology to its farthest reaches. What Lucchesi was doing in his Sardinia-based laboratory was the stuff of science fiction.

In an ironic twist, Grimsdóttir and Fisher attempted to start their own doppelgänger factory, writ small, by hacking into Lucchesi's mainframe and stealing what they needed: an atomic-scale tracking beacon that Fisher could deploy at a distance and Grimsdóttir could monitor remotely. The most promising approach came from one of Lucchesi's projects, code named Ajax, which involved molecular, photonic-crystal-based robots designed for microscopic electronic repair. Of course, as did most nanotechnologies, Ajax had a plethora of collateral applications, including the signal-hijacking of silicon microchips.

Once Grimsdóttir had extracted the details of Ajax from Lucchesi's mainframe, she turned the project over to her own private laboratory, deeply firewalled within Third Echelon, which set out to transform Lucchesi's robots into microscopic, and therefore untraceable, beacons designed to infiltrate cell phones, laptop and desktop computers, modems, broadband routers—anything that used microchip technology to transmit digital data—and send a prearranged burst transmission using the host device's own internal circuitry. Alone, each Ajax robot was ten nanometers, or one hundred thousand times smaller than the head of a pin; the number of bots required to hijack the average silicon microchip was 125—in all, smaller than a virus.

"So what's the problem? Your lab geeks leave the door open?" Fisher asked.

Grimsdóttir laughed. "Not quite that simple. We're missing a line of code. We've got the bots working like a charm—we can program them to magnetically gravitate to anything with whatever EM signal we choose; they infiltrate, congregate, and diffuse where they're supposed to, but they don't transmit."

You think Lucchesi left it out?"

"Yes. We don't know why. Maybe he didn't have it finished when we hacked in, or he held it back for security reasons."

"How long is this line of code?"

"Four thousand or so characters."

"Long line. You've tried to hack back into his mainframe?"

Grim nodded. "It's not there."

"At four thousand characters it's not something he memorized," Fisher observed. "Which means he's got it stored somewhere else—somewhere not linked to his mainframe."

"Agreed."

"So I'm going to Sardinia."

"Already got your flight booked."

24

AN afternoon Iberia flight took him from Madrid to Milan's Malpensa Airport for a charter connection to Olbia on Sardinia's northeastern coast, where he drove inland on the E840 until he reached the small town of Oschiri. Whether it was coincidence or sentimentality, Fisher didn't know, but according to Grimsdóttir's biographical brief on Terzo Lucchesi the doctor had been born in Oschiri. He'd built his cutting-edge laboratory two miles from Oschiri, on the arid hills overlooking the Coghinas Reservoir, a location that had as much to do with water access as nostalgia, Fisher guessed. Nanotechnology fabrication produced copious amounts of heat; without fresh cooling water . . . Fisher hadn't done enough research to know what happens to superheated nanotech, but he doubted it was pleasant.

Fisher drove into Oschiri, found a restaurant from whose terrace he could see the Lucchesi laboratory, and ordered lunch. While waiting, Fisher, again playing the lookie-look tourist, snapped photos of the countryside around the facility. As laboratories went, the building was architecturally impressive but petite: a white cube measuring two hundred feet to a side and sixty feet tall, with mirrored slit windows on each floor at five-foot intervals. *Six stories aboveground,* Fisher estimated, *and an unknown number underground.* At least one, judging from the massive cloverleaf of water conduits that climbed the side of the reservoir before disappearing into the angled hillside beneath the laboratory. That much piping translated into a lot of water, and a lot of water required machinery. As for exterior entrances, Fisher counted two, both on the east side of the building: one pedestrian door and one garage door complete with sloped loading ramp.

During his approach to Oschiri, Fisher had seen signs of neither a police nor a military presence, which told him Lucchesi had pulled off a minor miracle beyond those he creates in the lab: He had managed to keep the Italian military and intelligence communities at bay. As it seemed unlikely neither entity was unaware of Lucchesi's work, Fisher guessed this meant he was placating them with marvels peripheral to his nanotech work or that he had promised them something juicy in the future.

Or Fisher was simply wrong, and Lucchesi had a

company of 9th Parachute Assault Regiment troopers inside the cube.

AFTER lunch Fisher followed the SS392 northwest out of Oschiri and to the reservoir. The winding road took him within three-quarters of a mile of the laboratory before curving north along the shore, over a bridge, then east, following the contour of the reservoir before curving once again, this time north into the mountains. He stopped the car, turned around, and retraced his course to Oschiri.

He'd confirmed his suspicion: There were no boats to be rented on Coghinas Reservoir. If he wanted to exploit the laboratory's natural weaknesses, he'd have to do it the hard way.

AN hour later, back in Olbia, Fisher drove to the airport, found the FedEx pickup desk, and collected the box Grim had sent him. In a hurry, Fisher had decided against visiting another cache, which was in San Marino, on the opposite site of Italy's boot. He drove to his hotel, unpacked the box, and powered up his OPSAT. As promised, Grim had left him an update:

1. Team returning to U.S. pending your results.

Fisher was under no illusion: With Kovac still breathing down her neck about whether he, Fisher, was verifiably dead, Grimsdóttir might soon reach a place where she had to either actively continue the ruse or manufacture evidence that Fisher was still alive. Perpetrating the lie would give Kovac cause to fire her; coming up with new evidence would send Hansen and his team back in the field. Fisher would have to consider his options.

2. Started covert investigation: Ames's finances, history, communications, etc.

Ames had lied about the source of the information that had sent the team to Vianden, and Ames had probably ordered van der Putten killed to cover it up. Why? If not Third Echelon, who was Ames's master? Where had he truly gotten his information? For these two questions, the finger seemed to point to Kovac, but they had no proof. Lambert had believed the corruption ran deep and high within the U.S. intelligence community. Could Kovac be among the bad eggs, or was he simply a bitter bureaucrat with an ax to grind with Grimsdóttir?

3. Details thin re Lucchesi facility: none available. "Mystery Question" still remains.

At this message, Fisher smiled. Terzo Lucchesi was perhaps the best-known *unknown* in Italy, a Howard Hughes–like figure whose secretive research and lifestyle had kept the collective tongues of the tabloids wagging for a decade. Not even Third Echelon's reach had shed any light on Lucchesi. What Fisher and Grimsdóttir had dubbed the Mystery Question was this: How exactly did Lucchesi fund his research?

4. Signs at Aariz Qaderi home of pending departure. Attempting to electronically penetrate
   target computers for further information.

5. Detailed inventory of 738 Arsenal theft.

Fisher scanned the list and immediately realized Zahm hadn't been exaggerating: In both quality and quantity, the weapons in the 738 Arsenal were staggering and apparently perfect, if not improved, versions of the original systems:

French high-impulse thermobaric mortar and grenade rounds

South African Milkor MGL (multiple-grenade-launcher) systems

Heckler & Koch HK416 assault rifles

Swiss TDI Vector close-quarter-combat machine pistols

American Intelligent Munitions System (IMS) land mines

British AS50 .50 sniper/antimatériel rifles

American Mk44 Bushmaster II 30mm chain guns

American XM307 Advanced Crew Served Weapons (ACSW)

Swedish ADWS (acoustic direction weapons system)

British Starstreak High Velocity antiaircraft missiles

Fisher continued reading until he reached the bottom of the list, then read it a second time, counting as he went. Sixty-two different systems or weapons and hundreds of thousands of rounds of ammunition—all with three things in common: They were cutting-edge, they were portable, and whichever terrorist group got its hands on the 738 Arsenal could wreak havoc on any armed force in the world.

ITEM number four was Fisher's most immediate concern. Aariz Qaderi was their only known auction attendee. If he left before Fisher could nanotag him, they'd have no hope of tracking him to the meeting and the 738 Arsenal would be lost. Fisher considered his options and realized he had none: On his own, with standard technology, he would lose Qaderi.

He needed the final line of code for Lucchesi's nanobots.

25

HAVING traveled so far, so quickly, through so many time zones, Fisher's internal clock was scrambled. Though he knew better, it seemed there hadn't been a day in the past two weeks that he hadn't been waiting for nightfall to either leave his hotel or hostel and go on the run or don his tac-suit and go about his business.

Tonight was no different. He caught a few hours of sleep before ordering room service, then walked out to his umpteenth rental car. He dropped a new backpack, containing his new equipment loadout, into the trunk, then left Olbia and headed south, arriving in Lucchesi's hometown forty-five minutes later. As before, he followed the SS392 northeast, but where the road turned north toward the bridge, Fisher took a dirt tract heading south. Following prompts from his Garmin, after three miles he slowed down and doused his headlights. Ahead, to the right, an acre-sized clump of trees appeared against the night sky. Fisher let his car coast to a stop before the gravel driveway. Predictably, the farmhouse looked different from ground level than it did from Google Earth, but the overgrown weeds, dilapidated barn, and empty animal pens had been clear enough, and now, looking at the sign on the chain spanning the driveway, he knew there was no mistake. The farmhouse had been foreclosed upon six months earlier and had been vacant ever since.

Fisher got out and walked to the chain and found it was padlocked to an oak tree on either side of the drive. It had been done sloppily, however, with both loops set too high and the chain drooping to low. After a brief search, Fisher found a pair of fallen branches with the right configuration and used them to lift the chain off the ground. He drove through, stopped, and got out and kicked the branches away, then pulled behind the barn and shut off the ignition.

He checked the Garmin once more. *Good*. A short walk followed by a not-so-short swim, and then the real challenge would begin.

BEHIND the boarded-up farmhouse Fisher found a dry creek bed that meandered down through the hills toward the reservoir. In the wan glow of his night-vision goggles the landscape looked alien, the slopes around him barren, save for the occasional tree rising in silhouette against the sky. After thirty minutes of walking, he heard the lapping of water ahead, and soon the creek bed fanned out into a V-shaped alluvial plain. Directly ahead lay the mouth of a finger inlet.

Fisher stopped and checked his OPSAT. Lucchesi's laboratory, shown on the map screen as a pulsing red square, lay a quarter mile to his south over a series of dunes. His route, however, would be indirect.

He walked down to the water's edge and took a moment to check his belt and harness, his SC holster and SC-20 sling, and his gear pouches, then waded out until the water reached his chest. He kicked off the bottom and set out in a steady sidestroke.

He'd estimated the mouth of the inlet at eight hundred yards. So ten minutes after setting out, the sand-and-rock walls of the inlet disappeared and he found himself in the reservoir proper. On his hip, he felt the OPSAT give three short vibrations, signaling the first waypoint.

He stopped swimming, lifted his digital compass to his face, and rotated in the water until the blue numerals read BEARING 237. He found a landmark—the lights of a house or cabin—on the headland a half mile away and started swimming toward it.

The second leg was short, not quite eight hundred feet, which he covered in three minutes. The OPSAT buzzed on his hip and he stopped for a compass check, this time rotating himself on a bearing of 121. Lucchesi's lab lay deep within this next inlet, around four S-shaped curves. As the crow flies it was a mile; in the water it would be almost twice that.

* * *

FISHER'S sidestroke ate up the distance at a slow but steady and energy-conserving 2.5 miles per hour, or 220 feet a minute. Around him the erosion-slashed hills rose steeply from the water, and as the inlet narrowed, first to a half mile, then a quarter, then a hundred yards, the cliffs seemed to grow higher, until he felt as though he were swimming among half-sunken skyscrapers. Finally, after forty-five minutes, his OPSAT buzzed again, this time two quick signals followed by two long ones. He stopped swimming and let himself float, still, for a moment as he caught his breath.

He lifted the compass to his face to double-check his mark and made a slight adjustment until the numerals read BEARING 087. He unslung the SC-20, brought it up to his shoulder, and peered through the scope, zooming and adjusting until he spotted, two hundred yards ahead, the upper corner of Lucchesi's cube peeking out from behind a curved cliff face. Illuminated by the moon and set against the dark sky, the corner was startlingly white. Fisher saw no lights, either outside or in. He slung his rifle and continued on.

He stopped again at a hundred yards and could now see most of the cube sitting atop its hill. Still no lights. Fisher zoomed in with the SC-20's scope, looking for indications of security—paths worn into the ground around the laboratory, protrusions on the walls or along the roofline that might indicate security cameras or sensors. . . . He saw none of these. An EM/IR scan once he got closer might reveal something, but from here the laboratory looked abandoned.

Could it be? Fisher wondered. Could Lucchesi have closed the laboratory without anyone knowing? By all accounts, the man virtually lived here, only occasionally leaving for brief, mysterious stints; similarly, his handpicked staff of eight scientists lived on-site in two-week shifts: four on, four off. Here again was a by-product of hurried mission preparation. Had he the time, he would have known by now the comings and goings of staff, visitors, and repair and maintenance personnel; he would have studied security procedures, lighting schedules, the frequency with which doors opened and closed. . . . *Spilled milk,* Fisher thought. You came to a mission with what you had, not what you *wish* you had. Adaptability, not technology, was a Splinter Cell's bread and butter. The latter could fail you, the former rarely.

Fisher kept swimming, angling toward the far cliff until he rounded the bend and the laboratory came into full view. Now, too, he could see the water-cooling system: four silver conduits, each three feet in diameter, rising forty feet from the surface before turning forty-five degrees and plunging into the earth beneath the facility. Fisher zoomed in on the water at the base of the conduits and saw a slowly swirling vortex. *First sign of life,* he thought. If work wasn't going on inside, there would be no need for cooling water. There was only one way to be sure. He donned the Trident goggles and scanned the cube, the feed-water system, and the cliff, and saw nothing. Not so much as a blip on the EM scan, and on the infrared the laboratory showed as a dark block. The building's white exterior, combined with whatever insulation the architects had chosen, had made the structure all but thermally invisible.

Goggles still on and set to night vision, Fisher started toward the conduits in a slow breaststroke, and with each passing foot his sense of déjà vu increased until finally the cause popped out of his subconscious: another mission, another place. The Burj al Arab hotel in Dubai. *Another set of water intakes,* Fisher thought. Of course, the Burj al Arab's conduits had been monstrous, driven by battleship-sized screws. Then again, he'd known what to expect there; here, he knew nothing.

Less thinking, more doing, he commanded himself.

When he was twenty feet from the conduits, he felt the first tug of current, gentle at first, then more insistent as it drew him into a counterclockwise spin. He made one revolution of the conduits, then two. On the third he reached out and touched the closest conduit and was rewarded by an immediate slowing. He reached up with his opposite arm and snagged one of the brackets that joined the conduits. His body came to a halt and he hung still for a moment, feeling the undertow on his legs. Through the corrugated walls came the rhythmic thrumming of the pumps. The tempo seemed muted, as though the system was operating at nominal power. He pressed his ear to the metal. The rising water sounded hollow and spasmodic.

He extended his right leg, straining, until his toes found the lip of the conduit's mouth. There was no protective grating in place. Bad for unwary fish but good for him. From here on it was pure guesswork. If the pumps were strong enough to lift him, he would end up pulped on a propeller or pinned against a filter grate until the power was either decreased, which would drop him back down the conduit, or increased, which would drown him.

Fisher took a deep breath, released the bracket, and knifed beneath the surface. He immediately curled himself into a ball, waited until he felt himself slip into the mouth of the conduit, then straightened and spread his arms above his head. His right hand touched something hard, a protrusion—a ladder rung. *Maintenance ladder.* He latched onto it, twisted his torso, and slapped his left hand onto the rung. Water rushed past his body in fits and starts; over the whoosh he could hear the pumps straining to clear the obstruction. He chinned himself up, found the next rung, and climbed until his feet found purchase. He pressed himself against the wall. The pump smoothed out and returned to normal.

He started climbing.

IN the cascade both his night vision and headlamp were useless, so he relied on his sense of touch, taking the rungs carefully and slowly until he felt the conduit turn inward on its forty-five-degree angle. Now on a near-horizontal plane, the water flowed along the bottom, occupying half the conduit's volume. Fisher crawled forward, arms braced against the rungs as the river rushed past his legs.

He reached a left-hand juncture. He followed it, and after another four or five feet came to a manhole-sized butterfly valve. He pressed his hand to the valve and felt nothing. He pressed his ear against it. Nothing. He turned around, rolled onto his back, and pressed his feet against the valve, slowly increasing the pressure until it flipped open. He flipped himself around again and wriggled headfirst through the opening. Another five feet brought him to the neighboring conduit. There, no water was flowing. He flipped on his headlamp, turned right, and kept crawling. After forty or fifty feet his headlamp picked out a short, vertical ladder leading to a hatch. Knees braced against the ladder's uprights and one arm curled around a rung, he snaked the head of the flexicam through one of the hatch's airholes. The fish-eye lens revealed pipes, stanchions, a concrete floor. . . . It was the pump room. Fisher retrieved the flexicam, then gently lifted the hatch and climbed through.

26

THOUGH much of his view was obscured my machinery, piping, lighted control panels, and stanchions, it appeared that the room ran the length and breadth of the laboratory above; the banks of gray metal storage cabinets along the walls told him it also served as a storage area. Aside from sporadic blinking lights from the control panels, the space was dark. The only sound came from the throbbing of the pumps.

With just his head jutting from the hatch, he scanned the room, pausing first on the most likely spots for sensors and cameras before checking the rest. He spotted twelve cameras—one in each corner and two spaced along each wall. All were fixed and, judging from the Tridents' EM, nonoperational.

Curiouser and curiouser, Fisher thought. Privately run or not, this facility dealt with arguably the most sophisticated technology of the twenty-first century, and yet he'd seen not a single active security measure. If Lucchesi was calling the shots, why would he decline to protect his life's work? The special operator's part of Fisher's brain whispered *trap*, but he discounted it. An ambush, to what end? And why wait until he'd penetrated the facility?

Fisher climbed out of the hatch, closed it behind him, and moved among the pipes and stanchions until he reached a steel door set into the wall. A quick check with the flexicam revealed an alcove and a set of stairs leading upward. He could see a wall-mounted camera on the next landing—it, too, was dead. He opened the door, crossed the alcove, and started up the steps until he reached what he assumed was the first-floor landing. Here the door was made of reinforced steel, with shielded hinges and a biometric keypad lock. Fisher was reaching for his OPSAT when he stopped and, on impulse, pressed down on the door handle. It clicked open. He eased the handle back to its original position. He checked the jamb. There wasn't enough space for the flexicam. He gave the door an EM/IR scan. Nothing. He pressed his ear to the door. Silence.

Too much good news, Fisher thought, and drew his SC pistol.

He pressed himself against the wall on the door's knob side, eased the door open an inch, and braced it with his foot. He raised the SC to chest height, aimed the muzzle at the gap. He waited. Ten seconds. Thirty. A full minute.

No ambush, no shots, no rushing of armed security personnel through the door.

The hell with it.

Fisher swung the door open, peeked around the corner, and found himself staring into a dark, cavernous space.

HE flipped on his night vision and looked around. The lab was in fact six stories tall but contained no floors, at least not in the traditional sense, but rather concentric, spiraling catwalks connected by narrow gantries. The slit windows cast stripes of pale light over the walls and catwalks and floors, leaving Fisher with the sensation that he'd stepped into a giant colander.

Hulking pieces of equipment dominated the floor, some of them tall and narrow, rising thirty and forty feet; others squat and featureless save a few control panels and LED displays. Clear acrylic tubes crisscrossed the space, entering and exiting the machinery at odd angles. Nothing looked familiar to Fisher, but he was unsurprised. The manufacture of molecule-sized devices would of course require specialized equipment and procedures.

After performing his now token NV/EM/IR scans, and once again coming up with nothing, he began moving through the space until, finally, he found a raised platform of white Lexan tiles in the northeast corner. Measuring roughly thirty feet square, the platform was surrounded on three sides by railing, while the wall side was dominated by a row of computer workstations. In the center was a rectangular chrome-and-glass conference table. Fisher was about move to ahead when his subconscious spoke up again: *Complacency.* He stopped, backed into the shadows beside one of the machines, and flipped on the night vision.

A lone figure was sitting in a chair before one of the workstations. The broad shoulders and height told Fisher it was a man. He sat hunched over, elbows resting on his knees, face cupped in his hands. SC raised and extended, Fisher crept ahead to the platform steps, then stopped.

"Don't move," Fisher whispered. "I'm pointing a gun at you."

The man obeyed, save for a slight lifting of his head so he could see who was talking.

"Who are you?" the man said in Italian.

"I was going to ask you the same thing."

"I am Terzo Lucchesi," he muttered halfheartedly.

"You don't sound sure."

"He sent you to kill me. So kill me."

"No one sent me to kill you."

Lucchesi sat up in his chair. Light from one of the slit windows reflected off wire-rimmed glasses. "You're American." Lucchesi switched to English. "Why did he send an American? Were you cheaper?"

"Raise your hands above your head," Fisher ordered. None of this felt right.

With a fatalistic shrug, Lucchesi raised his hands. "Are you a good shot? Please tell me you're a good shot."

"For the last time, I didn't come here to kill you. Ask me about it one more time and I'll start rethinking my plan."

"I don't understand, then. Who are you? Why are you here?"

"Let's get some lights on," Fisher said, taking a little of the edge from his voice. "Anything goes wrong, I'll shoot you in the kneecap."

"All right," Lucchesi said hesitantly, and reached his hand toward one of the monitors.

"Wait." Fisher mounted the platform steps and side-stepped around Lucchesi until his back was facing the wall and he could see the rest of the facility. He knelt down, making himself a smaller target. He flexed his rear foot, readying himself to spin should targets present themselves. "Go ahead. Carefully."

Lucchesi tapped a series of buttons on the keyboard and, above, a series of halogen pendant lights glowed to life, illuminating the platform like a stage; then slowly more lights came on throughout the space until it was bright as daylight.

Lucchesi took in Fisher's tac-suit, Trident goggles, face half covered in his balaclava, and tilted his head to one side as though he'd just seen a dodo bird. "My, you must have been expensive."

Fisher sighed and lifted the SC, taking aim on Lucchesi's forehead. The Italian raised his hands and nodded apologetically. "Sorry, sorry . . ."

"What's going on here?" Fisher asked. "Why are you shut down? Where is everyone?"

"In order," Lucchesi replied, "absolutely *nothing* is going on, we are shut down because we are broke, and everyone has gone home."

"Explain."

"My funding has been revoked."

"The military?"

"My father."

"Say again?"

"My father decided—and I quote—'you've wasted enough time on your invisible robots and bugs.' That was just his excuse, though."

"Who's your father?"

"You have heard of Graziani Motors, yes?"

Fisher nodded. Since the early 1950s Graziani Motors had specialized in custom-made sports cars. Special-order Graziani coupes began at eight hundred thousand dollars. At the age of seventeen Calvino Graziani started the company in his garage in what was then the village of Sassari; now seventy-four, Graziani remained at the company's helm. Conservative estimates put his net worth at 14.2 billion.

Before Fisher could ask the next obvious question, Lucchesi said, "When my parents divorced, I was a teenager. I took my mother's maiden name in protest."

Fisher was running on instinct now, having decided against simply demanding the Ajax code from Lucchesi. Perhaps it was the vulnerability Fisher saw in the man, or genuine sympathy, or both, but his gut told him there might be a better way of skinning this cat.

"You said something about your father's excuse. . . ."

Lucchesi gave another shrug. "It doesn't matter."

"Tell me anyway."

He studied Fisher for a moment. "I think you

Americans call this the 'bartender effect.' You know, you tell your secrets to a complete stranger who happens to be serving you drinks. Or holding a gun on you."

Fisher lowered the SC to a forty-five degree angle but kept it pointed in Lucchesi's general direction.

"I should have expected that my father wasn't helping me out of the goodness of his heart," Lucchesi said. "He has none of that. He gave me just enough money to build this place, hire the best people, and make some progress before springing his trap. I was to start making nanotech-based weapons for his new start-up company. Father wanted to become an arms dealer, you see. Evidently, fourteen billion dollars isn't enough."

"So you refused."

Lucchesi shrugged. "We argued. I tried to stall, I tried to compromise, and then a couple of days ago he pulled the plug, as you say. I came back from Milan and found this." He swept his hand across the expanse of the laboratory. "Everything shut down. My staff gone. Every scrap of data removed from the mainframe. They pulled every hard drive, took every CD and USB flash drive."

"Why didn't you just go along—give him something so you could keep working on your own projects?" Fisher thought he knew the answer to this question, but he wanted Lucchesi to verbalize it so the man's moral compass snapped back into focus.

"I got into the nanotech field to help people. To help the world. I inherited that weakness from my mother—if you listen to my father, that is. A soft bleeding heart with his head in the clouds."

There it is, Fisher thought. "What if I told you I might be able to help?"

"You? Hah! I'm a dreamer, not an idiot. Anyone who dresses like that and carries the weapons you carry is more like my father than me."

"You should know better than to make broad assumptions, Doctor. Sometimes you have to do a little bad to do a lot of good. Hear me out."

Lucchesi wagged his head from side to side, thinking, then said, "Why not?"

LEAVING out names and places and the specifics of 738 Arsenal, Fisher outlined his goal: help stop a massive arms deal from taking place and round up some of the world's most dangerous terrorists. "It's probably not quite what you had in mind," Fisher said, "but as you're fond of Americanisms, what you've got here is lemons."

Lucchesi smiled. "So I should make lemonade."

Fisher nodded.

"How do I know you're not lying to me?"

Fisher made a snap decision. He holstered his SC, took off his Trident goggles, and removed his balaclava. He looked Lucchesi in the eye. "I'm not lying."

Lucchesi held his gaze for a long ten seconds. "No, you're not, are you?"

"The kind of people you're worried about would've stopped talking a long time ago."

"I will trust your word on that. So these weapons . . . They are bad?"

"Very. And the people who want them are worse."

Lucchesi considered this for a few moments, then stood up, ran his hands through his disheveled hair, and said, "What do you need?"

"AJAX?" Lucchesi said after Fisher explained what he needed. "I abandoned that months ago."

"We didn't."

"Too many bugs. We couldn't get it to work with enough chipset brands."

"Define 'work.'"

"There were too many variables in the maintenance protocols. The bots would find their way to the correct location, then get stuck in a feedback loop. Even the simplest maintenance tasks crashed them."

"What if they only had one task?"

"Wait a moment. . . . You said, 'We didn't.' What does that mean?"

"We built our own version of Ajax. But we ran into a problem."

Lucchesi smiled. "Ah, the fail-safe code. That's what you came here for. They refuse any execute commands you give them?"

"Right."

"What is this one task you want them to do?"

"Use whatever internal communication hardware and software they come across to send out a burst transmission."

"Like GPS coordinates, perhaps?" Lucchesi was smiling more often now, warming to his new task. At Fisher's nod, he rubbed his hands together. "Interesting . . . So you essentially want them to phone home. What kinds of hardware?"

"Laptops, desktops, cell phones, PDAs, GPS devices—anything that communicates electronically."

"Which is everything nowadays, yes? Oh, this is wonderful!" Lucchesi shook his finger at Fisher. "You see, this is the problem with scientists. We tend to overthink problems. Often, instead of reducing, we add. . . . You have schematics for me? Code?"

"I can get it. But that doesn't solve our problem—the line of code we need was confiscated along with everything else."

"Hah! One line of code—what was it, six or seven thousand characters long?"

"Four."

"Four!" Lucchesi waved his hand dismissively. "I can write that in a few hours. Come on, come on. Get me the data. I want to play!"

IT took several exchanges on the OPSAT before Grimsdóttir accepted the unusual course Fisher had chosen and acquiesced. When the schematics and code finally appeared in the OPSAT's download folder, attached was a note from Grim:

You're mellowing in your old age.

While Fisher had been communicating with Grim, Lucchesi had trotted off to a nearby file cabinet, retrieved a fifteen-inch MacBook Pro, and returned to the platform's central conference table.

Fisher asked, "I thought you said—"

"They found it. There's not a file left on it, but we don't need those, do we? What media does that gadget accept?" Lucchesi asked.

"You name it."

Lucchesi fished into his pants pocket, pulled out a 16 GB microSD card, and tossed it to Fisher, who inserted it into the OPSAT's multiport and began the download process. Fisher sat down at the conference table.

"So you took quite a risk, yes?" Lucchesi asked.

"How so?"

"I assume men in your business aren't encouraged to *ask* for anything. Plus, you've shown yourself to me. I could identify you—I won't, of course, but I could."

Fisher found himself liking Lucchesi. The man was a pure scientist, a man without guise or ulterior motive. Fisher rarely met such people in his line of work. Outside his own environment Lucchesi was probably socially maladroit. In his element he was perceptive and amiable.

"I know you won't," Fisher replied, keeping any inflection from his voice.

"So these weapons and these men . . . What happens once you've tracked them?"

"Bad things."

"Ah, the good kind of bad things."

"Right."

The OPSAT beeped. Fisher removed the microSD card and handed it to Lucchesi, who plugged it into an adaptor, and then into the MacBook's USB port.

For ten minutes Lucchesi stared at the screen, scrolling, pausing, typing random notes, until finally he looked up. "Very elegant. Your people did this?"

"More or less."

"I'm impressed. And they got the bots to work—all but the execute command?"

"Yes."

"I'll need one more thing. That person you were talking to on the other end of your device . . . They have access to databases? The Internet?"

Fisher smiled. "You have no idea."

ON its face, Lucchesi's request was daunting: He needed the specifications of every piece of hardware that matched their parameters and had been manufactured in the last decade. When Fisher put the question to Grimsdóttir, she simply typed back:

What format?

Fisher put the question to Lucchesi.

"XML spreadsheet should do nicely."

An hour later the OPSAT chimed again. Fisher read the screen, then looked up at Lucchesi. "Done."

"You're joking with me."

"No. Give me the card."

Grimsdóttir's data took up two gigabytes of space on the microSD card. Lucchesi spent a few minutes scanning the spreadsheet, then shook his head in wonder. "Amazing. You have a powerful friend there. Okay, I'll get started. There's a break room off the second-tier catwalk. Would you mind terribly much making coffee?"

"Twist my arm," Fisher said, then got up.

LUCCHESI was as good as his word. Three hours after he started, he gave the keyboard a final, definitive tap, then pushed away from the conference table with a heavy sigh. "Done. Can your people run the simulation?"

While Lucchesi went to the bathroom, Fisher plugged the microSD card into the OPSAT and uploaded the code to Grimsdóttir. She replied:

Team already called in; standby. Ninety minutes to run sim.

Fisher and Lucchesi passed the time talking. It was, Fisher decided, one of the most surreal missions he'd conducted: He infiltrates a high-tech nanotechnology laboratory, finds it abandoned except for the chief scientist, who is sitting alone in the dark, dejected after being financially cut off by Daddy, and now they are sitting together, like old friends, over coffee.

The OPSAT chimed again. Fisher read the screen, smiled, then turned it so Lucchesi could see the message:

Sims complete. Green across the boards.

Lucchesi clapped his hands once, stood up, did a victory lap around the conference table, then shook Fisher's hand and sat down again. He leaned across the table, his eyes wide. "So what now?"

"I go do my job and you . . . You're broke?"

"Broke?" Lucchesi chuckled. "No, no. I sold a few patents here and there—Apple, HP, Kodak . . . Miniaturization processes. Very rudimentary, but profitable."

"Enough to restart—"

"No, not enough for that. But enough that I can take some time and gather my thoughts. Can you at least let me know whether Ajax worked as designed?"

"That I can do."

"I have a villa in Tuscany. I can give you the address." Lucchesi stopped and smiled. "I don't suppose you people need addresses, do you?"

Fisher smiled back. "We'll find you."

27

"YOU took a hell of a chance," Grimsdóttir said on the LCD screen.

"I disagree," Fisher replied. "In essence, it was agent recruitment. Lucchesi had vulnerability and I recognized it. And he struck me as a decent guy in a bad situation. Grim, that's what case officers do."

"But he saw your face. He knows—"

"You're going to have to trust me on this. It isn't a problem."

Soon after leaving the laboratory—through the front door, with a departing wave from Lucchesi—Fisher had walked the half mile cross-country to the farmhouse, gotten in his car, and driven back to his hotel in Olbia.

En route, a message from Grimsdóttir appeared on the OPSAT:

Athens. 754 Afroditis, apartment 14.

Fisher boarded the first available flight the next morning and arrived at the safe house in the early afternoon.

Grimsdóttir shrugged. "I trust you. With age comes wisdom, I suppose."

Fisher smiled. "Go to hell. What's the latest with Aariz Qaderi?"

"Still in Grozny, but he's moving somewhere. His entourage is there, extra bodyguards. . . . It fits his pattern."

"As soon as you can get me the updated bots—"

"They're already headed your way."

"How?"

Grimsdóttir chuckled. "FedEx, if you can believe it."

The shipment method did in fact seem incommensurate with the nature of the package, but aside from sending a Third Echelon courier with the proverbial handcuff-equipped briefcase, Grimsdóttir's choice made the most sense.

"Be there tomorrow morning," Grimsdóttir added.

"Where are you with Kovac?"

"He's pushing. The German rescue workers found your car in the Rhine, but, of course, no body. Evidently most floaters in that area of the river eventually surface in the same general area. The fact that your corpse hasn't yet has got them scratching their heads."

"How much time can you buy me?"

"Two, maybe three days."

Fisher considered this. "I'll find a way to get Hansen and his team back in the field. If I do it right, it'll keep Kovac off your back and solve another problem for us."

"Such as?"

"I'll let you know when it works. *If* it works."

CUTTING the timing very close, Grimsdóttir's package arrived an hour before Fisher was to depart for the airport. He had just enough time to inspect the contents. Grimsdóttir's techs had installed the bots into six reengineered gas-grenade cartridges—two equipped with aerogel parachutes and a CO_2 dispersal system, and two with the standard impact actuators—and eight SC pistol darts. In stacked pairs, the larger bots fit neatly into three miniature, partially functional cans of shaving cream, the darts into a large-barrel ballpoint pen. Satisfied, he stuffed one can of the shaving cream into his carry-on bag and two into his checked bag. The pen went into his jacket pocket. He ran down to the waiting cab.

Thirty minutes later, as the driver pulled up to the departure level's curb, Fisher's iPhone chimed. He checked the screen. A text message from Grimsdóttir:

Grozny airport mortared this a.m. Closed to all traffic.

Our friend headed Tbilisi via ground transport.
ETA three hours. Attempting to locate destination. Will advise.

"Damn," Fisher muttered.

"Eh?" asked the driver.

Fisher glanced at the meter, gave the driver the fare
plus a tip, then told him, "Circle around."

As they pulled out, Fisher used the iPhone's browser
to check the Lufthansa website. He punched his search—
flights from Athens to Tbilisi—and got more bad news:
The shortest flight was nearly eight hours and didn't
depart for five hours. Aariz Qaderi would likely be long
gone before Fisher even reached Tbilisi.

After three more circuits of the airport, and three more
tips, Fisher got another text message from Grim:

Friend had to book Tbilisi departure with known
account.
Leaving Tbilisi at 1325 hours on Turkish Airlines flight 1381 for Bucharest, Romania. Arriving Henri Coandă International Airport 1815
local.
Stand by.

Two minutes later:

Olympic Airlines flight 386 leaving Athens 1610,
arriving Bucharest 1720.

With luck, he'd touch down fifty-five minutes before Qaderi. He texted back:

At airport. Heading Bucharest. Keep advised.

"Attagirl, Grim," Fisher murmured.

"Eh?" said the driver. "Again?"

"No, pull over."

INSIDE the terminal he walked straight to the Olympic desk and booked the second-to-last seat on flight 386, then checked his bag, went through security, and found his gate. He sat down in a quiet corner, set his alarm for 3:20, then pulled his cap over his eyes and went to sleep.

AT three his iPhone trilled; the screen read UNKNOWN. He answered. Grimsdóttir said, "It's me."

"Where are you?"

"Don't laugh, but I'm at a pay phone."

Fisher didn't laugh, but the image was amusing: Anna Grimsdóttir of the NSA and Third Echelon reduced to using a pay phone to make a secure call.

"Did you dry-clean yourself?" Fisher asked, only half seriously.

"Yes."

"Tell me about the bots."

"The six grenades will have the same range as a regular

gas grenade and same hang time as an ASE. They'll either disperse on impact or thirty seconds after the aerogel chute deploys. The darts are disperse-on-impact, too. They all rely on kinetic energy, so you have to hit a hard surface."

"Range?"

"Variable. Remember, the Ajax bots gravitate to strong EM sources, so you're aiming for hardware, not people. For the grenades, dispersal range is twelve to fifteen feet; for the darts, about half that. They need to be airborne for full effectiveness. Depending on the surface, when the bots hit the ground, friction will negate their EM homing: rough surfaces completely; smooth surfaces . . . it's hard to say."

"I'm going to need equipment. What do we have in Romania?"

"A cache in Piteşti and one in Sibiu."

"Both too far for me to go there and get back before Qaderi lands."

"In that at least we caught a break," Grimsdóttir replied. "I happen to have Vesa Hytönen in Budapest doing an errand for me. He should be boarding a flight to Craiova in about ten minutes. If he hauls ass, he can get to the cache and reach Bucharest about the same time you're touching down. I'm texting you his toss-away-cell number."

"Been thinking about Qaderi. This can't be his destination."

"I agree. If he's on his way to the auction, Bucharest is going to be a waypoint. Whoever's running the get-together would make sure the guests are clean coming in."

"And if he never leaves the airport?" The chances of Fisher getting even the SC pistol through security were nil. He might have more luck with a dart, but without the kinetic energy supplied by the SC, would the bots disperse?

"That's the other piece of good news. When he had to reroute from Grozny to Tbilisi, Qaderi used a different credit card to book the ticket—an account number we hacked about four months ago. He's booked a rental car at the Bucharest airport—Europcar. We can't count on our luck beyond that, though. He'll change cards."

"Then I'd better not lose him," Fisher replied.

FISHER'S plane was ten minutes late taking off, but it caught a tailwind and made up five minutes in the air. He landed at 5:25. As soon as he was clear of the jetway he dialed Vesa Hytönen's phone. It rang eight times but no one answered. Fisher waited five minutes, then tried again. This time Vesa picked up on the third ring.

"Is that you?" he asked Fisher.

"It's me." It occurred to Fisher that, in all their meetings, Vesa had never once used Fisher's name, neither his first nor his alias surname. Another of Vesa's idiosyncrasies. "Where are you?" Fisher asked.

"On the E70 heading south. I'll arrive at the airport in roughly fifty minutes."

"Hold on." Fisher found an arrivals/departures board. Turkish Airlines flight 1381 was on time. Fisher checked his watch. Vesa would arrive ten minutes after Qaderi touched down. Fisher did the mental math: three to five minutes to deplane; five minutes to reach the Europcar desk. . . . It was unlikely Qaderi had checked baggage. Fisher asked Vesa, "Do you know where the Europcar exit is?"

"No, but I'm confident I can find it."

"Do that. Call me when you're here."

FISHER spent the next forty minutes familiarizing himself with the airport, making sure he knew, backward and forward, the routes Qaderi could take from the gate to the Europcar desk. He was stopped twice by airport security, which checked his passport and boarding pass. He explained that his friend was late picking him up. At 6:20 Fisher found an arrivals board and checked flight 1381; its status read "at gate." He strolled over to the ground-transportation area and waited.

Ten minutes later Qaderi appeared, coming down an escalator with a bodyguard in the lead and one in tow. All three were dressed in conservative blue suits: executives traveling on business. The bodyguards were good, scanning ahead, to the sides, and behind with an economy of motion that told Fisher they were muscle with brains. This was good in one respect alone: They would react in predictably professional ways.

As the group moved toward the Europcar desk, Fisher's phone trilled and he answered. "Go ahead, Vesa."

"I'm here. The attendants are urging me to move on, however."

Fisher checked his watch. "Drive once around, then park and lift your hood. "Tell them you're having car trouble."

"Okay."

Fisher disconnected.

Qaderi himself took care of the paperwork at the rental desk. Fisher waited until the clerk handed Qaderi the ubiquitous trifold envelope, then turned and headed for the exit marked with the Europcar logo. He crossed to the lot, nodded at the attendant, and walked down the rows of cars to the exit. Ahead he could see Vesa standing beside a powder blue compact Opel, talking to another attendant.

"Vesa!" Fisher called. "There you are! Is she giving you trouble again?"

Vesa turned, and he stared at Fisher for moment before answering. "She? Oh, yes, the car. Something's wrong with the . . . the, uh . . ."

"The starter? Again?"

"Yes."

As he reached the car, he gave the lot attendant a friendly clap on the shoulder. "We'll be out of here in two minutes." He had no idea if the attendant spoke English, but as he opened his mouth to protest, Fisher smiled broadly and made a shooing motion. "Don't worry about us. We'll take care of it. Thanks."

He turned his back on the man, said, "Get in," to Vesa, then ducked under the hood. The attendant loitered a moment, then shrugged and walked away. Fisher leaned out and looked past him, back down the row of cars, where Qaderi and his companions were being led to a Mercedes-Benz S-Class. Eyes fixed on Qaderi, Fisher kept tinkering with the engine, wiggling hoses and tapping on parts, until he saw the Mercedes' reverse lights come on.

"Try it now," Fisher called.

Vesa turned the ignition, and the engine puttered to life. Fisher slammed the hood, gave the attendant—who had turned back around—a wave, then climbed in the passenger seat and told Vesa, "Go."

28

"**NOT** too fast," Fisher ordered, then adjusted the rearview mirror so he could see Qaderi's car. "Let them pass you."

"Okay," Vesa said nervously.

"You're doing fine," Fisher said.

"Your case is in the back."

Fisher glanced over his shoulder and saw the familiar Pelican case lying across the seat. He said, "First chance we get, I'll let you out and you can hail a cab."

"I can help. I can drive. I am a good driver."

Fisher shrugged. "If that's what you want." Fisher clicked on the dome light, leaned back between the bucket seats, and punched the correct code into the case's pad. He was rewarded with six green lights, a beep, and three mechanical clicks. He reached in and groped around until his hand found the butt of the SC pistol. He pulled it out and closed the case, then loaded the Ajax darts.

Qaderi's Mercedes passed them and got on the E70 and headed north toward Piteşti, where it joined the E81 and continued north into the foothills of the southern Carpathian Mountains. As night fell, and the Mercedes passed Râmnicu Vâlcea, the highway joined with the Olt River as it wound its way deeper into the mountains, through the villages of Călimăneşti, Brezoi, Balota. . . .

"I think he's heading to Sibiu," Vesa said.

"Why do you say that?"

"It's the next biggest city. The man we're following doesn't strike me as someone who enjoys drives in the country. He's a man of purpose."

"You have a good eye."

"It's just logic."

"How far is it from Bucharest to Sibiu?"

"Two hundred thirty kilometers."

About 170 miles, Fisher thought. The Mercedes' range was far greater than that, so there was little hope for a refueling stop.

At Căinarii Mari, the Mercedes' taillights flashed once, twice; then Fisher saw the car's headlights swerving right, taking a fast turn over a bridge.

"Don't slow down," Fisher said. "Keep going."

"They're going to lose—"

"They're checking for tails. Trust me."

As the Opel pulled even with the bridge, Fisher darted his eyes sideways and caught a glimpse of the Mercedes, its lights now off, doing a U-turn on the bridge.

"Were they there?"

"Yes."

"Do you think they spotted us?"

"I don't know. We'll know shortly."

Three minutes passed; then the Mercedes' headlights reappeared in the rearview mirror. Fisher watched closely, trying to gauge its speed; it was gaining ground but not at an alarming rate. Over the next fives minutes the Mercedes continued closing the gap until it was a foot from the Opel's bumper.

"What's he doing?" Vesa said, hands tightening on the wheel.

"Relax. When they pass, make sure you glance at them."

"What? Why?"

"Because it's the natural thing to do when a car rides your tail like a maniac, then passes. Glance at them, gesture, get mad."

Fisher pulled his cap down over his eyes and nose and laid his head back on the rest, letting it go loose as though he were napping. "Let me know when they're passing."

"What if they shoot at us?"

"Then we know they spotted us. The first shot usually misses," Fisher added. "It's harder than the movies make it look. You'll have a second or so before the second, better, shot comes."

"I am not reassured."

"You're doing great."

"He's getting ready to pass us. He's in the other lane," Vesa reported.

"How fast?"

"Not too fast."

"Did he signal?"

"Yes."

"A good sign," Fisher muttered from under his cap.

"They're coming even with us."

"Give them the okay sign?"

"The what?"

"Form your thumb and forefinger to make a circle. Do it."

Vesa complied. After a few moments he said, "They're pulling ahead."

Fisher looked out from under the brim of his cap.

"What did that mean?" Vesa asked. "The circle."

"You called him a zero. Or, worse, an asshole."

"Oh."

Predictably, Qaderi's driver mostly obeyed the speed limit, never straying more than a few kilometers per hour under or over. Vesa's Opel had no cruise control, but he did a good job of keeping the car at a steady pace.

"What are we going to do?"

"Wait. And hope we get a break."

THEY did, twenty minutes later, as they rounded a bend in the river and pulled into the town of Râul Vâlc. Again

Fisher saw the Mercedes' brake lights flash a few times, but this time the turn was done slowly and evenly. A hundred yards back, Fisher could see the Mercedes had stopped at a gas station/convenience store.

"Drive past," Fisher ordered, and Vesa complied.

When the lights of the convenience store disappeared behind them, Fisher said, "Turn right here. Stop." Fisher reached up, toggled off the dome light, and opened his door. He climbed out and pushed his seat back into its fully reclined position. To Vesa he said, "Get back on the highway and keep heading north. Stay five miles under the speed limit. When the Mercedes passes you, wait until it's out of sight, then turn around and come back for me."

"And if they don't pass me? If they take another road?"

"I'll try to let you know. If it happens, get back as fast as possible. Go on, now."

Fisher slammed the door and started walking back to the convenience store.

HE had no plan and no time to come up with one, so he kept walking, trusting his training and his experience to recognize an opportunity.

The lights of the convenience store appeared ahead. Ten feet before the sidewalk ended at the driveway, Fisher remembered his cap. He took it off and tossed it into the bushes, then turned into the parking lot. He jammed his hands into his coat pockets, hunched his shoulders, and loosened his gait, letting his right foot slap unevenly on the asphalt. The Mercedes was beside one of the pumps. One bodyguard stood pumping gas. The other stood just inside the store's front door. Qaderi was nowhere to be seen.

Fisher could feel two sets of eyes on him, but he ignored them and kept walking, head down, until he reached the door, which he pulled open weakly. He shuffled past the bodyguard and headed toward the self-serve soda pop area. He bumped into a candy bar display and turned to set it straight; in the corner of his eye he saw the guard had turned toward him. His suit coat was unbuttoned and both hands were clasped at his belt. It was a classic ready-gun-hand pose, but Fisher couldn't be sure if the man was armed or simply stood that way out of habit.

Fisher lifted a cup from the stack, stuck it beneath the ice chute, then the soda machine. Somewhere at the rear of the store came the sound of a door opening, then closing. Footsteps clicked on the linoleum. Fisher didn't look up. He took his half-filled cup and shambled to the counter, where he dumped out a handful of euro coins, mumbled something incoherent, then turned and headed for the door. Qaderi was coming down the aisle toward him. Fisher ducked his head and sipped at the straw. The bodyguard took a step toward Fisher, simultaneously blocking and slowing down his principal. To his credit, Qaderi reacted as a good client, taking the hint and pausing behind his guard, who watched until Fisher had pushed through the door and turned right down the sidewalk, past a stack of bundled firewood.

Now, Fisher thought. He stopped and plopped down on the curb, knees bent and shoulders hunched as he brought his soda straw to his lips. Directly across from him, twenty feet away, was the Mercedes. The second bodyguard stood at the hood of the car. Fisher waited for the guard to look away, then pulled the SC from his waistband and tucked the barrel between his left thigh and the sidewalk, with the butt hidden by his leg.

He heard the ding of the convenience-store door opening. Qaderi and his guard appeared in the corner of his eye.

Transitions were the most dangerous times for VIPs and, as a result, the time when bodyguards are at their most alert. While moving from a car to a building and back again was when most assassination attempts took place. Qaderi's two-man detail had a lot of open space to scan, and Fisher's presence had complicated matters. Was this disheveled idiot with the soda what he seemed or something more? If the latter, was he working alone or with someone else, a gunman who was hoping the bodyguards would fixate on Fisher and make a mistake? All of these questions and more were racing through their heads as Qaderi headed for the car. Both men were in full scan mode now—heads rotating as they checked angles and fields of fire and blind spots and the soda drinker sitting on the curb. . . .

Qaderi's guard reached the Mercedes three steps ahead of his principal and opened the rear door. The guard looked up, glanced at Fisher, then away, scanning the rest of the parking lot. Fisher flicked his eyes to the

guard standing at the hood of the car. The man was looking over his shoulder, checking the street side.

Now.

Fisher dropped his right hand down, behind the soda
cup, grasped the butt of the SC, drew it, and raised the
barrel. He fired.

The dart was moving too fast for him to track its
course, but decades of range time and combat missions,
and hundreds of thousands of rounds of expended ammunition, told him the shot had struck home: the lower seat
cushion just above the door's inner kick panel.

Fisher let the gun dangle, twisting his wrist so the SC
was again hidden by his thigh. He raised the straw to his
lips and took a slurp and waited for the guards or Qaderi
to react. They didn't. Qaderi ducked inside the Mercedes
and sat down. The guard slammed the door shut and
got into the front seat. Five seconds later the driver was
behind the wheel and the Mercedes was pulling out.

"THE bots are live and tracking," Grimsdóttir said four
hours later. With no safe house within Fisher's vicinity,
she was once again calling on a pay phone. Fisher had
found a cheap hotel on Sibiu's outskirts, and then sent
Vesa back to Bucharest. "Qaderi is in the air and headed
east. We'll know more in a few hours."

"That's good news."

"How did Vesa do?"

"You might want take a closer look at him, Grim. He's

got good instincts, and he's cooler under fire than he thinks he is."

He recounted their tailing of Qaderi's Mercedes from Bucharest to the convenience store in Râul Vâlc, Fisher's tagging of Qaderi, and Vesa's return forty minutes later.

"I'll give it some thought. What's your plan?"

"I've got an old, not-so-good friend in Odessa—Adrik Ivanov. He used to be a medic in the Russian army. He's got a gambling problem, or at least he did a couple years ago. I doubt that's changed. He'd roll his own grandmother for ten bucks and turn me in for even less. If you got a tip that I showed up on his doorstep asking for medical treatment, would Kovac buy it?"

"Yes."

"Okay. Give it a few hours, then call in Hansen and his team and brief them. Keep it sketchy for now. I'll move tomorrow morning and let you know the particulars. I need to get Hansen someplace I can handle him."

29

FISHER'S Carpatair flight landed at one thirty the next afternoon, and Fisher went through his now-familiar routine of renting a car and driving to the local DHL office to pick up his equipment box. He then drove to Ivanov's last known address, a duplex near the Tairov cemetery. A woman working in a tiny garden in front told Fisher that Ivanov spent most of his leisure hours at a pub near the Chornoye More hotel. Initially suspicious, she warmed to Fisher as he asked her questions about her garden—the soil, pests, and the best time to plant tomatoes. In short order he discovered that Ivanov had added alcoholism to his list of vices and that he worked as a night watchman at a LUKOIL warehouse annex at the city's northern industrial docks. Fisher thanked the lady and followed her directions to Ivanov's pub, where he parked outside and waited.

At four Ivanov emerged from the pub and shuffled his way to a nearby tram stop. Fisher followed the tram back to Ivanov's duplex, then called Grimsdóttir with an update.

"Hansen and his team are due into Odessa at ten tonight. He'll check in when they change planes in Frankfurt."

"Keep it vague. Tell them you're running down Ivanov's particulars. I need to get a look at the warehouse first."

"Got it. Sam, have you given any thought to the worst-case scenario?"

Fisher chuckled. "Grim, look what I've been doing for the past year and a half. You're going to have to be a little more specific."

"I mean Hansen. What if he doesn't buy it? What if he decides not to play nice—to try to take you?"

Fisher had already given this considerable thought. Except for perhaps Ames—who would, with luck, soon be irrelevant—the rest of the team would follow Hansen. Where he went, so went the team. And while finishing this mission would be much easier with their help, the equation was very simple: From Odessa on, he couldn't afford to have Hansen and his people hounding his steps.

"Are you asking me what I think you're asking me?" Fisher said.

"I guess I am."

"Grim, this arsenal can't get loose. That's my litmus test. If Hansen falls on the wrong side of it, so be it."

AT five Ivanov reappeared, wearing gray pants and a gray shirt with his name embroidered on the pocket and a white on red LUKOIL patch on each shoulder. He walked back to the tram stop and boarded. Fisher followed. Alcoholic and gambling addict or not, Ivanov knew his tram schedule. At 5:50—ten minutes before the start of his shift, Fisher assumed—the tram pulled to a stop.

The LUKOIL warehouse was set back from the road, just a hundred yards from the beach, amid a quarter-mile cluster of other warehouses, most of them displaying FOR LEASE signs in Cyrillic. Carrying a lunch pail and an olive drab canvas messenger bag, Ivanov crossed the road and disappeared down a dirt alley between two brick buildings. Fisher continued down the road, then did a U-turn and found a parking lot from which he could see the alley. Fifteen minutes passed, and then a man dressed in gray pants and a gray shirt appeared at the mouth of the alley. He waited for a break in traffic, then jogged across the road to the parking lot in which Fisher sat. Ivanov's fellow watchman climbed into a rust-streaked white ZAZ with a cracked windshield and drove away.

Fisher got out and went for a walk through the warehouse complex. Whatever purpose it now served, it had clearly once been part of a refinery hub: Like the roots of a giant tree, cracked, half-buried oil pipelines ran through the lot down and disappeared into the sand at the water's edge. After a few minutes of walking, Fisher found the LUKOIL annex—a graffiti-covered, redbrick building with neon blue doors and a recreation yard at the rear, complete with horseshoe pit, a swing set, and a jungle gym. A thick, ten-foot-tall line of privet bushes encircled the lot; here and there sumac trees jutted from the cracked concrete. The warehouse was relatively small: fifteen hundred square feet, give or take.

He walked back to his car and texted Grimsdóttir:

In place. Dispatch team to below link upon arrival. Confirm tactical comm protocols.

He included a hyperlink to a Google Earth map with a red pushpin atop the LUKOIL warehouse. She replied five minutes later:

Will alert upon touchdown. Good luck.

The team's current OPSAT frequencies and encryption codes followed, then:

Q appears heading to Moscow.

Fisher checked his watch. Four hours.

With Qaderi on the move, Fisher didn't expect to be in Odessa long enough to warrant checking into a hotel, but with four hours to kill, and running on a sleep deficit, he also knew he needed to take advantage of the downtime. After a frustrating iPhone search, he finally located a nearby parking garage. He drove there, took the ticket from the automated kiosk, and found a dark, empty corner of the garage. He switched his iPhone to vibrate, then set the alarm, tucked it under his thigh, and went to sleep.

SOME time later the iPhone buzzed against his leg, and it took him a few moments to realize it was not the alarm but an incoming text-message notification. He checked the screen. It was from Grim:

Team plane arriving early—2140 hours.

Fisher checked his watch. *Twenty minutes early,* he thought.

HE was back at the parking lot outside the LUKOIL warehouse twenty minutes later. Two police cars were sitting in the parking lot, both with the lights flashing. As Fisher drove past, he glanced out his side window and saw four cops standing over a pair of men who lay spread-eagled on their bellies. Two blocks south Fisher turned right, found an empty spot near the curb, and pulled over and doused his headlights. The minutes ticked by, and the cop cars remained in the parking lot. Finally, at 9:20, the two suspects were hauled to their feet, stuffed into the backseat of one of the cars, and driven off. Fisher waited five more minutes, then returned to the lot. He grabbed the SC pistol and his lock-pick set from the Pelican case, got out, and trotted across the street to the alley. The only lights came from the main road, and after twenty feet of walking, these were blotted out by the bushes. Another twenty yards brought him within sight of the warehouse; it, too, was dark, save for a single security light over the rear neon blue door. Fisher stopped and crouched down to watch at the corner of a neighboring building.

Behind him he heard the soft squeal of car brakes. He glanced over his shoulder to see a police car slowing to a halt. Fisher took two quick steps, crabbing around the corner and missing the car's spotlight by a half second. He pressed himself against the wall. Had he been seen? Ten seconds of silence passed. Then he heard the mechanical *chunk* of the car's transmission being engaged. Moments later tires crunched on gravel. Fisher looked around. Down the wall to his left was a stoop leading to a door. Ahead and to his left, the door to the LUKOIL warehouse. Between them, an eight-foot brick wall. Fisher sprinted to it, jumped up, caught the edge with his fingertips, and chinned himself up. He then hooked his right foot and, using his arms for leverage, did a one-leg press until he was standing upright. The ledge was narrow, no more than six inches. Arms extended for balance, he tiptoed to the roofline and hopped up, then lay flat and went still.

Preceded by its headlights, the police car appeared in the alley. It stopped. The horn honked twice, then twice more. After ten seconds the door to the LUKOIL warehouse opened and Ivanov emerged. He waved to the police car, then walked over and leaned his elbows on the driver's door and started talking to the occupants. Fisher could hear nothing of the conversation, but Ivanov's body language was relaxed. A friendly check-in by the local police. They chatted for another five minutes, then Ivanov stepped back and gave the car's roof a friendly pat as it backed down the alley out of sight. Ivanov walked back to the warehouse, opened the door with a key from a ring on his belt, and disappeared inside.

He checked his watch: 9:35. Hansen's plane would be touching down in five minutes. They would have no bags and a rental car already arranged. How far from the airport to here? Fisher cursed himself for not checking. It couldn't be more than twenty minutes, he decided, which put their arrival at roughly 10:20.

Fisher hopped back onto the wall, then to the ground, and trotted to the warehouse door. He was about to get out his pick set when he decided to try another approach. He pressed his ear to the door. He heard nothing. Using his fingernail, he scratched at the steel. Waited. Scratched again, this time more loudly.

On the other side of the door he heard a voice grumble something, a curse, then feet clicking on concrete. Fisher stepped left, against the hinge-side wall, and pulled the SC from his waistband. The door opened; Fisher lifted his palm, rested it against the steel. When he saw the crown of Ivanov's head appear, he gave the door a shove and got a satisfying grunt in return. As Ivanov stumbled backward, Fisher came around the door and gave him a light heel kick to the chest, sending him sprawling. With a thump, Ivanov landed on his butt and stared up at Fisher. Even from ten feet Fisher could smell the alcohol on Ivanov's breath.

"Hi, Adrik," Fisher said pleasantly. He raised the SC level with Ivanov's chest.

Ivanov blinked several times as though waking from a deep sleep, then muttered, "Sam?"

"Yes."

"Is that you?"

"Yes." Fisher backed up, snagged the doorknob with his left hand, and swung the door shut. He looked around. The warehouse was divided down the right side by twenty-foot-tall rack shelves filled with boxes and crates. On the left, a glassed-in office occupied the far third of the wall. Closest to Fisher, fifty-five-gallon drums labeled in both Cyrillic and English—cleaning solution, floor stripper, sweeping compound—sat stacked three high.

"Why did you kick me?" Ivanov asked.

"Just my way of saying hello."

"You're not still mad, are you, about that thing in Minsk?"

"No, not mad. It just put our relationship in a different light."

"I'm sorry about that. I am. I had these guys after me—"

"I know. You can make it up to me, though."

"Stop pointing that gun at me."

"Are you going to behave?"

"Yes, of course."

Fisher lowered the gun but didn't put it away. He extended his left hand to Ivanov and helped him up. "What do you want?" the Russian said.

"You're going to get some visitors in a little bit. I need you to do a little acting."

"What kind of visitors?"

"The kind that hurt bad actors."

"Ah, Sam, don't—"

"Just play it like I tell you and nothing will happen to you."

"Can't I do something else? I have a sister in Karkiv—"

"Shut up, Adrik, and listen. . . ." When Fisher finished explaining what he wanted, he had Ivanov repeat it several times until he was satisfied. "One last thing," Fisher said. "Friends or not, if you burn me I'll shoot you dead. Do you believe me?"

"I believe you."

30

WHILE Ivanov sat in his office and sulked, Fisher found his perch, the second tier of the central rack shelf. He climbed up and rearranged boxes and crates until he had a blind from which he could see the whole warehouse. Aside from a blind spot to the right of the office, and one around the main door, he had clear fields of fire.

He settled down to wait.

NOT *bad*, the logical part of Fisher's brain thought twenty minutes later as the warehouse door swung open silently and Ben Hansen stepped through and to the right, SC pistol extended. They'd picked the lock without a sound. Right behind Hansen appeared Gillespie, then Valentina,

Noboru, and finally Ames. On flat feet, Ames and Valentina rushed the office and swarmed Ivanov, who was on the floor with a gun to his head before he had a chance to open his mouth. Using hand signals, Hansen ordered Gillespie and the other three to search the warehouse. Once done, they gestured back, *all clear*, and Hansen called, "Clear. Okay, bring him out."

Ames frog-marched Ivanov from the office and gave him a too-rough shove, sending him, belly first, to the concrete before Hansen. Ivanov tried to raise himself to the push-up position, but Ames stepped forward and rammed his heel into Ivanov's butt, shoving him down again. Gillespie and Noboru each shot Ames an irritated glance.

"Enough, Ames," Hansen ordered. "Leave him be."

Ames offered a smarmy grin. "Just trying to soften him up a bit, boss."

Hansen ignored the sarcasm. He knelt before Ivanov and helped him to his knees. "Are you Adrik Ivanov?"

"Yes, I'm Ivanov. Who are you? What do you want?"

"We're looking for a man," Hansen said. "An old friend of yours named Sam."

"I don't know any Sam."

"Yes, you do. He's been here."

"No one's been here. I work alone. I came on at six o'clock and haven't seen anyone since—"

Hansen cut him off: "You owe some people money."

"Hey, no! I paid them two months ago."

"Maybe so, but the people we're talking about don't keep paper records. They prefer computers. Computers can be hacked, records changed. Are you understanding me?"

"No. What are you saying? Computers . . . what computers?"

"Tell us what we want to know or we're going to make it so you owe a lot of people a lot of money."

"You can't do that."

"We can. And we will. You got a visit tonight from an old friend," Hansen repeated. "Tell us what he wanted."

Fisher knew Hansen was bluffing; he *knew* nothing. Still, the authority in his voice left little room for doubt.

Ivanov shrugged and spread his arms in bewilderment.

Hansen pointed at Valentina and said, "Make the call. Let's start him out at three hundred thousand rubles. What is that, about ten thousand dollars?" He looked at his companions for confirmation.

Noboru nodded and said, "Yeah, ten thousand, more or less."

Valentina got out her cell phone and started punching numbers.

Ivanov cried, "Yes, okay, fine. He was here."

"When?" Hansen asked.

"About an hour ago."

"What did he want?"

"He was hurt. Something wrong with his ribs. He said he needed someplace to sleep. . . ." Ivanov's voice trailed off. He sighed with just the right amount of solemnity.

Attaboy, Fisher thought.

"Go on," Hansen said.

"I gave him the keys to my apartment."

Hansen spent the next five minutes firing questions at Ivanov—was Fisher armed, did he have a car, was he alone?—until seemingly satisfied that he'd wrung the Russian dry of information.

"You can forget about this visit," Hansen told him.

"Believe me, I will. What about—"

"If you cross us, I'll make the call. You'll have every Russian mobster in Odessa looking for you. Understand?"

"I understand."

Hansen nodded to the others, and they began heading toward the door. Hansen went last, taking a moment to help Ivanov to his feet. "Stay off the phone, too."

"Yes . . . yes . . ."

Hansen headed for the door.

Come on, Adrik.

"Hey, you're Hansen, aren't you?"

Hansen turned back. At the door, the others did as well.

"What?" Hansen said with some edge in his voice. "What did you say?"

"He told me to give you a message."

"What?"

Ivanov glanced toward the others. "In private."

Ames barked, "That's crap! What the hell is this? Hansen—"

"Quiet." Then to Ivanov: "Tell me."

Ivanov shook his head. "He told me, only you. Listen, I've known Sam a long time, and, to be honest, he scares me a lot more than you scare me."

Ames chuckled. "Well, dummy, in about fifteen minutes good old Sam is going to be dead or tied up in our trunk. If you got an ounce of brains, you'll—"

Hansen interrupted. "Everyone outside." Ames started to protest, but Hansen shot him a glance. Fisher couldn't see his face, but clearly it worked. Ames snapped his mouth shut and filed out with the others. The door banged shut.

"What's the message?" Hansen asked.

From the rack, Fisher fired once, sticking a dart in the side of Ivanov's neck. Even as he fell, Fisher adjusted his aim to Hansen. To his credit, Hansen exercised the better part of valor, discreetly raising his hands above his head.

Without looking around Hansen said evenly, "Hey, Fisher."

"HI, Ben," Fisher replied.

"I guess this is what you'd call a rookie mistake."

"Mistakes are mistakes. They happen. How you handle them is what counts."

"I'll keep that in mind. What are we doing? What's this about?"

"Carefully, pull out your SC and lay it on the floor."

Hansen did so and was about to slide it away with his foot when Fisher stopped him. "Too noisy, Ben. Nice try, though. Interlace your fingers and place them on your head. Take ten steps forward."

Hansen didn't move.

"I won't ask again. I'll just dart you and this will turn ugly before it's started." Hansen paced forward the ordered number of steps. "Now turn and face the office." Hansen complied. "On your knees, ankles crossed."

Once Hansen was in position, Fisher climbed down the rack ladder and came up behind Hansen, stopping ten feet away. Hansen turned his head and said over his shoulder, "You've been a pain in my ass, you know."

"Sorry about that. It was necessary."

"Is that what you want to talk about? That there are extenuating circumstances? That you didn't really kill Lambert?"

"No, I killed Lambert. He asked me to."

"Bull. You've been jerking us around for weeks—you, Grimsdóttir, and Moreau—but as far as I'm concerned, you're a run-of-the-mill murderer."

"You sound angry, Ben."

"Damn right I'm angry. You've run us ragged. Five of us, and we never even came close."

"You came close. More times than you know. You almost had me in Hammerstein."

"No, I didn't. You pushed me into a split-second, no-win scenario, and you knew I'd hesitate." He chuckled. "You know what gets me? I don't even know how you . . ." Hansen turned his head back forward and his voice trailed off.

Even as Fisher was doing it, taking that natural step forward to catch the tail end of Hansen's words, alarms went off in his head. *Mistake.* Hansen had started the conversation, built some animosity, then injected some amiability and piqued Fisher's curiosity with the trailing sentence.

A well-laid trap, Fisher thought, as Hansen levered himself upright and spun on his heel, instantly cutting the distance between them by seven feet. Fisher brought the SC pistol up, but the motion of Hansen's lead arm, coming toward him in a flat, backhanded arc, told Fisher it was too late. The shot would go wide. The knife Hansen surely had concealed in his fist, its blade tucked against his inner forearm, was a half second from his throat. Fisher resisted the impulse to backpedal or duck. It would be what Hansen expected, and Fisher couldn't afford to find himself in a protracted, noisy wrestling match with the young Splinter Cell. It was a fight he couldn't win, especially when the rest of the team rushed back in to investigate the commotion.

Instead, Fisher took a quick sliding step forward, his right hand coming up to block Hansen's knife arm, while his left hand, formed into a fist with his thumb extended, shot forward and plunged into the nerve bundle in Hansen's armpit. Hansen's eyes went wide with pain. His momentum faltered. Fisher clamped down on Hansen's knife wrist, then spun on his heel, around Hansen's back, using the momentum to pull Hansen around and off balance. He slid his left hand down, joined it with his right on Hansen's wrist, then pulled it toward him, torquing the wrist joint at the same time. Fisher could feel the bones and ligaments beneath Hansen's skin twisting, stretching. . . . Hansen gasped in pain. The knife clattered to the floor. Fisher kept moving, however, using his own momentum to keep Hansen stumbling forward until he spun once more, this time changing direction, swinging Hansen's arm back over his head, while side kicking his feet out from under him. He landed with a thud, back flat on the concrete. Fisher dropped his weight, jamming his knee into Hansen's solar plexus. All the air exploded from Hansen's mouth. His face went red as he tried to suck air.

Fisher reached behind him and grabbed Hansen's knife. Even before seeing it, he knew the feel of its haft, its balance. . . . It was Fisher's own Fairbairn Sykes World War II–era commando dagger. A gift from an old family friend, the FS had for years been Fisher's lucky charm. After Lambert, he'd been forced to leave it behind.

Now Fisher laid the FS's blade across Hansen's throat. "This is my knife, Ben. Why do you have my knife?"

Hansen was still gasping for air. Fisher waited until finally Hansen wheezed out, "Grimsdóttir."

"Grim gave you this?"

"Thought it . . . thought it would bring . . . luck."

Fisher smiled at this. "How's it working for you so far?"

Hansen took a deep breath. "Keep it."

"I'm going to get off you. Lie there. Don't move. Once you've got your breath back, I want you to do me a favor. After that, we call 'time in.' Deal?"

Hansen nodded.

"Your word on it," Fisher pushed.

Hansen nodded again. It took another thirty seconds before he fully recovered. "Jesus, what the hell did you do to me?"

"I'll take that as a rhetorical question. Are you ready to hear the favor?"

"Yeah."

"Call Grimsdóttir. Ask her about Karlheinz van d
Putten."

"The guy that gave us the Vianden tip? Ames's contact?"

"That's him. Make the call."

Hansen fished his cell phone from his pocket and hit speed dial. A few moments later he said, "It's Hansen. Yeah, I'm with him. . . . I'm supposed to ask you about van der Putten." Hansen was silent for a full minute as Grim spoke. Finally he said, "This is on the level? No more games? Okay, got it. I'll hear him out." Hansen disconnected and looked at Fisher. "She's says you're going to answer all my questions."

"As best I can."

"She also said to tell you, 'Sorry about the Fairbairn Sykes.'"

Fisher laughed. "Sure she is. First things first. Call your team. Tell them everything's okay and that you'll get back to them shortly."

Hansen made the call on his SVT, then disconnected.

"The Vianden ambush tip came from Ames, who claims he got it from van der Putten. You know that's bogus, correct?"

"I'm taking it on faith for the time being."

"Fair enough. I found van der Putten dead, his ears cut off. That was Ames covering his tracks."

"If not van der Putten, where'd he get the tip?"

"Kovac, we believe."

"Kovac? That's nuts. Ames is working for Kovac? No way. I mean, the guy's a weasel, but—"

"Best-case scenario is that Kovac simply hates Grim and he wants her out. What better way to undermine her than to catch me without her? Here's how it'd be played for the powers that be: Kovac, suspicious of Grimsdóttir, puts his own man on the team dispatched to hunt down Sam Fisher. Grimsdóttir's inept handling of the situation allows Fisher to escape multiple times, until finally Kovac's agent saves the day. Same scenario at Hammerstein. Kovac called in a favor at the BND."

Hansen absorbed this for a few moments. "What's the worst-case scenario?"

"Kovac's a traitor and he's working for whoever hired Yannick Ernsdorff. Up until I went off the bridge into the Rhine, Kovac had been getting regular updates from Grim. The moment it became clear to him that I was heading to Vianden—and in Yannick Ernsdorff's general direction—he got nervous and Ames's tip miraculously appeared. Think about it: After I lost you at the foundry in Esch-sur-Alzette, did you have any leads? Any trail to follow?"

"No."

"That's because I didn't leave one."

"Okay, some of what you're saying makes sense, but Kovac a traitor? Grim suggested that a while ago, but that's a big leap."

"Not too big a leap for Lambert. It's why he asked me to kill him. It's why I went to ground. He was convinced the U.S. intelligence community, including the NSA, was infected to the highest levels. Have you ever heard of doppelgänger factories?"

"No."

"They're secret Chinese factories dedicated to cloning and improving on Western military technology. The Guoanbu steals schematics, diagrams, material samples— whatever it can get its hands on—then feeds them to doppelgänger factories for production."

"Sounds like an urban legend."

"Lambert didn't think so. He thought they were real, and the Guoanbu was getting help from the inside: politicians, the Pentagon, CIA, NSA. . . . No one's willing to admit it, but when it comes to industrial espionage, the Guoanbu has no peer. You don't get that lucky without help."

"So, Kovac—"

"That, we don't know yet. Here's the important part: Yannick Ernsdorff is playing banker for a black-market weapons auction starring the world's worst terrorist groups. Grim and I call it the 738 Arsenal—named after the doppelgänger factory it was stolen from."

"And you know this how?"

"I found the crew that did the job—a bunch of bored former SAS boys led by Charles 'Chucky Zee' Zahm."

"The writer?"

"You can add professional thief to his resume," Fisher said, then explained about Zahm and his Little Red Robbers. "Zahm had proof of the job, including a complete inventory of the arsenal."

"What kind of stuff?"

"I'll show you the list later, but suffice it to say we can't let the 738 Arsenal get away from us. Ben, you might have even seen pieces from the arsenal."

"Come again?"

"The doppelgänger factory that Zahm hit was in eastern China, near the Russian border. In Jilin-Heilongjiang, about a hundred miles northwest of Vladivostok and about sixty miles from a Russian town called Korfovka."

At the mention of Korfovka, Hansen's eyes narrowed. "I was there. A while ago."

"That's where Zahm claims he delivered the arsenal."

"When was this?"

"About five months ago."

"I was there before that. The mission went . . . bad."

"That happens," Fisher said carefully. "It seems you got out okay."

Hansen was nodding vaguely. He stopped and studied Fisher's face. "I got out because somebody helped me. Stepped in at just the right moment."

"Lucky break."

"Yeah . . . lucky." Hansen shook himself from his reverie. "This is a tall tale, Sam. Doppelgänger factories, Chinese replica weapons, this auction, Kovac . . ."

"Truth is stranger than fiction."

"This cat-and-mouse game we've been playing has been for Kovac's benefit."

Fisher noted that this was a statement, not a question. Hansen and his team had already realized their strings were being pulled, but not why.

"Correct," Fisher said. "He forced her to put a team in the field. If she refused, she'd be out, and all the work we'd done since Lambert's death would be gone. I had to make it look good—keep you guys close, but not so close I couldn't work. Without some minor victories and near misses, Kovac could have called Grimsdóttir's plan a failure, and she'd be out."

"This explains why she's been jerking us around. She's been juggling a lot of balls," Hansen said. "Back to Kovac. If he's not just an asshole but an asshole *and* a traitor, and he's working for Ernsdorff's boss, then . . ."

"We couldn't afford to have him know I was on to Ernsdorff or the auction."

"But Kovac knew you were there. Wouldn't he have already pushed the panic button?"

"Probably. And the first thing Ernsdorff and his boss would have done is check security. I didn't leave any fingerprints when I hacked Ernsdorff's server; none of the auction attendees have disappeared. . . . As far as they can tell, all is well. We suspect the auction is days away; they're at the point of no return."

"Yeah, you don't invite the world's worst tangos to one location, then tell them at the last minute to turn around and go home."

"No, not with these kinds of stakes. And this is where you come in, Ben."

"You mean we get to stop playing straight man in your comedy road show?"

"Exactly. Yesterday I tagged one of the auction attendees. A Chechen named Aariz Qaderi."

"CMR, right?" Hansen asked. "Chechen Martyrs Regiment?"

"That's the guy. I tagged him. He's headed east into Russia—on his way to the auction, we hope."

"Hold on. All the attendees will be scrubbed before

they reach the auction site. Any kind of beacon or tracker will be found."

"Not the kind we used." Hansen opened his mouth to ask the obvious question, but Fisher cut him off. "Another time. Trust me: You can scrub all you want and these trackers won't come off."

Hansen shrugged. "What's our plan?"

"You get your team in here and brief them. Once they're on board, we start moving east and wait for our trackers to phone home."

"What about Ames?"

"We'll deal with him later. For now he's part of the team. We include him in everything."

"What about his cell phone? And his OPSAT? He'll try to contact Kovac."

"Let him. Grimsdóttir's made modifications to his phone and OPSAT. Every communication he makes beyond our tactical channels will go straight to her. She'll be playing Kovac and anyone else Ames has been talking to. He'll get voice mail, but Grim will respond to texts. Your phones aren't Internet-capable, right?"

"Right." Hansen smiled. "I like it. I like the plan."

"I thought you might. One thing, though: One of us has to stick to Ames like glue. If he slips away and gets a message out another way, we're done."

"Understood."

"How do you want to handle your people? I'd prefer to not get shot in the confusion."

Hansen chuckled. "I'll see what I can do."

* * *

FISHER sat along the office's back wall, the lights off. Ivanov, with a second dart in his thigh for good measure, lay on the floor before him. Hansen dialed his cell phone and recalled the team. Once they were inside he told them Grimsdóttir had come clean, then gave them the *Reader's Digest* version of the story Fisher had laid out a few minutes earlier, save any mention of Fisher, his mission, Ernsdorff, Zahm, Qaderi, or how they were tracking him. These last two items Fisher had decided to hold in reserve.

Hansen fielded twenty minutes of questions and gripes before, finally, the team cooled off and seemed to accept its new mission. "One last thing," Hansen said. "We're taking on a new member. He's going to be our team leader from this point on."

The griping started again.

"Who the hell . . . ?"

"Why would Grimsdóttir make a change at this point . . . ?"

Fisher took his cue and walked out of the office. Gillespie saw him first, did a double take, then reached for her gun. Hansen called, "Stand down, Kim. Everybody— hands at your sides."

"You gotta be kidding me," Ames said with his greasy smile. "Look who it is."

Noboru said, "Ben, what's going on?"

"I think I'll let Mr. Fisher explain that."

31

FISHER'S overt reentry into the Third Echelon/
Splinter Cell community took place not at the National
Security Agency in Fort Meade, Maryland, amid back
slapping and handshakes, but in a warehouse in Odessa
amid the suspicious stares from a group of twentysome-
things who, up until thirty minutes before, had been
bent on taking Fisher dead or alive. And judging from
the glares aimed in his direction, it appeared most of
Hansen's people had been leaning toward the former
choice. Predictably, once Fisher finished talking, Ames
was the first to express his misgivings:

"I don't buy it. Not a bit of it. This is just another
circle jerk."

"To what end?" Fisher asked.

"What? What's that mean?"

"For what purpose?"

"Who the hell knows? You people are nuts." Ames turned to Noboru, Valentina, and Gillespie. "Don't tell me any of you are buying this."

No one spoke immediately. Then Kimberly said, "I do." Then, to Fisher: "That night at the foundry . . . I almost shot you. You know that, don't you?"

Fisher nodded.

"You and Grim could have told us," Noboru said. "We would have held up our end and made it look good. Screw Kovac."

"We couldn't risk it," Fisher said. "If he got even a hint that you guys were holding back, he would've canned all of you—including Grim. It had to be done this way."

Valentina said, "Why tell us now, Mr. Fisher—"

"Sam."

"Sam," she repeated. "Why tell us now? Seems to me you didn't have much trouble keeping us at bay. Why not keep up the ruse?"

"Two reasons. One, to stop this auction I'm going to need your help. There are too many variables, too many unknowns. We won't know until we get there, but my gut tells me this isn't going to be a one-person job. And two, when I went off the bridge at Hammerstein I bought myself some time, but I knew they'd find the car but no body. Kovac would get suspicious and accuse Grimsdóttir of . . . anything. Any excuse to get her out. If I resurface, you guys get deployed and Kovac has to back off for a while."

"How did you survive the bridge?" Gillespie asked.

"Dumb luck and an OmegaO unit. I kept the windows shut and the car floated downriver. On the bottom, I waited to the last minute, then put on the OmegaO and got out."

Ames said, "Well, I'll give you this much: You've got brass ones, Fisher."

"Since we're reminiscing," Noboru said. "That was you at the Siegfried bunkers, right? You took out those two guys?"

"Yes."

"Why'd you do it?"

"Why wouldn't I?"

"I don't know. . . . One less person chasing you."

Fisher shook his head. "High price for that."

Noboru considered this, then said, "Well, thanks."

"Don't mention it."

"Now that we're in on the con," Valentina said, "we're going to have to be *real* careful about what gets back to Kovac. If he's involved with this auction stuff, he can't get even a hint of what we're doing. If he's not involved but wants Grim out, we can't give him any reason."

"Agreed," Fisher said. He looked around. "Are we good?"

There were nods all around, except for Ames. Hansen saw this and said, "In or out, Ames? Either you're with us, or I'll kick your ass back to Fort Meade."

"You'd like that, wouldn't you?"

Hansen didn't answer but offered a half grin.

"Yeah, okay. I'm on board. We don't have to hug or anything, right? I ain't doing that."

"Idiot," Gillespie muttered.

Fisher said, "Any questions?"

"I have one," Valentina said. "You said the guy you're tracking looks to be heading into Russia, right?"

"Right."

"If the auction's taking place on Russian soil, we have to consider that the government might be involved. If that's the case, we could find ourselves up against the Russian army."

"Anything's possible," Fisher agreed. "Let's cross that bridge when we get to it."

"Or die on that bridge when we get to it," Ames shot back.

THEY waited until Ivanov regained consciousness; then Hansen and the others left, while Fisher made sure his old friend/not friend had suffered no ill effects. He gave Ivanov fifteen hundred rubles—about five hundred U.S. dollars—for his trouble, called them even for the trouble Ivanov had caused him in Minsk, and left with the Russian's assurance that he was only too happy to forget the last two hours of his life.

Outside they split into two groups of three and checked into hotels near the passenger port terminal. Fisher, Gillespie, and Ames took the Mozart Hotel; Hansen, Noboru, and Valentina, the Londonskaya Hotel a couple blocks away.

Once in his room, Fisher texted Grimsdóttir:

Mission accomplished. Call for details.

His phone trilled ten minutes later. Fisher answered and said, "Another pay phone?"

"Outside a 7-Eleven," Grim muttered.

"Oh, the degradation," Fisher replied.

"Smart ass. How'd it go?"

"Complicated. Hansen took a little hands-on convincing, but he came around."

"Was that before or after he called me?"

"Before. The rest of the team's on board, too, including Ames. He grumbled, but I imagine he's thrilled at the idea of being able to give Kovac a blow-by-blow."

"If he tries Kovac, he'll get voice mail, and vice versa. He'll turn to texting soon enough; then he's ours. What we still don't know is how deeply Ames is involved. If Kovac's linked to the auction, that doesn't necessarily mean Ames is."

"We'll know. When the time is right, I'm going to have a heart-to-heart with him."

"Why doesn't that sound as friendly as it should?" In the background Fisher heard a double bing. Grimsdóttir said, "My other phone. Wait." The line clicked into silence. She returned half a minute later. "Qaderi just left Moscow, heading east to Irkutsk."

"How do you know that?"

"The bots are into five devices in Qaderi's group: a laptop, three cell phones, and one satellite phone.

They're all pinging, so the GPS coordinates are triangulated down to an eight-foot circle. They had him placed at the gate assigned to an Irkutsk flight."

"Score one for Terzo Lucchesi. Flight time?"

"Six hours, fifty minutes."

Fisher checked his watch and did the time-zone conversion. Irkutsk was six hours ahead of Odessa. With flight time that would put Qaderi there in thirteen hours, or at one in the afternoon Irkutsk time.

"How fast can you get us there?" Fisher asked.

"I'm on my way back to the office right now. I'll text you."

Grimsdóttir disconnected and Fisher called Hansen with an update. "Thanks," said Hansen.

"How's the mood over there?"

"Still a little stunned, I'm guessing, but I gotta be honest: None of us is gonna miss chasing you around. You taught us some tough lessons."

"We had a saying on the Teams: The more you sweat in training, the less you bleed in combat."

"I'm a believer. Listen, Sam, I'm at the ice machine. I think I may have solved one of our problems."

"How's that?"

"I'm bunking with Ames. He left his phone sitting on the bathroom sink. I knocked it into the toilet. He didn't notice it for ten minutes. It's dead."

Fisher chuckled. "How'd he take that?"

"As you'd expect. I feel better knowing his only option is the OPSAT now."

"Agreed. I'll call you when I hear back from Grim."

* * *

SHE called fifteen minutes later. "Best I can do is a Czech Airlines flight leaving at 4:00 A.M. your time, with connections in Prague and Moscow. You'll touch down in Irkutsk eight hours behind Qaderi."

"Unless the auction's in Irkutsk, he'll be traveling from there. I'm guessing car or train."

"Gut feeling?"

"Partially. Irkutsk is a big city, but it's still Siberia. It's about as remote as you get, and if I were holding this kind of auction . . ."

"Where better," Grim finished.

"As long as our bots keep phoning home, we'll be able to find him. Book the flights. I'll gather the troops."

32

"YOU tried to wash me out, didn't you?"

The words penetrated Fisher's dozing mind and he opened his eyelids. He turned his head and looked at Ames in the aisle seat. The rest of the team was spread throughout the cabin. "What's that?" Fisher asked.

"I said that you tried to wash me out of the program."

"Are you asking me or telling me?"

"Asking."

"The answer's no. I helped train you and I submitted my evaluation. That's it."

"But you didn't give me your stamp of approval."

"Doesn't work like that."

"But you're the man, the legend." Ames's voice dripped with sarcasm.

"I told them I thought you had the skills and the intelligence for the job but not the temperament. I haven't seen anything that changes my mind."

"Hey, the hell with you. I've done damned good."

Fisher shrugged, then closed his eyes again.

"What's the plan, anyway," Ames asked, "when we touch down?"

Fishing. "Depends on what our friend is doing. Wherever he goes, we need to be there."

"And who is this guy? What did you say his name was?"

"I didn't."

"What, you don't trust me?"

"Nobody else knows, either. It's compartmentalization, Ames."

"How're we tracking him?"

"Pixie dust." Fisher had to suppress his smile. His statement was almost closer to truth than fantasy.

"So let me get this straight: You won't tell us who we're after or how we're tracking him, and we don't have jack for a plan."

"That's about the size of it."

"Great, just great."

IT was after ten at night when their plane began its approach to Irkutsk International Airport. Having spent the last three hours of the flight staring out the window at thick cloud cover, Fisher was surprised to see an expanse of white. For as far as he could see the terrain was clad in moonlit snow. While they'd been traveling east, a late-spring snowstorm had come in from the west. Located so close to the Angara reservoirs, the airport had its own microclimate that left the area fogged in for much of the year, and with the drop in temperature, that fog had turned into a frost that clung to trees and telephone poles and power lines. Three years earlier an S7 Airlines Airbus A310-300 had crashed here, overshooting the runway before smashing into a concrete barrier and exploding. Of the 203 passengers aboard, only 76 survived.

"Just our luck," Ames said as the aircraft's gear squelched on the runway. "A Siberian blizzard."

"This is a win for us, Ames."

"How do you figure?"

"Our friend probably arrived just as the storm started rolling in. Everything would have slowed down until the plows started rolling. This storm might have cut his lead by half."

CUSTOMS went slowly but smoothly. Stripped of their wristbands, the team's OPSATs were taken for PDAs, which in essence they were. Fisher had divvied up the Ajax shaving-cream cans, giving one each to Noboru and Hansen. The darts, still inside his barrel pen, were inside his carry-on rucksack.

Fifty minutes after they landed the team pulled onto the airport's approach road in a pair of Lada Niva SUVs. The snow had stopped falling, but the clouds to the southwest were dark with moisture. More was coming. In the lead SUV, Fisher checked his iPhone's signal and was pleased to see five bars. Siberia or not, Irkutsk was still a metropolitan area, boasting six hundred thousand in the city itself and another hundred thousand within a fifty-mile radius. Irkutsk would lack many of the conveniences of a Western city of comparable size, but he and his team were far from being in the boondocks. Past that fifty-mile radius, however, was another story.

At the first sight of an open diner, Fisher, in the lead SUV, pulled into the lot. They went inside. The place was empty. The hostess gave them a "take your pick" shrug of her shoulders. They took the booth nearest the door. Fisher waited for the waitress to deposit the water glasses and silverware and leave before saying, "We've got some legwork to do. We need weapons, equipment, and cold-weather gear."

"Caches?" Gillespie asked.

"Nearest one is three hundred miles north of here in Bratsk. That's a single; the nearest multiple cache is . . . too far. We're going to have to get inventive. Noboru, you did some work in Bratsk once, right?"

"How did you? . . . Never mind. Yeah, I spent a couple of weeks there a few years ago. Great town. A lot of gray cinder-block buildings. Very Soviet."

"Can you make some calls? We'll need a local contact."

"I'll see what I can do."

Fisher nodded. "Who's got the best Russian?"

"I do," Maya Valentina said immediately.

"We've got OPSATs but no SVTs or subdermals. We're going to need to improvise. I'll give you a list. You and Kimberly hit electronics stores and hobby shops."

"Got it."

"Hansen, you and Ames find some army-surplus stores. Look for cold-weather and camouflage gear and anything else we can use."

Hansen nodded. Ames shrugged.

Fisher's iPhone chimed, signaling a text message. It was from Grimsdóttir:

Q halted at lat 53°50′15.61″ N, long 108° 2′35.13″ E, 210 miles northeast Irkutsk.
No movement three hours.
Stand by.

Grim had hyperlinked the latitude and longitude. Fisher clicked on the link and Google Earth opened and zoomed in. Qaderi's location put him on the western shore of Lake Baikal. Fisher shared the update with the group.

"What the hell is he doing there?" Ames asked.

Hansen said, "That's what we're here to find out."

They talked for a few more minutes, then got another text from Grim:

Road blocked at Q location (Rytaya River estuary) for last six hours. Plows working. Estimated time to clear, six hours.

"We just got another break," Fisher said, then explained. He checked his watch. "We're not going anywhere tonight. Let's find a place to settle in and wait for daylight. If we get on the road by noon, we'll only be four hours behind our target."

"Our yet-to-be-named target," Ames corrected.

"You'll know when you need to know," Fisher replied.

AS arranged, Fisher and Hansen met in the hotel's lobby an hour after they checked in. Aside from the desk clerk, who stood leaning over the desk with his head in a paperback novel, they were alone. They found a seat on one of the settees. The lobby was a pastel nightmare of light blue upholstered furniture, peach carpet, and gold curtains.

"Ames is pushing hard for information," Fisher told Hansen.

"That could mean nothing. He's that way—always trying to get over on people."

"Could be. When we're closer to catching up with Qaderi, I'm going to give everyone a few more details. If Ames has been waiting until he has more to feed Kovac, that should do it. Since he hasn't got a phone, he'll try the OPSAT."

"Then do we get to string him up by his ankles?"

"Something like that. In the end we're going to need him to cooperate, so we can't do anything . . . permanent to him."

"But he doesn't know that."

Fisher returned Hansen's smile. "No."

WITH their body clocks scrambled from the flight and the rapid jump in time zones, the team awoke at seven and met in the lobby as planned. Beyond the revolving doors was nothing but white. Snow had begun falling again since a few hours before dawn, and now a foot of it lay on the ground.

The restaurant was just opening. They found a large round table near the back, and then helped themselves to the buffet and filled up on eggs, sausage, bacon, black bread with butter, blini with sour cream, and assorted pastries. This could be the last time they would have a regular meal until the mission was over, Fisher told them. Where their target seemed to be headed there would be no grocery stores or fast-food restaurants.

Over coffee Fisher once more went over individual assignments. There were a few questions, but aside from Ames, who wore his characteristic sneer, the team members were steady and focused, and Fisher could see the glint of anticipation in their eyes as they talked.

At eight, they parted company and set off on their missions.

FISHER had left to himself the toughest and most critical task: finding a way to deploy the Ajax bots. Without either an SC pistol or SC-20K assault rifle to provide kinetic energy, the darts and grenades were all but useless.

Using his iPhone's map application and the hotel's broadband wireless connection, Fisher quickly came up with a list of four businesses in the area that might serve his purposes. A little cajoling and a hefty tip convinced the day manager to put the hotel's shuttle and driver at his disposal for a few hours. None of the shops had what he was looking for, but each had plenty of almost-right odds and ends. A trip to a hardware store near the hotel rounded out his shopping list.

He was back in his room by eleven. As planned, Noboru knocked on his door a few minutes later. "How'd you do?" Fisher asked him as they sat down.

"Okay. The stuff isn't Third Echelon quality, but what is?" Noboru handed over a list and Fisher scanned it:

Groza OTs-14-4A-03 assault rifles: 4

SVU OC-AS-03 sniper rifles: 2

PSS Silent Pistol with armor-piercing jacketed-steel core ammunition: 6 × 600

Fisher looked up. "These are Spetsnaz weapons—current issue?"

"Yep." Noboru gave Fisher a "don't ask" half smile.

The Groza was a noise-suppressed, short-barrel assault rifle designed for urban combat; the SVU was essentially an improved version of the Russian SVD Dragunov sniper rifle; the PSS had been specially created for special operations soldiers. With its internal automatic bolt mechanism and subsonic SP-4 gas-tight ammunition, the PSS was one of the quietest handguns in the world.

Fisher read the rest of the list: an assortment of fragmentation, smoke, and stun grenades; spotting scopes; night-vision headsets; binoculars; gas masks; Semtex plastic explosives and detonators—and then a surprise.

Again Fisher looked up at Noboru. "An ARWEN," he said. "You got an ARWEN."

"My guy had one. Wanted twenty thousand for it. I talked him down to eight."

The ARWEN 37 was a classic SAS weapon originally manufactured by the British Royal Small Arms Factory. While far from recently issued, the ARWEN was compact, light, and offered an array of offensive options, including composite-plastic less-than-lethal Impact Baton Rounds; Pyrotechnic Irritant Rounds containing either CS or CN gas; Barricade Penetrating Rounds designed to punch through doors, windows, and thin walls before dispersing their gas; and finally Muzzle Blast Rounds, which spewed CN or CS gas directly from the ARWEN's barrel.

"Good work," Fisher said. "Hansen tells me you've got a knack for weapons improv. Give me those."

Noboru looked at the two cans of shaving cream he was carrying, then handed them over. "Oh, yeah, what's the deal? Ben just gave them to me, told me to bring them."

Fisher went into the bathroom, got the third can, then placed them all on the desk. He took the pen from his pocket, unscrewed it, and carefully spilled the darts next to the cans, which he then dismantled to reveal the six Ajax grenades. Using his index finger, he drew one of the darts to the edge of the table and slipped it back into the pen. "Regular dart," Fisher explained.

"Those are SC-20 grenades," Noboru said.

"Close, but not quite."

Leaving out any mention of Lucchesi, Fisher summarized for Noboru the Ajax project and why it was necessary. "The man we're tracking is our guinea pig. So far Ajax is doing what it's supposed to do."

"This isn't a joke?" Noboru asked.

"No."

"Who else knows about this?"

"On the team: you, me, Hansen. And that's the way I want it for now."

Noboru's eyes narrowed. "Why?"

"Because that's the way it is. You have a problem with that?"

"No. I'm cool. Okay, what am I improving?"

Fisher went to the bed and upended his shopping bags, dumping the contents on the mattress. "I need you to take all this and cobble together two launchers for the Ajax grenades and darts."

Noboru walked to the bed and stared. "These are paintball guns."

"I know that. Can you do it?"

"It's all CO_2 powered?"

"Right. I need a hundred feet of range for the grenades and half that for the darts. And I need them to hit with enough impact to trigger the dispersal mechanisms."

Noboru walked back to the desk and was about to reach out for one of the grenades when he stopped and looked questioningly at Fisher. Fisher nodded. Noboru picked up a grenade, studied it for thirty seconds, then did the same with a dart.

"Can you do it?" Fisher asked again.

"Yeah, I think I can. I'm going to need tools."

Fisher pointed to another shopping bag sitting in front of the chest of drawers. "Get started. Call if you need anything. I'm going to check on the others. We leave in an hour."

33

LAKE BAIKAL

FISHER had been to Lake Baikal before, but only once, and it had been more than a decade ago. Despite the blowing snow, his second glimpse of it was as shocking as the first. If not for being landlocked, Baikal would be a sea unto itself, with a shoreline that measures twelve hundred miles—long enough to stretch from New York to the middle of Kansas—and a length of more than four hundred miles. It holds 20 percent of the world's entire freshwater volume.

"Deepest lake in the world," Gillespie said, staring through the windshield from the passenger seat.

"Yeah?" Ames said from the back. "Exactly how deep?"

"Almost a mile," she replied, then went on: "Over 330 rivers feed it; it's fifty miles across at its widest point. If you drive at forty miles an hour, it'd take you ten hours to go from the south end to the north."

"Yeah, that's big, all right."

"And old," Fisher added. "Almost twenty-five million years."

"And you claim our guy's somewhere around here?"

Fisher nodded and checked his OPSAT; they were fully operational now, having been synced and updated by Grimsdóttir back at Third Echelon. Qaderi had started moving again two hours earlier. He was now a hundred miles north of the Rytaya River estuary, and two hundred miles ahead of them.

"Sun's going down soon," Ames said. "What's the plan?"

"Depends on our target," Fisher replied. "If he keeps going, so do we."

QADERI did keep going, until just after seven, when his signal stopped in Severobaikalsk, a town of twenty-seven thousand about twelve miles from Lake Baikal's northern tip. With nightfall, the wind began gusting more heavily and the snow picked up. Shortly after nine they pulled into a shantytown of hunting huts on Cape Kotel'nikovskiy that Grimsdóttir had spotted, via satellite, earlier in the day. The lights of their SUVs washed over a dozen or so thick canvas yurt-style tents built on wooden platforms.

The pine trees, blanketed in snow, stood shaggy and formless around the clearing.

"Why the hell are we stopping?" Ames asked, climbing out.

"Roads are icing up," Fisher replied.

"What is it, you lose your nerve?"

Valentina walked past, heading for the yurts. "Take a look at the map, Ames. For the next fifty miles, were down to one lane—most of it running along cliffs above the lake. You wanna go for a swim, suit yourself, but not us."

"How do you know our target hasn't stopped at the auction site?"

Fisher said, "You don't go to the trouble of coming to Siberia just to gather in a population center."

"And if you're wrong?"

"There are at least a dozen more guests coming. The storm's going to delay some of them. Relax, Ames. Take a breath."

THEY hauled their gear into the sturdiest-looking yurt, which had eight wooden bunks with thin straw mattresses situated in a circle around a potbellied stove. Valentina and Ames found a pair of kerosene lanterns, hanging from the crossbeams, and lit them. Written in Cyrillic, a handwritten sign on the post read,

Honor system. If you stay here, leave something: money, supplies, etc. Together Siberia is home; separate, a hell.

Ames said, "Yeah, well, if they ain't got a decent can around here, I'm going to leave 'em something, all right."

"I saw some outhouses at the edge of the clearing," Gillespie said. "West side."

Fisher caught Noboru's attention, gestured for him to follow, then went back to one of the Ladas to retrieve a couple boxes of rations Fisher had left behind. "How'd you do with our project?" Fisher asked.

"Good. I think. I worked on it on the backseat until about an hour ago. Told Maya they were flashbang launchers. I've got two pistols and two launchers. The pistols are single shot; no magazine, and you'll have to reload a CO_2 cartridge every time. Good news is, the range and velocity are there. The launchers are the same deal, but they take two cartridges, and to get even close to a hundred feet you'll have to use a high trajectory—fifty degrees or more."

"Good work," Fisher said. "We're not going to get a chance to test them. Give me a number. Best guess."

"Ninety percent chance they'll work as designed."

Fisher smiled. "Ninety, I'll take."

"I gotta tell you, Mr.—I mean, Sam. I gotta tell you: Keeping this from the rest of the team doesn't sit right with me."

"I'd be worried if you were okay with it. Hang on. You'll know why shortly."

BACK in the yurt, Fisher announced, "Let's get some sleep. We'll be moving again at first light or when the wind and snow let up, whichever comes first."

He got nods all around.

Gillespie held up her olive drab sleeping bag. "Ben, where did you get this thing? The rest of the gear's okay, but this thing . . ." She laughed. "It looks like it's from the Cold War. It *smells* like it's from the Cold War."

Hansen chuckled. "It's all the surplus store had. Got a bargain, though. A dollar a piece."

From his bunk, Ames called to Fisher, "Hey, boss."

"Sam will do."

"Okay, sure. Explain it to me again: This arsenal— why aren't we just blowing the hell out of it? I mean, we've got Semtex. Why not just rig the whole lot of it and call it a day?"

"Two reasons," Fisher replied. "One, I doubt whoever arranged this auction is stupid enough to keep it all in a big pile; we're talking about tons of equipment. We don't have enough Semtex for that. Two, these people are going to be our Trojan horses. Once they leave here, we'll track them wherever they go. In the space of a week, we'll learn more about these groups' logistics and transport routes than we've learned in the last five years. When they arrive at their destinations, we mop them up, along with anyone else we find."

"That's all assuming the bad guys don't find your trackers."

"Safe assumption."

"It's a big decision for you and Grim to be making on your own."

Hansen said, "Make your point, Ames."

"No point. Just sounds like Sam here's going a little cowboy on us."

"I'll make you a deal," Fisher said. "If this all goes to hell and we're both still around when it's over, you can say you told me so."

THIRTY minutes after the lanterns were turned down the yurt was filled with sounds of snoring. Fisher waited until eleven, then sat up. Two bunks down, Hansen was doing the same. Fisher nodded at him and got one in return. Silently they put on their cold-weather gear, then padded over to Ames's bunk. Fisher reached into his jacket pocket, unscrewed his pen, and dumped the lone dart into his palm. Hansen moved around to the head of Ames's bunk and knelt down. Carefully Fisher reached out and pricked Ames below the ear. Hansen clamped his hands over Ames's mouth until he stopped struggling and lapsed into unconsciousness. While it was more guess-work than science, Fisher had worked with the darts long enough to know that Ames had gotten a fractional dose. He'd be under for ten or fifteen minutes.

Working together, they lifted Ames from his bunk and laid him across Hansen's shoulders, fireman-style. Hansen headed for the door of the yurt and slipped outside. Fisher waited five minutes, then lit one of the kerosene lanterns. One by one he shook awake Gillespie, Noboru, and Valentina. All three were alert and upright in five seconds.

"What's up?" Noboru asked.

Gillespie noticed the empty bunk. "Where's Ames?"

"Get your gear on and grab your OPSATs," Fisher commanded. "It's time for show-and-tell."

FISHER led them across the clearing, where they mounted the steps to one of the four-person yurts and slipped inside. Dangling from the center beam was a kerosene lantern, its sputtering flame bright enough only to illuminate Hansen's face beside it. He reached up and turned the knob until the yurt was filled with yellow light.

Wrists and ankles bound to the bed frame, Ames lay spread-eagled on a bunk in the center of the space.

34

"**JESUS,**" Valentina muttered.

Gillespie turned to Fisher. "Sam, what is this?"

"Better you hear it from Ames."

To Hansen, Noboru said, "And you're okay with this? I mean the guy's a weasel, but . . . *this*?"

Hansen said, simply, "It's necessary."

Fisher looked at Gillespie, Valentina, and Noboru. "I want you to listen carefully: You're going to have to trust me. When Ames wakes up, it's going to get ugly. Then it's going to get uglier. Nobody interferes. Once you know what's going on, you'll understand. Agreed?"

He got delayed but firm nods all around.

Fisher said to Hansen, "Go get it."

Hansen slipped outside, was gone for a minute, then

returned carrying a two-liter bottle filled with liquid. He set it at Fisher's feet, then resumed his spot by the post.

AMES woke up five minutes later. Groggily he tried to sit up once, then fell back and tried again before rotating his head and staring at the flex-cuff around his right wrist. He blinked at it, then lifted his head and checked his feet. He lay back again. He turned his head and saw Fisher.

"What is this? Why the hell am I tied up?"

Fisher was mildly surprised that Ames hadn't started cursing and thrashing.

"Are you awake?" he asked.

"Yeah, I'm awake. What did you do to me?"

"I darted you."

"Why?"

Fisher didn't answer but simply nodded at Ames's bound limbs.

"Why?" Ames repeated.

"You're a traitor," Fisher said.

"That's crap! I'm a Splinter Cell just like you guys!"

"You're nothing like us. When you went to the outhouse, you made a call."

"How'd I do that? My cell phone is in the Irkutsk sewer system."

Fisher held up his OPSAT. "With this."

"That's for tactical comms. It routes to us, and the op center back home. You can't—"

"You can text with it if someone teaches you how. Somebody with enough power to bypass the system."

"This is stupid. . . . Check my OPSAT. Check if I did what you're talking about."

"You cleared it," Fisher said. "Lucky for us, I have a transcript."

Fisher nodded at the rest of the team and pointed at their OPSATs. In unison they studied their screens. It took thirty seconds. Gillespie said, "This is Ames."

"Yes," Fisher replied. "Talking to Kovac at Fort Meade—but not actually Kovac. Grim intercepted the message. Ames gave up everything—our location, the make and model of our vehicles, our weapons, what few details he had about the auction and our plan to track the 738 Arsenal. . . . Everything."

"Why?" asked Noboru.

"Ames has been working for Kovac for a while. We're not sure how long, but we're about to find out." Fisher went on, telling them the truth behind the Vianden ambush and Karlheinz van der Putten. "Since he got my position from Kovac, he needed a scapegoat. Since he worried I would go visit van der Putten, he had the man killed."

"You have proof?" asked Valentina.

"We have van der Putten's financials. No deposits before or after Ames says he paid for the Vianden tip."

"But how did Kovac know you were headed to Vianden?" asked Gillespie.

"Actually, we don't think it had anything to do with Vianden. It had to do with the guy I was there to visit—an Austrian named Yannick Ernsdorff. He's the banker for this auction we're chasing. Kovac was nervous because he and Ernsdorff are working for the same man."

"And who is that?" asked Noboru.

"We don't know."

"Does he?" Valentina asked, nodded at the prone Ames.

Ames barked, "I'm not following *any* of this, you idiot! I don't know *anything*! Fisher's making this up. He doesn't like me. Never has. He's—"

Fisher cut him off. "Best case, Ames is working for Kovac so he can push Grimsdóttir out. Worst case, Kovac is a traitor and he's helping whoever is behind this auction. Either way, Ames has been betraying you from the start."

"It's worse than that," Hansen added. "Ames thought he was talking to Kovac on the OPSAT. He probably knew Kovac was going to pass on the information. When we reached the auction site, we would've been walking into an ambush."

"That's a lie!" Ames shouted. "I wouldn't do that. Hey, Maya, come on! Nathan, man, we're friends. . . ."

Gillespie said, "There's a lot of 'ifs' in there, Sam."

"True. We can settle this pretty easily. We know Ames is working for Kovac. We have the proof. What we need to know is whether Kovac's just an ass or a traitor, and whether Ames is in on it."

He nodded at Hansen, who walked to the canvas wall, picked up the straw mattress lying there, and shoved it beneath Ames's bunk. Fisher leaned down, picked up the two-liter bottle, and unscrewed the cap. Almost immediately the stench of gasoline wafted through the yurt.

Ames's eyes went wide. "No . . . no!"

"You've got a thing about fire, don't you?" Fisher asked. "Your family died in a fire, didn't they?"

Gillespie said, "Sam . . ."

Fisher kept going. "You saw it, too. Watched the whole thing."

Ames was rapidly shaking his head from side to side.

Fisher tipped the bottle over Ames's body and soaked him from head to toe. Ames sputtered and coughed and began bucking against his restraints. The bunk banged on the wooden floor. Ames started babbling, his words running over one another.

Fisher told the group, "Unless I'm wrong, Kovac gave Ames the name of the man we're tracking. Aside from him, there are only three people who know it: me, Hansen, and Grimsdóttir." Fisher knelt down beside the bunk. "Ames," he said quietly. Ames kept thrashing. "Ames!" Fisher barked.

Ames stopped abruptly and looked at Fisher, who said, "Tell the name of the man we're tracking or I'm going to set you on fire."

"Aariz Qaderi," Ames said without hesitation.

Fisher stood up, tapped a few keys on his OPSAT, then nodded to the others, who studied their screens. Gillespie said, "I'll be damned."

"Son of a bitch," Noboru muttered.

To Ames, Fisher said, "Ben's going to ask you more questions. Answer him."

Ames's eyes were glassy, but he nodded emphatically.

Fisher nodded at Hansen, then led Noboru, Gillespie, and Valentina outside. They started back toward their yurt. Gillespie touched Fisher on the elbow and waited for the other two to get ahead.

"Tell me the truth, Sam," she said. "Would you have done it?"

"All that matters is that Ames believed I would."

"Answer my question."

Fisher considered the question. "Interrogation's an art, Kimberly. To be good at it you have to be able to stuff parts of your mind into boxes and use only the parts you need. The part I used in there would have done it. The part in charge of actually letting go of the match . . ."

Fisher shrugged and walked away.

35

"THINK he's going to be okay?" Noboru asked from the passenger seat.

It was an hour before dawn, and they'd been on the road for ninety minutes, having packed up as soon as Fisher realized the storm was abating. A hundred yards behind, the headlights of Hansen's SUV bounced over the rutted road. Somewhere in the blackness out the side window were the waters of Lake Baikal.

As he had been since the interrogation, Ames lay in the cargo area, flex-cuffed, gagged, and wrapped in a sleeping bag. After he'd finished questioning Ames, Hansen had done a decent job of washing away the gasoline, but still the stench of it filled the Lada's interior. Hansen had learned nothing more from Ames. He knew no details about the auction or who was behind it. As for his association with Kovac, however, Ames did not disappoint. As Fisher had suspected, Ames and Chuck Zahm were at least partially cut from the same cloth: Ames had meticulously documented the relationship, including digital voice records that Ames swore would put Kovac on the gallows beside him.

"Ames is a survivor," Fisher replied. "Like him or hate him, you have to respect that. Before we know it, he'll snap out of it and be pissed off again."

"That sounds almost sympathetic."

Fisher shook his head. "Sympathy and respect are different things. Once they throw Ames in jail, I'll be happy to throw away the key."

A few minutes later both their OPSATs beeped. Noboru checked the screen. "Qaderi's moving. There must be a little lag time. He's already outside Severobaikalsk. Wait a second. . . . He's heading south, back toward us."

"You're sure?"

"Yeah."

"How far?"

"Thirty miles. Should we tell Hansen?"

"He knows."

Fisher pressed the gas pedal down, and the Lada surged ahead.

"Still heading south," Noboru reported five minutes later.

The minutes and the miles ticked away, and slowly the

one-lane road widened and veered inland, away from the shore and behind a screen of pine trees. Sheltered from the wind and spray, the road lost its coating of ice. They were able to increase speed to fifty miles per hour, bumping over the washboard surface.

"Twenty miles," Noboru reported. "Sun's coming up."

Fisher glanced out the passenger window. Through the trees, a pinkish orange glow backlit the mountains.

Seven minutes passed and Noboru announced, "Ten miles," then a few minutes after that, "Five miles."

Fisher checked his OPSAT screen and muttered, "Come on, where are you?"

"What?" asked Noboru.

"That."

The Lada's headlights swept over a left-hand split in the road. Fisher slammed on the brakes, eased up, then began pumping them as the Lada slewed right, then left, then corrected and came to a halt thirty feet beyond the split. Fisher glanced in the rearview mirror. Hansen's SUV was fifty yards behind, sitting broadside in the road. Fisher put the transmission in reverse. Hansen took the hint and straightened out and began backing up. Fisher stopped, cranked the wheel to the left, and pulled onto the left-hand road. Hansen followed. The road took them up a grade, then through a series of S-curves. Fisher kept his eyes on the road but occasionally glanced out the passenger window.

"Look sharp," Fisher ordered. "They should be along anytime now."

Fisher reached down and shut off the Lada's head-lights. Behind him, Hansen did the same. They rounded another curve, and to the right and below, through the trees, they could see a small lake no more than a half mile across. The rising sun glinted off the flat, calm waters.

"Sludjanka Lake," Noboru announced.

On the opposite shore, another Lada SUV was heading south.

"That's him," Noboru said.

"Yep."

"Where's he going, though? The auction site?"

Fisher didn't answer. He got out and Noboru followed. Hansen and the others had done the same. They met between the cars at the edge of the road.

"Auction site?" Hansen echoed.

"Maybe," Fisher said. He lifted his binoculars and watched the Lada's progress. "Can't see who's inside, but unless he dumped his computer and phones, it's Qaderi."

Suddenly, from inside the Lada there came three over-lapping orange flashes. The SUV slewed sideways off the road, then back up, and coasted to a stop.

"Holy crap!" said Gillespie.

Fisher zoomed in on the Lada and waited. After thirty seconds the front passenger door opened and a figure emerged. The man turned around, leaned back into the car, and then came out with a briefcase. He slammed the door shut and turned around. For a split second his face was illuminated by the sun. It was not Qaderi. Nor his bodyguards.

"What the hell is this?" Hansen muttered.

"I think Qaderi just got uninvited to the auction," Fisher replied.

WITH his back to Fisher and the group, the man knelt down beside the Lada and opened the briefcase. He rummaged around for several minutes, then closed the briefcase and stood up. He loitered around the Lada as though waiting for something. Ten minutes passed. Then, to the east, came the thumping of helicopter rotors. They saw the mist on the lake's surface ten seconds before the helicopter appeared. Flying at twenty feet, the robin's-egg blue and white Sikorsky S-76 swept over the Lada, banked south, and then stopped in a hover and touched down astride the road a hundred yards away. The cabin door opened, and four men in black coveralls jumped out and sprinted to the man standing at the Lada. Without a word passing between them, the man got back into the Lada and the four men began pushing. Once the SUV was pointing at the Sludjanka Lake, the driver climbed out and helped the other four until the Lada was rolling at ten to twelve miles an hour. With only a slight bump as it went over the berm at the edge of the road, the SUV plunged into the water and sank from sight.

The five men sprinted back to the Sikorsky and climbed aboard. Thirty seconds later the helicopter was heading east over the lake. Fisher and the others stood in silence until the sound of the rotors faded.

"They must have known Qaderi was tagged," Valentina said.

"But not how. That briefcase they took was Qaderi's. I saw it in Romania. Everything that can identify him and his bodyguards is inside—including their phones and his laptop. If their Lada's ever found, they'll be John Does."

"So that's what the guy was doing when he was kneeling," Gillespie said. "Checking for beacons."

"Safe bet." Fisher told Valentina and Gillespie about the Ajax bots. He checked his watch. "Grim briefed him two hours ago. Just enough time for him to pass along the message. She left out any mention of Ajax, though, and he would have assumed she meant standard, Third Echelon–issue beacons."

Hansen was studying his OPSAT's screen. "The bots are heading due east at 150 miles an hour."

"We're still in the game," said Gillespie.

"What now?" asked Noboru.

"We hide."

HANSEN was the first to spot it on their foldable, topographical map of the area, an abandoned Stalin-era mica mine built into the cliffs a mile west of the lake. The dirt tract that led from the lake to the mine was littered with boulders and axle deep in a snow-mud mix the consistency of oatmeal, so it was an hour before they pulled into the clearing before the mine's entrance. Fisher backed in his SUV, followed by Hansen. Everyone climbed out.

"Okay, now tell us: Why are we hiding?" Noboru said.

"They killed Qaderi because Kovac reported the trackers. Grim told Kovac we were still in Irkutsk, and the weather was causing problems with the GPS. That's why the Sikorsky didn't look for anyone tailing the Lada. My gut tells me they'll be back—about the time we'd arrive if we'd left Irkutsk when Kovac thinks we did."

Hansen said, "You and Grim put some thought into this, didn't you?"

Fisher nodded.

"How long do we wait?" asked Valentina.

"Depends on where the Ajax bots go and how long it takes the Sikorsky to leave."

THEY got the answer to their first question two hours later, when Hansen called out from where he was sitting against the tunnel wall. "They're back." After leaving the site of Qaderi's execution, the Sikorsky had flown lazy figure-eight patterns up and down the lake's eastern shore and the foothills beyond. "Looks like its touching down. Thirty miles due east of us, about one and a half miles inland from Ayaya Bay."

Fisher got the topographical map, unfolded it on the Lada's hood, and found the spot Hansen had indicated. It sat two-thirds of the way between Ayaya Bay and a smaller V-shaped lake called Frolikha. "Middle of nowhere," he said. "The perfect spot for a black-market auction."

"I don't see any roads," Gillespie said.

"You're right. We're going to need a boat."

* * *

THE Sikorsky returned shortly before noon and spent two hours flying up and down the shoreline, using Slud-janka Lake as a datum. Several times it passed directly over the cliffs outside the tunnel entrance, but it neither slowed nor descended.

As the afternoon wore on the team members grew restless, pacing the tunnel, checking and rechecking their equipment, and cleaning weapons. Fisher gave them something to do, briefing each on what they would be carrying when and if they found the auction site. He'd gotten the same reports before leaving Irkutsk, but the task broke the monotony.

"Communications." Gillespie began laying out the equipment. "We'll all have hands-free, voice-activated headsets and microphones. We synced them to the OPSATs. They're not SVTs or subdermals, but they'll get the job done." She donned one of the headsets; it was a commercial cell-phone model with a dangling micro-phone and a miniature alligator clip. "The audio pickup is decent, but there's a half-second lag in the voice activa-tion. Also, you need to cup the microphone, bring it to your mouth, and whisper."

"We also jury-rigged a flexicam," Valentina said. "It's primitive—no night vision, EM, or infrared, but the pic-ture's fairly clear."

"Good work," Fisher said. "Ben?"

Hansen laid out their makeshift uniforms: wool-lined black cargo-style pants and heavy black sweaters, a dual layer of silk long underwear, fingerless mittens, and full balaclavas.

Fisher nodded, turned to Noboru. "Time to unveil your project."

Noboru walked to the Lada, pulled a duffel from the backseat, and returned. He laid out the modified paint-ball guns and launchers and ran through the operation and specifications. "Hold on," he said. "Forgot the CO_2 cartridges."

Moments later he called, "Ah, *goddamn it . . .*"

"What?" Fisher called.

"Better come see for yourself."

Fisher and the others walked to the rear of the Lada. Noboru was standing beside the open tailgate. Fisher felt his stomach lurch. He leaned into the cargo area and looked around.

Ames was gone.

AFTER passing out the Groza assault rifles, Fisher left Hansen and Valentina at the tunnel entrance and took Noboru and Gillespie deeper into the mine. A few hundred yards in, at a triple branch in the tunnel, they found a pair of flex-cuffs lying on the ground. They each took a tunnel and searched for fifteen minutes before meeting back at the branch.

"Nothing," Noboru said.

"Me neither," replied Gillespie. "I counted nine side tunnels in mine. There have to be other entrances. We can check the map, then split up and find a way around the cliffs—"

"No," Fisher said. "Forget him."

"Forget him?" Noboru repeated. "This is Ames we're talking about. After what he did—"

"We've got what we need from him. He's irrelevant now," Fisher said. This was only partially true. Ames had given Hansen the location of his insurance stash against Kovac, but if the case ever saw the inside of a courtroom, without Ames a conviction was uncertain. Right now, however, his team didn't need such worries clouding their thinking. "Focus on the mission," Fisher told them.

THEY waited until nightfall, then packed up and left the tunnels, picking their way back down the rutted tract to the main road, where they turned north and drove until the lights of Severobaikalsk came into view. They pulled off the road, shut off their engines and headlights, and waited for another two hours until, slowly, the town's lights began going out.

"Early to bed, early to rise," Gillespie muttered.

"Not much nightlife on a Tuesday night in Severobaikalsk," replied Noboru.

Fisher started the engine. "Let's go steal ourselves a boat."

36

WITH its hundreds of river outlets, Lake Baikal's surface generally stays ice free until mid-January and clears by the end of May, but this year was an exception, Fisher found as they reached the middle of the lake and the first pancake ice chunks began scraping down the hull. In both boats the team members looked around warily. From his seat in the bow Fisher spread his hands in the baseball "safe" signal. The ice was too brittle and thin to damage the hulls of their johnboats. So shallow were their drafts that in the worst case the flat-bottom rectangular craft could skim over the ice with little trouble.

As it was still early in the season, the tiny Severobaikalsk marina had offered them few choices of transportation: sailboats, fishing trawlers with diesel engines, or skiff-sized craft like their johnboats. The electric trolling motors were virtually silent, if not particularly powerful: After two hours of travel they were only halfway to Ayaya Bay.

Fisher donned his night-vision headset again and did a 360-degree scan. He saw neither lights nor shapes. They had the lake to themselves. A hundred yards off the bow he could see a low fog clinging to the water's surface. He looked left, caught Hansen's attention, and gestured for him to steer closer. When their gunwales were within a few feet of each other, Fisher whispered to Gillespie in the seat behind him, and she threw across the painter, which Noboru secured to the cleat.

The fog enveloped them.

WITH no points of reference except for occasional glimpses of the neighboring boat in the swirling fog, time seemed to slow. In Fisher's boat Gillespie had moved to the stern to help Valentina navigate; Hansen and Noboru had teamed up in the other. The steady hum of the electric motors had a lulling effect on Fisher. The days and weeks of being on the run, of infrequent and insufficient sleep, were catching up to him. He leaned over the side, scooped up a handful of icy water, and splashed his face.

He checked his OPSAT. *Five miles to go.*

AT two miles Fisher signaled to Valentina to cut the engine; Hansen heard this and did the same. They drifted ahead until the boats came to a halt and began gently rocking. For ten minutes they sat still, listening. They heard nothing but the lapping of water against the hulls. Fisher scanned with the night vision and saw nothing

At two-minute increments over the next half hour they repeated the process—engines off, glide to a stop, listen, scan—until Fisher's OPSAT told him they were at the mouth of Ayaya Bay. He ordered the motors lifted and the oars broken out.

They began paddling.

CONCENTRATING on even, silent strokes rather than speed, the last two miles to the beach took another hour. With an extra pair of hands, Fisher's boat pulled slightly ahead, and when his OPSAT's distance reading scrolled down to a hundred yards, he stopped paddling and untied the painter connecting the boats. On the slim chance there were guards posted, he didn't want to risk the johnboats bumping into each other. The gong of aluminum would travel clearly over the water.

He started sounding for the bottom with his oar. Sixty feet from shore, the tip plunged into mud. Fisher handed his oar back to Gillespie, then slipped over the side into the water. Hansen followed a moment later, and they began towing the boats until the water was only waist high. Noboru, Gillespie, and Valentina climbed out and helped drag the boats onto the sand.

Quickly and quietly, they unloaded their gear, ran a final weapons and equipment check, and donned their packs. Fisher checked his OPSAT. As they had been since early afternoon, the Ajax bots showed as a tight cluster two miles inland, sitting between them and Lake Frolikha. Again, Fisher found himself wondering where in the middle of thick, almost impassible Siberian forest did someone find a suitable spot for the auction. They would soon know.

He looked at each of the team members and got nods and thumbs-up signs in return.

In a staggered single file, they set off into the darkness.

WHAT none of them knew, and none of their maps showed, was that the area between Lake Frolikha and Ayaya Bay was part of the Great Baikal Trail. According to the sign they found higher up the beach, the non-profit, volunteer-driven project hoped to create a series on interconnected trails that circumnavigated the entire lake. Six years into the task, the trail was halfway done.

This again raised the issue of why this area had been chosen for the auction site. Admittedly the area was remote and the hiking season had not yet fully begun, but to go as far as holding the auction in Siberia only to place it astride the Great Baikal Trail . . . Something didn't add up. Even so, Fisher knew better than to overanalyze the gift. The trail would not only save them hours but also the effort of blazing their own path.

Taking fifteen-minute turns walking point, they made quick progress, covering a half mile in twenty minutes despite frequent stops to look and listen for signs of guards. By 3:00 A.M. they had closed to within a quarter mile of the Ajax signal. Fisher resumed point and led them forward until the trees began to thin and they found themselves at the edge of an oval-shaped meadow. In the moonlight stalks of brown grass and weeds jutted through the foot-thick blanket of snow. On the north side of the meadow sat a square, cinder-block hut with a rusted sheet-metal roof.

Fisher called Hansen up and whispered, "Take Gillespie and circle around to the east side of the meadow. Check for signs of foot traffic, sensors—anything out of place."

"Got it." Hansen collected Gillespie and they disappeared back down the trail. Noboru and Valentina moved up beside Fisher. He gestured to them to scan, and all three started panning their binoculars across the meadow. Twenty minutes passed, and then Hansen's voice came over Fisher's headset: "In position. No off-trail foot traffic, no sensors, no guards. There's something interesting at your eleven o'clock, though, in the center of the meadow."

"What is it?"

"I know what it looks like to me, but you better check for yourself."

Fisher adjusted his binoculars to the appropriate area and zoomed in. "Got it," he confirmed. He'd missed it the first time, but now the parallel ruts in the snow were unmistakable. Helicopter landing skids. "Our missing Sikorsky," he said.

"My thought as well. We're right on top of the touch-down coordinates."

The Ajax hadn't left the meadow. There was only one place they could be.

"Move back to the hut," Fisher told Hansen.

When both teams were in position, Fisher took a final look through the night-vision goggles, then whispered, "Move in."

In unison Hansen and Gillespie and Fisher and his two cohorts stepped from the trees and started toward the hut, their Grozas held low at the ready. As arranged, Hansen circled behind the hut, Fisher in front, where they joined up. A faded metal sign with red Cyrillic letters read METEOROLOGICAL STATION 29. The hut had only one entrance, a heavy steel door set into the cinder block; like the roof, it was pitted with rust. Fisher crept up to the door, then turned, signaled Hansen forward, and pointed at the door's padlock.

It was brand-new.

37

FISHER knelt down before the lock and realized it was more than brand-new. It was a Sargent & Greenleaf 833 military-grade padlock—six-pin Medeco biaxial core, anticutting and grinding ceramic inserts, liquid-nitrogen resistant.

"This must be one special meteorological station," Hansen whispered. "Can we pick the lock?"

"If we had a few hours, maybe. Semtex would do the trick, too, but we'd probably have company before the smoke cleared. Fisher stood up and backed away from the hut. "Not big enough," he said.

"What?"

"It's not big enough to hold the 738 Arsenal."

"Maybe we're wrong. Maybe it's not here."

Fisher shook his head. "Why did the Sikorsky land here? And why the lock? If the arsenal isn't here, then it's just Qaderi's laptop and phone sitting inside this hut."

"That may be, but we're not getting past that door."

"Let's find another one, then."

They retreated to the trees and crouched down in a circle. Fisher briefly explained what they were looking for, then assigned each of them a search area. "One hour. If we don't find anything, we regroup here."

FORTY minutes later, Valentina called, "Got something. Three-quarters of a mile north of the hut. Placing a marker on the OPSAT now."

They converged on her position: a narrow, six-foot-deep ravine bordered by scrub pines. Fisher whispered to her, "Where?"

"Dead ahead, about twenty yards. See that rock outcrop sticking up beside the stump?"

Fisher followed her outstretched arm with his eyes. It took him a moment to see it—a nearly perfect circle of melted snow around the outcrop. Fisher signaled for the group to wait, then donned the night-vision goggles and crept ahead. He was still six feet away from the outcrop when he felt the warm breeze. He continued forward, extended his hand, and stuck it into a niche in the rocks. His hand touched something metal.

* * *

IT took minutes of painstakingly quiet work to move the rocks away from the air vent. It was roughly the size of a manhole cover and consisted of steel crossbars. Fisher stuck his fingers through the gaps and felt around the edge. He found neither a locking mechanism nor alarm wires. He pointed to Noboru and together they squatted over the cover, gripped the bars, and lifted. It came free. They crab-walked it a few feet away and gently set it down. Fisher put his NV goggles back on and leaned into shaft. Beyond ten feet he saw nothing but darkness.

Gillespie already had her rope coil detached from her pack. Hand over hand, she lowered the end into the shaft. She stopped and reeled in the rope, counting turns on her arm as she went. She held up three fingers, then five fingers. *Thirty-five feet to the bottom.*

Fisher gave her the nod.

ONCE they had the rope tied off to the trunk and measured out thirty-five feet, plus another five for safety's sake, Gillespie severed the remainder and tied the rope to a Swiss seat rappelling harness. After a few adjustments, she secured herself in the seat, gave the group a nod and a smile, and lowered herself into the shaft.

A minute later her voice came over their headsets. "Down and clear."

Fisher went next, followed by Valentina, Noboru, and

then Hansen. Having already cleared the space with her night vision, Gillespie had set one of her LED flashlights upright on the concrete floor, casting a pale cone of light on the ceiling.

The room was ten feet long and roughly triangular, with the ceiling angling away from the overhead shaft to a half wall into which was set a doorway. Running down the middle of the floor was more vent grating. Warm air gusted past them and rushed out the shaft above. Somewhere below they could hear the faint pumping of machinery. Fisher turned on his headlamp and walked through the other door. He emerged thirty seconds later.

"It's a utility room. There's another door. I checked the circuit panel. Some of the lights are on somewhere."

"More signs of life," Hansen said.

"How big is this place?" Noboru wondered aloud.

Fisher replied, "Judging by the panel, damned big. There were a few hundred switches. A service tag read March of '62."

"Almost fifty years old," Valentina said. "Cold War era. What do you think—bunker, test facility?"

"Either or both. Let's pair up and do a little recon. Hansen and Gillespie; Noboru and Valentina. Stay sharp and stay in touch. Any trouble, we collapse back here."

"That leaves you on your own," Hansen observed.

Fisher smiled. It was strange to hear a fellow Splinter Cell talk about solo work as if it were an aberration. *Kids these days.* Then again, he reminded himself, there was something strange about working and living alone and considering that normal. He'd been under too long.

"I'll get by," he said.

ONCE through the utility-room door they found themselves in a wide, low-ceilinged corridor. On the concrete floor painted lines in fading green, red, and yellow led away in both directions. Stenciled on each line were what looked like three-letter Cyrillic acronyms. There were no lights. Everyone donned their night-vision headsets.

Fisher flipped a mental coin and pointed the others down the corridor to the left; he would take the right. With nods, the groups parted company and headed out.

FISHER hadn't gotten fifty feet before Hansen's voice came over his headset. "Sam, I've got something you'll want to see." He checked his OPSAT and saw the four of them were clustered together in the main corridor, fifty yards to the south. "On my way," he replied. When he got there, he found the group standing before the wall, shining their flashlights on a four-foot-square Plexiglas placard. It was a map of the facility.

The complex resembled a geometric cloverleaf. At its center was what looked like four concentric circles; Fisher leaned closer and read the faded label: RAMP TO LEVELS 2, 3, 4. Situated in each quadrant around the ramp were the clover's leaves, each one called a "zone"; each of these was divided into four "areas." Running between each zone was a corridor like the one in which they stood, and inside each zone smaller halls divided the four areas. *Squares within squares,* Fisher thought. The Soviet military had always been fond of geometry.

Gillespie stepped closer and read the Cyrillic labels beside each zone: MEDICAL, ELECTRONICS, WEAPONS, BALLISTICS. "It's a test facility. I assume ballistics means missiles and rockets."

Fisher nodded his agreement.

"This place is massive," Noboru said. "Take a look at the scale."

At the bottom of the map was a gradated line in alternating gray and black. Each unit indicated fifteen hundred meters, or five thousand feet. Using his index finger and thumb as calipers, Fisher measured the complex from end to end. "Twelve hundred meters," he announced.

"That can't be," Hansen said. "That'd make it a square mile."

Valentina replied, "Four levels. Four square miles."

Fisher did the mental math. "The east side of this place runs under Lake Frolikha." He tapped the placard. "Ballistics and electronics. If you were experimenting, you'd want access to water for cooling and fire suppression." He turned to the group. "We'll clear it as it's laid out, by zone and level, starting here and moving down. He assigned Hansen to the medical zone, Valentina to electronics, Gillespie to weapons, and Noboru to ballistics. "I'll loiter at the ramp area and play free safety. Questions?"

There was none.

"Lights off. Night vision on. Let's go."

AT the ramp they found a freestanding elevator shaft that presumably led to the hut they'd found in the meadow. Fisher took his post beside the ramp railing while the others split up and disappeared down the corridors leading to each zone. Fisher listened to their progress over his headset: *"At the entrance to the weapons zone . . . flexicam negative . . . entering zone. . . ."* One by one, over the next few minutes, they each reported *clear* or *no activity*. Hansen was the last to report in. "Sam, meet me in level one medical zone."

"On my way."

In the greenish white glow of his night vision, Fisher found his way to the correct corridor. Two hundred yards away he saw a figure crouched beside a door. Hansen raised his hand and Fisher walked to him.

"Some weird stuff inside," Hansen said.

"Describe weird."

"See for yourself. It's clear."

Fisher stepped through the door and found himself in yet another corridor, this one narrower. Fisher poked his head through the door of the first area. It was a laboratory: long black workbenches, sinks, rolling stools, and gray metal shelf units along the walls. Fisher clicked on his flashlight. In the narrow beam he could see that the shelves were full of glass jars of varying sizes. Some were empty, some filled with amber or yellow liquid, and some containing formless, organic-looking blobs.

Fisher moved on to the next area. It was a hospital ward. Dozens of steel-framed beds were bolted to the walls, each equipped with shackles at the head and foot. Rolling IV stands stood clustered in the far corner like stick-figure mannequins. The floor was covered with litter, towels, and skeins of gauze bandages. A bank of X-ray light boxes lined one wall like a row of dark windows.

Fisher moved on to the last two areas and found more of the same: laboratories and hospital wings. He returned to the main door and crouched down beside Hansen, who asked, "Human experimentation, you think?"

Fisher nodded. "There were a dozen or so gulags within a hundred miles of here. There'd always been rumors of prisoners disappearing and either never coming back or coming back . . . different."

"Christ Almighty."

"Did you get to the end?" Fisher asked, pointing down the corridor.

"Yeah. It's a ramp to the outside. It's been plugged with enough cement to make a Wal-Mart parking lot."

Fisher spoke into his headset: "Status report."

The rest of the team checked in with an all-clear. They regrouped at the ramp a few minutes later. Gillespie said, "Found an indoor target range—fun lockers, sandbag tables, a lot of pretty-good-sized chunks taken out of the concrete walls."

Valentina reported, "Standard electronics stuff: cabinets, testing benches, old capacitors, switches, wiring . . ." She looked at Noboru.

"Blackboards and drafting tables are all I found," he said. "What about you, Ben?"

Hansen explained what they'd found in the medical zone.

Gillespie muttered, "Okay, now I'm officially creeped out."

"Big shop of horrors," Valentina replied.

"Let's keep going."

AT staggered twenty-foot intervals they started down the ramp. It was wider than it had looked above, almost fifty feet from the wall to the guardrail—large enough, Fisher suspected, for the transport of heavy equipment, including rocket engines.

Forty vertical below level 1, the ramp opened into level 2.

Suddenly Fisher raised a closed fist. Behind him the others stopped and crouched down. Fisher pointed to his ear, then toward the railing overlooking the next level. He signaled to wait, then crept up to the rail and looked down. After a minute he returned to the group, gestured for them to follow, and led them a safe distance down the corridor.

"Two guards stationed at the entrance to the ramp below. Both armed with AK-47s. No night vision that I could see."

"Where there are two, there are more," Hansen said.

"Agreed. Let's check this level and regroup here."

Over the next half hour they each searched their assigned zones and found more of the same: experimental equipment and supplies. Noboru was the last to report in: "Sam, come down to ballistics."

"Coming. Everyone else regroup." He got three "rogers" in reply. As he had with Hansen, Fisher found Noboru standing outside the main entrance to the level 2 ballistics zone. Fisher stepped through. Instead of finding four areas divided by hallways, he found a man-made cavern. Measuring roughly two football fields in length and width, the area was filled with row upon row of engine-test scaffolding ranging in size from a VW Beetle to a commercial bus and each equipped with truck-sized tires. Fisher did a rough count and came up with thirty-six units. Four of them still held rocket motors.

"Check the far end," Noboru said.

Fisher got out his binoculars and zoomed in as best he could with the night-vision goggles. Near the east wall, more than an eighth of a mile away, were what looked like four garage-sized concrete sewer pipes lying on their sides and spaced evenly across the width of the space. The wall behind the pipes was charred.

"Blast funnels for rocket exhaust," Fisher guessed.

"Yeah, that's what I thought, too, but I'm not talking about that. See the dark lump between the second and third funnel?"

Fisher panned the binoculars and zoomed in. It took him a few moments to realize what he was seeing—a pyramidal stack of military-grade Anvil cases. "I'll be damned." Then, over the radio: "Everybody converge on ballistics."

38

THERE were twenty-eight cases ranging in size from footlocker to armoire. All were secured by the same Sargent & Greenleaf 833 padlock they'd found on the door to the hut.

"This isn't all of it, is it?" Gillespie asked.

"No. Unless Zahm's inventory was wrong, I'd say this is about a third."

"They're pretty well sealed," Valentina remarked, running her hand over one of the cases. "Sure the Ajax bots can get inside?"

"We're talking about a fraction of a hair's width," Fisher replied. "They'll get in. Everybody get behind me and back up." Once they were a safe distance from the cases, Fisher pulled Noboru's makeshift Ajax pistol from his pack and loaded a dart. He took aim on the ceiling above the Anvil cases and fired. The pistol emitted a barely audible *pfft*. The dart bounced off the ceiling, bounced off one of the cases, and rolled until the case's steel edge stopped it.

They stood in silence for a full minute. While Fisher hadn't expected fireworks, the dispersal of the Ajax bots was nonetheless anticlimactic.

Standing behind Fisher, Noboru stared at his OPSAT screen. "Nothing yet."

"Wait for it." Grim had said it could take up to five minutes for the Ajax bots to fully disperse and infiltrate.

"What if there's no power for them to gravitate to?" Hansen asked.

"Just about every weapon or system on the inventory list is equipped with some form of EPROM—erasable programmable read-only memory—a low-power battery for housekeeping functions like date, time, and user settings. And if it doesn't have an EPROM, it's not one of the higher-end items. If we lose it, no disaster."

Noboru said, "I've got action. Something's pinging in there. Another one . . . three more . . ." He looked up. "I'd say our first live-fire exercise is a success."

They gave the area one last quick search, then headed for the door. From inside one of the blast funnels Gillespie called, "Check this out." They walked through the funnel to where she was standing. "Watch your step," she said. "It's gotta be extra venting for the engines."

Fisher stepped forward and looked down. In the darkness they'd failed to see the gap between the funnels and the wall. It was hard to judge depth through the night-vision goggles, but he suspected the vent extended to the lowermost level.

BACK at the ramp, Fisher pulled Noboru and Valentina aside and whispered, "The guards are yours. Knives if you can manage it; PSS pistols as backup."

The both nodded.

Again Fisher led the staggered column down the ramp. At the halfway point he called a halt, gestured for Hansen and Gillespie to take up overwatch positions, and then gave Noboru and Valentina the nod. Grozas slung and secured, they continued down the ramp. Fisher crept to the railing to watch their progress. He slung his own Groza and drew his PSS and extended the barrel through the railing, making sure he had a clear line of fire on each guard.

As trained, Noboru and Valentina moved with exaggerated slowness, pausing between each heel-to-toe step until they were within ten feet of the guards. In unison, they stopped. Stepped forward. Stopped. When they were each within an arm's reach of their targets, they stood up, took a fluid step forward . . .

Hands clamped over mouths and knives came up. The guards slumped down, dead. Noboru and Valentina dragged the bodies back up the ramp to where Fisher was crouched. He nodded to Hansen and Gillespie, who came forward and took the bodies the rest of the way up the ramp. They were back five minutes later.

"Stashed them in medical," Hansen whispered to Fisher.

"Apt," Fisher replied.

THEY kept going, pausing only briefly at the next ramp's railing so Fisher could check the next level. He pointed to his eyes and his ears and shook his head, then gave the split-up signal. Over the next ten minutes Gillespie, Noboru, and Valentina checked in. Fisher ordered them back.

Noboru crouched down and said, "Found another stack of Anvil cases. They're tagged."

"How big?" Fisher asked.

"About the size of the first one."

"Two down. One to go." Fisher radioed Hansen: "Status report."

"Stand by." Two minutes passed, then: "Coming back."

When he rejoined the group, his face was red and flushed. "We've got company. Medical's been turned into a barracks. I counted a couple of dozen beds, all occupied."

"The attendees?" Noboru guessed.

Fisher nodded. "The hosts wouldn't be bunked with the guests."

"Maybe he's not here yet," Valentina offered.

"Maybe. We've got one more level to check. With any luck, we'll tag the last batch of cases and be back to Severobaikalsk for breakfast."

Behind them, a familiar voice broke the silence: "Not gonna happen, dickheads."

* * *

EVEN before Fisher turned around, the expressions on Valentina's and Gillespie's faces confirmed what his ears had told him: *Ames.*

Valentina muttered, "He's got a grenade."

"Armed?"

"Can't tell."

Fisher whispered, "Distance?"

"Sixty feet," replied Gillespie. "He's right on your six o'clock."

It was a long shot, especially off a quick heel turn, but not impossible. Still, having never used the Groza before, Fisher put his chances at only 70 percent.

Ames said, "Don't even think it. Don't even turn around. I go down, so does the grenade. No way you'll cover the distance in time."

Fisher noted that Ames's voice was still relatively soft. *He wants something.*

Gillespie said, "He's moving. Coming ahead . . . six o'clock . . . seven . . . eight. Forty feet. He's at the ramp railing. *Damn!*"

"What?"

"I can hear you whispering," Ames replied. "Turn around and you'll see what."

Slowly Fisher rotated on the ball of his foot, simultaneously raising the butt of the Groza closer to his shoulder. Hansen mirrored his movements. The entire group was now facing Ames. Gillespie and Valentina tried to crab-walk sideways to expand their fields of fire, but Ames stopped them. "Nope. Not another step."

Ames stood at the railing with his grenade hand extended over the ramp. He took a few steps closer, but his arm never wavered. If Fisher took the shot now, he wouldn't miss, but there would be no stopping the grenade. The explosion would bring everyone inside the complex down onto them.

"What do you want?" Fisher asked evenly.

"Just wanted to let you know you were right about me. I am a survivor. You figured your little gasoline trick sent me over the edge, didn't you?"

"How long did it take you to get out?" Fisher asked.

"An hour. Good thing I'm skinny. Some of those tunnels were tight. While you were hiding from the helicopter, I was flagging it down. It took a little talking, but I finally convinced them of who I was."

"And you waited for us."

"Right."

"Do they know we're here?"

"No. I wanted to make sure I saw it all happen. I told him you were still in Irkutsk."

"Him?" Fisher repeated. "Who?"

Ames smiled. "You've met him. In fact, he told me you had him in your hands and you let him go."

Fisher's mind flashed to the guards Noboru and Valentina had killed. The faces had looked familiar, but he'd dismissed it. He shouldn't have. He had seen them before.

In Portinho da Arrábida, at Charles "Chucky Zee" Zahm's villa.

39

AMES, having read Fisher's expression, was nodding. "Yep. That's him."

Hansen said, "Who?"

"Zahm," Fisher replied.

"You're kidding me."

Fisher shook his head.

It made a certain sense. Though he'd had no overt clues at the time, Fisher could now see his psychological assessment of Zahm made him an obvious candidate for the man behind the curtain. A born envelope pusher, he joins the SAS but finds the adrenaline rush of covert soldiering only temporarily satisfies his addiction, so he leaves and decides, on a whim, to become a bestselling novelist, but this, too, isn't enough. He rounds up some former comrades and goes into the business of high-end thievery only to find himself still restless, so he raises the bar. He breaks into a secret Chinese laboratory, steals five tons of weaponry, and invites the world's most dangerous terrorists to an auction at an abandoned Soviet complex in the middle of Siberia.

To the average person, insanity. To Zahm, just another day.

What Fisher didn't know, and might never know, was Zahm's purpose at the Korfovka rendezvous with Zhao and Murdoch. He'd probably been laying the groundwork for the Laboratory 738 heist and the auction.

"Where is he?" Fisher now asked.

"Around."

"You can still do the right thing," Hansen said.

"I could," Ames conceded.

He lifted his opposite hand in a fateful gesture. Even as Fisher's eyes instinctively flicked to the hand, he thought, *Distraction*.

"But I won't," Ames finished.

He dropped the grenade, turned, and sprinted up the ramp.

40

FISHER jerked the Groza to his shoulder and focused the crosshairs between Ames's shoulder blades, but he was gone an instant later, around the curve of the ramp.

"Down," Fisher commanded, and dropped flat. The others followed suit. Two seconds passed and then the *crump* of the grenade's explosion echoed up the ramp.

Hansen asked, "Up or down?"

"Down. We've gotta tag the last of the cases."

"Gonna be trapped."

"Bad luck for us," Fisher shot back. He turned to Noboru. "You have the ARWEN?"

"Yeah."

Fisher pointed down the corridor to the medical zone. "In about ten seconds they're going to come charging.

Don't wait until you see them. First sign of footsteps, you put two gas canisters downrange. Got it?"

"Yep."

To Valentina and Hansen, Fisher said, "You're with Noboru. Anybody comes through his gas cloud, put 'em down. They'll back off to regroup. When they do, leapfrog down the ramp and meet up with us. We'll try to hold the ramp intersection. You three split up and check the zones for the rest of the arsenal. Questions?"

There was none.

"Good luck."

You're with me," Fisher told Gillespie. They got up and sprinted to the down ramp. "Everything's a target," he shouted. "If it's alive, kill it. Two rounds, center mass, then move on."

"Got it."

THEY were halfway down the ramp when gunfire from below peppered the walls above their heads. They veered right, away from the railing, and kept going. Behind him Fisher heard a plastic *tink tink tink* and turned to see a fragmentation grenade rolling down the ramp toward them.

"Down!"

He spun on his heel, scooped the grenade with his free hand, and shovel tossed it over the railing.

"Grenade!" a British-accented voice called, followed by the explosion.

From the level above came the double *fwump* of Noboru firing the ARWEN. Voices shouted, then the overlapping chatter of Valentina and Hansen firing their Grozas.

Fisher called to Gillespie, "Keep moving," then plucked a flashbang off his harness and pulled the pin. She did the same. They rounded the corner, tossed the grenades, dropped to their knees until they heard the explosion, then got up and moved into the blinding light, guns up and tracking for targets. He kept Gillespie in the corner of his eye, instinctively closing or opening the distance between them to keep an overlapping field of fire.

"Clear," Fisher called.

"Clear," she replied.

Fisher heard Hansen's voice in his headset. "We're coming down. Four tangos down."

"Roger," Fisher replied

In unison, he and Gillespie turned right, checked the medical corridor for targets, then kept moving, following the curve of the railing. Fisher slowed their pace, taking slow, measured steps, controlling his breathing. He checked Gillespie; she was doing the same. They reached the head of the weapons zone corridor, paused, and saw nothing moving. Fisher turned to check their right flank and saw a figure charging at them from medical.

"Target!" he said, and squeezed off two rounds. The figure went down. "Moving." Groza still at his shoulder, he paced forward. Gillespie followed, turning in a half circle as she covered their flanks and rear. Fisher reached the corner at the corridor, paused, peeked around. A muzzle flashed in the darkness.

"Fire at the bottom of the ramp," Fisher advised Hansen.

"Roger. Coming down now."

Fisher saw the three of them appear down the ramp. He gave them a nod, then stuck the Groza around the corner and fired two shots down the corridor. Hansen, Noboru, and Valentina rushed forward and pressed against the opposite wall. Noboru dropped to one knee and aimed the ARWEN back up the ramp.

"How many?" Hansen asked Fisher.

"One that we know of."

"We'll take care of him."

Fisher nodded, and he and Gillespie backed away and kept circling around the ramp until they reached ballistics.

"Target!" Gillespie called. Fisher turned with her. They fired together. The figure went down.

"Are these Zahm's?" she asked.

Fisher nodded. "Unless he expanded his crew, he's only got three left."

From medical rose a double pop from a Groza. Valentina called over her radio, "Target down."

Fisher replied, "Hansen, you and Valentina clear medical."

"Roger."

"Noboru, can you hold the ramp?"

"Bet your ass."

From down the corridor to ballistics they heard a shout. Fisher stopped and crouched down. Gillespie did the same. "That's Ames," she said.

"You're sure?"

"Yeah."

Fisher radioed to Hansen, "Moving to ballistics."

HE and Gillespie headed out. A hundred yards down the corridor they heard Ames's voice again: "Shouldn't have left it sitting here alone, Chucky."

"Ah, bloody hell, you little weasel! Come down here so I can put a bullet in your brain."

"Can't do that, Chucky—"

"Don't call me Chucky!"

Fisher and Gillespie kept going until they were within sight of the main door. Pressed against the near wall, with Gillespie behind him, Fisher slid ahead until he could see inside. Like the ballistics zones above, this one was wide open, measuring several football fields in length, and filled with engine test stands and workbenches.

Fisher peeked through the door, then pulled back and said to Gillespie, "Zahm's at the far end of the room with his last two men. They're standing at the mouth of the middle blast funnel. Right inside the door there's a double row of workbenches running down the right-hand wall. Keep your eyes sharp for Ames. He's hiding somewhere. Ready?"

She nodded.

Fisher eased back to the door, lifted the Groza, and braced the barrel against the jamb. He nodded. Hunched over, Gillespie stepped around him and crept to the nearest bench. She took up a covering position, and he trotted forward to join her.

Zahm yelled, "Give it up, Ames. You ain't going to get 'em open."

"Don't want to!" Ames shouted back.

Gillespie whispered, "What's he doing?"

Fisher shook his head. "Don't know."

Hansen said over the headset, "Medical clear."

"Move on to weapons."

"Roger."

"Noboru?"

"All okay. I can hear them moving around up there but no action. I think they're trying to call the elevator. Should I—"

"No, leave them. We've got Zahm and we've got the arsenal. Not exactly the original plan, but it'll do. Hansen, once you're done clearing weapons and electronics, backtrack to Noboru and hold. As soon as we wrap up Zahm, we'll be there."

"Roger. And Ames?"

"He's dumb enough to have stayed. We'll take him, too."

LEAPFROGGING, Fisher and Gillespie made their way down the row of benches until they were within a hundred yards of Zahm and his two men. Fisher gestured for Gillespie to take the man on the left. She nodded and set up for the shot. Fisher fired first. His target went down. Zahm spun that way, then heard the second man collapse and turned back.

"Hi, Chuck," Fisher called.

Zahm turned around. He was holding a 9mm semiautomatic in his right hand.

"Lose it," Fisher ordered.

Zahm dropped the gun. "Fisher!" he called back with a wide grin.

"You just couldn't sit still, could you?" Fisher replied. "Couldn't have stayed in Portugal, enjoyed your villa and your mojitos and your boat."

"Boring. Too damned boring."

"Then you're going to hate prison," Fisher called.

"You can put me in, but you can't keep me there."

From somewhere in the space, Ames yelled, "You're both wrong!"

Fisher looked at Gillespie. "He's not in here."

"What?"

"The echo's wrong. He's above us—ballistics, second level. He's yelling down the exhaust shaft."

And then Fisher realized what was happening. He keyed the radio, "Ben, say position."

"Electronics. Just finishing."

"Move now, back to the ramp. You, Valentina, and Noboru get topside as fast as you can."

"What's going on?"

"Do it. Blast your way through whoever's up there, but don't slow down."

"Roger."

Gillespie asked Fisher, "What's—"

Ames shouted again: "Okay, Chucky, here it comes. . . ."

Fisher told her, "We're leaving. Move!"

From the far end of the space they heard a crash. They turned back to see an Anvil case bounce off the middle exhaust funnel and slam into the wall behind it.

Zahm spun around and stared at the case. "Son of a bitch! Ames, I'm gonna—"

A second case fell, this one the size of a closet. It struck the floor upside down and split open. Fisher saw a couple of dozen cylindrical objects skitter across the floor. Another case fell, then another, and then they were raining down the exhaust vent until the mound was taller than the funnels. Over the din, Zahm was shouting unintelligible curses. He stopped suddenly and stared at the debris.

Ames called, "Missed one. Here it comes."

A brick-sized white object dropped down the vent and disappeared into the pile.

"Ah, bloody hell!" Zahm called.

Gillespie said, "What?"

"Semtex," Fisher replied. "Run."

THEY were sixty feet from the door when the charge went off. A split second later a grenade detonated, then another, then rose a thunderous *whoop*.

Fisher felt a wave slam into his back. The air was sucked from his lungs. He tumbled end over end and slammed into a wall. He rolled over and looked around.

"Kimberly!"

He heard a groan near the door. She lay on her back, with her torso in the corridor and her legs lying across the threshold. Fisher pushed himself to his knees and stumbled toward her. He looked left. The back wall of the space was gone, along with the concrete blast funnels. Water gushed through the hole and surged across the floor toward them. Fisher reached Gillespie, grabbed her by the collar, and ran, dragging her out the door and down the corridor.

Hansen was on the radio. "What the hell was that?"

"Level four is blasted open," Fisher replied. "The lake's coming in. Where are you?"

"Near the top of the first-level ramp. There are about a dozen bad guys here. They're putting up a fight. The rest went up in the elevator."

"Hold on, we're coming. Gillespie's hurt. Can you spare Valentina?"

"She's on her way."

Fisher was halfway down the corridor. The ramp intersection was in sight. He glanced over his shoulder and saw debris and litter swirling through the ballistics door as if blown by a giant fan. The first of the water boiled through at knee height, but within seconds it rose over the top of the jamb and began climbing toward the ceiling.

He heard Gillespie mutter, "God Almighty . . ."

He looked down at her. Her eyes were open and she was blinking rapidly.

"Can you walk?" Fisher asked.

"The hell with that! I can *run!*" she shouted.

He released her collar. She rolled over, scrambled to her feet, grabbed Fisher's outstretched hand, and together they sprinted to the ramp, around the railing, and started up the incline. Behind them, the wave surged into the intersection, crashed over the railing, and slammed into their legs, shoving them sideways. Fisher went down. His nose shattered on the concrete. His vision swirled. He tasted blood. He spit, pushed himself to his knees. Ahead of him, Gillespie had stopped on the ramp. She saw him fall and turned back.

"No! I'm okay. . . . I'm up!" he shouted. "Keep going!"

Valentina came sprinting down the ramp, and Fisher shouted, "Take her!" and together she and Gillespie turned and kept going. Fisher gathered his feet under him, then slipped and skidded back down the ramp. The water crashed over his head, enveloping him. The world went muffled. Then he was sliding again. In the froth he glimpsed a straight line . . . a piece of steel. *The railing!* He slapped at it with his hand and missed. Tried again and, this time, managed to hold on. He reached up with his opposite hand, grabbed the next railing, and heaved. His head broke into the air. Behind him, the fourth level was gone, flooded up to the ceiling.

"Sam!"

Fisher looked up. Noboru was leaning over the railing with his hand extended and Hansen holding on to his legs. "Grab on!"

Fisher put his foot on the railing. It slipped off. Pain shot up his leg. He gasped. *Something wrong with my left foot,* he thought. *Broken.* He tried again, this time using his knee, and managed to climb halfway from the water.

With both arms braced on the railing, Fisher lifted his right leg from the water, pressed it against the top rail. Noboru's hand was eighteen inches away. Fisher took a breath, coiled his leg beneath him, and pushed off. His palm touched Noboru's; then he was falling again. He curled his fingertips into claws. Noboru did the same. Fisher jerked to a stop. Noboru's other hand was waving before his eyes. Fisher latched onto it with his free hand. Hansen began hauling them upward.

Together, they sprawled backward onto the ramp. They'd gained only a temporary advantage, he saw: The water was already rising around the curve.

"You okay?" Hansen asked, helping Fisher to his feet. "You're bleeding."

"I'm fine. Let's go."

Hansen and Noboru charged up the ramp and around the next turn. Fisher hobbled after them. "Sam?" Hansen called.

"Keep going!"

Hansen reappeared on the ramp. "Your foot."

"Fell asleep."

The water lapped over his ankles. Fisher stopped and looked down. His toes were almost pointing backward. The pain thundered in his head. He squeezed his eyes shut, then forced them open again.

Hansen started back down toward him.

"Ben."

The tone of Fisher's voice stopped Hansen in his tracks. "I can help you, Sam."

"Get everybody topside. I'm right behind you."

"Your foot's broken."

"I'm not going to argue with you. Go now, or the next time I see you I'm going to shoot you."

Hansen held his gaze for a few moments, then nodded, turned around, and disappeared.

THE water was shockingly cold. Fisher stood perfectly still, letting it surge over his calves, then his knees. The throbbing in his ankle tapered off. From the level above came the sound of Grozas firing. It went on for fifteen more seconds; then there was silence.

Fisher radioed: "Ben, where are you?"

"First level. Bad guys are either gone or dead. Elevator's out of commission. We're heading back the way we came in."

"Good."

"As soon as everyone's out, I'll—"

"No need. I'm coming up on the first-level ramp," Fisher lied. "I'm a minute behind you. Leave the rope for me."

Silence.

Fisher hobbled forward a few feet until the water level retreated to his knees

"Leave the rope for me," Fisher repeated.

"Roger."

He felt a wave of relief. Hansen and the others would make it. Knowing that, he steeled himself for what he had to do. He had no intention of standing on this ramp and waiting for the water to overtake him.

He took a deep breath, then a step forward. Pain burst behind his eyes. Another breath, another step forward. Each one got easier until he was clear of the water and twenty feet from the top of the ramp. He paused and patted his sides, looking for his Groza. It was gone. At the top of the ramp he saw a discarded AK-47. He fixed his eyes on it and kept going. *Ten feet . . . five feet . . .*

Pause. Breathe. Go.

Behind him the water had gained some ground, now lapping at his heels.

Five feet . . . He stopped, leaned down, and snagged the AK's sling with his fingertip and lifted it up. As a cane it was too short, but it took a portion of the weight off his ankle. He walked into the next level's intersection.

One more to go.

Hansen's voice: "We're out, Sam. Where are you?"

"Almost there."

Fisher pulled off his headset and tossed it away and kept walking.

The last ramp seemed to take hours. Hundreds of steps, but Fisher knew it couldn't have been more than minutes. The water dogged him, surging and retreating as it filled the level behind him, then finally rolling over his legs and staying there.

He reached the top of the ramp. Level 1. He took another minibreak, then turned right and started down across the intersection toward the utility-room corridor. He was twenty feet away when the floor trembled, then heaved upward. A crack shot threw the floor, splitting the corridor down the middle. Fisher started backpedaling.

A geyser of water burst from the floor, and the concrete began falling away into the chasm.

Fisher turned around, looked around. Directly ahead of him lay the elevator. *Out of service,* he thought numbly. He turned back. The utility corridor was gone; in its place a ravine filled with white water. It boiled up the walls and started rushing into the intersection.

No choice, Sam.

He started hobbling toward the elevator. He heard the wall of water approaching and could feel on his back the rush of cool air being pushed ahead of the surge, but he ignored it and kept his eyes fixed on the elevator.

He was ten feet from the door when the wave slammed into him.

— EPILOGUE —

HE felt a vague pang of guilt for not being excited at the prospect of having company, but he consoled himself with the knowledge that if he told them the truth, they would probably understand and even forgive him for it. They were friends, certainly, but not in the pure sense of the word. Of course, that predicament wasn't uncommon in a business where friendships were usually forged in the fire of hardship and tragedy. It was a strong, almost instantaneous bond, one that most people rarely took time to examine. The proverbial elephant in every room. He was cynical, that much he could admit, but whether that was his permanent mind-set or simply a bad habit that would fade with time, he didn't know. He would find out.

Fisher stepped away from the sunlit floor-to-ceiling windows and walked to his nearby leather armchair. He propped the cane against the arm and took a test lap around the room. The limp was almost gone and would eventually disappear altogether. Thanks to pins and screws and plates, the bones in his ankle were almost as good as new. His only reminder of the injury would be an uncanny knack for predicting rain. Given the alternatives, he considered it a fair trade.

The wave that had slammed into his back drove him headfirst into the side of the elevator-shaft wall, momentarily stunning him. When he opened his eyes, a second or half second later, he saw the partially open elevator doors sweeping past him. Acting on instinct, he shoved his arm into the gap, then made a fist and did a bicep curl until his shoulder was wedged between the doors. Having had no time to take a breath before the wave hit, Fisher found himself under five feet of water without an ounce of air in his lungs. He squirmed deeper into the elevator, his one good leg crabbing at the floor until he popped through the gap and he was able to stand. The water boiled at his chin. He looked up. His headlamp illuminated the ceiling escape hatch. He reached up. It was just out of reach, so he steadied himself, breathing deeply, oxygenating his blood as the water rose over his mouth, his nose, his eyes, and then he was submerged.

His headlamp flickered and went dark.

His fingertips touched the escape hatch, then his palms. He drew his knife and stabbed around the edge of the hatch, hacking away at the thin metal until it fell away and disappeared in the swirling water. He stuck both arms through the hatch, braced his elbows on the roof, and levered himself up and out. Water bubbled up behind him and began flowing over the elevator car's roof.

He tested the cable: It was thick with grease and grit. Half-a-decade old or not, the lubricant made the cable unclimbable. He looked around for a maintenance ladder. There wasn't one. Fisher knew what this meant: a ride up the shaft like a piece of flotsam. The trip took only a few minutes, but in the narrow confines of the shaft the water roiled and whooshed as air from the complex below sought escape through one of the few exits left.

When he drew level with the door, he found it closed, but ten seconds of levering with his knife opened a gap wide enough for him to squeeze both hands through; another twenty seconds and he was lying on the concrete floor of the hut. Water gushed after him and sloshed across the floor.

Bad to worse, Fisher thought. The hut was made of cinder block, the door of thick steel secured by a virtually indestructible lock. Fisher looked around. The inside was barren, just a floor, four walls, and a roof. Fisher caught himself. Not just walls—five-decade-old walls. He didn't need to find an exit; he needed to let the water make him an exit.

As the water rose past his ankles and then his knees, he hobbled from wall to wall, using the tip of his knife to test the grout between the cinder blocks. It wasn't until the water had reached his waist that he found the spot he wanted. He began chiseling at it, concentrating the knife's point on a quarter-sized spot. He stopped, stuck his finger into the hole. *Halfway there*. He jammed the knife back into the hole and hammered at it with his fist until his skin split and blood ran down his forearm. He switched hands and kept pounding.

The tip punched through. He pressed his eye to the hole. He saw bright sun.

The water reached his shoulders.

He thrust the knife back into the hole and began levering the haft in a circle, grinding away at the grout. A thumb-sized chunk of cinder block popped free, then another, and another. And then, with a sucking sound, the water found the hole and surged through. The water lapped at his chin and into his mouth. He sputtered and kept chopping at the block. The fifty-year-old grout began disintegrating. Horizontal and vertical gaps appeared, revealing daylight. The water level dropped an inch, then bubbled up again.

Fisher clamped the knife between his teeth, shoved both hands into the hole, and, using them as leverage, rammed his knee into the wall. Then again, and again, until his leg was numb.

A whole cinder block broke free and tumbled out. Fisher adjusted his aim and drove his knee into the neighboring block until it shifted sideways and slid halfway out. He drew his knee back, set his jaw, and—

A three-by-three section of the wall gave way and Fisher tumbled out onto the snow-covered ground and lay still. Hansen found him ten minutes later. Not content to sit on his hands at the entrance vent and wait for something that might never come, he'd left Gillespie to stand watch and taken the other team members on a perimeter search. Their first stop had been the hut.

FISHER watched the car pull down the driveway and stop beside the flagstone path leading to the front door. Fisher got there before either of them could ring the bell. Having left Washington two weeks after returning from Russia, Fisher had seen neither Hansen nor Grimsdóttir for three months. He'd stayed around only long enough to recover from the surgery on his ankle and sit through three days of debriefing.

Fisher invited them in. "Mojito?" he asked.

"Sure," said Grimsdóttir, and Hansen nodded.

"Head down to the deck. I'll meet you there."

Ten minutes later they were sitting beneath an umbrella overlooking the water. Hansen took a sip of his mojito and smiled. "It's good."

"They've grown on me," Fisher said.

"So this is it," Grimsdóttir asked, "the villa of the late, great Chucky Zee?"

Fisher nodded. "Thanks for that, by the way."

Through her contacts at Britain's Secret Intelligence Service, Grimsdóttir had enlightened the Serious Organised Crime Agency, or SOCA, about Zahm's nonliterary endeavors. From there Zahm's now-defunct criminal empire unraveled. Surprisingly, most of the jewelry and art and gems Zahm and his Little Red Robbers had stolen had never been fenced. SOCA found the bulk of the loot in a storage unit outside Setúbal. At her encouragement, the British Home Office had given Fisher a free, one-year lease on Zahm's villa.

"The least I could do," Grimsdóttir said. "I see they took his yacht, though."

Fisher smiled. "A few days after I got here some very polite gentlemen from the Home Office came and asked for the keys. It's okay. I've had enough of water for a while. Besides, if I change my mind, I've still got the rowboats."

"How's the ankle?"

"Getting there. How's Kovac?"

Two hours after his arrest for treason, Kovac had tried to hang himself in his cell but was saved by an alert guard. As it turned out, Ames's insurance cache had been more than enough to break the deputy director.

"Pliable," Grimsdóttir replied. "Officially, he retired after discovering he had colorectal cancer. Unofficially, he spends in his days in an FBI safe house answering questions and naming names."

"Is it going to do any good?"

Hansen answered, "Eventually. Lambert was right. This goes very deep. The good news is, the Laboratory 738 Arsenal is sitting at the bottom of a sinkhole near Lake Baikal. It's out of circulation. Permanently. Turns out Zahm leased the complex from one of the men I saw in Korfovka—Mikhail Bratus, former GRU. As for the other two, Yuan Zhao and Michael Murdoch, we're working on it. The auction guests didn't fare very well. Only six made it out of the complex, and all of them were scooped up by the FSB."

"Ernsdorff?"

"About a week after Baikal he disappeared, and he took a few hundred million in investors' money with him. Ten days ago they found in him a St. John hotel with his throat cut. Someone didn't appreciate his accounting methods."

"What about our old friend Ames?"

"No sign of him. If he's dead, somewhere in the sinkhole, we'll never know."

"And if he's alive?" Fisher finished. "He's not the kind of guy to hide forever. You and the others watch your backs."

"You, too."

"How are they, by the way—Nathan, Maya, and Kimberly?"

"All good. They send their regards."

They sat in silence for a few minutes, watching the ocean, before Grimsdóttir said, "Sam, if you want to come back, I can arrange it."

Fisher shook his head.

"Is that a no?"

Fisher looked around the deck for a few moments, then turned his face into the sun and took a deep breath. "That's an 'ask me again when my lease is up.' "

Turn the page for a sneak peek at
the other side of the story . . .
Coming December 2009!

TOM CLANCY'S SPLINTER CELL ENDGAME

Follow Ben Hansen's team in their
desperate race to corner Sam Fisher.

— PROLOGUE ——————

THE first blow loosened one of Ben Hansen's molars and sent his head wrenching to one side.

Captured . . . killed . . .

He never saw the second blow, only felt Rugar's pointed knuckles drive into his left eye.

Captured . . . killed . . .

Hansen's head whipped back, then lolled forward as warm blood spilled down his chin.

Now Rugar's screams grew incomprehensible, like panes of glass shattering across the hangar's concrete floor.

Make no mistake. If you're captured, you will be killed.

Hansen tugged at the plastic flex-cuffs cutting into his wrists and binding him to the chair. He finally mustered the energy to face Rugar, who loomed there, a neckless, four-hundred-pound, vodka-soaked beast crowned by an old Red Army *ushanka* two sizes too small for his broad head. He was about fifty, twice Hansen's age, and hardly agile, but at the moment that hardly mattered.

The fat man opened his mouth, exposing a jagged fence of yellowed teeth. He shouted again, and more glass shattered, accompanied by the rattling of two enormous steel doors that had been rolled shut against the wind.

Hansen shivered. It was below freezing now, and their breaths hung heavy in the air. At least the dizziness from the anesthetic was beginning to wear off. He tried to blink, but his left eye did not respond; it was swelling shut.

And then—a flash from Rugar's hand.

Captured . . . killed . . .

The fat man had confiscated Hansen's knife.

BUT this wasn't just any knife—it was a Fairbairn Sykes World War II–era commando dagger that had once belonged to the elusive Sam Fisher, a Splinter Cell few people knew but whose exploits were legendary among them.

Rugar leaned over and held the blade before Hansen's face. He spoke more slowly, and the words, though still Russian, finally made sense: "We know why you've come. Now, if you tell me what I need to know, you will live."

Hansen took a deep breath. "You won't break me."

For a moment Rugar just stood there, his cheeks swelling like melons as he labored for his next breath. Suddenly he smiled, his rank breath coming hard in Hansen's face. "It's going to be a long night for both of us."

Rugar's left ear was pierced, and the gold hoop hanging there caught the overhead lights at such an angle that for a moment all Hansen noticed were those flashes of gold. He realized only after the blood spattered onto his face that Rugar had been shot in the head, the round coming from a suppressed weapon somewhere behind them.

All four hundred pounds of the fat man collapsed onto Hansen, snapping off the chair's back legs as the knife went skittering across the floor. Hansen now bore the Russian's full weight across his chest, and he wasn't sure which would kill him first: suffocation or the sickly sweet stench emanating from Rugar's armpits.

With a groan, he shoved himself against the fat man's body and began worming his way out, gasping, grimacing, and a heartbeat away from retching.

He rolled onto his side and squinted across the hangar, toward the pair of helicopters and the shadows along the perimeter wall and mechanics' stations.

And then he appeared, Sergei Luchenko, Hansen's runner. The gaunt-faced man was still wearing his long coat and gripping his pistol with a large suppressor. An unlit cigarette dangled from his thin lips.

Hansen sighed deeply. "What happened? Why didn't you answer my calls?" He groaned over the question. "Strike that. I'm just glad you're here."

Sergei walked up to Hansen, withdrew a lighter from his breast pocket, and lit his cigarette.

"How about some help?" Hansen struggled against the flex-cuffs.

"I'm sorry, my friend. They sent me to kill you."

"Bad joke."

"It's no joke."

Hansen stiffened. "Not you, Sergei."

"I don't have a choice."

Hansen closed his good eye, then spoke through his teeth. "Then why did you save me?"

"I didn't. The kill must be mine. And . . . I didn't want you to suffer."

"This is not who you are."

"I'm sorry." Sergei withdrew a compact digital video camera from his pocket and hit the RECORD button. He held it close to Hansen. "You see, he is alive. And now . . ." Sergei raised his pistol.

Hansen cursed at the man.

There would be no life story flashing before Hansen's eyes; no images of his youth growing up in Fort Stockton, Texas; no scenes from his days at MIT, which he had attended on a full scholarship; no moments from that bar with the director, Anna "Grim" Grimsdóttir, who had recruited him out of the CIA to join Third Echelon and become one of the world's most effective field operatives—a Splinter Cell. No, there would be nothing as dramatic or cinematic as that—just a hot piece of lead piercing his forehead, fracturing his skull, and burying itself deep in his brain before he had a chance to think about it.

The gun thumped. Hansen flinched.

And then . . . Sergei collapsed sideways onto the concrete, a gaping hole now revealed in the back of his head.

Hansen swore again, this time in relief. He squinted

into the shadows at the far end of the hangar. "Uh, thank you?"

No reply.

He raised his voice. "Who are you?"

Again, just the wind . . .

He lay there a few seconds more, just breathing, waiting for his savior to show himself.

One last time. "Who are you?"

Hansen's voice trailed off into the howling wind and creaking hangar doors. He lay there for another two minutes.

No one came.

Tensing, he wriggled on his side, drawing closer to his knife, which was lying just a meter away. He reached the blade, turned it over in his hand, and began to slowly, painfully, saw into the flex-cuffs.

When he was free, he stood and collected himself, his face still swelling, the hangar dipping as though floating on rough seas. And then, blinking his good eye to clarity, he lifted his gaze to the rafters, the crossbeams, the pipes, and still . . . nothing. He turned back to the bodies and shook his head in pity at Sergei. Then he glowered at the fat man, who even in death would get the last laugh, since disposing of his body would be like manhandling a dead Russian circus bear.

There was still a lot of work to do, but all the while Hansen couldn't help but feel the heat of someone's gaze on his shoulders.

He shouted again, "Who are you?"

Only his echo answered.

— 1 —

MAYA Valentina saw it in the man's gaze, which flicked down from her low-cut blouse to her well-tanned legs to her feet jammed into a pair of stilettos. She tossed back her hair, which fell in golden waves across her shoulders, then put an index finger to her lips, as though to nervously bite her nail. Oh, yes, he liked the shy schoolgirl routine, and Valentina could pass for a freshman, too, though she was nearly twenty-eight.

"Hi, there. You must be Ms. Haspel," he said, drawing in his sagging gut and probably wishing his thinning hair were two shades darker.

She reached across the desk and accepted his hairy paw. "It's nice to meet you, Mr. Leonard, and thanks for the interview."

"Well, as I said, we only have one position to fill, so the competition is fierce. Please have a seat."

She settled down and leaned toward his desk, keeping her blue eyes locked on his. "Can I ask a question before we start?"

"By all means."

"Does the company have a sexual-harassment policy?"

His lip twitched. "Of course."

"Well, I've had some problems in the past."

"I'm sorry to hear that."

"Yeah, the one guy was married and claimed I was a stalker, which was totally not the case. The other guy kept saying I was making lewd remarks, and he even said I flashed my panties, and there's no way I did that."

He hesitated. "Are you serious?"

"Yes. I like to get dressed up for work. It doesn't mean I want to have sex with everyone I see."

He cleared his throat. "Of course not. But you should know that we have a dress code. Business casual."

Valentina nodded and gazed salaciously at him. "Is what I'm wearing okay?"

He swallowed before answering.

HANSEN was sitting in an SUV parked outside the four-story office building. The complex was comprised of ten equally nondescript buildings that were headquarters for a lengthy list of companies that were, according to an intel report, "assembling stacked layers of silver and nonconducting magnesium fluoride and cutting out nanoscale-sized fishnet patterns to form metamaterials."

Grim had explained that metamaterials held the key to developing cloaking devices to render objects invisible to humans. Leonard's company in particular was developing paint for military vehicles and fabric for military uniforms. This was all quite serious business, which was why Hansen could only shake his head as he listened to Maya and Leonard. What the hell was she doing? All she had to do was get hired.

Admittedly, she'd hated the tired old plan of playing dress up to ensure Leonard took the bait, so overplaying the role was her way of protesting. She wouldn't just be the attractive new hire; she was now the quirky sex addict who'd called way too much attention to herself. Hansen was a breath away from reporting her misconduct to Grim, but then he thought better of it and just sat there as Maya told Leonard she was always available for overtime and "after-hours" work. Hansen grimaced.

AT 10:05 A.M. Nathan Noboru parked his utility van at the curb outside William Leonard's seven-thousand-square-foot home. Sprawling front lawns, well-manicured grounds, and tree-lined brick-paved driveways unfurled to a grand entrance shadowed by twenty-foot columns painted in a glossy antique white. This part of southwest Houston was called Sugar Land, and it was sweet indeed: Multimillion-dollar homes were nestled among well-tended golf course greens and tranquil lakes. The senior citizen manning the neighborhood guardhouse had taken a perfunctory glance at Noboru's forged work orders and immediately waved him through.

With a sigh, Noboru grabbed his utility belt and started up the driveway. But then he slowed, furtively glanced around, and scratched his crew cut. He gazed out past the lawn toward the neighboring home, another mansion where an old man in a pink shirt and oversized sunglasses stood near his Mercedes, preparing to load a golf bag into his trunk.

Off to Noboru's left lay another spectacular three-story château with a tremendous brick facade and five-car garage. Noboru studied the windows, trying to spot the lens of a telescopic camera or other such observation device. Nothing. He continued on, but something wasn't right.

Or was it just his paranoia? Again. They weren't after him anymore. He had a new life now. He needed to believe that.

Noboru shifted up to the front door, made a call, heard the phone ring inside the house, and then he tapped a series of numbers into his phone and heard the rapid ringtone of the alarm being disarmed. He withdrew his double-sided lock-pick set and got to work. Three, two, one: The door opened—

And if the explosions hadn't started in the back of the mansion, he would've already been dead.

Twin thunderclaps resounded, and the ground literally shook beneath his feet as the door slammed back toward him, knocking him to the ground.

He rolled over, shot to his feet, and sprinted down the driveway. He might as well have been back in Kaohsiung City, chased through the crowded streets by Horatio and Gothwhiler, the night air humid, the sweat pouring down his face. Several more explosions ripped through the house, and he stole a look over his shoulder as huge windows burst outward, sending showers of glass to the driveway while flames shot through the holes and wagged like dragons' tongues.

He reached the van and whirled around. Clouds of black smoke backlit by more roaring flames now devoured the entire mansion, while fiery debris floated down like confetti and got trapped in the thick canopy of leaves and limbs.

The old man who'd been loading his golf clubs was now backing out of his driveway. He stopped, climbed out of his car, and hurried over while dialing a number on his phone.

Noboru's mouth fell open. This was supposed to be a pathetically simple entry to place electronic eyes and ears. In fact, he'd balked over how rudimentary the whole operation was (he was entering through the front door!) and had loathed the fact that Director Grimsdóttir was wasting his talents on such a menial task. He had only been employed by Third Echelon for less than a year, but didn't his four years with Japan's Special Operations Group, their own Delta Force, count for anything?

Apparently not . . . but what was going on now?

Were Horatio and Gothwhiler tailing him? Did they know he'd be here? Were they trying to finish the job?

If the others learned about them, about Noboru's *real* past, he would never be trusted. Grimsdóttir had promised him a new identity, a new life, and utter secrecy.

A voice crackled in the nickel-sized subdermal embedded in the skin behind his ear; it was the Grim Reaper herself. "Nathan, I'm looking at the satellite feed—"

"I know! I know!" Noboru ran back to the van and yanked open the door. "Ma'am, you'd better call Hansen!"

VALENTINA was about to stand and thank Leonard for the interview when the man's BlackBerry rang.

"Please, let me take this, but wait," he said. "I want to introduce you to the rest of my staff."

"All right."

He shifted away from the desk and headed toward the window.

Suddenly, Hansen's voice came through her subdermal. "Maya, get out of there. Now!"

Even as she gasped, Leonard cried, "What? Oh, my God!" into his phone.

"I'm sorry, Mr. Leonard. I need to go."

And with that she started for the door, which suddenly took a bullet, the wood splintering as she ducked and craned her neck to see two more rounds punch through the office window, the first striking Leonard in the chest, the second in the shoulder. Blood sprayed across the back wall as Valentina dropped to her hands and knees, drew her SC pistol from her purse, and crawled toward the door.

She chanced a look back at Leonard, lying there, bleeding, reaching out to her, his mouth working, a word barely forming: "Please . . ."

ALLEN Ames was on the building's roof when the shooting began. He'd been up there only as an observer, gathering intel on the comings and goings of visitors to the building and hoping to get some up-close-and-personal pics of at least two of Mr. Leonard's "special" friends from Beijing.

Ames felt at home on rooftops. He'd grown up in Brooklyn and had spent years atop apartment buildings, hanging out with his friends, getting drunk, and dreaming of a better life that would help him forget about the fire . . . about the screams from Mom and Dad, about Katy's face at the window, looking at him, coughing . . . until she fell backward into the flames.

Now, twenty years after that fateful night, Ames was staring down through the telescopic sight of his sniper rife. The shooter had set up on the roof of a building across the street from Leonard's and had only revealed himself to take the shots. He'd been in Ames's sight for all of two heartbeats before he'd vanished behind the air-conditioning units. Ames had been on the roof since sunrise, and he'd neither seen nor heard the shooter's approach, so the man might have been there even longer and had obviously cloaked his heat signature.

Ames cursed, slung the rifle over his shoulder, and muttered, "I'm going after the shooter."

The SVT, or subvocal transceiver, a butterfly-shaped adhesive patch on Ames's throat, just north of his Adam's apple, picked up his voice so it could be broadcast over the channel for all, including Grim, to hear.

Ames took off running for the stairwell door, wrenched it open, and began storming down the steps. At just five feet eight and 140 pounds, he was the fastest runner on the team; still, that didn't stop the others from quipping about his size. Oh, they never ridiculed him to his face, but he overheard their remarks. He didn't care. He knew he was ten feet tall when standing on his skills and charisma. Moreover, with a little gel worked into his unruly blond hair, he easily added three inches.

How many staircases had he mounted during his tenure as a New York City cop, back at the old four-eight precinct? Too many to count. And just when he'd grown so cynical that he thought he'd abandon public service forever, he'd joined the NSA and become a police officer in Fort Meade, Maryland. They'd given him a nice milestone recruitment incentive, and the money and new mission had lifted his spirits. While there, he'd been tapped for Third Echelon—despite his lack of a special-forces background—and so here he was, back to racing down the stairs, trying to help out his fellow Splinter Cells who, of course, had no idea what he really was.

"You don't have the temperament for this job," Sam Fisher once told Ames during a particularly brutal training session.

Fisher was a very good judge of character.

* * *

A motley crew of overweight soccer moms hopping around like sea lions in spandex, and another group of fifty-year-old cougars who'd left their rich husbands to lust after group fitness instructors half their age, had crowded into the Gold's Gym fitness room for the morning's body-combat class.

Under the harsh glow of overhead lights beaming off the waxed wooden floor, the class was in full swing, with the instructor, Greg, booming into a headset while techno music blared from speakers taller than Gillespie.

Kimberly Gillespie had donned her workout gear and stood within a meter of Mrs. Cynthia Leonard, the fabulously wealthy wife of the team's target. The first break in the music finally came, and they stole a moment to towel off and gulp down their water.

"You're really good at this," she told Cynthia.

The woman smoothed back her bleached-blond hair, then blotted sweat off her chest, her impossibly perky boobs threatening to explode from her tight top. "Thanks, I've been doing it for a while. Takes time to learn all the punches and kicks. But you look like you've had some training."

Gillespie smiled. "A little bit."

"I like you're accent. You're not from Houston."

"North Georgia."

"And I love all that red hair and your freckles. You know, I once dated a man who said he stopped for blondes and brunettes, but he took two steps back for redheads."

Gillespie chuckled under her breath. "I tend to scare away most men. They don't step back. They run."

"All right, ladies, break time is over," cried Greg.

"My Lord, he's a real drill sergeant," said Gillespie.

"Yeah," Cynthia agreed. "But look at that ass."

The remark reminded Gillespie of army boot camp, of her old friend Lissette who helped her get through the misery by making jokes and lusting after all the sergeants. The army had allowed Gillespie to escape from Creekwood Trailer Park and her father's grocery list of emotional problems and addictions. She'd finally been able to make a name for herself as an intelligence analyst who advised special-forces teams and operations.

Four years in the army, then another four years at University of Central Florida, to earn a degree in civil engineering, had prepared her well for a career with the NSA. When she was handpicked by Grim to join Third Echelon was one of the proudest moments of Gillespie's life. Someone had finally noticed her, recognized her skill set, and appreciated her sarcasm and take-no-prisoners attitude.

As they were about to move forward and prepare for the next phase of punishment, Cynthia glanced down at the BlackBerry sitting atop her purse and shifted back to take a call.

Gillespie assumed the fighting stance, then turned as Cynthia suddenly rushed from the room.

Penguin Group (USA) Inc.
is proud to present

GREAT READS—GUARANTEED

We are so confident you will love
this book that we are offering a
100% money-back guarantee!

If you are not 100% satisfied with
this publication, Penguin Group (USA) Inc.
will refund your money!
Simply return the book before
January 3, 2010 for a full refund.

To be eligible for refund, please mail the book, along with a
copy of the receipt, your address, and a brief
explanation of why you don't think this is a great read,
to the address listed below.
We will send you a check for the purchase price and sales tax
of the book within 4–6 weeks.

Great Reads Guaranteed/ATTN: Dept RP
Penguin Group (USA) Inc.
375 Hudson Street
New York, New York 10014

Offer ends January 3, 2010

Coming in January 2010

Tom Clancy's

HAWX®

WRITTEN BY DAVID MICHAELS

The world of warfare is changing. More and more national armies are being replaced by private military contractors (PMCs).

Troy Loensch is a screwup. He joins the U.S. Air Force and, with some difficulty, learns to work together with the other pilots. But Troy's career is derailed when his program is taken over by Firehawk, a PMC. When the CIA comes to Troy and asks him to investigate Firehawk, Troy agrees—but what he uncovers could be more dangerous than he ever imagined.

M522T0709